THE DROPSHIP

The Dropship

WELCOME TO THE ISLAND

Danny Kylstra

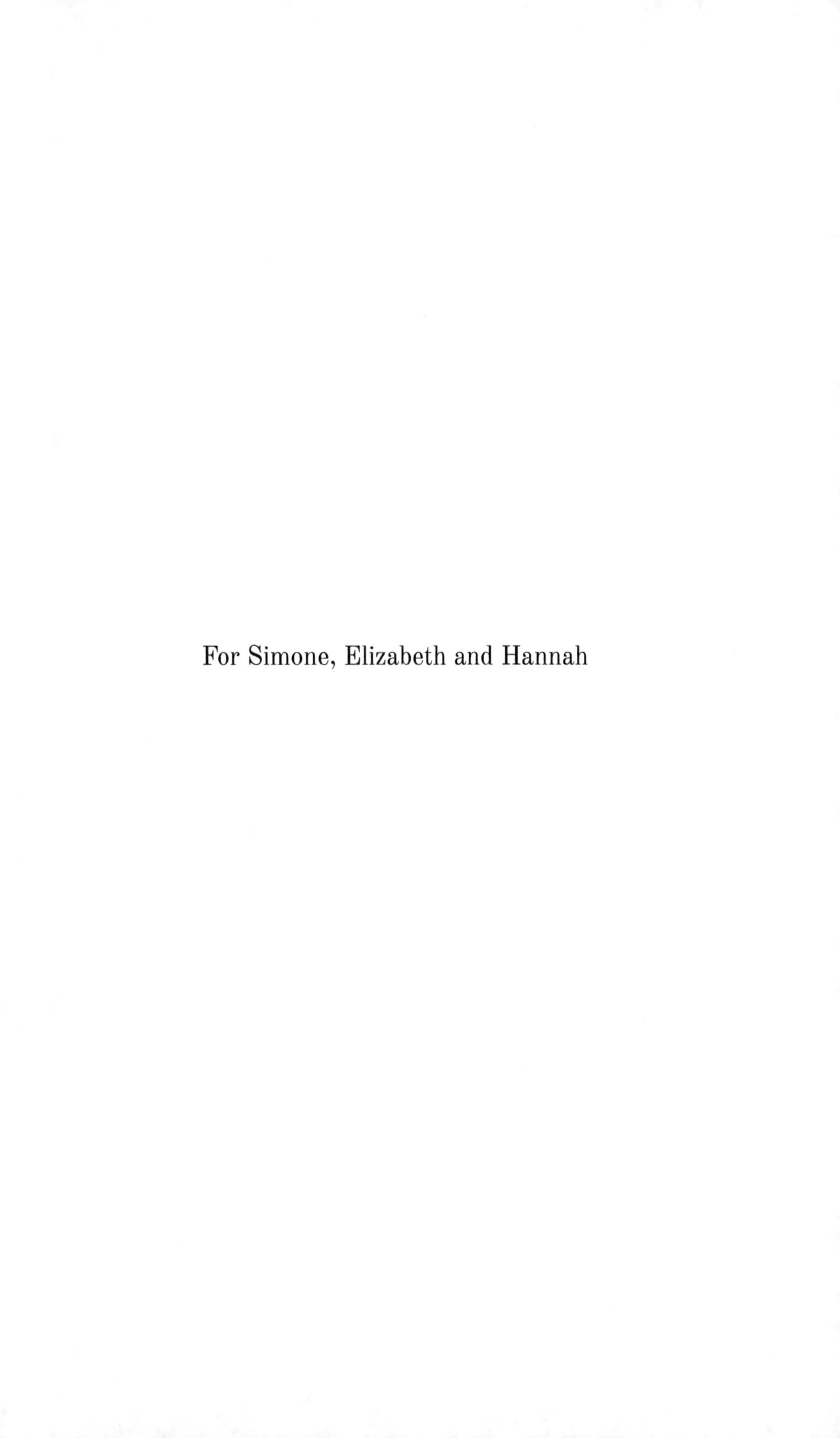

For Simone, Elizabeth and Hannah

Prologue

"This is what we need to do." Joseph Kahn began. Joseph was a senator who was trying to make his way up the ranks to become president. He was a tall slim built man in his twenties, with thick black hair parted to one side, one eye green and the other blue, and a long fat nose. "This war has changed the way our country works, unemployment is at record numbers, our debt is dangerously high. Many places due to the destruction and devastation, are now inhabitable, those areas that can still support life cannot afford to have anyone that doesn't want to be a proper member of society...."

The crowd made up of mostly members of the press, listened in silence, microphones in hand, waiting to hear his solution.

".... therefore, I have put forward a proposal to the rest of the government, that we find an island for mid-level criminals, aged between sixteen and thirty-four. While their crimes are not vicious in nature, they are criminals regardless, and we can no longer support them just sitting in jail..."

A member in the crowd rose-up in applause, which was all the encouragement most of the crowd needed, they then joined in.

Joseph raised his voice, "...Everyone knows we cannot support our prison system as it is, it is too crowded. My plan is simple, we use an uninhabited Island to drop the criminals onto. They will live their lives there. If they don't want to live by the laws of this country, this island will give them their own. If they don't wish to be a valuable member of society, we will just simply relocate them."

Some of the crowd rose-up in cheers again. Joseph moved to the side of the podium, his assistant Laura Wick, went up to the microphone, "We will now be taking some questions."

A woman with thick-rimmed black glasses and blonde hair in a bun stood and asked a question, "My name is Jenny Crossword, I work for the Daily Instant. What about food, water and other necessities? Without that, you're basically dropping these people on an island and forcing them to starve, that's basically a death sentence anyway, isn't this an out of sight, out of mind solution?"

Joseph went back to the podium and answered the question, "Yes, thank you. I understand your concern. The answer is quite simple, food and supplies will also be dropped on the island each month. These supplies will be donated by various Charity's, and businesses further reducing the cost to our taxpayers"

An old man, much older than the rest of the crowd stood up, he had grey hair, balding through the middle. As soon as he stood up it was obvious that he was quite frail. "I have a son that is currently in Jail," he announced. "He didn't have a job, all he did was steal some food for his family, what will happen to my son?"

Joseph took a deep breath looked at his assistant, placed his hand over the microphone and quietly, but in a tone suggesting his annoyance asked her. "This was only supposed to be for the press. What is he doing here?" He then looked at the crowd, more toward the man and quickly thought of an answer. "Anyone with a sentence, longer than a year, will be sent to the Island as well!"

The answer horrified the old man. "But…but I'll lose my son."

The crowd looked nervous and annoyed, they didn't know what to make of the announcement. "Next question, please?" Laura asked for Joseph.

Another reporter, a woman with a pen in her blonde hair stood to ask a question, "You say dropped down, what do you mean by that?"

"All the prisoners will be taken in 'Supply Dropships.' Where they will land on the island in a processing centre and then released to do their own thing," Joseph replied, grateful for an easier question.

Another reporter, a balding man with some grey hair stood. He pushed his thin, brown rimmed glasses up along his nose, then asked his question. "Isn't this forcing them to fight over those supplies? Once they have been processed, there won't be any laws. You're basically going to let them go on their own and fend for themselves!" His voice started to get more emotional. "These people aren't on death row, but you are taking their lives from them and by doing so, you are punishing their families and friends." The anger in the tone of his voice could be heard. "This is cra...." He was then cut off mid-sentence.

".... Thank you that will be my last question." Joseph just stared at the man, he was in disbelief that someone could think his idea was horrible. "If these people don't want to follow our laws, our way of life then they need to face harsher punishments, they think they can do what they want and only end up in jail with the government supporting them, I say it ends now!" He yelled and slammed his fist on the podium. "We need to come down hard on them." Joseph then walked away from the podium, his arms raised looking like he was declaring victory. Half the crowd booing and the other half still cheering.

*****

Wednesday the 11th of April 2085, two months after his original announcement, Joseph put on another press conference, this time he was standing in front of a brand-new Dropship. "I'm proud to say this is the day that my glorious bill to help solve our budget crisis has come into effect. While the vote was close, I'm glad to see that common sense prevailed." He then turned around and looked at the Dropship, waited a few seconds then turned back and spoke again into the microphone. "I'd like to present to you, The 'Dropship' that will take our first prisoners to their new home."

The Dropship was a silver metallic oval with large wings on either side, window panelling on the front, where the cockpit could easily be seen. It had a tailgate at the back with a ramp leading from the ground to the inside of the cabin.

Ten people were being marched behind the press conference by five armed guards. Not one of the prisoners looked at the cameras, which were broadcasting their march onto the Dropship for the world to see.

"I am proud to announce our first Dropship will be leaving today, towards the Island." Joseph paused for a moment and smiled. "Which you can understand for security reasons, the location will be kept a secret, each month another dropship will be sent to the Island. Today I present the first ten prisoners, who are going to be sent to the Island." He then began to name the Prisoners and their crime.

Marty Mater- string of robberies.

Holi Lens – Theft.

Nicky Bright – Arson.

Sam Instant - Violent Protestor.

Mitsi Tors - Attacking police officers.

Brooke House – Tax Avoidance.

Wade Saver - Drug dealing.

Jay Cona – Fraud.

Missy Speaker - Spent longer than maximum time aloud of six months on welfare.

Daman Biguy – Bribery and Corruption.

*****

Joseph's plan had been working perfectly, six months after the original ten prisoners, or *"The Original 10,"* as they were branded by the media, were marched onto the first Dropship. Joseph was becoming more popular within the ranks of government, making his way higher. Election time was about to come up, and as his popularity had not fallen since his controversial plan was first announced, he saw this as the best chance for him to run for President.

The night before the election, there was a knock-on Joseph's front door. Two police officers arrested Joseph and charged him with Fraud. The arrest meant that he could not be elected for office until all charges had been dropped. That wasn't to be, as he was found guilty and was sentenced to the Island. His 'Glorious Bill,' as he put it, had become his own nightmare.

1

Minin Woobry glanced at the calendar and smiled. Today's date was marked with 5 small hearts. It was the evening of the 26th of Feb 2095, the fifth anniversary of Amber Cleen and himself. Amber a 23-year-old, short woman with silky brunette hair, sharp blue eyes, and a small pointed nose, was wearing a long red dress over her curvy body. Minin, a 22-year-old man, decided on a black collared shirt and cream coloured pants. He even combed his usually scruffy, dark hair. He looked in the mirror, to make sure it was sitting as it should, he glanced at his face, looking over his average nose, and his dark brown eyes, before double-checking that the collar on his shirt was even. He was ready.

Date nights were something that they were usually unable to do, with the busy lives that they both lead. They would normally work anywhere between sixty to eighty hours a week at the Lens Corporation. A huge multinational company, where they both worked and met. Amber was a Personal Assistant and Minin was an errand runner in the law department. Working with different schedules made it hard to organise much time together. What time they did have, they usually spent at home, relaxing and enjoying each other's company.

Neither of them wanted to do anything extravagant, so they both agreed to do something casual, just a movie and a meal. The simple act of spending some time with each other while being out of the house and not having to worry about their jobs was appealing enough. The place they had picked for the meal was Ruby 7's, a small little café located a few blocks from the cinema where the movie would be shown.

Its location was not the only draw to Ruby 7's, they enjoyed the food there, and the fact it was the place they had their first date, made it their favourite place. Tonight, they chose their usual order. Amber had a Caesar Salad. While Minin had Steak, cooked medium as always.

The conversation was mainly reminiscing over what had happened to them over the past five years, meeting each other by accident at a work meeting, going on their first date, buying a house together, talking about marriage. Tonight was the night Minin was going to take that step. His plan, go to the movies, followed by a walk to the top of Sunny Towers, the highest tower and look out over the city, the view at night was glorious. He would then get down on one knee and propose.

They had finished their meals and the conversation had gone on for a while without either one realising it. Minin glanced off at a clock behind Amber and saw the time, it was 20:45, the movie was scheduled to start at 21:00. "We better get a move on, or we're going to miss it". He announced.

Amber agreed and they both got out of their seats, paid their bill, and made their way outside, it was pouring with rain. Amber opened her umbrella and without hesitation began to walk fast. Amber was ahead of Minin, she knew that he would be right behind her. Minin's umbrella had gotten a little stuck, once it was open he started walking fast to catch up to Amber but he was quite a distance behind.

As Minin hurried along, he saw an alleyway and looked through it. It looked as though it would lead them directly to the Cinema. He knew this way would save them plenty of time, so he called out to Amber. "Amber!" He shouted out, but his voice was drowned out by the heavy rain. "Amber!" He shouted again, even louder, again she didn't hear him. Then he screamed out, "AMBER!".

She had barely heard him but turned around to see what the commotion was about. "What's wrong?" She called out, her voice also not making it to Minin's ears.

He motioned for her to join him, which she did. "This alley will get us there quicker, instead of going all the way around," He told her once she was closer.

Amber looked down the alley, she wasn't so sure it was safe, something inside was telling her not to do it. "I don't know, it doesn't feel right, I want to see the movie as much as you do, but I don't think an extra five minutes will kill us." She took out her phone and checked the time, 20:55. "Ok, we'll take the alley." She said, knowing they would miss the start of the movie if they didn't.

They started making their way down the alley, wet posters were hanging from the outside walls of the buildings, most being for 'The Changed,' The movie they were on the way to see. Other posters were for bands and shows being promoted. The further they went the more uncomfortable Amber got with their shortcut. They walked past two people, that appeared to be living in the alley, which was unusual. The world they lived in didn't have this. A law was passed about eight years ago, that meant all people without a job and home, had to submit to the local shelter, to be sorted into suitable community service type jobs, so the government were paying them for at least doing something. This forced people to try harder to get a job or be given whatever job the city had available. It was a way to save on welfare payments and get job positions filled that no one else wanted. Both Amber and Minin knew that the homeless people would have ended up on the Island if they had been caught.

The two of them continued walking, they could see the lights from the Cinema getting bigger and brighter. They knew the journey was going to be over soon enough. Amber looked at Minin, "I still have a bad feeling about going this way, but I'm glad I'm with you." She told him with a smile as she gripped his hand.

They took a few more steps. A voice came from behind them. "The lady was right to be scared, you should have followed your gut." The two of them turned around and saw a desperate looking man in a trench coat, a tilted hat angled over one of his eyes, the other eye was black. Scars covered the part of his face that could be seen. In his cotton gloved hand, he was holding a pistol, which was pointing right at Minin, though his hand was rather shaky. He was slightly taller than Minin but with a thin, malnourished frame.

Both Amber and Minin put their hands in the air. "We don't want any trouble," Minin assured the man.

He disabled the safety on the pistol to tell them he was serious. "Give me your money, phones and anything else I can sell!" He demanded, his hands shaking slightly more.

Amber noticed the shaking, she knew the man was nervous. She thought he was only trying to scare them and looked him in the eye. "No, we're not giving you anything, piss off!" She yelled, trying to be brave and walking closer to the Gunman.

The Gunman tightened his grip on the gun, with his finger firmly on the trigger, any more pressure, would set the gun off. "Don't come any closer!" He yelled, shaking a bit more. "Just give me what I want!" He shouted at them.

Minin decided to help Amber. "Move away, we're not giving you anything," He told him. "You leave, this will be the last of it, no cops, especially not the Island." He said, hoping the threat of the Island, would be enough to scare him away.

"I'm not going to no island." The Gunman replied nervously. "That ain't for me, that's why I need your stuff to sell, so give it to me, NOW!" He was now furious.

Amber sometimes had more bravery than smarts. She moved in closer, trying to show that she wasn't scared of the demand. It was at that moment the Gunman pulled the trigger the rest of the way, a loud gunshot echoed through the alleyway. The bullet penetrating Amber's chest, she knew right away she had been hit. She fell to the ground quickly, although still conscious.

Minin dived down, lifting her to comfort her. He didn't know what to do at this point, his brain shut down. Amber was just looking up at him not saying a word.

The Gunman started to pace around, looking worried. "Look what you made me do. I didn't want to do that." He knew things had gotten out of hand, much worse than he had planned. He aimed the gun back at Minin's head. "Give me the money and everything now!" He screamed at him, not knowing what else to do.

Minin was still frozen after what had happened and didn't respond. He was still just holding Amber in his arms and looked up at the man, tears streaming from his face over the woman he loved.

The Gunman was now desperate for everything to fix itself, he needed the money and anything else valuable and he knew he couldn't let Amber or Minin go and let anyone know what had happened. He pulled the trigger, the gun jammed and misfired.

Minin flinched as he closed his eyes, and it dragged him back to the here and now. He had to focus on finding a way to get himself out of trouble and to get Amber to safety. The Gunman became distracted whacking the gun with his hands trying to get whatever jammed the gun loose, to be able to fire it again. He turned his back while continuing to whack the gun. Minin put Amber on the ground softly, hoping it wouldn't be the last time he held her.

Minin lifted himself and ran towards the Gunman as fast as he could. He knew he needed to take the gun off him, he just grabbed onto it with his right hand and pulled, hoping the surprise would be enough to make the gunman let go.

There was no such luck, the Gunman held on as hard as he could, doing everything to not give it up. Minin threw a punch from his left hand while his right still had hold of the gun. The Gunman did the opposite threw from his right and held with his left, punches were being thrown back and forth between the two.

Minin eventually threw a punch that shocked the Gunman enough for him to let go of the gun, but the force of trying to get it made Minin swing his arm back and launch the gun away towards where Amber was laying.

The gun fired a bullet, missing Amber but close enough that she felt it whiz by. The gun was no longer jammed. The Gunman ran towards the gun wanting to pick it up and take control of the situation and get what he came for. Minin grabbed the Gunman and wrestled him to the ground.

Amber picked up the gun and aimed it at the two of them, she was becoming increasingly groggy from the shot she had received. Minin and the Gunman saw her aiming and sprang apart, knowing she could hit either of them in the state that she was in. She fired the gun towards the Gunman and missed.

The Gunman wasn't going to take another chance to be hit and ran toward Amber hoping to take the gun off her. Minin ran after him hoping to catch up and stop him getting to her. The Gunman ran, lowering himself into position and picked the gun up out of her hand, he stopped, turned around, beginning to aim the gun towards Minin.

Minin still had momentum and got close to the Gunman and spear tackled him to the ground, releasing the gun in the process back towards Amber who then started dragging herself towards the gun.

Police sirens began to sound over the sound of the pouring rain. They were getting louder, relief washed over Minin, he knew in his mind that this would be over soon, and the police can take over, he just had to keep the Gunman from getting the gun.

Both men were wrestling on the ground trying to get the upper hand on each other. The Gunman grabbed Minin's head and slammed it the ground, enough to unlock them both. The Gunman could now make it to his feet and ran towards the gun and Amber.

Amber picked up the gun and fired it once more, this time hitting the Gunman in the stomach and he fell shaking.

Minin returned to his feet and ran towards Amber, he cradled her once more. Amber looked up at him and smiled. "You did good today, you did so well. I love you."

Tears fall from Minin's eyes. He looked at the Gunman, who was trying to crawl away.

Amber looked at the Gunman crawling away, she lifted the gun and took a final shot. The Gunman stopped moving. Minin looked into her eyes, she looked deep into his. "Don't let them get to you." She told him as she closed her eyes and took a final shallow breath.

Anger surged through Minin, he knew the Gunman was to blame for what had happened. He let go of Amber, took the gun out of her hand, stormed to the Gunman, he looked at him, but the Gunman was already dead.

Minin looked up, snapping out of his fury and saw two police cars and four police officers hiding behind the cars. Their guns were drawn and ready to fire. Minin dropped the gun, his hands were shaking, he had no idea how long the police had been there, but he knew how it must have looked to them, standing there holding a gun and two dead people laying on the ground. He put his hands over his head and knelt to the ground. The police swiftly moved in and arrested Minin.

2

Minin's day in court was the next day. He was being tried with two counts of murder. The only thing they had told him was that the police had seen the shooting of the gunman and not much else. Minin's only hope was that the jury would see his side of the story.

Minin was well aware of how the trial system worked, he had to learn it as part of his job. It was a four-person jury of two women and two men, a judge proceeding it, and a guard on standby. Minin would be asked to give a statement over what had happened, any witnesses would do the same then the jury would have twenty minutes to decide. Then the sentence would be handed out. This system was designed to make the whole procedure efficient and be over within a day. A system designed to save time and money.

Minin was seated at the front left of the room, to the right was the police officers that witnessed the shooting. In front of Minin would be where the judge would sit. To the side of the judge is where the jury sat.

Minin's jury comprised of a large, older, balding man with a scruffy beard, wearing a suit, sitting at the front of the 4-seat booth. Next to him a young blonde woman with thick red glasses wearing a neatly ironed grey business suit, with a pale blue blouse. Seated behind her was a middle-aged woman with hair that was bleached blonde and in need of a touch-up. She was sitting there in a yellow dress that looked too big for her. In the final seat, sat a man that looked to be in his 20s, with dreadlocks, dressed as though he was ready to go to the beach. The four of them were looking at Minin, with judging eyes. It seemed they had made up their minds about him before the trial had begun. Minin didn't like his chances.

The guard, a chubby man wearing a muddy green uniform, walked to the front of the courtroom. "All rise for the honourable, judge Cleary." Everyone stood up. The judge walked into the room, he was short and wearing a black robe that was three sizes too big, huge eyes, tiny lips and a long nose. He got to his seat and sat down, the guard then announced, "You may be seated".

As everyone resumed their seats, Judge Cleary read over some papers that were on the desk. He looked up at Minin, shook his head disapprovingly and then looked at the papers again. He looked up again at Minin and began. "Case number 685367, Minin Woobry vs the city with 2 charges of murder. Defendant, how do you plead?"

"N...not Guilty." Minin's nerves made his tongue feel thick in his mouth, making it hard to talk.

The Judge replied. "Ok, let's begin, stand up and state your name please."

Minin got out of his seat and stood up, his voice could tell anyone he was nervous. "My name is Minin Woobry, your honour." He said shaking from the nerves.

The Judge stared at him. "You're charged today with murder, this is a very serious charge, that will result in the death penalty if you are found guilty. Do you understand this?"

"Yes, I do," Minin replied, not taking his nervous eyes off the judge.

"Ok, now please tell the jury what happened on the night of the Twenty-Sixth of February 2095."

"Minin told the story to the jury, his voice became less nervous as he went on. "... I wasn't the one to pull the trigger, I had the gun at the end, and I was very upset and angry at the man. I thought about shooting him, but he was already dead, taking the decision from me. Seeing the police brought me to my senses. I understand why you may think I killed this guy, but I was really only trying to protect my girlfriend and myself, and that is the truth of what happened." Minin then sat down, hoping what he had said was believed by the jury.

The judge then asked the room. "Is there anybody present today, that bore witness to the events leading to the death of Amber Cleen and Harry Ralph?" The judge then looked around the room, waiting for someone to respond.

An old man with a short white beard, dressed in an old dirty trench coat, stood up from a seat and walked to the front of the room with a slight limp. "If I may your honour? I saw what happened."

The judge peered down at the old man before addressing him. "Alright, for the jury, please state your name."

The old man looked at the jury. "My name is Jonas Wheel."

"Thank you, Jonas. Now please tell the room what you saw happen."

"I was in the alley with my friend, we saw Minin and Amber walk by."

Minin realised that Jonas was one of the homeless people that he saw before the attack. He was shocked that he would risk being arrested himself by coming forward as a witness. He wasn't sure whether to be relieved that someone could finally back him up, or worried that his one witness would not be seen as credible.

Jonas continued. "I didn't see the beginning of the fight, but when it began, it was loud. It was definitely heated. I walked over to see both Minin and Harry fighting over a gun, I hid behind a garbage bin. I didn't want to get involved, but I kept watch. The fight was back and forth. Eventually Amber had the gun." He paused as his eye began to twitch. "Sorry, I have this medical condition." He then continued. "From my angle, it looked like that guy." He pointed straight at Minin. "Pulled the trigger, to defend himself and his girl."

Minin's blood ran cold at his words.

"So, let me get this straight." The judge probed. "You saw Minin pull the trigger, to defend himself?"

"That's right, protecting Amber and himself."

"Do you have anything else to add?"

"No, your honour."

"Ok, please be seated."

Minin sat confused, he didn't pull the trigger, but this person said that he did. He knew this wasn't a good situation. He breathed deeply and slowly, concentrating on each breath, to make sure he didn't pass out. "How could this be happening?" He asked himself quietly.

The judge and jury were scribbling notes furiously. Once the judge had finished what he had written he then spoke up once more. "I now call upon one of the police officers at the scene, to give their version of events".

A tall female uniformed police officer stood her hat under her arm. Her grey eyes and an average nose rounding off her features was brought to the front of the room and took a seat next to the judge. "Please state your name?".

The officer smiled to the jury and proudly announced her name. "My name is Sergeant Claire Buxom, your honour."

The judge then continued. "Please tell everyone what you saw when the incident occurred".

"When my partner John Knight and I had arrived at the scene of the incident, a female, who we now know as Amber, was lying on the floor with a bullet wound in her Chest. Two men were fighting on the ground, one being the defendant, the other was the deceased man. The now-deceased person was able to get himself off the ground and try to run towards the gun, and the wounded Amber, shot the now-deceased man in the stomach".

A smile came over Minin's face, what little she did say so far matched up with his own story perfectly. He thought this might save him from the charges.

Officer Buxom continued her story. "Another squad car arrived at this moment with two more officers, Ada Bottle and Kim Medicine. As the defendant then approached Amber which blocked our view, what we could see was Minin's arm move up and the gun was fired. Minin then got back up from the ground and approached the now-deceased male, we now know as Harry Ralph and stood over him while holding the gun. The defendant then noticed us, dropped the gun, raised his arms behind his head and knelt for us to subdue him.

The judge then asked another question to the officer. "From what you saw, do you believe it was Minin or Amber that shot the man?"

The officer took a deep breath and answered, "I can't be sure your honour."

"That didn't quite answer the question, just to make it perfectly clear, do you believe this man to be guilty of murder?" The judge said pointing to Minin.

"What I believe is that Harry Ralph was shot in self-defence, I just can't be sure who pulled the trigger."

Minin couldn't believe it. The person that was on the prosecution, was saying he could be innocent. A sense of relief came over him.

The other three Police officers all gave their own accounts of what they had seen, each one backing up the what the first had said, and that they could not be sure who pulled the trigger. Once the officers had all given their statements, Minin could only hope that the judge and jury would have enough doubt to drop the murder charge.

The judge then announced. "All the statements have been said, it is now time for the jury to deliberate, they will have twenty minutes to decide." At his words, a frosted, sound-proof glass barrier went up around the jury box to give the jurors privacy while they went over the statements and notes and come to a decision. The decision that could change Minin's life forever.

Each passing minute felt to Minin like an hour. After twenty minutes, he would find out his fate. His thoughts were going around and around in his head. One minute he was convinced that he would be found guilty of murdering one, or even both of them, and he would be sentenced to death. His next thought that he would be set free. He was innocent, how could they not see that? He would surely be able to get on with his life, well, a life that he would have to endure without Amber in it. That thought made part of him hope to be found guilty. He could not imagine a life without Amber. During this time, the idea it could be something else didn't come to his mind at all.

A bell rang from the jury box, telling the jurors they had two minutes left to decide. The sound of the bell seemed to make option three come screaming to the front of his mind. No, they couldn't possibly send him there, could they? No, he was innocent, surely this couldn't happen. Just like that, horrible images filled his head. Images that his mind had created, based on stories and rumours. He knew, if he was not charged with murder, he would not get the death sentence. Which left only one other option. The Island. It was a place of no return. No-one that had been sentenced to the Island ever came back. His home, his family, his friends, his job, all gone. He had already lost Amber, surely life couldn't be cruel enough to take everything else from him too. He was innocent after all.

The barrier surrounding the jury box then came down. Pulling Minin to the present. The judge spoke up. "People of the jury, have you reached a verdict?"

All of them had a synchronised answer. "Yes, we have your honour." One of the jurors, the large man in the suit with a scruffy beard, handed a note to the judge and sat back down.

"Thank you." The Judge says to the jury. He then began to speak to the room loudly. "On the charge of murder, the jury has found the defendant, not guilty!" Automatically, a huge wave of relief came over Minin, like the weight of the world had come off his shoulders, but the judge continued. "However, you admitted to being in possession of a firearm and had the intent to kill."

The weight that had lifted moments ago not only returned, but had tripled, and was now pushing squarely on his chest. He couldn't breathe. His fear threatened to drown him. He put his hand over his head, the word "No!" repeating, bouncing and echoing.

"Minin, please stand up." The judge said. Minin hadn't noticed that he had sunk to the floor. He gingerly got to his feet, holding on to his chair for support. Scared of and fairly certain what was coming next. The judge began. "Your charge has been downgraded from murder to possession of a firearm and intent to kill. This is not a charge which I can issue a jail sentence for, therefore I can only sentence you to one thing. Minin Woobry, I sentence you to spend the rest of your life on the Island!"

Just like that, Minin had lost everything. "This can't be happening". He started rocking back and forth. Based off everything he had been told or read, this would be a fate worse than death. The judge then continued. "You will be taken there on the next Dropship." Then with the thud of his gavel, Minin's fate was sealed.

3

After the trial, Minin was placed in a local jail cell on his own, which contained a small square window, a single framed metal bed, and a metal toilet. One wall was steel barred, the others were all stone. He wouldn't stay here long, as the next dropship would be setting out the next day. All he could think about was what Joseph Kahn had said about the prisoners on the Island. *"They are criminals regardless, and we can no longer support them just sitting in jail any longer..."*

Every news crew imaginable covered the first departure of prisoners towards the Island. Each of the Original Ten was treated as a celebrity, even though all were convicted criminals. Every single bit of information about them was made public. Now, like most people, Minin could only remember the basics.

Each month a new news article would be out announcing who was on the Dropships. After a few months, unless there was a reason, most people didn't take notice or even care. Minin couldn't tell you about most people sentenced to the Island except for The Original Ten and three other exceptions. One being a protester called Charlie, who had found information about the Island and was going to reveal it all, he was arrested and charged with treason against the state. Normally this would have been charged with the death sentence but the court figured a more fitting sentence would be to go to the Island he was going to reveal.

The second person was Mark Brockly. Minin remembered him for two reasons. The first, he was on the verge of being the World Heavy

Weight Mixed Fighter Champion of the world. He was in his fight for the championship, his opponent was on a streak of twenty-four fights without a loss. If anyone was going to beat the champion, it was going to be Mark. The fight went further than just beating his opponent in the ring, he ended up killing him by accident. Mark was charged with manslaughter. The second reason Minin remembered Mark was from a news report stating that the Dropship, scheduled to drop Mark and other prisoners on the Island, had had a takeover attempt, but was destroyed before it had been completed. All prisoners and anyone working on the Dropship was killed. This caused a major change in the way the Dropships were operated. From then on, the ships were all unmanned.

The third was Joseph Kahn. The man that had developed the idea of the island. His arrest made shockwaves around the world.

Minin didn't know much about the Island itself but knowing that prisoners were willing to take over dropships rather than go to the island and the fact that threatening to reveal what was happening on the island, was enough to get you sent there, worried Minin considerably. Charlie clearly was so horrified by what he found out about the Island, that he wanted everyone to know and to put a stop to it. Minin did find himself wondering though, *'Could it really be that bad or was it made like this to scare anyone into not wanting to go to the Island in the first place?'*

Minin knew he would need to get some sleep, the next day would be stressful enough, he didn't need his exhausted mind making it worse. He laid on his bed, it wasn't comfortable in the slightest, but he supposed it would be luxury compared to the ground or whatever was going to be ahead of him after tonight. Minin kept waking through the night, the thought of what the Island could be or what was in store for him, just kept playing on his mind.

He woke up the next morning, he estimated he may have gotten two or three hours sleep. The sun was shining harshly through the window that wasn't covered, the beam of light shining directly onto his head. Minin looked around to get his bearings, there was a clock with a calendar on a wall outside of the steel bars of his cell. It displayed 06:18 am on the 28th of February, he moved his head out of the way of the sunshine and just laid on the bed. Time had passed and Minin looked at the clock it was now 6:29, he put his head down again.

A siren began and a red light on the roof that he had not noticed before was now flashing. Minin didn't know what this meant, he wondered whether he had done something wrong by moving, was there a sensor around knowing the way he was laying? Two male guards wearing white uniforms were walking towards the cell. Both men were holding batons. One had a stubble like beard, the other was clean-shaven, both looked young and both overweight. Both had small rounded glasses covering their eyes and barely-there haircuts. If it wasn't for the stubble-like beard, Minin wouldn't be able to tell them apart.

One of the guards stood near the door of the cell while the other walked to the side out of view. "Get up out of the bed, with your hands behind your head and kneel down." The guard with the stubble-like beard demanded from near the door.

Minin didn't know what was going on and hesitated, not sure if it was him they were talking to for a second.

The guard who was becoming annoyed then said. "Get up out of the bed, on your knees and hands behind your head. I'm not going to repeat it again."

Minin did as he was told as quickly as he could. He stayed in this position, waiting for the guard to make his next move.

The guard kept looking around the room and eventually turned to where the other guard was hidden, "Open it up" he called out. There was a clicking noise, and he moved some of the bars which slid out of the way with ease and went in the cell, rushing to get behind Minin. The second guard now came back into view with his hands behind his back and stood at the door.

The guard behind Minin got out a pair of handcuffs and used them on Minin, first connecting his right wrist and pulling it down behind his back, he then pulled his left arm down connecting it to his wrist. The guard then lifted Minin by the wrists in such a forceful way that he had no choice but to stand or have his shoulder separated in the process. "Move!" The guard commanded and marched him to the door where the second guard was located. The second guard looked Minin up and down and smiled. Minin decided to smile back hoping whatever the two of them are going to do to him will be less severe, but the guard brought a think pillowcase from behind his back and shoved it over Minin's head. It was so thick that Minin was plunged into darkness. "Time to go, the Dropship is waiting for you." The Guard behind him said as both guards march Minin off.

They walk for a few minutes, eventually, Minin could feel a cool breeze and assumed he was outside. He could hear the rumble of an engine close by. It got louder as he continued walking. He was then pushed, landing on something metal, he could hear a different type of engine noise, he was inside of the van.

Minin was shaken around as the vehicle moved off. He began calling out, "Hello." There was no answer. "Hello, is anyone out there?" but still no answer. Minin stayed quiet and still, knowing he couldn't control what was happening to him and knew he had no choice but to go along with it. The trip was rough, the vehicle jumping all around the road. It soon got rough enough that it knocked Minin onto the floor, hitting his head, and causing the pillowcase to rip slightly, enough for him to see through the hole. He lifted himself and looked around. He was in the back of a van. There was a window, which he could see that the van was going along a busy highway. although he had absolutely no idea where he was heading.

The van pulled off the highway and made its way into an industrial area with buildings all around. The van stopped suddenly with a jerk, and the engine turned off. A loud Humming noise was coming from outside the van. The door of the van was then opened, two new guards were standing there. They had the same haircut as the last two, and look similar to the other guards only slimmer. They grab Minin out of the van forcefully, neither one noticing the hole in the pillowcase.

In front of Minin was something he had only seen on television before, a Dropship, but what surprised him most was that it wasn't alone.

There were at least ten Dropships he could see. All of them, the same rugby ball shape, with wings protruding out the side. From the front, they looked more like silver grey rounded blimps. The noise coming from the Dropships was deafening, each making a low rumbling noise. The Dropships engine was so much louder than what he thought, as all he had seen of the Dropships had been on television.

Minin's attention was dragged away from the ships when the guards stopped in front of a table. Sitting behind it was another Guard who looked completely different to everyone else, his hair was longer, his eyes small and judging, his body type told Minin that one of his hobbies was going to the Gym, he was holding a clipboard. "Who's this?" He shouted trying to project his voice over the Dropship's engines.

"Minin Woobry, he was only registered yesterday, he might be on the last page." One of the Guards holding Minin replied.

'So prisoners are ordered by date?' Thought Minin.

The guard flipped through the pages. The guard found the name and scrolled his finger across the page, "He's on ship B, it's going to is-land A."

This caught Minin off guard. 'Island 'A'? Did this mean there was more than one island, could that have been one of the secrets Charlie had been arrested and sentenced to the island for knowing?

"Thanks." The guard replied. Both guards grabbed Minin again and dragged him to the dropship he was assigned. They went to the back of the ship where the tailgate was down, ready to take its human cargo on-board.

The three of them marched up the tailgate to an area that looked like it belonged on a cargo plane, not a dropship for people. The only difference was the seating, which was big, metal seats secured to the walls, five on each side. Connected above the seats looked to be a rail, that went to the back of the Dropship, back towards the tailgate. In the middle, it was mostly empty except for the occasional wooden crate.

Both the guards rip the pillowcase off Minin's head, giving him a clear view of the area. There were no windows, which Minin guessed was so the prisoners wouldn't be able to see where they were going.

Minin was placed on the furthest seat inside, next to a door, which he assumed was the cockpit. He was locked in by a metal strap that was wrapped around his chest, another around his arms, then on his legs, another to his waist and then torso. He could barely move, let alone escape.

Both guards went over the straps three times to make sure he was locked in. Once they were satisfied, they started to walk back out of the dropship. One of the guards shouting out, "Good luck kid, you're going to need it." As they walked away, they both started laughing.

Another prisoner, a man with a star tattoo over his right eye, and dyed blond hair limped onboard, with two more guards. The prisoner was placed into the seat across from Minin, strapped in, and checked over three times, then the guards walked off.

This happened for another five prisoners until a Blonde man with bulging muscles was brought on board to his seat, he looked at it and shook his head. "I'm not sitting there." He told the guards firmly and began to swing his body around, one of the guards lost his grip on the prisoner and was slammed into the floor. The guard composed himself and pulled a small metal pole from his pocket, he got up and swung it at the prisoner hitting him in the left temple, knocking the prisoner out. Both guards picked him up without hesitation and slammed the prisoner into the seat, locking him into position swiftly. Once again, the guards went over the prisoner three times and left.

More prisoners came on board each being placed into their seats until the tenth and the last prisoner came on board. A woman with spiked fiery red hair, that looked like it had been badly dyed, who seemed barely old enough to be sent to the Island, looked at the Blond prisoner that tried to escape. "What happened to him?" She quizzed the guards that brought her on-board.

"The same thing that'll happen to you if you don't sit down." One of them told her in an impatient tone.

She sat down, then was strapped in and went over just like everyone else. Everyone just sat there in silence. All ten seats were filled, four women and six men, just sat in silence waiting for what will happen next. Finally, a chubby short man with a clean-shaven beard boarded the Dropship, he was silent, going over everyone's straps one last time. Once he had finished checking all ten he walked out of the back shouting out. "Ok this one is good, let 'em go."

The room was silent, none of the prisoners knew what was going on, and none wanted to make a sound just in case they ended up like the blonde prisoner. A minute past, which seemed like an eternity to Minin. Then the lights all turned off, the only source of light coming from the open ramp at the back, which was beginning to disappear as the door slowly closed. Minin said his final goodbye internally, to his home and his life as he knew it.

A different set of lights then turned on, they were red, illuminating the room just enough for everyone to see each other and not much else. "How nice of them to let us see." Came from a voice in the room that Minin didn't recognise. This got a chuckle out of some of the prisoners.

A deep humming noise began to sound below them, it got gradually louder. Minin guessed that this was the engine and the dropship was about to leave. The ground began to shake, the walls and floors began to rattle as the dropship began to move, confirming Minin's suspicions.

The prisoner sitting next to Minin turned to him and said. "Looks like we're in for a bumpy ride." Minin didn't say anything and just nodded agreeing with the prisoner.

Minin looked around at the others, all of who were curious about what was happening. Anyone that was scared of the future managed to hide their fear. Minin guessed that they could no longer show weakness. Once this journey had finished, it was survival of the fittest.

The dropship began to rise from the ground, the shaking of the room began to get more violent as it rose, the engine getting louder as it lifted itself. The engine then went silent, everyone in the room took notice, all having a look of concern and thinking. *'Had the engine failed? Are they going to fall back down to earth? How far above the ground were they?'*

For the moment, the ship just seemed to be floating in the air, then everyone started to feel like they were being sucked towards the back of the ship, the dropship was beginning to move forward, Its destination, the Island.

4

The sucking feeling began to subside, the prisoners now all seemed a little less concerned. The person sitting next to Minin and the person next to him started a conversation. On the other side of the cargo area, in the seat in the middle was a man who had short spikey bleach blonde hair and wrinkles under his eyes. He wasn't enjoying the flight in the slightest, he began screaming, saying, "Let me out of here, I'm innocent, I don't deserve this!" repeatedly.

Eventually the passenger next to him, a short man, with long dread-locked hair, just turned his head towards him. "Shut up!" He screamed at him.

This made him quiet for a few minutes but eventually, he couldn't take the silence anymore and began to shout again. The short man resigned himself to the screaming next to him and didn't yell at him again.

Minin decided to concentrate on the two talking to each other next to him, the noise of the 'screamer' made it hard to listen but he could hear some things they were saying. As their conversation continued it became obvious the two sitting next to Minin had known each other before the trip, they had known each other through friends, catching up on old times but had not seen each other in a while.

"This is crap, this island is a charade, all I did was steal some bread to feed my family. I wouldn't have had to do that either if they helped me get on my feet." Said the person sitting next to Minin.

"Tell me about it, Sam...." replied the person next to him. "....They're going to screw everyone that's sixteen to thirty-four, everyone will eventually end up there."

"We're all screwed anyway. I'll tell you a secret, Hayden. I heard when they drop you on the island, there's no parachute's, they just drop ya, you're dead as soon as you hit the ground...."

Minin was shocked at what he had heard and needed to hear more.

Sam continued his story ".... That was one of those things Charlie was going to reveal. Basically, if you're a criminal you're given a death sentence anyway. They just don't show your death in front of everyone."

"Well, we're never getting off the island anyway," Hayden replied. "Might as well put us out of our misery."

Focusing on the talking between Hayden and Sam did help to block out the screaming. Although with what they were saying, he started to wonder if he would have preferred to hear that instead.

The conversation continued for a little while longer, the lights inside the cargo area then turned on, completely illuminating the area. Screamer stopped his screaming, he was distracted just like everyone else trying to work out what was happening. A siren noise of three long WHOOP's which were deafening sounded over speakers that were located all over the room. Everyone on board was relieved when it stopped.

After five seconds an announcement came over the speakers. "Attention passengers, this unmanned dropship is about to open its hatch, please be aware that the seats which you are locked into have an attached Parachute and will be ejected with you, landing you safely on the island. You will not be unlocked out of them until the very final moment before you are ejected from the dropship, the seat belt over your chest and waist will be your only connection left to the seats and the Parachute, anything else will be disconnected".

Everyone inside the cargo area looked around at everyone else. Minin thought the announcement was a joke and thought to himself. *'They're going to land, it's just a scare tactic.'*

Then the back of the dropship began to open, the roar of the air rushing in made it impossible to hear anything else. It was now clear that the dropship was definitely not going to land. Outside was blue, with light clouds shooting past the back as the dropship went past. Minin could just see the ocean at the back of his vision, he didn't think they had gotten to the island, then he remembered what the passengers sitting next to him said, that they just drop them into the ocean, and that was it.

Minin then saw a white light start to flash violently above the seat of the person closest to the hatch of the dropship, on the opposite side of the cargo area. Minin started to look all around the seat wondering what was going on, it looked as though a clamp still connected the seat to the rail.

The straps holding anything except for the waist and chest disconnected themselves, then the clamps holding the seat disconnected and retracted behind the rail. The seat was now sliding towards the back, becoming faster as it got close to the opening. The seat got to where the hatch had opened, the seat was now loose swaying towards the open air, then launched into the blue wonder.

Everyone on board had seen what had happened. Screamer began to scream once again, so loud that even the deafening roar of the wind, wasn't enough to fully block him out. "I don't want to do this, let me out, it's not fair." He just kept repeating over and over.

The seat next to the first was next. Its light began to flash. The same thing happened as the first person until they were launched into the air. This kept happening, each person being disconnected one after the other until eventually, it was 'Screamers' turn. Minin looked at him, he had pure fear on his face, he didn't want to be launched into the unknown. The light started flashing above his, but it was green. It didn't make sense to Minin why this one would be any different to the others. But just like the others he was detached, and rolled to the edge, till he was gone.

Minin looked back into the opening, where he could see the water before, he could now see what looked to be the edge of an island, *They must have been dropped onto the land.'* He thought. This island was the one they were going to live on.

Minin looked at the row of people remaining on his side, knowing the person furthest along was the next to go, but they didn't get released, the dropship just kept moving forward. After a minute or so everyone just looked at each other, none saying anything, but all had the same questions. What's going on? Where are the rest of them going?

The hatch at the back of the ship started to rise halfway, *'They must be going somewhere else'.* Minin thought. The dropship then began to tilt to the left, Minin then knew the answer, they were not going somewhere else, they were turning around.

The dropship took some time to level itself out as the hatch at the back lowered into the same position as it did before. The light above the person next in line then flashed, this time it was white again, Minin then realised the different light colours must mean that the person is the last inline before the dropship turns. The next person in line was disconnected from the ship and launched out towards the island. Same thing as before, each time a person would be let go and put out into the openness.

It was now Sam's turn, who looked at Minin and shouted, "Well I always wanted to go skydiving." He was then launched out.

While everything was going on, Minin hadn't had a chance for his fear of heights to set in and it had now registered. He started to breathe heavily, his heart rate skyrocketed, and there was nothing he could do. He looked at the person across from him, who slid out into the unknown, and knew it was now his turn. He was breathing to the point of hyperventilating, he knew this wasn't good for him, and forced himself to slow down, even though it was difficult.

He looked up waiting for the light, it flashed green, he was the second last to go. Minin closed his eyes, he didn't want to see what was next, he heard the clamps disconnect, and then the scraping sound of the sliding, and a slight slowdown of movement with the straps being removed, then the shaking that he knew was from no longer being connected to the safety of the dropship.

The wind rushing all over his body, he knew he was now floating towards the ground. It felt like the trip was going to be over quickly, then an explosion sounded behind him, and he was jolted backwards like the seat had brakes and slowed his descent immensely. A piece of metal flew past him towards the ground, it looked like a backing of the seat. As Minin slowed, his chair changed position and he was now sitting like it was a swing, slightly swaying in the breeze. The fear of the descent no longer worried him as much and he could now open his eyes and look at what was around him.

Minin looked around at the island below, beaches around the outside, the forest wall almost surrounding the beach, then open grasslands, rivers flowing in the middle, it looked almost uninhabited if not for the huge manmade tower three-quarters of the way across, with two rivers looking as though they were coming out of it, one reaching to a waterfall. To Minin this didn't look too bad. He thought, *"Well there could be worse places I could be trapped.'*

Minin then looked around the sky trying to find everyone else that was ejected from the dropship, he could see parachutes, all coloured red, floating towards the ground, there was at least twenty of them. Underneath them, there were metal crates but no people. In the distance, he could see a green Parachute, *'could that be another person?'* Minin looked up at his Parachute and it was green too.

Minin continued to look around desperate to find someone else that was making their way to the earth. There wasn't another single green parachute to be found, then he looked below him to his left and saw a metal piece falling, it was bigger than the piece that fell off Minin's chair, he looked closer at it and noticed a pair of shoes, then arms came out from the sides, this was a person falling to the island, their parachute had not deployed.

Minin remembered the colour of the light that flashed before he came out of the dropship, his was green, the same colour as 'Screamers'.

Everyone else had white, was the other Parachute *'Screamers'*? was everyone else doomed?

The forest area Minin had seen when he had first opened his eyes was getting closer, this was where he was going to land. The tops of the trees were now close enough that any second he was going to hit them. He was there, as he got further in, he missed each branch of the trees by mere millimetres, having what looked to be a direct path to the ground. The descent then stopped with a cracking noise. Minin was still in the air attached to the seat and chute. The Parachute was now tangled to the trees.

Minin did all he could to dislodge himself, he kept trying to swing and move around but was unable to. His only chance was other islanders that could come and rescue him, but would that be a good idea? He didn't know anything about the island, was it completely lawless, everyone for themselves, or worse? Was everyone now a cannibal? Was he going to be tonight's dinner?

Minin sat dangling in the air for some time then heard a noise coming from below and behind him, it sounded like voices. He couldn't see anyone, but the voices were getting louder. He strained his eyes and could just make out three people walking towards him. He could see them now covered by the shrubs and trees.

"There he is." A man said while pointing at Minin. Minin stayed quiet, not sure what would happen if he said anything. Were they allies or enemies? As they got closer he could see the man that spoke was wearing nothing but ripped cargo shorts, he had a somewhat toned body and a bushy beard. A woman appeared next to him, she had long red hair, she was shorter than the man that called out. Coming behind her was another man, he looked younger than the other two, with short cut hair.

The three of them stood below Minin just looking up at him. The woman looked at the younger man and pointed toward Minin. "Climb up and see what's connecting him". He obliged and began climbing another tree close by, making his way up quickly. It was clear that he had climbed the tree many times. The woman and the other man were still on the ground talking to each other. Minin was unable to hear what they were saying as they just start randomly laughing.

Minin began to worry a little. Are they deciding if he will be roasted or boiled tonight?

The climber returned to the woman and starts waving his hands around, not making a noise, pointing at things, but no words.

The woman then said, "So if he holds a branch and we cut, he should be stable?"

He starts nodding indicating she was right.

Minin had no idea what to make of this. Are they cutting him out while he holds the branch or cutting into him while he holds the branch and then they leave him to die once they have everything they need from him?

The woman handed the younger man a huge knife and he began to climb, she looked to the other, "Go up there and get him to swing over to you, or if he doesn't he's fallin' to the ground, that'll be fun for him." She laughed and he joined in.

The older man then went to another tree and began to climb it, got to the same level as Minin, putting his arm out and called. "Swing over to me." Minin could see him better from this angle, his face had a few scratches, his tan wasn't from the Sun, he was naturally like this, his eyes were as dark as his hair, which was messy. Minin instantly assumed Shampoo and conditioner was something of a luxury here. The arm that was reaching out was toned but didn't look bulky.

Minin stayed quiet and didn't do anything, unsure if he should or not.

"Look." The man continued. "You're safe with us." He paused for a moment, smiling. "We have plenty of food at the camp, we haven't resulted to cannibalism...." he paused and smiled "...Yet." He began to laugh and held out his hand. Minin cracked a smile, the joke eased his worry a smidge, and he began to swing, back and forth till he grabbed the man's hand, and pulled towards the trees. "Ok, hold onto the tree. Callum is going to cut the chute."

"Ok, do it," Minin replied.

The man shouted to the top of the trees. "Ok, do it." There was a cutting noise above them, it stopped, and the ropes connected to the still-attached seat fall towards the ground below pulling Minin with it. The man then looked back at Minin. "Ok, hold on tightly." He pulled a knife out of his pocket and cut the straps around Minin's body, the chair fell to the ground with a loud crash. "Can you climb down on your own?" He asked.

Minin nodded. The word, "Yes", barely audible from his mouth, and the man began to climb down. Minin following slowly afterwards, being careful with every step. Once he was on the ground he curled up, thankful he survived. After a few minutes, he looked up and saw three people standing over him. The third person who cut the Parachute ropes put out his hand to get Minin from the ground, Minin taking it.

The woman in the middle of the three said to him. "Hi." She pointed to the man that was on the level with Minin. "This is Hunter." Then to her other side, the man that helped him from the ground. "This is Callum, and I'm Hayley. Welcome to the Island." She said with a smile.

Hayley standing between Hunter and Callum, looked even shorter, they were about the same height while she was a head shorter than them. She had grey eyes, a few small freckles over her face, a smile that was warming to Minin, her nose was average, her clothes were in tatters, her white button shirt looked as though it needed to be replaced rather than repaired, her shorts were ripped to the same degree.

Callum's hair looked as though it had only recently been cut, which Minin thought wouldn't happen on the island, his eyes dark and his hair colour darker, didn't wear a shirt and wore board shorts that looked brand new.

Minin didn't know what to make of the three of them, but he also didn't have any reason not to trust them. He sat quietly for a second thinking, he then said, "Hi," Still not completely sure if he should make a run for it.

Minin then remembered a photo he had managed to sneak into the dropship with him and got it out of his pocket. It was a picture of Amber, from one of their first dates, Minin was having trouble with managers at his work, and Amber wanted to cheer him up, so she wrote on the back. 'Never let them get to you'. Minin would always look at the picture if he needed to be cheered up, or if things had gotten hard. Looking at it now. It helped him, he definitely couldn't let anyone or anything get to him now that he had arrived.

Hayley peered over his shoulder, "You're going to need all the inspiration you can get here," She advised. "If the guards didn't manage to get it off you before, you best make sure you never lose it."

Hunter looked Minin over, "You look hungry," He said. "After a big day like this you could use something to eat, we'll take you to our camp."

Minin smiled at that, he didn't expect everyone to be nice, everything he had heard about the island was that it was filled with savages and was a free-for-all, but here, standing in front of him, were three people trying to help him out. "Thank you." He replied.

They all started the walk to the camp, Minin wondered what the camp would look like, and if there would be others, then Hayley, as if reading his mind, said, "It's not that bad here, it definitely has it's challenges, but if you are with the right people, the island isn't a bad place." She said with a smile.

Hunter then continued, "What she means to say is that, 'We are the right people." He turned his head so that he was looking at the huge tower in the distance, the tone in his voice suddenly changed. "… And there are a lot of people that aren't."

Minin didn't know what to take from that message, for all he knew the three taking him could be the bad guys and are trying to impress him before they do something, and the Tower could be a sanctuary. The Tower in the background began to glow green from the top. "What's happening?" He asked.

All three looked as confused as Minin, they had not seen anything like that in their time on the island, Hayley answered the question. "I don't know and to be honest I don't really think I want to know." She touched the back of her neck, a faint red glow reflected from her hands. "No good ever comes from that place." She said nervously.

5

That afternoon everyone was sitting around the campfire on wooden seats made from old logs, "I'm so glad you wanted to come with us," Hayley said, "Drop day is usually the worst, no-one has any idea what is going on, landing inside a camp area is usually a lot easier."

"I've only been here a few hours, I'm still getting used to it," Minin admitted. "I've never lived like this in my life, I've never roughed it, I think the worst was staying at a three-star hotel once."

Hunter laughed, "Some parts of the island are rated negative three."

"Exactly," Minin replied. "I'm just going to have to get used to it. It'll take time, trust me I'm grateful for everything."

"We're glad, for most people it takes about a month," Hunter replied.

Hayley then spoke, "We'll give you something special on your first drop day." She then paused, "That's if you stay".

"Why wouldn't I stay here?" Minin wondered.

"You don't have to stay here, it's not like the tower." Hayley paused for a moment. "Where they choose if you stay or go. You're free to make your own choice with our camp."

Minin didn't know what to say at first but after a moment, "I'm not leaving this camp, I wouldn't survive on my own." He admitted as he smiled, then adding. "What do you mean? 'Something special on my first drop day' isn't today my first and only drop day?"

Callum started to wave his hands to get everyone's attention, they all looked, he then started to draw in the dirt, a badly drawn picture of a dropship and people coming down then wrote the number zero.

"What he is trying to say…." Hayley explained, "…. Is that when you first get to the island, that's your original drop day, sort of like your birthday. Each one after that is counted, so next months drop day will be called your first drop day. We don't have clocks or calendars here, so it's hard to keep track of birthdays, ages or how long we've been here, so we measure time by the drop days." She smiled, then added. "So today your counter begins."

Hunter then spoke. "I'm about one hundred but you start to lose count after a while."

"And I'm Twenty-Eight drop days." Hayley announced, "Or about two years 4 months."

Minin then turned to Callum who was looking at the ground shyly, Hayley spoke for him. "We don't know, he never dropped inside the camp, we think he might have been a Freelander that wanted to join a camp. We just don't know, since he can't talk. Unfortunately, somethings that he tries to say to us, we can't fully understand." Her words made Callum look a little defeated, Hayley went and put her shoulder on him. "But we don't care, he's family and we love him regardless, even if we don't know how many drops he is."

Minin thought for a moment. He saw how it was making Callum feel, so he wanted to change the subject. "I want to see the rest of the island, I want to know about the home that I'll be on for the rest of my life."

"We'll do that tomorrow," Hayley said with a nervous smile. "I'd rather not go anywhere from the camp, but a little bit out into the Freeland's won't hurt us." She said trying to smile. "It's getting late now, we'd only be out for a moment."

"Thank you," Minin said, seeing she wasn't happy over the idea.

Callum passed a cup to Minin, it looked like it was coffee, he was pleasantly surprised, he didn't expect to get anything like this, he took a sip, the taste was good. Minin nodded at Callum. "Thank you."

"Tell us about yourself," Hunter then said. "If you're going to be here for a while, we might as well get to know you."

"Well, I work for a place called Lens corporation."

Hayley interrupted him for a second, she made coughing sounds as she spoke. "Worked."

Minin became quiet for a second, reality once again set in. Hunter looked at Hayley annoyed. "Ok, I'll change the question, "What's one thing you would love to do?"

"I'm not really sure," Minin answered. "Can I think about for a bit?"

"Sure. I'll answer instead," Hunter replied. "I've always dreamed of being a pilot. Flying all over the world, visiting all sorts of countries and seeing new cultures. I reckon that would be interesting. It's one of the things that I don't know how to do and I would love to learn it." He then turned his head towards Hayley. "What about you?"

"Fire a gun, I've never done it before. Not at anyone, just tin cans or a target," She Clarified. She looked up and stared deeply into the fire. "Although maybe just one person, Daman." She said, continuing to stare at the fire.

Minin didn't know who Daman was, thoughts began to run through his head. '*Could this Daman be the reason she was on the island?* Minin then looked at Callum, he wasn't sure if he was going to be able to get an answer for the question from him.

Next to Callum was a pile of magazines, he picked one up and began to flip through it quickly. He found a picture of a man with a woman who was knocked out in his arms walking through a fire to save her and showed everyone. The three looked but didn't understand, they kept shaking their heads. So Callum started to flip through the magazine once more and stopped on a picture of a war scene in the trenches with the troops going over into the battlefield.

The three looked at Callum thinking about what the pictures meant, Hunter then took a guess. "You want to be a hero to someone?"

Callum nodded, Hunter was correct.

Hunter then spoke again with a smile. "It'll take some getting used to, but once you work out what Callum is saying, we can communicate pretty easily." He then turned his attention to Minin. "Ok, we've had our turn, now it's yours."

Minin thought for another second. "When I was a kid, I always loved reading comics about superheroes. I could just zoom into their world, I was able to forget about what was happening in our own for a while. They helped people if they're in trouble. It would be great for something like that to happen, especially on an island like this." Minin realised it sounded childish and felt embarrassed by saying it. "It's stupid I know."

Hayley snapped. "That is so incredibly stupid, that's so dumb, I don't even know where to begin with…" She was furious with what Minin had said as though there was steam coming from her ears. "I can't believe you would say something like that.… How dare you?" She stormed off.

"What was that all about"? Minin asked the other two completely confused over what he had said.

"I have no idea," Hunter answered. Both Callum and himself had a look of shock on their faces, "We've no idea, she's never gone off like that, that was really strange for her."

Minin ran after her, he knew he needed to do something, he caught up to her quickly, "I'm sorry, I don't know what I said, but I'm sorry." He said to her desperately.

She turned around to him, she took a deep breath, her eyes were filled with tears. "I'm sorry I went off at you like that."

Minin couldn't believe it, for a moment he thought that he had done something horrible, but she was apologising to him. "I still don't know what I said."

She grabbed his hand and began to walk back to the campfire, they both sat. "I might as well tell you all something that I haven't said to anyone on the island." She paused for a moment. "It was my brother."

"We didn't even know you had a brother," Hunter said, "You never mentioned it."

"I didn't want to, especially when I first got here. I didn't know who to trust, and when I did, I just never spoke about it". She replied. "When

I was about ten, he would read comics all the time. He loved them, he had the same dream as you Minin. He wanted to become a superhero to save people who were in trouble. When he was ten he got sick, I mean really sick. He eventually became terminal and died. That was the reason why I became a doctor, when you said you had the same dream as him it hit me hard. It made me miss him that bit more, hearing his dream repeated." She then turned her head toward Minin. "I'm so sorry I went off at you."

"It's ok," Minin said with a smile.

Everyone was quiet for a while, no-one knew what to say. Callum then clapped his hands together to get everyone's attention. He put them together and laid them on the side of his head, indicating he was going to get sleep.

"Yeah, that's probably a good idea," Hayley replied. "We're in for a big day, Minin's first day out in the Freelands."

"You'll be bunking with me," Hunter announced to Minin. "At least until we can work something else out."

"Head to toe?" Minin asked not entirely sure how it would work.

"There's a mattress on the floor, it'll only be temporary." Hunter said, "Anyway I'll go get it ready." He then left toward his hut.

Hayley just sat looking at the fire sobbing, her eyes full of tears, that she kept wiping away, Minin looked at her. "Are you ok?" He asked.

"I'll be fine, thank you," She said quietly. "I just miss him sometimes." She looked up at him. "You will want to get some sleep, tomorrow is a big day."

"You sure you're going to be ok by yourself?"

"Trust me I'll be fine, I'll head to bed soon."

6

The next morning, Minin woke up early, he didn't sleep much. He kept dreaming about his arrival on the island. The same things kept replaying in his dreams every time he closed his eyes, Amber losing her life, the unfair trial and then the fall onto the island.

Minin looked around, Hunter was still asleep, it was obvious he wasn't going to wake up anytime soon. Minin got out of his bed and walked out of the hut he was in. To either side of the hut were two other Huts. One belonging to Callum and the other to Hayley, Each hut was facing the Campfire. From the front, they looked like tiny houses, made from pieces of wood of all different sizes and colours, the front door being the largest part.

Sitting at the campfire was Hayley, she looked tired, Minin walked up to her. "Did you even go to sleep last night?" He asked.

"I only just got up, I don't sleep much but I do get enough." She replied. She handed him a blue mug, "Here this will help you wake up."

Minin took the mug, inside was black coffee. "I honestly didn't think I would get something like this on the island, now I've gotten coffee twice in less than twenty-four hours."

"Don't get used to it. We don't usually bring it out that much. The same goes for alcohol, they're just too rare to waste."

"I'm addicted to coffee," Minin replied. "I usually drink like fifteen cups a day."

Hayley laughed slightly, "You'll be lucky to drink fifteen a year, well that's one advantage for you, your caffeine addiction will subside." She said smiling.

Minin smiled back looking down at himself, his clothes were dirty, that's when he realised he didn't have a chance to shower or change in the last few days. "Do you have any other clothes and is there a shower?"

"If you want to wash there is a beach out there, just make sure you don't swim out too far," Hayley told him. "As for your clothes, get used to wearing them. The dropships don't give out much of that kind of stuff, plenty of other junk, but not many clothes."

Minin didn't know what to make of it, he knew that there would be a short supply of clothes. "But what if my clothes start to wear out too much?" He asked.

A voice from behind them both then called out. "There's a short supply but we never run out." They both turn around, Hunter was at the door of his hut. "We'll give you some to change into but you're going to want to get used to wearing the same day in day out."

Minin started to nod his head, accepting what he couldn't change. The three of them began talking around the campfire and began to have breakfast, toast made from freshly made bread that had been made the day before while waiting for Callum to wake up.

"This toast is amazing," Minin said. "How do you get something this fresh, I knew coffee was asking for a lot, but bread, I just can't believe it." He continued in amazement.

"Callum made the bread, he knows how to make a lot of things," Hayley replied. As if on cue, Callum then woke up looking like he was fully refreshed for the day. He pointed at the path from which Minin had entered the camp the previous day.

"Don't you want some breakfast first before we head out?" Hayley asked. Callum just shook his head. "He never has breakfast," Hunter said, "But we always ask, just in case he ever changes his mind"

"We'd be pretty shocked if he did say yes though," Hayley then mentioned.

Callum pointed again at the path, looking eager to get going. "Ok, ok, we're going," Hayley replied. "I don't understand why your so excited, it's not like we force anyone to stay in the camp if they don't want to, besides you're always going on little trips for days at a time."

"He's probably happy going with someone else." Hunter then said.

Hearing that Callum wandered the island regularly, made Minin think that the island couldn't possibly be that bad, and all the things he had heard were probably just rumours.

Hunter then spoke. "Looking at the weather, I don't want to be out that long, it looks like it's going to pour down soon."

Minin wanted to explore the island all he could but noticed the clouds Hunter was talking about. He nodded and agreed, knowing he could explore the island when he was ready in his own time. "How far out will we go?" He asked.

"Not far," Hayley announced. "We'll show you a little bit of the Freeland's then come back."

Everyone got up from where they were and began to make their way along the path, after five minutes of walking Minin stopped, everyone did the same. They knew what he was doing, in front of him was the chair that he sat in when he arrived at the island, broken into pieces, this was the area he first landed. The same dream from last night came rushing into his head.

Hayley put her arm around him. "The dreams won't go away, there are less of them, but they don't go away. You just have to remember you survived each time they affect you." Minin took a deep breath and started to walk, thinking that the best thing for him to do was to walk away from the reminder of that nightmare.

It wasn't long before they all got to the edge of the path, Minin could see a red metal arch as high as the trees, beyond that, the clearing, which to him looked like it was beautiful. It had green grass that went on for ages, surrounded by trees of all different colours. Paths all around leading to different areas. Exactly what he had seen when he was landing on the island.

An hour had passed, the clouds were getting heavier, the sound of thunder began to rumble in the distance. "Alright, time to head back." Hayley announced, "Let's get home before we get too wet."

Minin, Callum and Hunter, all agreed and they began to make their way home. They took a different path to the one that they came out on. It wasn't long before they spotted something in the distance, Minin rushed toward it. It was a wooden crate connected to a red parachute. "What's it doing here?" Minin asked.

"It's a supply crate," Hunter said, as he and Callum began looking around. "I wonder what's inside?"

Hunter, Callum, and Hayley took a corner of the crate, each knowing exactly what to do with it. "We're not low on supplies, but who knows when we'll get another?" Hayley said. They all look at Minin, it took them a moment to realise he didn't know their procedure. "Grab the other corner," She told him.

Minin walked to the spare corner, they all lifted. "What do we do with it?" He asked.

"We're taking it back to the camp, then we'll open it and find out what it's got," Hayley told him. "If we're lucky it might have those clothes you wanted this morning."

The four of them began to walk toward the camp, the crate was heavy, but not enough that the four of them couldn't handle the weight. As they got to the entrance of their camp it began to rain. A voice called out from the distance. "You there, stop!" Hayley, Hunter and Callum freeze obediently, they knew the voice. Minin didn't know and was slower at listening to the command almost causing the crate to lose balance. "Put the crate down." The voice called out.

"Minin, do what he said," Hayley said quiet enough that only he could hear, and they all put the crate down.

"Now turn around and look at me," The voice called out. They all do what they are told. Walking toward them was a man wearing an all-black business suit, his hair neatly cut, and clean-shaven. He was average in height. A look that Minin felt would be out of place on the island. With him were five other people, a little taller, wearing white pants and white long sleeve shirts, black balaclavas covering their whole head, except for two eye holes. They were carrying a cart containing four other supply crates.

Callum, Hayley, and Hunter all just stood there, straight and still, as he began to approach. Minin was not sure who the person was but could see everyone else's fear in the way they were doing things and joined them. They all looked like they were part of a military line up about to begin a march.

The person wearing the black business suit then stopped in front of them. "Hayley, Hunter, Callum……" He said as he walked in front of them. "…..And someone I have never met. Enlighten me, what is your name?" He asked Minin.

Minin was confused, how could someone who spoke so well, make the three of them so afraid? "Ahhh…." Minin paused for a second. "Minin… My name is Minin."

The man in front of Minin put out his hand, wanting to shake it. Minin shook, knowing that if his friends were afraid of him so much, he best make the best impression he could and if shaking his hand would keep the man calm, that would be a smart move. "My name is Daman Biguy, it's nice to meet you," He told him, his voice sounding very pleasant.

He then turned to Hunter, his tone suddenly changed. It was now incredibly serious. "How many crates did you get for me this time? You've been here the longest out of everyone, you can tell me." He then turned to Minin, turning his nose at him. "I'd ask your friend, but he seems to be new, probably doesn't know enough about the island and how things work, I'll let him off this time but it's best you get him up to speed."

Hunter didn't pause, his voice sounded nervous. "Just one this time, it landed close to our area."

"Just one crate? That isn't enough for three of you, let alone four," Daman declared.

'This man doesn't seem to be evil, he feels sorry for us.' Minin thought, 'But why are they so scared?'

Daman smiled. "I'm going to give you a crate, we have plenty this month." He then turned toward one of the guards and clicked his fingers. One of the guards began to unhook a crate from the cart, the four other guards then move the crate in front of Daman, then proceed to walk back to the cart. Daman then went up to the man that released the crate and asked him. "Do you know where their area is?"

"It's right behind that line of trees sir." He answered, pointing to the tree line.

"No, that's not right," Daman replied, sounding annoyed. He then pulled out something that looked like a smartphone from his pocket.

The man in white started to shake in fear knowing he answered wrong and was going to pay dearly. Minin got a glance of the screen, it showed a radar with yellow dots. Daman moved the screen, the dots moved with it, he then pressed one of the dots. A bright red flash shone from the back of the neck of the man who closed his eyes knowing his fate. Everyone looked at him as he fell to the ground having a fit, his body then suddenly stopped.

Daman looked at the other people that were accompanying him. "That land, like everything on this island, belongs to me, never forget that." He announced. He then looked at the four standing in front of him. "Don't forget that favour I did for you today." He then turned to the guards that arrived with him, pulled out his index finger on his right hand and did a circular motion with it. They all began to run off with the cart quickly.

The rain began to get heavier, the body of the dead guard was lying lifeless on the ground, blood began pouring from his nose.

Minin knew from then that Daman wasn't to be messed with.

7

Six months of living on the island had passed. Minin marked each day on the wall of his own hut by adding another notch to his tally, it was now one hundred and eighty, which was close enough for him to say he had now been officially on the island for six months. To make it easier, he did six down, then one across, each one representing a day of the week. It was the best way he could think of to figure out the date, he estimated that it was July nineteenth. Minin looked around the hut, on the same wall as the tally, was a picture that Minin drew of the island from his memory of falling from his dropship which was beginning to get tattered and limp on some of the corners.

Minin turned around again and looked at his bed, it didn't look particularly great and was barely holding together. The mattress was made from old clothes sewn and stuffed together, but like his housing situation, it was a lot better than what some had, which was nothing.

Next to the bed was a bedside table made from old driftwood. It had a stack of paper, which was used much like a journal. Which described life on the island, each day would include things like the weather, to try and figure out where they were in the world. This had not gone as well as they had hoped as the weather except for the occasional day was pretty much the same temperature-wise since he arrived, the only difference was if it had been raining, so he could only guess the island was somewhere tropical. The journal also included what had happened during the day and information on the people of the island, Minin also secretly hoped that someday, he would be able to leave and the journal would just be a memento of the time spent on the island.

On top of the journal was the picture that Minin was able to sneak onboard the dropship. Amber was in front of a lighthouse and smiling, it was one of the last photos he had taken of her, Minin received the printed version from Amber as an anniversary present. He kept it hoping that it would be able to keep him sane and thought of life before the Island. Sometimes it would work, other times it broke him down knowing what he had lost. Sometimes he wondered why something so personal like this was never confiscated. In fact, nothing was ever taken off him, the only explanation Minin could come up with was they sent you to the island with whatever you had on you no matter what it was. It wasn't like he was ever going to get off the island.

There was a knock on the door. "Hey, are you ready? It's time to go," It was from Hayley. Minin knew what 'Time to go' meant. Today was 'drop day'. The day when dropships come over the island from the mainland and dropped more supplies and people to the island. "I'll be out in a minute," Minin called out. "I just have to get a shirt on."

Hayley didn't care about the shirt and busted into the hut without a second warning, the shirt wasn't the only thing Minin wasn't wearing, he was just in blue boxer shorts. Minin just stood there, he wasn't shocked, this wasn't the first time she had done that. He was positive this wasn't going to be the last time either.

"I've come into your room, what?..... Once or twice a week now since you got here." Hayley asked him. "Each time I expect you to be ripped and have a major 'beach body.' And each time, without fail, I'm disappointed. It's not like you can sit around watching TV all day, I'm glad you've learnt to tan though." She then began laughing. Minin discovered making jokes was Hayley's way of coping on the island. Everyone had a coping mechanism and that was hers.

"What's the weather like outside?" Minin asked. "It looks clear, not a cloud in the sky, another day in paradise …. if it wasn't for Daman." She replied, looking a little less bright than before.

Minin got a pair of khaki shorts and pulled them on, along with a t-shirt with a witch printed on it, and a pair of old shoes. They stepped outside, it was hot, hotter than normal with the usual high humidity and just as Hayley had said, it was a cloudless blue sky, stretched out above as far as the eye could see.

Minin's hut looked directly at the campfire. All four now encircling the campfire. Except for the two of them, the camp was empty, not a single other soul around. Minin was usually the last one to wake up, everyone else usually had to wait for him. "Where is everyone?" Minin enquired, thinking that it was strange.

"I decided to do something a little bit different, I'd go get you and hope the rest would be ready in time and meet us here. I guess that plan didn't work. Callum won't be too far off, probably exploring the island for a little bit..." Callum's way of coping on the island was to explore "...and Hunter is at the beach again...." Hunter coped by keeping his mind occupied, trying to figure out how to get off the island. "... I'll head to the forest and call out for Callum, you head down to the beach and bring up Hunter. We'll meet here again in ten minutes." The two of them broke apart, going their separate ways. Minin took the path going through a shallow number of trees and shrubs, Hayley through the thicker part.

Everyone took part in drop day. The only reason someone wouldn't be able too if they were sick and couldn't physically take part. Their camp didn't have many crops and they couldn't live or eat without supplies, so they were forced to trade with other camps. Everyone had to help, this was one of the only rules for the camp if they wanted to stay.

The path Minin took was short, the trees were lower to the ground, shrubs taking up most of the space surrounding the walking path, which had been cleared. He arrived at the beach. Either side of him was just sand and water as far as he could see, if it wasn't for a few footprints in the sand it would look like it had never been occupied by anyone. Out in the sea, there was a rock formation that looked like a fallen bridge. Standing in front of Minin at the water's edge was Hunter.

"What have you got there?" Minin asked.

Hunter was holding what looked to be a miniature raft, "I just built it". It was tiny and made from driftwood, with a tiny engine attached. "I'm going to float this out, if I get the right trajectory, I'll have our way out," Hunter replied with a smile.

"Well try it," Minin said encouragingly, even though he was highly doubtful this would work. This wasn't the first time Hunter had done something like this, and he doubted it would be the last. But Minin encouraged Hunter anyway, just for the slight chance that it may work. The moment Hunter had arrived on the island, he tried coming up with ways to leave. Minin sat down, there was no point in standing, as this would take a while.

Hunter put the raft into the water and pushed it out over the waves, it floated out, moving reasonably quickly along the path that Hunter had chosen. The furthest anything had gone was the rock formation. When that happened Minin had never seen Hunter so happy. He thought he'd figured it out. When that raft got close to the rock formation, it was blown up, only small pieces that floated back to the beach remained. This time was no different, the raft plodded along the top of the water for about fifty metres when it exploded.

The first time when Minin saw that happen, Hunter explained that there were missiles in random places under the water, that could detect anything that it identified as a vessel or person. If they tried to get too far from the island, it would believe it was an escape attempt and launch, resulting in the attack. Hunters theory was that the missiles might have a blind spot which he would be able to exploit.

Hunter put his hands over his head in disappointment, rubbed his hands over his face, then looked at Minin. "You'll figure out a way to get off the island eventually," Minin assured Hunter, trying to cheer him up, even though he thought it was a fool's errand.

"One day, one way," Hunter replied. "Is everyone up at the camp yet?"

"Not yet, Hayley came and got me out of bed, she went into the forest to get Callum, who's gone off again. It wouldn't surprise me if they are both there waiting for us by now."

The two of them make their way back to the camp and just like Minin had predicted, the other two were sitting waiting for them to return. "Bout time you two got here," Hayley said to them. "Callum came into the camp right away, only forgot the time by a few minutes, you two are running late."

Both Hunter and Minin looked at the sky, they didn't believe that they weren't late. Usually, the dropships never came onto the island until the sun had been overhead and it didn't even look like it was close. "We're not late." Minin tried to say back.

"Not now, but we still need to wait, it's not always a sure thing when the dropships come, you both know that," Hayley replied. "Now stand up and look sharp, when our new friends arrive," she said, trying to joke again.

The two of them sat down on the seats that were around the campfire, they didn't want to waste any energy while waiting for the dropships. They needed all the energy they had to bring the crates back into the camp. Callum sat next to them, bringing out a packet of cards, the back was coloured green from his pocket, he also knew that the wait for the dropships could be a while. He began dealing out a hand then clapped his hands, trying to get Hayley's attention to see if she wanted to be dealt in as well. She waved him off and continued to look at the sky waiting for the first sign of a dropship she could see. They continue to play for a few hours as the sun went overhead.

The only things that you ever saw or heard flying over the Island were the dropships. The island itself was a no-fly zone, only the dropships being permitted to fly overhead. The exclusion zone was so large that no plane could even be close enough to be heard or seen at any other time.

A rumbling whooshing sound came from the beach area of the camp, all four of them knew what the sound was. The three stop playing cards and pack up the deck and all stand up waiting for the first glimpse of the dropship.

"It's coming from the east this time, let's head to the beach and see it go past," Hunter suggested. The dropships usually were on the same path, but occasionally it was random. If it came from the east, it would come overhead of the camp first rather than the rest of the island.

"Let's go," Hayley replied with both Callum and Minin agreeing.

The four of them ran toward the opening of the beach hoping to get a glimpse of the dropship first. The whooshing noise was getting louder, but none of them could see anything coming their way. A few minutes' passed and still no sign of the Dropship, just the noise getting louder.

Minin then saw a dot in the sky coming toward them. "Look over there," he pointed in the direction. "That's it," he announced. The dot gained size until it morphed into the familiar rugby ball shape of the dropships. The noise of the engine started to become deafening.

"Almost time for the drop," Hayley announced with a smile on her face. "I love this, we are getting our supplies and new people."

A siren began to blare, the first sign that the door at the back of the dropship was about to open. "I never understood why I couldn't hear the siren when I was still inside the ship," Minin asked curiously.

Hunter turned his head. "No-one knows, it's strange you can hear the engine, just no sirens from the inside, it's never made sense to me either."

The dropship was nearly overhead, Callum pointed to the sky and made a line with his hand. He waved his arms over his head trying to tell everyone which path the dropship was taking. He believed that it would be overhead. The dropship got close. He was right, everyone would be able to see the underbelly of the Dropship as it passed by.

The Dropship went over with the back open. The first crate of supplies came out, close to the border of the camp. "That's ours, it's gotta be within our camp area," Hayley said, hopeful but with desperation in her voice.

More crates fell out as the Dropship moved further away from them. Every one counted as each one fell to the earth. "2....3.........20." Which was the last one.

"There weren't any people, it usually drops people first, doesn't it?" Minin asked with concern, thinking something had gone wrong with the drop, just as the dropships began to go out of sight. The noise of the engine, the only remaining clue that it was nearby.

"It's rare there isn't anyone on board, but it does happen," Hunter said, trying to calm him. "I've seen it a couple of times, just supplies, no people. It's not the end of the world, trust me, if there are fewer people on the island, that's fewer people we have to share the supplies with. Just remember that."

Hayley continued, "Don't get so worried, the ship hasn't turned around yet, there still might be a chance for it to drop people, maybe it's droppin' them last. Could be a small drop of people this time." The noise of the Dropship's engines began to get louder again. It was making another turn towards the island. Hayley grabbed Minin's arm and shook it in excitement. "This is it, it's got to be the people coming," She began to jump up and down. "I can't wait, I hope someone joins us this time."

Minin didn't understand why this day made Hayley so excited. To him this was just life on the island, once a month new people and supplies arrive. The first couple of times he'll admit that he was excited but the excitement had turned into a routine for him. "Can anyone see anything?" He called out as the Dropship came back into view as soon as he asked, it was faster than usual. "It's in a bit of a rush, isn't it?"

The back was still open. The chairs that the new Islanders sat on while in the dropship start rushing out, quicker than any time anyone had seen before. There was no gap between people falling out the back before the next started, everyone was standing and looking on in horror.

"Why the hell is it going so quick?" Hunter screamed out in confusion, "I've never seen this before, this isn't right?" Before anyone knew, six people had come out of the dropship, the back then closed and headed away from the island.

"Can anyone see how many parachutes opened?" Minin asked, thinking more about the people that came out rather than the timing. He couldn't see a difference from the colours of the parachutes from the people and those of supply crates from the angle he was looking.

Callum waved his hand around, showing two fingers.

"That's how many I thought as well," Hunter replied, knowing if they both were correct four people had just lost their lives.

Hayley's excitement had worn off after seeing everything that had just unfolded. The speed at which everyone had been ejected was too quick. She put her hand up and pointed at one of the Parachutes. "That one's close to the supply crate that came into the camp, we have to go for them."

"It's going to be close, even if they didn't land in our area," Hunter replied.

The Parachutes continued to fall until they became obscured by the surrounding trees and bush. "It's time to go," Hayley announced.

All four immediately began the journey to find the supply crate and the person that may have landed within their borderlines. They found the first crate close to the middle of the camp, just at the beginning of the path that went out toward the Freeland's. It looked like it had fallen hard and was cracking on the sides. Minin and Callum both knew the drill that they needed to pick the first crate they see and take it, so they both went over and claimed it.

"Leave it," Hunter instructed. "It's close enough to the camp that we don't have to worry about someone coming in and taking it. If there is another crate that's further away or we come across the person, it's better for us to get them first, that crate isn't going anywhere," he explained with a smile. This hadn't happened before but neither one argued, knowing that he was more experienced in this situation and they were sure he was right about it.

The four of them continued to walk towards the entrance, it was getting close. It looked like it was going to be clear and the crate that had come into their area was going to be the only thing this drop-day was going give to them. They eventually got to the borderline, half in and half out was another crate, all four rushed to it. They wasted no time getting it back over the line and into the camp, each one taking a corner and lifting it.

"It's lighter than usual," Minin said. "It's not exactly light-light but it's lighter than they usually are."

"It doesn't mean whatever is inside can't be useful to us," Hayley replied. "I just wished we found the person," she continued sounding disappointed.

"They would have landed just outside the camp area, there's a good chance once they get their bearings that they'll walk into the camp, you can make your introduction then," Hunter said to her, hoping to get the crate back quicker.

Hayley stopped moving. "Let's look for them."

While the crate was lighter than usual, just standing was beginning to take its toll on everyone. "Rules are rules. If anyone lands in the Freelands they are on their own unless they come into the camps." Hunter explained. "These are rules from all the camps. Don't worry they'll come in," he reassured her. Hayley was disappointed with what he had said, she didn't try to hide it but she knew this was the way it was.

Everyone continued the walk back, Minin heard a faint cracking noise coming from the trees above them and stopped the group. "Did anyone else hear that?" He asked them. Everyone started looking around hoping to hear something. The cracking noise got louder, everyone had heard it. They put down the crate and looked around hoping to see what was making the noise.

Callum pointed to an area just to the left, there was a seat and what looked to be a woman sitting in it. She wasn't awake, no-one could see if she was breathing or not.

"Do we go up there?" Minin asked not knowing what to do in the situation. During his time on the island, no-one had ever landed within the area.

"Usually Callum goes up and checks if they're ok. He's the lightest except for me, but I'm not good with heights." Hayley said.

Callum climbed up a nearby tree as quickly as he could, getting to the woman and checked on her. He looked down at the ground and put his hands together, laid them on his face, telling everyone that the girl was alive but had passed out.

"She's probably knocked out, or passed out from the shock of the drop," Hayley informed them. She then asked Callum. "Can you get her down on your own?"

Callum carefully examined how she was connected to the seat and the tree for a few minutes, going over every strategy in his head and the potential for them to go wrong. He weighed up the situation then pointed to himself and nodded his head to everyone waiting below.

"He's going to do it himself, let's get under him and get ready to catch, just in case," Hunter directed Minin. They all moved into position. Minin noticed that they could see Callum properly from this angle, Hunter just smiled noticing his confusion. "And that's why Hayley stays where she is."

Callum began to unhook the woman. Everything was fine until she slipped. "Get ready guys," Hayley called out.

Hunter and Minin braced themselves but Callum grabbed her just in time. He lowered both himself and the woman as low as he could. Eventually, he realised that he had misjudged and must pass her to those on the ground. He looked at Hunter, who already knew this. He nodded back at Callum, as Callum let go of the woman.

The woman landed softly in the arms of Hunter. Callum came down just as quickly as he went up. As he did the woman began to stir. She looked up into Hunter's face, she didn't know what to make of him, she just stayed quiet and began to look around nervously.

"Put her down. She obviously doesn't like a stranger carrying her," Hayley said. Hunter gently lowered her to the ground. Minin, Hayley, Callum and Hunter all go over to the woman. She was young, with a slim build and long blonde hair, her nose button-like, with a tiny smattering of freckles. There were scratches all over her face from landing in the trees. She was wearing small yellow shorts and a white crop top. She stared at all four in fear.

Minin soon realised as to what might be going through her mind. The same thing that was going on when he first arrived on the island and saw everyone. "We're not going to eat you, we're not going to harm you," He said, trying to calm her. But the woman still looked very wary.

'CRACK.' A branch began to break above everyone. "It's coming from the tree that was holding both the woman and the chair. We've got to move, the seat is going to fall." Hayley commanded everyone.

Everyone except the woman moved out of the way. She was calmer than before but she was still slightly paralysed from the fear. She looked at the seat that was threatening to fall onto her. She began to breathe heavily, knowing in her mind that this was dangerous, but her body wouldn't let her do anything about it.

Minin looked at the woman and realised the same thing. Without a second of thinking, he ran toward her and picked her up out of the way. The seat fell crashing to the ground, shattering into hundreds of pieces. Just missing them both.

Minin looked at the woman, "Be glad your shoot opened, if not that would have happened long before now."

The rest join them, Hayley said to the girl with a smile. "Happy drop-day, Welcome to the island." The girl then fainted again.

Hayley looked over her for a minute. "She'll be ok, she's clearly shaken up, a bit of rest and she'll be fine. Although she is going to have to harden up. This place will eat her up if she doesn't." She looked directly at Minin. "You take her to the camp and get her to lie down, we'll get the supplies and follow you over. If she does wake up and remembers what had just happened, maybe she'll be a little more trusting of you. Then hopefully she'll warm up to us in time." Minin picked the girl up and began to walk to the camp.

"Are we going to look at the supplies when we get back?" Hunter asked.

"No, remember our rule, everyone in the camp has to be present for the supplies, and she is one of us now, and I doubt she'll be awake before the sunsets.

8

The sun was beginning to set. Callum had already set up the nightly fire, Hayley had taken her seat waiting for everyone, Minin was the first to join her. "How is our new friend doing?" She asked.

"She's still out of it, I was having a look at her scratches while she was asleep, they seem like they aren't going to cause her any trouble, you are welcome to double-check though," He replied.

"I trust you," she replied with a smile. "If there was a problem I'm sure you'll let me know, we'll just let her rest for the night. If she wakes up anytime soon, she'll at least be able to get some dinner after such a long eventful day."

Hunter joined them. "It's getting a bit cool isn't it?" He said. "How is our new friend doing?" He asked.

"She's good, a bit shaken up but I'm sure she'll be fine after she's rested up," Minin replied.

"I'll get onto making a hut for her as soon as I can, you're still good with sharing yours? That is unless she wants to become a Freelander?"

"It doesn't bother me, it's going to take getting used to having to share a hut again, but I'll get used to it."

Hayley cut in. "If it gets too much and you don't want to share with a girl anymore, I'll swap huts with you," she said jokingly, trying to see if the comment would get a reaction out of him.

"Doesn't bother me in the slightest." He paused then smiled, "Sounds like you're a bit jealous that I've got a roommate?"

"I'm not jealous, I just don't want you freaking out if you see a bra and panties on your floor."

"Who's to say they don't belong to me?" Minin said with a slight smile. "Maybe she wants to share?" They all began to laugh. It took a moment for them to calm down. "Where's Callum? I just realised I didn't eat any lunch. I don't know about you guys but I'm starting to get hungry."

"He shouldn't be too far behind. He's probably getting something from the food supply shed," Hayley responded. "I'm getting hungry myself."

At that moment, Callum came out from near his hut, holding the handles of two cast iron pots. Hunter called to him, "Aren't they heavy? Do you need some help bringing them down?"

Callum just shook his head, he wasn't struggling in the slightest. He placed the pots into the fire, away from the centre in mostly just hot coals and then sat next to Hunter. He looked at everyone and started rubbing his arms, indicating he was getting cold.

"You're right, it's going to be a chilly one tonight," Minin replied.

Suddenly there was a broken – glass smashing noise coming from inside Minin's Hut. Everyone looked in that direction but they couldn't see anything from the outside.

"Minin, let's have a look," Hayley instructed. "It might be the girl. She might have woken up and freaked out again not knowing where she is, I'll come with you." She looked at Callum and Hunter. "You two stay here and make sure dinner doesn't get ruined."

Both Minin and Hayley hurried over to the hut. Minin opened the door, there was smashed glass on the floor, but the girl was still asleep. They both went to the smashed glass and inspect it. It was the picture frame containing the picture of Amber, that had sat in the window.

"It must have blown over in the wind," Minin announced. He lifted the frame, took the picture out and inspected for damage. "Nothing's wrong with the picture, so that's good, we'll have to get another frame though," He continued as he found a dustpan and brush then began to clear up the mess. "I better do this just in case she wakes up and walks around."

Hayley looked over the girl. "I wouldn't worry about it in a hurry, if I had to take a guess, I'd say she is going to be crashed out for the whole night," She said. "I think everyone is like that on the first night or two. No one wants to wake up, everyone is under the impression this place is a nightmare." She paused for a moment. "It's not that bad as long as you don't cross the wrong people." She looked at Minin and smiled, "You were the same when you landed, once you went to sleep you tried staying in bed as long as possible, Callum as well and I tried to stay asleep as long as I could, once I got out of the Tower. I'm sure Hunter was the same. It's probably worse for him, he's been trying to leave since I met him."

"Hunter's been here longer than the rest of us, there weren't that many people here when he arrived. In those days it must have been pretty much everyone for themselves, I couldn't even imagine the stuff he must have seen before the crowds moved in." Minin mentioned.

"I'm not going to argue with you there." Hayley went to the girl, looked over her and began to check her scratches. "Are you sure you're going to be ok with someone else sharing for a bit?" She asked Minin seriously. "I know how much you and Hunter fought when you both had to share when you came into the camp. When Callum shared with me it was a lot more peaceful."

"I'll be fine, I don't think it will be anywhere near as bad. Hunter just liked his own space was all and he had a place for everything. I came along and changed that, he's just set in his ways." Minin shrugged his shoulders, "It made him build my hut quicker, he probably thinks to give me the spare bed was a punishment after all the arguments we had."

Hayley finished looking over the girl. "She's fine if you want to head back to the fire. There's not much else we can do here, Dinner will probably be ready soon anyway, let's go."

They returned to the fire, and just like Hayley had predicted, the dinner Callum had prepared was about to be served, it was vegetable soup. He had five bowls all with spoons and ladles, four of which were filled.

"Looks like you guys made it in time." Hunter exclaimed, "You guys decide to take a detour somewhere?" Smiling and pointing at the forest suggesting they went there romantically.

Hayley and Minin were used to these suggestions, Hunter and Callum believed something was going on between the two of them. "Didn't have time for that, way too exhausted after today's exciting activities, besides Minin's hut is a lot more comfortable, didn't want to scare the poor girl if she woke up," Hayley replied jokingly back. They were just close friends as far as she was concerned.

Minin felt the same but played along with the joke as well. "I tried to make a move but she turned me down, I don't understand either, look at me." He moved his hands down his body, "I'm gorgeous". Everyone began laughing.

"Umm…. Hi," a soft shy voice came from the direction of Minin's Hut. Everyone turned around to see who it had come from. It was the girl, "You were the people that found me, weren't you?"

Hayley went to the girl, who looked nervous and not entirely sure of what was going on. "Yeah, we found you strapped to your seat and helped you out."

"Then the seat fell, but you…" She pointed to Minin. "…. got me out of the way." Her voice still indicating that she wasn't sure whether she had dreamed any of it.

"That's right, he did" Hayley confirmed.

"I'm sorry, I'm not sure, it seems all so unreal."

"That'll last for a while, what's happened to you will take time to get used to, but I assure you this place is very much real."

The girl looked back at the hut where she had come from. "I got woken up by some people talking, one of them sounded like you and then there was another voice."

"That would be me," Minin said. "You were sleeping in my hut, it's got the only spare bed for guests, so we've put you in there for now.

If you stay with us, you'll end up with your own hut eventually." He paused for a moment, "Sorry for waking you."

"It's ok, I wasn't sure if I should come down here and meet with you all and say thank you, or if you were going to do something to me and I should make a run for it." The girl explained, still looking nervous.

Hayley lead the girl to near the fire and got her to sit down. "You're safe with us, trust me," she said with a smile. Callum got the other bowl for the girl and ladled some soup, then proceeded to hand it to the girl. "That's' Callum" Hayley continued.

"Thank you." She said with a smile as she took the bowl.

He smiled and nodded back to say you're welcome.

"He's mute, so don't take his silence as rudeness, he might not talk, but he listens really well, so if you want a shoulder to cry on, he's the man to do it," Hayley explained. "Everyone has a job in our camp, it's one of our rules. If you want to stay here you're going to have to do the same, Callum is our chef and lookout."

The girl had a confused look on her face, "I can understand being a cook but how can he be a lookout if he can't talk? I just don't see how that works. Wouldn't a lookout require him to shout out or scream or at least something to warn people if there is danger coming?" She then realised that she may have offended Callum then added. "I'm sorry."

"Don't worry that won't have offended him, he's quite aware of what his limitations are without a voice. If he needs to he can make a lot of noise, trust me if there is danger about he'll be able to warn you." Hayley continued smiling at Callum who began banging on a pot with the ladle loudly, making noise. "See."

Hayley then pointed to Hunter. "The guy with the bushy beard, that's Hunter. He's the builder, repairer, general handyman of the camp. He was our first...."

Hunter interrupted her. ".... she's right, I can pretty much build anything. If you need it built and I have the parts, I can do it. Just give me a bit of time is all I ask."

Hayley continued. "Before he came to the island, he was.... a bit of everything.... weren't you?" She said trying to think of the correct words to describe him.

Hunter then took over. "I'll explain, it's a bit confusing for anyone else. I'll try and keep it short. Before I came to the island, I was special, I have the ability to learn anything and just do it, give me instructions on building a miniature house and I'll put it up without a struggle, without having to go back to the instructions once. I decided to use this ability to learn a new thing every few months. I figured I could use this to eventually 'Find my calling'. But after a few months, I was able to master it then I would get bored of whatever it was, then move onto something else. A few years had passed and I moved onto learning about computers and everything from building to programming them. As this went on, I discovered their 'finer arts', like hacking. Like everything else, I was able to pick up that skill quite easily. Eventually, I got a job for Big-Bank Inc. as an internal hacker trying to find flaws in the system. This lasted quite a while, but like everything else, I eventually got bored. I decided to give myself a little extra 'bonus' on the side. I did this by funnelling money out of other accounts and putting them into mine. I made a lot of money out of this. It was simple, all I would do is take a little out of someone's bank account then move onto the next one, each time I would add a little bit more to the amount I had taken, I eventually got greedy and started taking more. Their bosses found out that someone was taking the money and the chase was on. It made me excited and I wanted the chase to last, so I kept taking more out, I eventually got too cocky and made a mistake putting an extra bit of code into what I was doing which revealed who I was. I was sentenced to the island to pretty much get me away from any computer."

The girl looked amazed at what Hunter had said. "So you're truly happy being away from computers and the internet and not being able to learn something new?" She asked him trying to get more information. "Well, I always got bored and lazy once I mastered a subject, here I've got to learn it without a textbook or google, so it slows me down enough to make it last that bit longer."

"That's fair enough" The girl responded. She then looked at Minin, "What about you, I'm now curious about everyone, why are you here?"

"My Name is Minin......" he began and told the girl the story of how he arrived on the island. "....And that's how I ended up here," he concluded. He then realised something, "I know you from somewhere, don't I?"

"You probably do..." she said with a smirk. "...And I think I heard that story on the news, but they didn't say you ended up on the island, said that there was controversy or something." The girl hesitated for a moment. "I could be wrong, there are so many stories that get onto the news about who and who doesn't end up on the island, I could have mixed them up or something, I don't know." She said thinking she had sounded foolish. "What's your job anyway?"

"I'm the...." He stalled, not knowing what his job was.

Hayley cut in, "He usually just helps everyone else with their jobs, he's a bit of everything."

The girl nodded then looked at Hayley and smiled, "What's your story?"

Hayley smiled back, "You've heard two of our stories, I think it's only fair you tell us yours."

The girl took a deep breath, "That's fair, it's not going to make a difference if you know or not." She then took a deep breath. "My name's Tiffany, in, well...now I'll call it my old life, I was a swimsuit model, I was in high demand, every magazine wanted my picture on their covers."

Minin then interrupted her, "I knew, I knew you from somewhere! I had an old co-worker who has posters of you all over his work station. He was practically in love with you...." He stopped, knowing what he had said could have sounded bad. "...I don't think he was a stalker or anything though."

"I didn't have any stalkers or know of any that I did have. The island will certainly stop them If there were any," Tiffany said, starting to sound more confident. "*Anyway I was always busy on shoots, then it came to my last shoot, I was in an apartment, there was me, the photographer, her assistant, and a couple of people who I didn't know. I assumed they must have owned the apartment since they were so casual about being there. The shoot's theme was 'high-class partier' or something like that, and was designed to look like someone who was rich and partied all the time. So they had all sorts of things lying around, one of them looked like white powder, I assumed it wasn't anything bad, just make-believe, so I didn't think anything of it. We were halfway through the shoot and then the banging at the door began, the photographer got annoyed by all the noise and instructed her assistant to see what all the fuss was about. He unlocked the door and slowly opened it, just as one of the random people yelled for him not to. A flood of police came charging into the room, telling everyone to get on the floor. They arrested everyone on the spot, charged with drug possession. My trial was three days later, enough time to test the white powder, it turned out it was real."* Tiffany began to tear up over the memories. *"Every single person that was in the room at the time turned against me and said the drugs were mine and I wanted them at the apartment and I was using them during shots, which wasn't true. I've never touched the stuff, but since they testified against me, it was just my word against everyone else's. I was convicted and sent here, I'm not sure what happened to anyone else."*

Minin understood how she felt, he was on the island because everyone had said something against him. Hayley went over and hugged her, "Don't worry, if you stay with us, none of us will screw you over like that." Tiffany stopped crying at that moment, not sure what she meant. "What do you mean if I stay with you? I'm stuck here aren't I?"

Hayley explained, "It's true that you're stuck on the island, but that doesn't mean you have to stay at our camp, we hope you do, but you're free to go if you want. You can try to make it on your own like the Freelander's or hope that another group takes you in. It's up to you really, we hope you stay with us."

"Freelander's, other groups?" Tiffany's face showed she was confused.

"Don't worry about any of that for now, we'll explain more about the island tomorrow, it's been a big day, a huge one for you. The first day is always the hardest."

Tiffany thought about her options and decided right there, "I'll probably stay with you guys." She said happily, "My skills back home were posing and looking good on magazine covers, I've never killed an animal for survival, never made a campfire, living here is all foreign to me...please don't kick me out if I stuff up," she said trying to make a joke.

"We're not going to kick you out," Hayley assured her. "You'll have the same job as Minin, at least until we can find something you are good at. You won't be able to stand around looking pretty but you'll do something that can help us." Hayley decided to change the subject. "You said your story, now it's my turn... My name is Hayley and before I got to the island, I was a doctor, it's probably why I'm the camp's medic."

"And don't forget leader," Hunter said, adding in.

"Anyway...unlike here, where it's the occasional cuts, few bruises, I was working in a big insanely busy hospital, stress was a huge deal with what I did, but I never turned to use drugs. My addiction to overcome the stress of the world was gambling. We had a casino not too far from the hospital that I was working at. After every shift, I would go there for anywhere up to three or four hours to destress. Anyway, I kept losing until I was broke, but by this time, I was hooked and each day I needed my fix, I didn't resort to stealing off family or friends, so none of them knew I had a problem, the way I got around it was by having access to the drugs at the hospital. I started selling, it was just a small amount, just enough so I could play a few more hands, but I kept losing. I soon realised I had a problem, but I didn't want to get help, I just needed the fix and to play a hand and win. Then it would make it all better, especially if I won big, but my luck wasn't that good and I kept losing. While this was happening, I sold more drugs. I didn't realise each time I was getting the drugs I was being recorded. Eventually, the hospital asked me about it, I confessed everything hoping they would help me. They didn't, I was charged and convicted with theft and drug dealing, and sentenced to the island, I guess it helped me as I don't have a gambling problem anymore." She finished.

"What about being the leader, that didn't explain that," Tiffany asked.

"Well that comes with the territory of being in the hospital, you either had to be giving the orders or be the one taking them. I was always the one giving them, when I arrived here it's no different, none of the boys seems to have a problem with me calling the shots... or they haven't said anything." She looked around at the other three, none of them made any indication that they disagreed.

"I'm not going to argue with that," Tiffany said. She then thought, "I must warn you though, I called the shots when it came to my photos, they came out the way I wanted and if I didn't like them, whoever had taken them heard all about it," She said and began to laugh. She then looked at Callum. "What about Callum? Everyone else has had their story, what about his?"

"That's a bit hard," Minin said. "Since he can't talk, communicating is hard as it is. We don't know much about his story." Callum heard what he said and looked embarrassed.

"If he doesn't talk, what about sign language?" Tiffany enquired, she then began to sign, 'my name is Tiffany, what did you do before the island?'

Callum looked at her and shook his head confused.

"He doesn't know sign language," Minin said. "The only reason we know his name is Callum is that he could write that name in the sand and dirt. A lot of other things he has tried to say to us gets muddled up in translation. We think whatever made him not be able to speak has made everything else communication-wise hard for him." By this time, Callum was looking down at the ground, what Minin was saying was getting to him. "Anything Callum does say we have to concentrate on. We may never know his story......" Minin smiled at Callum, "......either way, he's our friend and we wouldn't change that." He said hoping to cheer Callum up a bit.

Callum looked up but with a fake smile, trying to show it wasn't affecting him. He looked at the pots that were on the fire and realised the soup on the inside was beginning to burn and moved them out of the fire.

"Well, I think now we've introduced ourselves," Hayley announced. "Tomorrow will be a big day I think, we'll get those crates open and have a chance to see what's inside."

9

The next morning Minin had woken up earlier than usual. He knew why, he could hear Tiffany tossing and turning in her bed, it was clear she was having a nightmare. He had no doubt what the nightmare was, it would be the same one that affected him on his first night, it was the same one that he had when he had nightmares. While the details are different for himself, he didn't doubt for a second that the nightmare was how she ended up on the island. He had a choice to wake and release her or let her sleep through. He thought for a second, but then she was no longer tossing and turning, but looking quite relaxed, he decided against waking her. She now had a smile on her face, the dream had changed from the nightmare to something more pleasant, and letting her sleep and relax would be a better option for the time being, she might not get this again for a while.

Minin got himself out of bed and put on his clothes. He looked over Tiffany one last time, she still looked peaceful, so he left the hut and headed toward the campfire, which was still embers and smouldering coal but not flames. Sitting next to the pit was Hayley, she still didn't sleep much.

"How was her first night? Did the Nightmare happen for her?" Hayley asked, even though she already knew the answer.

"She's sleeping fine now, she was tossing and turning before though," Minin replied.

"The entry to the island is hell. No-one knows that your drop is a lottery, everyone thinks they will at least survive until they hit the ground…." Hayley paused for a second, "Well I guess the lottery part is technically true, but you know what I mean."

"I know what you mean, either way, I'm going to let her sleep for now."

Hayley nodded her head, "We'll wake her, once everyone else is. Both the boys are still out of it. I have a good feeling about these crates, I'm sure we won't have to go into the Freeland's," she announced.

Minin didn't like Hayley's *good feelings about crates.* In his experience, normally it did not turn out well, but just like Hunter trying to get off the island, he was encouraging. "I'm sure that there won't be a problem," he told her.

Just then, Callum made his way to the fire, he looked at the two of them and made a bowl and a spoon motion, asking if either one of them would like any breakfast.

"I'm good," Hayley replied, "I just finished having some."

"I'm right, thanks anyway, I'll get my own after." Minin always made sure he would get his own in the morning, even though Callum's job in the camp was the cook. He thought he could at least get his breakfast every morning. Callum nodded his head to tell them he understood then took his seat at the fire.

"That's one of them up," Minin announced. "Just one more and then our *'guest of honour.'*"

It wasn't too long before Hunter made his way out from his hut, he looked like he had just woken up. "Morning," he said to them all. He rubbed his eyes attempting to wake himself up more, "Is Tiffany awake yet?"

"Tiffany's still asleep," Minin answered. "I'll go get her up in a moment."

Hunter looked behind his Hut towards a shed, which contained all the food they had stored. "I might go get some breakfast while she wakes up," he announced. Callum tried to get the breakfast himself. "No, you stay, I'll get it," Hunter said, then began to walk off.

"I better go get her, since everyone is up now," Minin said and headed towards his hut.

"No problem, we'll be waiting here for everyone," Hayley replied.

Minin went inside the hut. Tiffany was awake and sitting up on her bed, she was looking around, unsure of herself, while her blanket was still covering her. She looked up at him, "I didn't know if last night was a dream or not, the drop just kept replaying in my head."

Minin put his hand on her shoulder, trying to comfort her. "The nightmares come less often over time," He said, then realised that he had just said exactly what Hayley had said on his first few days on the island.

She looked at him disappointed that they don't stop but was happy he didn't lie to her about it either. "When I woke up last night, I didn't know if yesterday was a dream or reality."

"This is very much real life, you just have to make the best of it," Minin said with a smile. He then looked outside the door, "Everyone is ready for you, we're about to open the crates unless you want something to eat first."

"I think I'll be all right, but thanks anyway," Tiffany smiled. She then removed her blanket. Minin was taken aback, she was wearing nothing but red underwear, she didn't seem to care that Minin was in the room with her.

Minin politely looked away and said "Uhhhh... I'll give you some privacy."

"It's all right, you guys helped me last night, I didn't feel so out of place before I went to sleep. I then had the nightmare which woke me, that made me feel out of place." She thought for a moment, "I wanted to feel normal, and I feel more comfortable wearing not much to bed. It helps me sleep and reminds me a little of home." She then smiled cheekily, "Besides, I'm used to not wearing much when I work."

Minin understood the need for the comforts of their old life, "I try thinking of the good things in my old life whenever I go to sleep, It helps me relax. I also think of the good times that I've had here too."

"If I think of my old life, it's usually my first best friend, Shaun, we would do anything for each other. He was the reason I got my first modelling contract, he encouraged me, even though I knew it would make things hard between us not being able to see each other, we tried everything to stay in touch, but eventually, it just became too much. I hoped one day once it all slowed down we could get the friendship back together, but…" She shrugged her shoulders, "…. It's not going to happen now, is it?" Without missing a beat Tiffany tried to change the subject, "What's the go with you and Hayley, you two make a nice couple, how long have you been together?" She said with a smile.

Minin looked back at her and smiled, "There's nothing going on, we're just friends and it probably won't be any more than that."

Tiffany got out of the bed and began to look for the clothes she was wearing the previous night. "That's a real shame, she's cute, and I'd go for it if I was you. You never know what's going to happen." She told him with a smile as she put on her pants and t-shirt. "I'm all good to head to camp if you are?" She announced.

Hayley, Hunter and Callum were still waiting at the campfire. "Are either one of you going to have breakfast, before we begin?" Hunter asked.

"I might give it a miss for now," Tiffany replied.

"Yeah, I can wait till we have seen what's in the crates." Minin also replied, still trying to sound excited for Hayley.

"Awesome, let's head to it then."

The crates were in the holding bay. Located next to the path that lead to the beach. They were open tin-sheeted sheds, made from old supply crates. It was covered, so no-one had to worry about the elements.

All five began to make their way to the holding bay. Sitting underneath the covering were the two crates that were collected the day before, neither one looked like it had been dropped from the sky, they both looked brand new.

"What happened to the crates? They don't even look like they had been touched?" Tiffany asked.

"It's not real wood, just designed to look like it. It's some kind of metal, able to clean it's self after it gets dirty." Hayley explained.

"I wouldn't have the slightest clue why they would give us something like that. If it was me I'd use old crappy wood that's barely able to stay together," Hunter said. "But if it was old wood I'd probably have to keep fixing the sheds.

"They probably had pressure from the citizens to make it more humane, make it at least able to survive the trip, but you aren't interested in what they come in, are you?" Minin asked Tiffany, knowing she was more excited by what the crates contained, rather than what was holding them together.

Tiffany didn't answer, she was just staring at it, wondering how to get the crate open.

Hunter then handed her a claw hammer. "It's your first time, so you get to open it first." He wasn't sure if she knew what to do, so he explained. "Hook the end in and move it, it'll come apart if you give it enough of a yank, they might be made of metal but are easy to open."

She was excited and didn't want to look useless by doing it wrong, so she did exactly as he told her. She couldn't get the sides to come apart, she just didn't have the strength. "I can't do it," She said disappointed. The look on her face thinking she had failed.

Minin didn't want her to feel upset, so he grabbed the hammer and took over. "Don't feel so bad. I couldn't do it my first time either, it takes a bit of getting used too. You'll get there pretty quickly," He hooked the claw in and moved the handle back and forth. The side connecting to each other started to come apart revealing darkness from the inside.

Minin handed Callum the hammer to do the other side. He could get his side undone easier than Minin. Hayley was next and hers came off as well. The last side had nothing holding it, so Minin removed the lid.

Tiffany looked inside expectantly, but only saw dust. "It's empty, It's just a crate of dust." Her excitement turning into disappointment.

"It's always dusty for a bit, it needs time to settle," Minin said. "Moving and opening the crate probably disturbs it. We'll give it a few minutes while we open the other one."

Hunter now had the hammer, he began to open the other crate, but just like Tiffany, he couldn't do it. "This one is a bit stuck." He gave a frustrated laugh, "Must be old," he said trying to make an excuse for not being able to do it.

Hayley took the claw off Hunter and passed it to Tiffany, "Some people just don't get the hang of opening things," she said smiling.

Tiffany tried again, she paused, thinking, *'if Hunter can't open the Crate, how is she ever going to be able to?'* But tried none-the-less. It took a bit to budge but to her surprise, it came off. "I did it," she said proudly then passed the claw to Minin who removed his side, who then passed to Callum who got the last and removed the lid. Just like the last crate, it was dusty inside.

Minin returned to the first crate and had a look inside, Tiffany wasn't too far behind him and looked inside as well. She got herself inside the crate and started tossing everything about and announced confusingly, "It's all Magazines and newspapers, it looks like junk. How is that useful for us? I was expecting food or something we could use." She picked up a magazine called *'Celebrity gossip'* then dropped it in disgust. "Not anything like this," she continued. She then got out and headed towards the other crate hoping for something better.

Minin announced proudly to everyone, "Tradeable Crate." The other three hurried over and rummage through, with more excitement than Tiffany.

"Have a look at this," Hunter said as he picked up a magazine.

"We can get something huge for this," Hayley said as she picked another magazine herself.

The three of them start taking everything out of the crate and began stacking everything into order. Minin looked at Tiffany, who was now more confused than ever, began to explain what *'Tradeable Crate'* had meant. "This is all tradable, you'll be surprised what we can get for it. Not everything we get is going to be food or clothing or on the surface usable. Everything that comes to the island is donated and if we do get a crate, it's a lottery of what's on the inside. Things like this we can trade from another camp. *'One man's trash is another man's treasure'* as the saying goes, so even if we don't get something in the crate that we can use, what we do get can be traded to someone else."

She began to understand a little, "So it's like money?"

"Something like that. The magazines and whatnot, we think are supposed to show us what we are 'missing' from the outside world. They probably think it shows us what kind of hell we are in. But in reality, if it wasn't for certain people, this place would be heaven." Hayley replied.

"Certain people?" Tiffany asked sounding slightly nervous.

Minin paused for a moment. "I'll explain later. We have some work to do with the crate first. "See what they are doing," he looked at the others. "They are stacking them in the order which they think people would want them, and the value it will bring to us." Minin started to pick some magazines and place them in order, "Have a look and give us a hand, it's not that hard to work out, once it's done we'll move onto the next crate."

It took them a while but eventually, there were ten stacks all ready to be traded. "Ok time to move onto the next crate," Hayley announced.

Hunter was the first one to go over and look at it. "It's all electrical stuff, I call dibs on this," he said with a smile.

Everyone else came over and glanced, Minin looked at Tiffany. "Now this is what we call junk. Most camps have no power, they have no use for any of it." He smiled at Hunter. "Unless you can turn it into something else."

Hayley was looking in the distance and could see the tower. "But depending on where you are, it might be useful," she said nervously. She quickly changed the subject before Tiffany had a chance to ask what she meant. "We didn't get any food or anything, which means we should go into the Freelands and look for crates that haven't been collected yet?"

"It might be useless considering it's been a day since the drop, it's probably been all collected," Hunter said.

Tiffany then spoke before anyone else could answer. "What's wrong with these Freelands?" she looked and could see that no-one answered, "I want to see the Freeland's. I want to know the island I'm on."

Minin then remembered the first time entering the Freelands and how that had turned out.

Hayley smiled at her, "Going to another camp to trade is bad enough, they have their own rules that we need to follow. The Freelands themselves are just fine. It's just the people out there that make it a problem. The rules are different again. Well, there really aren't any rules. The Freelands are a free-for-all".

Hunter interrupted her, "You came at the perfect time, it's peaceful. When I came here it was anarchy, it was everyone for themselves, exactly what the island was designed for, come here and survive on your own. Everyone all had our own space and fought for it. Eventually, people started joining with others for bigger spaces and they became little communities. If you go into another camp you should abide by their laws. If you don't and you're lucky, they just throw you out but if you're unlucky something worse. It's completely up to that community. But that's only certain places, the Freeland's doesn't even have that, it's a free-for-all." Hunter looked Tiffany up and down. "I'll be completely honest, I don't think you would have survived if you were here during the early days."

Minin then added, "Or worse, you meet Daman Biguy."

"Who's that?" Tiffany asked. The name sounded familiar but she couldn't picture who it was.

Callum opened his hand then began to shake them in frustration, walking away from everyone.

Minin answered, "Callum's only met him twice and myself only once, he thinks he owns the island. No one seems to know that much about him, all we know is that he was one of the original Ten to be put on the island. A quick version of the story goes, that he killed the other Nine hence why he thinks he owns the island."

Callum came back with a piece of paper, a partial map that Minin had drawn of the island, the west side was blank. He began tapping on the picture of the tower.

"That's the Tower, Daman Biguy's area and for everyone's sake let's hope he stays there while we are out," Hayley said as she rubbed the back of her neck, her eyes show she was remembering something from her past. She turned around and showed everyone her scar and the barely visible red light underneath. She turned back around, a tear was streaming down her cheek. "It's a kill chip planted at the base of the skull, I think I was one of the last to get one. We think the supply ran out soon after, so you newbies won't get one, and I hope you don't, not that it's going to help you. He has other ways to kill people with or without a chip." She took a deep breath, "We should get going, the sooner we are back, the safer I'll feel".

"I'll go get some protection before we go," Hunter said, leaving toward the centre of camp but going passed further. He shortly returned carrying homemade slingshots, his hands so full, looking like he couldn't possibly hold anything else. Everyone took one from him. "Weapons are hard to come by, not that it's ever happened before but we might need something to protect ourselves with. We didn't use to take weapons but now that we have them I'd rather, Just in case." Hunter warned.

"That's the rule for anyone except Daman," Minin continued warning Tiffany. "If he or anyone from the tower comes, just stand still, and let them do their thing. Don't upset them. When I first met him, they said he was having a good day, it was scary enough as it was. The one time you meet him, he might not be."

"And how will I know that they are from the tower?" Tiffany inquired.

"You'll know. Let's just say they'll be a little bit different and you'll know right away"

10

They all began to make their way from the camp and into the surrounding forest, eventually arriving at the area which Tiffany first landed, the ground still wasn't cleared from the debris from the seat that was destroyed.

Just like Minin had done on his first Journey to the Freelands she paused looking at what she had survived.

"Take one last look," Minin said to Tiffany. "The island is about to get a lot bigger."

But she ignored him, she just stared at the ground, thinking the same as Minin had done, she could have been part of the debris if the four of them hadn't come to rescue her. A tear slid down her cheek, knowing what could have been and was thankful for what everyone had done. She composed herself and continued to walk.

They soon arrived at the very edge of the boundaries of the camp. The red metal archway as high as the trees show the difference between the forest and openness ahead. "This is the boundary," Hayley announced. "Each camp has something like the archway, a warning that you're entering someone else's camp, any further than this and we're in the Freelands." She walked through, everyone following.

Minin watched Tiffany's face as she looked around, her face lit up over what she was seeing, the rolling grassy hills, the oceans, she turned to her right, to see more of the same only in the distance was the tower, looming over the forest that was in front of it. It looked bigger than what it did from the camp, she stared at it for a second and turned again to what was in front of her. "This isn't a prison, this is heaven, I can't believe they send criminals here, this is picture-postcard perfect." She declared then began to run ahead, twirling and dancing as she went.

"It's good to see she's lightened up," Minin said to Hayley.

"It's going to come crashing down on her eventually, and that's the worst part about it." She replied, "but let her enjoy it while she can," She continued, "keep an eye out for anything that might look like a crate." She called out and everyone started to follow in Tiffany's direction.

It's not too long before Minin called out, "Hey! I found something," pointing down a hill to everyone's right.

Everyone ran to it, it was the remains of a crate. Hunter inspected carefully, "It hasn't been that long since it was destroyed, someone has raided this area recently and if they're this close to us, there's not much chance of finding somewhere they haven't been. It's probably too late to get anything, we might have to set a trade with another group, at least something small just to get enough supplies to last us for a month. The farmers enjoy magazines, let's use some of those." He suggested.

Tiffany began to look disappointed at this suggestion, she didn't want to end her first time in the Freelands so briefly. Minin could see her disappointment from her facial expression, "Let's give it another hour or so," he asked, hoping for Tiffany's sake they would agree. "If we find more supplies as well then the day isn't wasted, besides I don't know about you guys, but the weather is too good to head back early." He continued, hoping that would help his case.

Callum began to nod hoping for the same answer, Tiffany's smile returning. Hayley and Hunter didn't look as sure as everyone else, knowing what they might run into. Neither one was a fan of the Freelands unlike Minin and Callum for this reason, both preferring to stay in their own area but if they have to be out they wanted to be back just as quickly as they had left.

Tiffany and Hunter looked at each other, not sure what to say, Hunter just nodded at her, "Just an hour. Then we're going back with or without you," Hayley warned.

Minin was relieved, he knew the dangers and why the two of them wanted to go back, but he felt in his mind the danger was minimal and Tiffany should be able to enjoy what time she had here for as long as she could.

Tiffany began to dance around in the grass again thinking about the paradise she had fallen into. She grabbed Callum making him join in her dance. Even though he knew the dangers quite well, at least for the time being, he forgot them. Tiffany's excitement over everything became a pleasant distraction. Time passed, eventually, Tiffany and Callum stop dancing and spotted a metal grate surrounded by a thick layer of concrete. Grass and shrubs are covering most of it. "What is it?" Tiffany asked curiously.

"It's one of two entrances to 'The Bunker.'" Minin explained, "Most people don't know about this one. The other side looks like the opening to a bomb shelter. That side is a lot easier to get more people in, one day we will show you. It's our last resort if anything happens with Daman, no-one thinks he knows much about the place, and we hope that remains true. If anything happens and you get lost, go and stay here and we will find you."

Hayley interrupted them, "It's time to go, we've been out here for a while now, Hunter has been talking to me and wants to check one last area on the way back to camp, he thinks if there are any more crates, they will be there."

Minin replied, "Ok, start heading there we'll be right behind you."

"Ok, don't get too far behind," she replied. Both herself and Hunter began to head away from the other three, in a direction, just to the left of where the entrance of their camp would be.

Tiffany still looked at the bunker entrance, "This island is huge isn't it?"

"It is. I've never been inside the bunker, I've never been out of the camp for that long to look inside. If we could get rid of Daman we'd probably be able to see the whole thing." Minin began to laugh to himself, "We all can't live forever, I suppose," thinking that it'll probably be a long time before Daman was gone. "We better get going before we fall too far behind, you don't want to be on the receiving end of Hayley's rants if you can avoid it," He told her. Both himself and Callum began to snigger.

They caught up swiftly. Just as they did, they all see something standing right on the forest line, a crate not yet been touched, looking like it was newly dropped, everyone running to it. Without thinking Hunter, Callum and Minin go over and pick it up. "Ok head in my direction, it'll only be a couple of minutes' walk till we hit the boundary," Hunter instructed as they began carrying.

Tiffany was amazed that all three of them were in sync, knowing what to do with a crate. "You guys have done this before, haven't you?"

"Every few months we get lucky and find another crate out in the Freelands," Hayley replied. "Never usually here, Hunter used to find them all the time before the rest of us came. He would always try to persuade us to look along here as well when it was me and him. We found one or two that I can remember, ever since then nothing. My guess is that someone else knows they land here and they get them before we do. One of the unwritten rules of the island is that a crate on the Freelands belongs to anyone else until they get to their own camp, that includes when someone is carrying it so we should hurry back."

The two of them start to walk up to the boys. They all get close to the camp's boundary, everyone began to think they were home free with a third crate. A voice then called out, a voice that no-one wanted to hear, "Stop, that belongs to me, that's mine." It was a voice that made everyone's hair on the back of their necks stand up, everyone except for Tiffany, It belonged to Daman Biguy.

Like Minin when he first went into the Freelands, Tiffany didn't know who the voice belonged too. Unlike the others, she didn't stand still, she turned around to have a look at who the voice belonged too. Minin quickly grabbed and pulled her arm sharply to the ground to get her to stop what she was doing.

Daman was sitting on top of a horse, looking down on everyone, standing beside him was his personal bodyguard, and five other guards, who were pushing two trolleys which looked to be made for carrying the crates.

The bodyguard went over to the five and began to size them up. He was huge, compared to the people he was looking over, a mountain in size and height, completely muscle, his face looked stern like it wouldn't know how to smile even if he had tried. He was bald with tiny brown eyes, his nose squashed in. He was wearing blue gym shorts, which looked brand new and was shirtless. Everyone stood still as he went through and around them, even to someone who didn't know, it was obvious this was a man you didn't want to mess with, and if you tried to, he would have had the power to lift you up and split you in two without even breaking a sweat.

After what felt like an eternity, The Bodyguard stopped in front of Minin, got close to his face looking him up and down and breathed loud and hard enough to feel the breath over his skin. Minin had never seen him before but heard enough stories to know this was a man not to get on the wrong side of. He stayed perfectly still, hoping this was the right side to choose. What he was doing was part of those stories, he looks like he goes into a trance and looked you over, remembering every pore, scar, blemish that your face had. Learning about the look of, what Minin could only think of was his prey. Each second it went on, Minin became more nervous, a bead of sweat dripped from his forehead, all he could think of was that he hoped that it would finish sooner rather than later.

"Minin." the Bodyguard announce low and deep, quiet enough so that only Minin could hear. He came out of the trance and went over to Tiffany, she was now more than aware that this was serious and stood still, while the Bodyguard did the same to her.

Daman shouted at Tiffany, while the Bodyguard was still doing his thing. "Girl, what is your name?" She didn't respond, she didn't know if that would put her into any trouble. He then shouted at her louder. "Girl," he screamed at her, "I said what is your name, tell me now." His face becoming red with each word.

She eventually managed to stutter, "Tif…. Tiff.." She drew in a deep breath and quickly uttered, "Tiffany". She then began to sniffle and tears started to fall.

"Tiffany," The Bodyguard said, in the same tone as what he did to Minin. The Bodyguard moved away, back toward Daman. A feeling of relief rushed over the five as he walked away. He got to his boss and began to talk to him quietly enough so that no-one else could hear. "I know everyone here now, Minin doesn't look like it at the moment, but I think he's going to be a problem in the future, do you want me to take him out now? Let the rest know, you're the law?"

Daman looked up at Minin and smiled, then looked back down to the Bodyguard and talked to him quietly. "No, they all know I'm the law, he won't possibly be a problem for me, he's petrified of you, and you're a damn Kitten. I'm a lion compared to you, he isn't going to be a problem for me." He jumped off the horse and went over to the group. The relief they had quickly vanished. He stood in the middle of them and looked at each one of them. He cleared his throat and began to make a speech that had been clearly rehearsed. "Attention Group F, from now on any crates dropped from the ships that are outside your given area will now belong to myself and the tower. The crate you currently have will be taken from you. If you disagree with this…." He showed the kill chip controller from his pocket, "…further action will be taken."

Everyone didn't need any other information about what that meant, although they didn't like the idea either after they had done the work to find the crate, and he was just going to take it away, just like that.

Minin without thinking shouted, "This isn't fair, that's our crate you can't just have it. We need it, we need what's in it." He began to lie, knowing they still had the option to trade and hoped Daman would show pity on them just like the last time they had met. "We don't have enough supplies to last us until the next drop and you're just going to run off with it."

Callum's hand went into a fit of rage, he had the same idea as Minin, he wanted to fight back but had mixed feelings, knowing he needed to hold back. Everyone else just remained silent and still, they didn't want the trouble that this was causing.

Daman could see the fight in Minin, "You're only saying what you are because you don't have a chip, it'll be a very different story if you did…" he began to snigger. "…. Well you wouldn't be saying anything again," then waved the kill chip controller once more. "You say you don't have enough supplies? Don't bring extra people into your group, it's that simple. Let go of the girl, surely you haven't grown attached to her yet." Everyone on his side began to laugh at his comment, "Over-population on the mainland is one of the reasons why this island exists, surely you know that? You look like someone reasonably smart. You're smart, aren't you?" The Bodyguard then ran to Minin and went as close to his face as he could, Minin feeling every breath he took. "There are other ways to get you to comply, even if you don't have a chip," Daman continued.

Minin took a deep breath, slowly trying to calm himself. "You're right," he said shyly knowing that any other answer would be the wrong one.

The Bodyguard returned slowly walking backwards, staring into Minin's eyes, just waiting for the moment he could pounce if he said one more thing out of line.

Daman then continued what he was saying before, "I'm going to put that outburst down to a brain malfunction, don't screw up again. You may not have a kill chip in your head, but there are other ways to teach you why I'm not to be messed with." He began to look at the Body-guard who was making a bending shape with his hands. "Now walk away from the crate," he commanded the five.

Everyone did as he said, they didn't want any more trouble. They got far enough that the crate was a few metres away. Four of the guards that were accompanying Daman went to the crate. Each guard taking a corner, each holding metal suction cups that had a handle, which at-tached to the crate. A noise like a drill began, a tiny stream of smoke coming from the suction cups, the noise stopped and the guards picked the crate by the handle. They then walk to the trolley and place the crate down. The guards then began to push the trolley away.

Daman looked at the guards as they walk away, he then looked at the five just standing there powerless, "You see that? They do a little work for me, they don't argue about it, they keep their mouths shut and they do it. That's loyalty and I reward them for it. You all might want to talk with…." pointing to Minin "'.....*Mr brave*' here about that before we meet again, otherwise, something else might happen." His voice rose, "And it might not be to him."

Minin knew that this time he got extremely lucky over what had happened, talking back usually meant death from what he had heard. He also knew that the *'Loyalty'* those guards had, was more like slavery and the reward they had was keeping their lives.

Daman looked down at everyone for a few more seconds which felt like a lifetime. He wanted to watch them instilled with the fear of him just that little bit longer, he eventually turned and rode away. The Bodyguard waited a bit longer, he managed to crack a smile at all of them. Minin could only think he was doing this because of how lucky they were to survive an encounter like this.

The five of them just stood in silence, until eventually the group leaving had disappeared. They all turned to Minin in disbelief, except for Callum who was smiling, Minin could only imagine he was happy that someone had just stood up to Daman and lived to tell the tale.

The silence eventually lifted when Tiffany spoke up, "Who was that? and what was that all about?"

Hayley then spoke, "Yeah, what was that?" She was beyond annoyed. "You know the rules when he is here, you keep your mouth shut, you do what he says and he leaves quickly, you don't try to be a hero." She then pointed to Tiffany, "She doesn't know all the rules on the island yet, but you don't have that excuse, one press of a button, either I or Hunter get killed, you know that. You also know that damn Bodyguard of his is dangerous too, he can easily kill anyone that doesn't have a chip."

Minin already knew he had made a mistake before she had said anything. "I... I... I'm sorry ok. Is that what you want me to say?" He paused for a moment trying to explain himself. "But someone needed to say something, I'm sick of living in fear of him."

"Someone does need to say something and something needs to be done. But everyone wants to live just that little bit more," Hayley replied.

Callum threw a punch, then pointed to himself and then pointed in the direction of the tower, telling everyone he wanted to fight back.

"See, Callum wants something done, and so do I. Everyone says this place is paradise if it wasn't for him. Someone has to say something before it gets worse," Minin said, feeling good that someone else agreed.

"He could have killed any of us," Hayley argued. "One press of the button would have done that, he didn't need to kill you to show what he can do. He could have killed me or Hunter, The Bodyguard could have grabbed Tiffany and belted the crap out of her, and there wouldn't have been a damn thing any of us could have done about it unless we got killed ourselves." She paused as a few tears move down her face, "Do you understand now why we keep our mouth shut. He has the power and he knows it. We can't go against him, most of us will die without him taking a single step, what kind of revolution is that?"

Minin understood what she had said, though he didn't agree. "I'm sorry", he said although annoyed, trying to defuse the situation with her.

Hayley shooked her head, "It's fine," she replied abruptly, storming off toward camp.

"Let's just get back to camp, we have stuff we can trade, we'll use that," Hunter said, trying to find peace.

Minin knew he had to do something to make it up to Hayley, he felt the best thing for the moment would be to go over to her and try to talk it through. He began to run to her, getting a slight touch of the back of her arm. She turned around, her tears becoming a stream. "Just leave me alone," she shouted at him and began to run off. Minin stopped and looked at her while she ran. Tiffany followed her trying to catch up.

Minin stood still watching her go, he knew he had made a major mistake and it wasn't something that could be fixed easily. Hunter came over, "Let her go, she needs time to cool down, give her a few days, she'll be fine. This isn't the first time she has had a scare like that, she'll realise you didn't mean for it to turn out like that," he said reassuringly.

Minin didn't know what to say, he knew that Hunter was right, but regardless he didn't want the situation to be like this. "You're right," he replied and began the rest of their journey back, Callum following behind.

They arrived at the centre of the camp, just after Hayley and Tiffany. Hayley was no-where to be seen, Tiffany just standing around the campfire, looking down, the boys came over to see what she was looking at. A boy was laying down, curled up with his legs near his chest. Wearing cargo shorts and a ripped white t-shirt, "What's happened?" Minin asked.

"He's asleep," Tiffany replied, unsure if she should be worried or not.

Hunter went over to the boy and tapped him on the shoulder. It woke him harshly, he looked around confused, wondering where he was. "Wait...what's...happening?" He asked them.

"We could say the same thing to you. What are you doing here?" Hunter questioned.

The boy was nervous, he kept looking around like something was wrong. Minin recognised straight away that he was Screamer from his drop-ship. Minin never managed to get his real name. "Screamer, what is it? What's wrong?" He asked.

"You guys have to help me......we didn't get anything from this month's drop. We haven't had anything in months. We have a day or two worth of food left. We need your help," He begged them. "Remember I'm your drop brother...you need to help me," he continued. Minin knew he had to help him. Going through something as traumatic as Drop day together made the other people on your dropship feel like your own family, just like your camp did. The difference being those people knew how your drop to the island was. From Hunters drop-day, only three remained, Hayley also three, and Callum as far as he knew was the only one.

Hunter grabbed Minin by the arm, pulling him away from everyone and started to speak to him quietly enough so that no one else could hear. "Hayley isn't here, she's probably in her Hut, but if she was, she'd say the same thing, we can't do it. We barely have enough ourselves so we have to trade with the other camps. That's easy enough, but after today, I don't think any of us want to take the chance of seeing Daman anytime soon. Going to other camps to trade is a lot harder just in case we do see him since we have to leave the camp. Giving what we have to Screamer is going to make it that much harder if we don't have anything ourselves. I'm going to give the decision to you, make the right one," He warned as he released his grip.

Minin knew he was right and went over to Screamer and looked him the eye, took a deep breath. "Screamer," he announced in a calm serious tone. "We can't do it, I'm sorry, we haven't got much ourselves."

Screamer was disappointed, he looked up at Minin, his eyes telling him he was desperate. "It's Ronald, my name is Ronald," knowing he didn't know his real name. "You really can't help me out?" he said, hoping his answer would change.

Minin stood there thinking about what Screamer had said before, that his group hadn't been able to get anything dropped near their camp in a while. "What do you mean you haven't had anything in months? Hasn't there been a drop at your camp or at least close by? Why didn't you get something then?"

"No, the last few months when the ships came by, they drop crates and people on other parts of the island, then instead of continually dropping like it usually does, it goes near the tower and does a major drop of supplies there, you probably don't see it from where you guys are, it's like they can force it too or something." He explained.

Minin still didn't quite believe him, something from what he was saying just didn't add up in his head. "You're probably being paranoid," He told him. "We get a dry spell of supplies every now and then, in fact, we only got two crates this month, with nothing of use for us.

Maybe your camp is having one yourself?" He questioned him, hoping he would see they also didn't have anything.

It didn't work though, Screamer hated the fact he wasn't believed, "You guys don't see anything. You don't see anything once the ships are past your forest line." He started shouting at them, "I'm not crazy, I'm telling the truth, you guys stay in your own little bubble, in this area and only come out when it suits you."

Hayley could hear what was going on, she came out of her hut, remaining quiet, looking at what was going on.

Minin still wasn't so sure it was the truth or whether Screamer or his group were trying to get more than their fair share. It was one of the problems of the island, groups taking more than they needed. Minin knew his own camp wasn't innocent of that either, so Minin had to choose carefully whether to believe his story. Screamer quickly calmed down, Minin could see his eyes, they were desperate, weak, helpless, they weren't lying, they were begging, 'help me please.'

Minin thought everything over for a moment and decided to help. He knew it wasn't going to be a popular choice. He hadn't seen Hayley arrive to ask her opinion so he looked at Hunter. Without saying anything Hunter knew what was going on, he didn't like the idea, he thought it was the wrong one but he also knew he gave the decision to him.

Minin then announced, "We'll give him something, it'll only be small, and it's only something you will be able to trade with someone else, but at least it'll give you a chance." Screamers eyes lit up a little, relief, evident in his face, Minin continued, "But…. we need something in return though, we can't do this for free."

At that moment, Screamers smile faded and his eyes lowered, this wasn't a part he wanted to hear, and the desperation that he had in his voice came back. "I haven't got anything to trade. I told you that we haven't got any food ourselves, this is why we need you."

At that moment, Hayley spoke up, "You or your group owe us a '*no questions asked I.O.U*', take it or leave it?" The sound in her voice made obvious to the fact she wasn't happy Minin was prepared to give something of their own away, when she like everyone else knew they were lacking. But she knew an 'I.O.U' would be highly valued in the future if ever the group need to cash it in.

Screamer stood there thinking over his options, he didn't know what he was getting but had to give an I.O.U up for it. He thought for a second and realised he had no choice but to accept, "Ok."

Everyone in the camp except for Tiffany knew accepting an I.O.U was a true desperation move, you wouldn't do it unless you truly had no choice. Hayley wanted to make sure he knew what he was getting himself into, "What we give you it'll be small, won't be much value but it'll get you something from another camp and in return, we get an I.O.U. Are you sure you accept?"

Screamer continued to shake his head, "I've got no choice, it's this or starve to death. At least with you guys I know you're only going to call it in if you have to, you're not Daman. You know yourself that getting something with him just isn't worth it. Last month a girl from our group, Stephanie, went to see if she could get at least one crate from him, everyone warned her not too, begged her even. We haven't seen her since but we did have a crate delivered to us, it was half empty, barely lasted us a week. I don't know what deal she made with him, but I don't like whatever it was."

Once the deal was done Minin realised that the sun was beginning to set and dusk was starting to fall, "Ronald, stay here the night," he offered. "Head off in the morning, have dinner with us tonight," he said, trying to show that there weren't any hard feelings between the two after the deal."

Screamer thought for a moment. "Ok, I'd like that," he said, taking the offer. "It'll be nice to have something more than just enough to scrape by like we usually do in my camp," he said with a smile.

"By the sound of it, it's going to be a lot more," Minin replied with a smile.

Callum walked off knowing what to get for that night's dinner, he prepared it and everyone took their seat. But the night wasn't the same as normal, even though the tension from the day had subsided, it was the quietest night in a long time.

11

Minin woke the next morning, to him it didn't feel like a regular morning, although everything seemed as though it was normal with nothing out of place. Tiffany was still asleep in her bed on the other side of the hut. He had a quick look out the window before he got dressed, it looked as though it was a normal day. He eventually shrugged whatever feeling he had, thinking it must have still been guilt over what had happened the day before and decided to get dressed and head outside.

He walked to the campfire, Callum must have just woken up next to it, he looked like he could go back to sleep at any moment. "Did you sleep out here?" Minin asked.

Callum pointed at his hut, put his hands together and put them on his head.

Minin thought he had meant he had slept in his hut but being out here told him otherwise so he took another guess, "Screamer took your hut for the night?"

Callum started to nod, he was right.

"Why didn't you get a tent or at least a sleeping bag or something if you gave up your hut for the night," Minin asked.

Callum just shrugged his shoulders and smiled. Sleeping outside didn't bother him in the slightest.

Minin then proceeded to ask him. "Where's everyone else?"

Once again Callum shrugged his shoulders then pointed to the huts, he didn't know for sure but took a guess.

Minin agreed with him, he thought for a second as to why Hayley wouldn't be up yet when she was usually the first to rise. "Do you think it had something to do with yesterday, that they are avoiding the place or even me?" He asked, hoping Callum would have the answer.

Just like the question of where everyone was, he didn't know the answer and as such shrugged his shoulders once more.

Minin once again thought about what he could do to try and make things better, he didn't want any of his friends to be annoyed or angry with him, especially Hayley when all he did was try to help his drop-brother and stand up for what he thought was right. He knew on the island trying to get a gift or even an 'I'm sorry' card was near impossible. And that could only happen if he tried to go to another camp unnoticed, hoping they had something like that he could trade for. But that would not be ideal since everyone was already going to other camps to trade, leaving earlier might be taken the wrong way, especially if he was needed to help transport items that were going to be traded.

Callum tapped Minin on the shoulder, this took him out of his train of thought. Callum then made the bowl and spoon motion with his hand, asking if he wanted any breakfast. That's when Minin realised what he could do, it was only small but at least it was a gesture of good-will. He was going to make breakfast for everyone. "I'm going to make breakfast" he announced to Callum

Callum was taken aback, he was always the cook when he was around and anytime Minin had made something in the past, it wasn't great, to put it nicely. He tried to say nicely, "Are you sure? I can do it no problem," by pointing to himself and smiling.

But Minin didn't want to take notice, he was determined and that was it. Minin walked away from the campfire towards the north end of the camp. Callum began to look worried but decided to let it go, in the hope that this time he would be wrong.

It wasn't long until Minin got behind Hunter's hut. It was still quiet, Minin was sure that he should have been hearing something going on since Hunter was always making something inside, so he assumed he was still asleep. Nether the less he walked past and entered the animal pen. The animal pen took up most of the northern area of the camp. The animals inside were taken from the island itself. There were three cows, ten chickens and two goats. Minin had never asked how the camp or even the Island had acquired them, he never saw the point.

All the animals were oblivious to Minin walking around in their area, just ignoring him. He went to the chicken coop and checked the nests, finding twelve eggs. He grabbed them and made his way out, knowing he wouldn't need anything else here. Before he left he had a quick check over everything, nothing seemed out of place.

Minin knew he needed more than what he currently held, twelve eggs were not going to do it for everyone, and knew that the freezers should have something in it he could use. He went back to the campfire, dropped off the eggs, and headed past Callum's Hut in the south of the camp, he walked past noticing Screamer wasn't making a sound and assumed that he must have still been asleep like Hunter was. Once again, he didn't want to disturb him and just walked on past, getting to the tin-sheeted sheds with the Fridges. There were three fridges on each side of the shed which were connected to Solar Panels and batteries that Hunter had made over time from anything he could get. It was one of the things Hunter was proud of making, unlike other camps they didn't need to throw out or consume anything that might perish quickly from the trades or supply crates. At the back of the shed were two fridges side by side. Minin went over to one of the freezers and opened, and saw only a small number of frozen items inside, mostly meat. Minin had hoped he would find some bacon inside but this one only contained Steak. He went to the other, hoping it would have what he needed, once again there wasn't much inside, but this time he was in luck, it contained just enough bacon to be able to use for the breakfast.

Minin knew that with the freezers being so low that would mean the group would eventually have to Trade with Carmen the only qualified butcher on the Island that he knew of, she was part of the all-female camp. The other option being, use their own animals but that would require a fee of half the animal to the female camp, and giving up that much wasn't something anyone wanted to do lightly.

Minin decided that would be something for the group to have to worry about at a later point and returned to the campfire. The fire was no longer just embers burning, it was now gaining momentum. On Approach, he saw that Hunter had now arrived, "Good morning," Minin cheerfully said to him, hoping that any problems from the previous night had gone away.

"Morning," Hunter replied, sounding like he had not long woken up. "Callum said you're making breakfast for everyone."

"That's right."

"Are you sure you don't want Callum to make it?" He replied, trying to sound nice, knowing that the food wouldn't be anywhere at the same standard that Callum would make.

"Nah, I'm going to make it. After yesterday this is the least I can do for everyone," Minin replied.

"Are you sure?" Hunter said unsure that Minin's cooking would actually help.

"Yeah, it's no problem, I'm just about to get some pans and start," Minin replied, hearing the worry in Hunter's voice. He attempted to assure him it wouldn't be a problem. "It's going to be bacon and eggs, not poison, I don't think I can screw it up."

"Ummm.….Yeah," Hunter said hastily, thinking that poison would probably be more edible than Minin's cooking.

Minin left the campfire once more, this time towards the west of the camp, near Hayley's Hut and just like the previous huts it was quiet. In Minin's mind, quieter than any other, at that point all he wanted to do was just go in and try to make everything better between them. But at the same time, he knew if that were to happen, it would probably make the healing process much worse. This was something he needed to take his time with, so he continued with his quest to get what he needed.

Going past the hut, he arrived at another tin-sheeted shed, this time with pots, pan, cups, anything cutlery like or something that could be used for cooking was stored on one side, on the other side was anything else that could be stored for trades and fun like toys and old clothes with an aisle way through the middle. Minin went through the aisle, grabbing five cups and five plates, putting them aside and then grabbed two pans. He looked around, knowing that the cutlery should have been there as well, he also knew that a lot of things go missing quite often. He looked again but couldn't locate anything of that sort. He took a mental note to ask if anyone knew where the missing items were. Minin didn't like the idea of having to cook with his hands but didn't have a problem eating that way though.

He found a box and put everything he needed in, then returned to the campfire, both Tiffany and Screamer had arrived. Callum, on the other hand, wasn't anywhere to be seen. Tiffany didn't look like she was upset over the previous night, but none-the-less looked like she had not gotten enough sleep, "Morning." She said, as she rubbed her eyes and yawned.

"Morning" Screamer also said, looking like he also didn't get enough sleep.

"Morning. I'm going to make breakfast this morning for everyone," Minin told them both, proudly, "is bacon and eggs ok with you both?"

Screamer looked pleased with this question, "I haven't had anything like that in…. well since I got to the island. We only usually have toast that's been made from whatever we can get from the crates or trades, it's usually horrible."

Tiffany smiled thinking it was a wonderful idea. She looked at Hunter who slightly shuddered.

"You're in for a treat then," Minin said. "Callum usually cooks, but trust me mine will be perfect," he looked around for a second, "Where is he anyway?"

Tiffanys face changed to a look of worry, "The last person that said trust me ended up selling me out and sending me to the island." She replied quietly to herself. She then continued louder, "Callum looked like he was going to get some firewood or something by the look of his hands."

"I still need to get the cooking plate, so I'll go get that, by then he should be back. I didn't see any utensils to cook with, you don't know where they are, do you?" Minin asked hoping for an answer.

"Probably with the cooking plate. I think Callum is trying to slowly relocate everything cooking wise into that shed, just so it doesn't look too suss just having a plate in there and nothing else," Hunter replied.

Screamer overheard, "What do you mean doesn't look suss?" He asked, thinking the comment didn't quite sound right.

Minin answered quickly before Hunter, "The shed looks empty is all." But he knew it wasn't the full truth and walked away from the campfire one last time.

This time he travelled east past his Hut, behind it was another shed. This one was empty except for a cast iron foldout cooking plate sitting in the middle and hanging on the wall were the newly relocated utensils. The other side was a table just sitting on its own, the back wall looked out of place, Minin knew exactly what it was. The walls were fake, behind it was an arsenal of makeshift weapons, all made over time, Slingshots, bows and arrows, crossbows, explosives. Minin went to the open wall and pushed it closed and thought that he was going to have to tell Hunter they needed to get a better locking system. This was something no-one in the group would want Daman to ever get a chance to find out about. This would land them in all sorts of trouble, although it would be the perfect start in bringing him down. No one believed that would ever happen though, the weapons only job was for hunting any wild animals within the campgrounds, but never taken on the Freelands. If someone from another camp were to find out, it could turn into a nightmare if they turned that information over. He hoped they wouldn't, but if the price was high enough, anyone has there selling price.

Minin checked over the weapons, everything was in its place except a slingshot, the one that Callum used every time. Minin knew not to worry as Callum liked to have it on himself even when he wasn't hunting, he figured this was one of those times, but just to make sure Minin would ask him, but only once Screamer had left. It would also explain why the walls were not in place, Callum must have not closed them properly when he came in the last time. Minin began to think it might be better if something was added that could close the walls itself making it a lot safer, something to ask Hunter to get onto, also once Screamer had left.

Minin lifted the cooking plate and the utensils and returned to the campfire, everyone was now sitting around including Hayley, talking like nothing had happened. Minin took this as a good sign that it was all looking good from here on out. The fire was burning better than it had before, Callum had brought back enough logs refilling their spare pile.

Putting the pans into the fire to warm up, Minin took his seat. Hayley turned to him, "You're right," she announced. Everyone looked at her, unsure what she meant. "You're right, we have to fight back against him, we can't live like this anymore."

Minin replied as he began to cook breakfast. "You're the last person I would ever think would say that, you've never wanted to cause trouble against the Tower, you'd rather keep your mouth shut. What happened?"

"I've had time to think it over last night. This island was designed so no-one person was in charge. Everyone was sent here to govern ourselves because they didn't want us back on the mainland, and he's taken upon himself to be the leader. We can't let him do that anymore, I'm sick and tired of living in fear of him."

Hunter stood up, looked straight over at Hayley with his eye's piercing at her in fear. "We can't do that, I don't know about you but I don't want to end up dead..." He clicked his fingers together sharply, "...Like that, we can't even get close to him to take the remote away from him. Then there's everyone else that doesn't have the chip, he'll just release whatever army to kill people with his weapons or just their arms, wouldn't surprise me if he has others like his Bodyguard, people that would fight for him at a drop of a hat that think they would get rewarded for their actions." He then looked at everyone else around the campfire, "Besides, look at them," pointing at Tiffany, Screamer, Callum and Minin. "They aren't no fighters, they're not even close. If Daman has an army, either way, we all die."

Hayley quickly fired a reply, "Or we die old. I'd rather die young and try and do something. This living in fear bullshit, it has to end."

Screamer interjected, "He can't kill us all, the ones without the chips at least. There's got to be enough of us to fight back, show him that we're not his slaves. This isn't his land it's all of ours, we just have to find enough of us to do it." His comment made it clear, that everyone else on the island thought the same, but no-one had the strength to do it. Everyone around the campfire began to cheer except for Hunter.

"What do you think we should do?" Hunter questioned. That one comment stopped everyone at that moment from rising up, meeting with the other camps and marching to the Tower. "It's only been, what? Eighteen months since the chips ran out of supply, there have been maybe one hundred people if you're lucky that have been dropped on the island and survived, and maybe a quarter of them are in the Tower with him, that leaves seventy-five and that's only a guess. Even then, not all of them are in camps. We can't just run up and ask them to join. And another problem not all of them are going to fight. The ones that will, are going to be lambs to the slaughter against him. I have seen that man do unmentionable things to people, I am truly scared of him since he holds my life in his hand. I don't want anyone to die by him, going up against him is insane, actually winning would be a damn miracle." He paused for a moment trying to compose himself, "I've been trying to work out how to leave the island the second I got here and so far it's failed but at least I can do that without getting myself killed." Everyone was quiet, they all knew that Hunter usually went quiet whenever something was said about Daman and what he had done to them. As if it was too traumatic and didn't want to remember anything, although he never mentioned what it was. "I want freedom from him like anyone else, but unless we can get that remote off him, we don't have a chance, end of the story. That's why I choose the escape option," Hunter said as he stormed off towards his hut.

Those around the campfire remained silent thinking about what Hunter had said. After a few minutes, Tiffany spoke, "This place isn't paradise. I've only just started to see below the surface, haven't I?" She asked not sure what else to say.

"You haven't even begun to start digging," Minin replied as he began to serve breakfast.

Everyone ate quietly, the tension and silence once more made its welcome. After a few minutes, the silence was broken, "I'm sorry but this is the worst," Screamer shouted. "It's bacon and eggs, how could you screw it up?" Minin didn't know what to say, "I'm sorry but I'd rather eat the bread they make in my camp."

Callum and Hayley began laughing knowing what they had gotten into. Tiffany, on the other hand, tried to be nice. "Well…. I wasn't expecting a five-star meal." She put the plate down after only eating a mouthful.

Minin couldn't believe that they were saying he thought it tasted perfectly fine, and just sat there in silence continuing to eat.

Screamer apologised, "I'm sorry but I just can't eat it."

"No-one can. I'm sorry Minin, but it's really bad," Hayley said. "Now do you know why we wanted to get Callum to make it?" She turned her attention to Screamer, "I'll get you that thing to trade."

"Yeah, I better head back to my camp," Screamer replied as Hayley went toward the shed with the cutlery in it. She returned swiftly, holding a cookbook in her hand.

"This is probably what we should give to Minin, but he'd probably won't read it anyway," She said laughing. If you don't trade it, you'll probably be able to make something to give to other camps, we have another copy." She explained and handed the book over.

Screamer took the book and stood, "Thank you for everything, you have no idea how grateful I am. I'll talk to my group, if you're serious about a revolt, I'll see if we have volunteers, not that I see any of them saying no," He said with a smile. "Maybe it'll stay a dream…." He said shrugging his shoulders, "…..Maybe it'll be the start of something new." And began walking off towards the exit of the camp.

12

"Ok, now that Screamer isn't here, let's get ready so we can trade. I want to be back before it gets dark," Hayley announced.

Minin looked around, "What about Hunter? Shouldn't we wait for him?"

"We've done it with four or less before, Hunter can miss out this time," Hayley replied knowing he had not had a chance to cool down and taking him with them wouldn't be the best idea. Callum and Tiffany began to walk to the shed with the crates, Hayley and Minin quickly followed.

The four arrived at the shed, Hunter was there looking over the piles of magazines and newspapers as though nothing had happened. Tiffany went to him. "Are you ok? You were fuming before."

He looked back at her and calmly replied, "I just needed a few minutes to calm down was all."

She looked back at him surprised, she didn't think someone who was that upset could recover so quickly, "Are you sure?" She asked, not completely believing him.

"Yeah, it's not a problem now," he replied, continuing through the piles.

Tiffany looked at everyone else, she didn't think his reaction was normal but the three of them were already starting to look through the piles, creating smaller piles that they could carry. She continued just looking at what they were doing, even though it looked like a simple task, she didn't want to pick something and look like a fool.

Minin looked up from his pile and noticed Tiffany standing there unsure what she needed. "You'll never survive if you don't get the good things first, we might try and trade as a group but sometimes you just have to be selfish and get something for yourself," He told her as he stopped and tried to pull her over.

Everyone else heard the comment and muttered that they agreed with him.

Tiffany stood still, looking at how they were making the piles, but her mind was still on Hunters recovery. She whispered into Minin's ear, "Is everything ok with Hunter, I'm not a psychologist or anything like that, but he shook it off a little too quick, he was fuming before he left."

"Some people recover quicker than others and unfortunately the reality of the situation is that you have to recover quickly, or it will destroy you. If you were a Psychologist, you'd never get a break, you'd be in too much demand with the nightmares and things we see, you just have to find that 'Happy Place' in your head that helps you recover quickly," He warned her. "Come on, the quicker we can get stuff to bring the quicker we can come back and relax again."

They both went to the piles, they all looked full, just a lot messier than the last time they had seen them. Callum handed a pile of magazines over to Tiffany, so high that she could barely hold them. He nodded and smiled, telling her that this was a good start.

Minin had a glance at what her pile contained, he could only see the top one, it was a celebrity gossip magazine called 'Celebs.' The headline read, 'Will they ever be free of the 'paparazzi?'. "That one will be good, someone will want that for sure," He told her with a smile.

Tiffany went over to a bench and put the pile down with a thud, some slid off each other onto the floor, revealing another copy of 'Celebs' but with a picture of Tiffany wearing a bikini, she picked it up to have a closer look, the headline, 'Exclusive - The *model* prisoner – What awaits inside the island for Tiffany Skye'. She went to open it.

"Don't read it, whatever you do, don't read it". Hunter warned. "This is your new life, trust me, don't let it get you down with what they've written about you, you're on the island now."

She stood there for a moment trying to decide to read or not. Callum put his hand out to try to take the magazine back, "Why did you give me this one?" She questioned him.

He shook his head, fiercely trying to tell her he didn't mean to.

"He wouldn't have done it on purpose," Minin explained. "He goes through and collects 'Celebs' Mag, he only scans the name of the magazine. He knows there are people at the Coasties camp that like reading that rubbish, he probably didn't see the picture or the headline."

She handed the magazine back to Callum, who put it in his back pocket and pointed to the fire telling them that he planned to burn it later. He then nodded and smiled.

Tiffany then picked up the other magazines without looking at any of them, "Don't let it worry you, you need to recover quickly," She said to herself. "Has everyone got what they need?" She asked, hoping to get to the burning of the magazine quickly.

"Yeah, I think we're all good," Minin replied, looking at everyone as they finished getting the last few things they could hold. With that everyone began to make their way from the shed and the middle of the camp. "I hope you'll actually be able to see the rest of the island without a problem," Minin continued trying once again to get everyone in a more hopeful mood. "The rest of the camps are pretty good, as long as you follow their rules."

Once Minin had finished, everyone could hear stomps on the ground, which were coming closer towards them. With each passing second, they got louder, everyone was on their guard waiting to see what or who was coming. Screamer appeared once more, once again with a look of fear on his face, his arms empty of what the group had given to him. "It's him, it's him, he's coming this way."

Screamer didn't need to explain anymore, everyone knew who 'he' was.

"How far away is he?" Hayley asked in a hurry, "Are you sure he is on his way here?"

"I'm positive he's coming this way. I saw him near the entry."

"Why were you still inside the camp?" Minin asked, forgetting about the danger for a second. "You should have been long into the Freelands."

"That's not the point, he's coming here, I don't know if he saw me or not but he's coming."

All five look at each other not sure if they should believe him or not. There had been times Screamer had seen hallucinations in the past. One such time was during the first week he had arrived, Screamer was positive he had seen a group of Guards, including Daman's Bodyguard from the Tower, talking to some of the islanders, they were all wearing green face paint, he could have sworn they were laughing and planning something but he wasn't close enough to hear what they were saying, he tried getting closer but they heard something and broke away from each other. Everyone was starting to think this could be one of those thoughts.

"He's still not happy over what happened yesterday," Minin announced hoping that Screamer was telling the truth and thinking this could be the only reason for Daman to be coming back. "He's coming back for revenge."

Tiffany then thought of a plan, "We run back to the camp," she announced. Everyone else looked at her, surprised that she was making a command. "Hide what we can, if we look poorer, he might pity us."

"It certainly won't be mercy," Hayley replied in a whisper, just in case that Daman was within hearing distance. She thought for a second, "I don't have another plan, let's do it." Everyone stalled, not sure what to do, "NOW," she said as her whisper got stronger. Everyone, including Screamer, ran back to the middle of the camp.

Hunter and Callum ran toward the shed with the crates in it. Hunter grabbed a sheet and concealed the crates. Callum gave him a strange look, knowing the concealment was obvious. "Well, I don't have another idea that we can do in a quick amount of time," he replied.

The two of them returned to the middle of the camp, everyone had taken a seat around the fire. Hayley looked at Minin and quietly said, "This time don't say a thing. Please, I'm begging you."

Minin looked back at her, he knew he wanted to say something once again, he knew that everyone did, but this time he would accept her request. "Ok, I'm not going to say a thing. You have my word".

Hunter took his seat next to Minin, while Callum sat on the opposite side. They both tried to act like nothing was happening. Hunter looked at Minin and waved his arms trying to get his attention, Minin looked at him, without being too loud he said, "Just act normal."

Minin couldn't understand why this was all happening, he had been on the island for this long but nothing like this had happened in his time. He had seen Daman, but only a day or two around drop-day. He didn't want to make much noise since everyone else was being so quiet but had to ask a question, "Has this ever happened before?"

"It used too. I didn't think it would happen again. Just before Callum first got to the island, he used to raid the camps for any new arrivals but since he ran out of kill chips he stopped. It's a bit of a relief actually, but I don't understand why he is on his way here now. It's not like we have anything of value for him," Hayley replied as she looked up at Hunter. "Do we?" She asked, thinking he may have made or collected something none of the group had known about.

"Nope, I have no idea. Anything he would want is kept quiet and hidden like always. Anything I've made wouldn't be of any use to him, he'd have better stuff in the Tower, I have no idea why he is coming."

Screamer became even more nervous, Tiffany gently put her hand on his forearm, "It's ok, I'm sure there's a perfectly good reason. I don't think he is after you," She assured him.

He looked at her, "I don't know what you guys did to him, but I've heard enough to know you don't piss him off." He said as he took a deep breath.

Minin knew they were right, they weren't after Screamer, they were after him. His slight act of bravery had put everyone in danger and he knew it.

It was at that moment, everyone could hear people walking towards the camp. It was confirmation that Screamer wasn't hallucinating, the confirmation they didn't want. As much as everyone tried to act normal, the knowledge that Daman or anyone from the Tower was on the way made it impossible. Usually, they would be talking around the fire as a minimum, here there was just silence, all anyone could hear was the footsteps coming towards them and the breathing from everyone waiting for the appearance.

Hunter had the perfect view of what was coming up. After what seemed like an eternity, his eyes and face opened, everyone knew exactly what that meant. He just stayed quiet hoping to not create attention. He could see every step until they stopped.

Everyone else could now see Daman with his guards, in the corner of their eyes, they didn't move either, just staring at the fire. Minin knew as much as he was told to 'act normal' this was the farthest from normal any of them could be. He turned his head directly into the direction of the men standing there.

"Everyone stand," Daman's voice commanded. "Don't act like you didn't know I was coming, you got warned," He continued with disgust. "Our friend Ronald warned you I was coming."

The mere mention of Screamers own name sent a shiver down his spine, he was paralysed and stayed on the ground while everyone stood up and turned, looking at the group in front of them, which was smaller than the previous encounter. Just three guards all wearing a black version of the guard's uniform and Daman Biguy.

Daman took his attention to Screamer, and questioned him calmly, "Ronald, why do you not stand?" While he spoke, Tiffany did everything she could to lift him herself. "Is it because you don't think I deserve even a little gratitude, for letting you stay here?"

As much as Screamer tried to lift himself, with each word being spoken he froze that little bit more. Tiffany was now yanking him with all her strength, just so that Daman would move away from the camp just that little bit quicker.

"I'm quite insulted. I allow you to stay in paradise. I haven't harmed or insulted you, have I?" He continued, questioning Screamer hoping to get an answer, still, there was nothing, just silence. He walked over to Tiffany and brushed the back of his hand over her face, "Your pretty little friend, the model here, has only been on the island for a few days now and knows that you show me some respect…" The feeling of his hand sent shivers down her spine. "…So why can't you do the same for me?" He continued as he brushed her face one last time and returned to his entourage. Screamer just sat there frozen. Daman's patients suddenly ran out becoming infuriated, he clicked his fingers and two guards ran over and lifted Screamer from the ground, bringing him in front of Daman, "What do you have to say for yourself?" He began to scream, "You disrespect me, you anger me, and you know that's not a good thing."

Screamer was speechless, all he could do was look Daman in the eye with terror, as much as he tried to apologise to save himself, nothing came out, his mouth refused to open his lips and body trembling.

Daman began to calm down, "You're afraid of me, I see it now, you're not trying to insult me, you're frozen by fear." He then smiled and looked at the other five standing around the campfire and announced proudly, "This man knows how it should be, he knows to fall into line, he's too scared to rise up or insult me, unlike the other day, as you all did." He looked back at Screamer, "Go back to your camp, I have nothing else to teach you." He then lightly tapped Screamer on the cheek with his palm, "Go back to your camp, tell them I was merciful to you. Teach them how it should be."

Screamer didn't know if this was real or if he had passed out and had been dreaming, either way, he wasn't going to take a chance, he began to move, no longer paralysed by the fear and ran as quickly as he could, not once trying to look back.

Everyone in the group began to think the same thought, *Did that just happen, he let someone go?* They then all thought it was an act and he would pull a gun on him and shoot him in the back as he ran, but that didn't happen. Screamer just ran away from view. They then all realised that they were now in the spotlight.

Daman looked at the group ahead of him, "Now our guest has left, onto business," He said calmly then just as quickly his tone changed and screamed a command, "In a line now." Everyone got inline swiftly, and just as quickly his voice became calm again, "I have figured out a way that you can make up for what happened yesterday." He then began pacing back and forth along the line-up, "I have a job for one of you," and stopped in front of Hunter. Hunter gulped in fear, hoping it was just temporarily, "I see what you have done in the past, what you do. I have found a use for someone of your talent, you're an asset to the island that can no longer go to waste." Hunter's face became even more fearful with every word, "Come with me now." Daman put out his hand, looking like he was trying to be a friend.

Hunter stood there for a second and just breathed in and out thinking about the offer. *'Go and leave my friends? Will I be killed for this? What is the plan?'* Hunter thought it over for a moment, he then said his answer. "No." He replied bluntly, "I don't want to." Everyone was shocked at the announcement, none more so than Hunter himself. All he could think was less than twenty-four hours ago he was willing to do whatever he could to make peace for everyone and here he was arguing about leaving the camp.

Daman was shocked, "This isn't a negotiation, the fact I asked you was just a formality. You're coming with us," he said as the anger in his voice began to rise.

Hunter once again replied, "No." Still not believing what he was saying and shook his head. "I'm staying here," he said, trying to not show fear in his voice. "These are my friends, I'm not leaving them."

Daman began to look as though there was steam rising from his ears and brought out the kill chip remote from his pocket. "Once again, not a negotiation," Looking like he was about to press a button.

Hunter refused to stand down as Callum took a step forward, knowing this might be the time for everyone to fight back.

The three guards standing with Daman realised this as well, drawing guns from the uniform, aiming quickly.

Minin saw the guns and just as Callum had done, he was ready to fight but knew their weapons were primitive compared to these.

"Don't take another step, or this will get messy," One of the guards warned. Callum took the warning seriously and stood back, as much as he didn't want to, but a blood bath wasn't on his agenda either. "That's better" The guard continued.

Daman then put a finger on the kill chip remote, he looked at the guards. "I need Hunter, I don't need Hayley," he said, getting his message out as to who will be the target.

Hayley heard the message, whatever fear she had endured the previous day, this was worse. She knew what was going to happen to her and it wasn't her fault. A tear began streaming down her face.

Daman began to slowly lower his finger to the button that would finish Hayley. "One last chance to save her life," He screamed at Hunter. "If her life doesn't matter to you then maybe theirs do."

The guards aim at the heads of Callum, Minin and Tiffany, each one ready to fire at a moment's notice.

Hunter looked around trying to think about what he could do to defuse the situation. He didn't know what else he could do, "Wait," he said pausing everything. "I'll do it," he announced. "But I want something in return."

That confused everyone, the number one rule for trading was that you didn't with Daman or the Tower. The one person that was more thrown off was Daman, but he was curious as to what the condition was, "You're making a deal with me? Well, this is new, go on then, what is it?"

"My friends," he moved his arms around showing all four. "They're free, anyone that comes into our camp is free. The camp becomes a refuge for anyone, you can do whatever the hell it is to anyone else, but here they are free. If you want me to come with you that's the deal."

Daman thought for a moment. "So, let me get this straight, I'll have you and this 'little' bit of the island is no longer touchable for me?"

"That's right," Hunter replied, nodding his head, pleased with himself thinking the deal might go ahead.

Daman took a breath. "That's all good and well, but I told you this wasn't a negotiation," He said calmly. "Anyone that tries to, ends up punished," His voice beginning to rise. "It isn't 'our camp.' It's 'my Island'. All of it is mine, your friends won't be free while they are here." He moved his finger a little bit closer to the button, "Come now or Hayley and your friends die, and I'll take you regardless."

Callum had heard enough. He wasn't going to let his friend get taken or himself and everyone killed without a fight. In the back of his mind he knew the dangers of what he was about to do, but he didn't care by this point, all his mind was telling him was *fight back, this is it*. He reached into his pocket slightly and grabbed onto the slingshot that was missing from the weapons shed, just enough so that the guards and Daman were unable to see it. He looked to the ground, seeing a handful of rocks just waiting to be used, he launched himself down and swooped them off the ground, taking the slingshot out of his pocket as he did and loaded one rock without pause, aiming it at Daman.

The guards without hesitation, all aimed their guns at Callum, both sides at a standoff. "Don't be stupid Callum," Daman urged him. "You have a slingshot, we have guns. This is a very stupid thing you're doing," He continued calmly. "You might hurt me, but they will kill you."

Callum just shrugged his shoulders. At that point, he didn't care.

"Don't do it, buddy," Minin said to Callum, "Let's all just think about it," He said trying to defuse the situation, thinking about the result.

"Listen to Minin," Hayley added. "He's right, we don't want any trouble."

Callum wasn't listening, he didn't want Hunter to go, he wanted Daman to leave. He eventually fired, letting go of the rubber holding the rock, hitting Daman on the temple, it was enough to knock him back and loosen his grip on the kill chip remote. Callum rolled on the ground quickly picking himself up and began to run, firing more rocks now at the guards, making sure he didn't stay in one spot.

The guards didn't hesitate and fired back, missing each time. Minin, Hayley, Tiffany and Hunter went to the ground trying to stay away from the showering of the bullets. "What do we do?" Tiffany shouted over the madness.

"Stay down as low as you can and try not to get hit," Hayley replied. Tiffany did exactly what she was told even making herself into a ball.

Callum kept running around firing rocks at the guards as quickly as he could load, eventually, he was out but he kept moving, he would get close to a guard, then move back, doing whatever he could to stay random and not get a bullet shot into himself. He eventually got close enough to leap into the air and punch a guard in the face, knocking him out. It was enough to make a path in front of him, he jumped into it and ran off, he knew he didn't have a choice, staying here would get him killed.

"Stop firing," Daman ordered. "His days are numbered, he can't hide forever, when we find him, bring him to me, he'll get what's coming to him."

"And if we have to kill him?" One of the guards asked.

"Just make sure I see the body." Daman then took his attention to everyone on the ground, everyone looked up at him, they could see steam coming from his ears, his hands shaking from the rage of what had happened, he wanted nothing more than to press the button eliminating Hayley and a hail of bullets into the rest. He lifted the remote and began to lower his finger. Hayley closed her eyes tightly, not wanting to see the end.

"Wait," Hunter screamed. "I'll go, just let them live. Please, I beg of you," he said hoping for a miracle.

Daman stopped, "Fine! I can see by the way they all cower on the ground. They are not much of a threat and they understand who the true leader is." He told his guards.

"That's right, not a threat at all," Hunter said, trying to agree with him.

"What about the rest of you?" Daman asked.

Both Hayley and Minin nodded, not agreeing that he was the true leader but just wanting everything to end. Tiffany just stayed on the ground not saying anything.

"Grab him then," Daman ordered the guards. They hoist him up from the ground, "March." He commanded Hunter, who didn't put up a fight and just walked away from the camp. Hayley and Minin watching as he disappeared with the guards and Daman.

Minin glanced over to Tiffany, who was still in her ball. She was shaking but hadn't moved from her position. "It's over, they're gone." He told her, but she stayed in her ball.

"Are you ok?" Hayley asked. A red liquid pooled away from her. Hayley knew straight away what the liquid was, as Tiffany finally uncurled herself, she had been shot in the back of her shoulder. The liquid was blood.

13

"It hurts," Tiffany said as she withered in pain.

"Ok, I need you to stay calm," Hayley responded, knowing instantly what to do. This wasn't the first time she had been around a shooting wound but the first since she had arrived on the island. "We need to lift her onto a bench, so I can inspect the wound," She said.

Minin looked around hoping to find something that would act as a bench, he kept looking around unable to locate anything, he then remembered there was a table in the shed that held the weapons, without even mentioning it he ran off, returning with the table. "You're a little too calm for this, you realise," Minin commented, noticing how calm Hayley was.

"This isn't the first time I've been around something like this you know?" Hayley explained. "Besides if I freak out, it isn't going to help, now grab her feet while I take her shoulders." They both got into position, "Ok when I count to three we are going to lift her. Ok, ready, one...two...three. Lift." They both lifted Hayley, placing her on the table.

"She was a lot lighter than I thought she would be." It was at that moment Minin realised that Tiffany hadn't said anything since he had returned getting the table. "Is she ok? She's quiet."

"When you were gone, I told her to concentrate on her breathing trying to get her to be calm, I think it's working. Without many pain killers available to us, anything I can do to not use them is going to help." While Tiffany was quiet, she kept shutting her eyes tightly, even though she was trying to breathe slowly, she had no luck forgetting the pain. "I need to go to my hut and get a few things, just stay here and make sure nothing happens to her," Hayley said.

Minin didn't know what to make of this, "And what if something does happen?" He knew what Hayley asked was a simple request, but wouldn't have the slightest clue what to do, if something did happen in the meantime, his background was an office worker not a medical professional like Hayley was.

"Prey that I come back quickly," She replied, shrugging her shoulders trying to joke. "But seriously it should be fine, I'll be as quick as I can be." She then ran as fast as she could toward her hut.

Minin looked at Tiffany, who now had her eyes open and held his hand, "This place isn't paradise," She said slowly. "But it's good to have friends like you and Hayley," She said as she continued trying to smile.

Minin didn't know what to say, he didn't want to look or sound like this was a bad situation, even though he knew it was. He had had only seen two people get shot and that was just before he had arrived on the island, any other shooting he had seen had been on television and never close enough to feel it. All he did was smile gently and reply, "It'll be alright, Hayley will patch you up and you'll be back to normal in no time."

Tiffany smiled, "She's a good girl, isn't she? Always being there for everyone." She took a deep breath, "I don't want her to feel threatened by me."

Minin didn't know what she meant by '*threatened by her,*' all he could think was the pain was making her feel delirious and she was unsure herself as to what she was saying.

Hayley arrived back, she was carrying a bag that was overflowing with items. It contained a first aid kit, pain killers, bandages. She started to take everything out and placing it carefully in an order which Minin didn't understand. "I have no idea if this is enough, but we don't have a choice," Hayley said as she was emptying the bag even more, eventually bringing out a bottle of home-made vodka. "The most important thing," she announced.

Minin didn't think it was the best time to be drinking, but he just went with it.

Hayley continued to place everything in the order that she thought she needed. When she finished, she took another look at Tiffany. The bleeding from the shoulder had slowed down, she thought this might have been a bad thing, "I think she has lost a lot of blood."

"You think?" Minin said, worried that Hayley might be worried about the task at hand.

It was at that point Hayley just stood there and froze, "I don't know what to do," she announced. "I lied to everyone."

"What do you mean you lied to everyone?" Minin didn't know what to think about her statement.

"I'm not a doctor, I was a nurse. I just wanted to sound better when I got on the island, this was my new beginning, now its caught up to me, and I can't do it."

"You can't guess?" Minin tried helping her, knowing time was being wasted for Tiffany, "You would have a better idea than anyone else."

"This is an actual surgical procedure, I've been in on surgeries before helping out, but never done the job."

Minin knew he couldn't stop her thinking this way, and didn't want to waste any more time. "Fine, if you can't do it, I'll do it myself, how hard can it possibly be? It's only a bullet in a shoulder, it's not like it's near a vital organ or anything."Minin picked up a needle and a vial with 'pain killer,' written on it. He inserted the needle and started to suck the painkiller. He took the needle and turned it upright, pushing the air bubbles out, then lowered the needle near the wound.

"STOP," Hayley screamed. "I'll do it," she announced. "You're right, I'll have a better idea on how to do it." Hayley inserted the needle into Tiffany's shoulder and pressed down, injecting the pain killer into Tiffany, "It'll take a couple of minutes to work," She announced.

Both Hayley and Minin just stood around in silence. Minin was still thinking about her announcement that she wasn't a doctor after all the times in the past that she had said. Hayley was looking over the wound, thinking about how she would get the bullet out. Tiffany began to become drowsy, it wasn't long before she had completely fallen asleep.

Minin looked at Hayley and realised what she was doing. "Do you have any guesses?"

Hayley looked back at him as she put on some rubber gloves. "I can't see any arteries, so I can't cut them, that's a good thing and the bullet is only in shallow." She shrugged her shoulders and shook her head, "The only thing I can think of is to use a clamp and pull it out, then sew her up."

"That's it?" Minin asked, not entirely convinced.

"Unless you have another idea?" She replied.

"I have no idea."

"Then let's get this done," Hayley said as she picked up a bottle with a small hose at the end. She pressed the bottle and water flows onto the wound removing some of the blood giving a better view of the bullet. Hayley picked up a set of metal clamps, she inserted them into the wound just enough that she could clamp onto the bullet with less chance of losing it while she took the bullet out. She clamped onto the bullet tightly and began to pull slowly out of the wound, the bullet coming as well. Suddenly Hayley lost the grip and the clamp disconnected with the bullet halfway out. Hayley smiled at Minin, "If I lost my grip at any point this is the best time to do it," she announced, reattaching the clamp and pulled the bullet the rest of the way out. Hayley then re-flushed the wound, re-examining for any shrapnel that may have come off the bullet, but was unable to see any. "I think that's it," She said, picking up a sewing needle and some fishing wire. "This isn't the best stuff but it will have to do." She finished stitching up the wound. "It's done," she announced.

"It's done?" Minin asked confirming.

"I've got the bullet out, I don't think there is anything else I can do. All we can do now is hope." Hayley then smiled finally realising what she had done, "I can't believe it. That was crazy, I actually did it," She said with a laugh. She then stopped, taking off her blood-stained gloves, she then fell to the floor with her back supported by the side of the table. "I did it, I've never done anything like that before," she paused for a moment then began crying.

Minin quickly went to the floor, putting his arms around her, "It's all over, she'll be fine." He said trying to console her, "She'll wake up and it'll all go back too normal."

"We're not out of the woods yet, I have no idea if it will be enough to save her, or if I've actually done it right," She replied sobbing.

"That was better than I could have ever done, she would have had zero chance if it was me, you saved her." He said thinking this would help her out of her slump.

She looked back at him, "You think I'm crying because I'm a fraud don't you?" She paused for a moment looking around, finding the vodka bottle then took a swig. "I always cry like this when someone isn't around."

Minin didn't know what she meant by this, "How did you not break down whenever you need to? Why now once it's done."

"I can turn it off, turn my emotions off for a while until it's safe to turn them back on. It's something I've had to learn when I was doing anything medical before I got here, it's happened plenty of times while I've been on the island, I wanted to burst out crying the other day when you talked back to Daman. But I waited till we got back to camp. When I went to bed I cried for hours, you probably knew about that one, I looked like crap when I got out of bed," She sniggered. "The first time we had a fight I did the same thing."

The first fight that had occurred between them happened after the first thirty days after Minin had arrived on the island. It was around the campfire. Everyone was celebrating Minin's first drop day. Hunter had made homemade vodka from the potatoes from the garden and everyone was drinking. During the day, the camp had traded with another group that came to the camp. Minin had made a mistake of giving the other camp too much without thinking about their own needs. During that time Hayley had put it down to a 'new campers mistake' and had left it at that. At the celebration, Minin asked the question of why they couldn't share everything. Hayley couldn't understand why he was so naïve, "If we give everyone everything, they will take it all, as much as there is a society of camps, it's still everyone for themselves." Minin couldn't understand that and thought they could share, and tried to explain himself, but Hayley couldn't see his point eventually storming off to her hut.

"That fight seems so stupid now, doesn't it?" Minin said, laughing slightly, "I was so dumb for thinking we could all share."

Hayley laughed thinking back at it, then suddenly went silent. A thought had occurred to her. She then spoke up, "He knows I wasn't a doctor, it's the only way I didn't stay in the Tower when he put my chip in, I didn't understand it until now. Every time I see him, I think he's coming for me and someone has spoken up and he can use me. I don't want to ever end up there, but he knows I'm not a doctor. I don't know how, but he said, *your pretty little friend, the model.* He knew Tiffany was a model, that's impossible unless he knows about everyone when they come to the island."

Minin thought about what she had said for a moment, "It's probably the same for Hunter and why he only just came for him now. He came here for using computers, there are no computers here. He didn't think he was of use until he found out what else he could do."

Hayley cried for another moment knowing that Daman was now more frightening than ever with what he knew. "We have to get him back. In one day we've lost Callum and Hunter, had Tiffany shot, we need to get everyone back and revolt. If everyone knew how much more dangerous he is, more are going to want to get on board for sure."

"I know we need to but I don't think it's going to be that easy," Minin replied. "You've told me plenty of stories about the Tower, and the only way out is if you're new and have a chip in the back of your head and that's if he lets you out. I want him gone probably as much as you do, but unless we can find a way to destroy the kill chip controller, Hunter's a sitting duck. As for revolting, people are still going to hide, as much as I don't want them to, but that's the way it is." Minin stopped talking for a moment and thought it wasn't so long ago that these ideas were coming from each other.

As for Hayley, she had stopped crying, thinking, staring into space. She knew Minin had thought what they need to do more than she had, it then hit her, "We get them on board, fight or flight."

Minin thought about it for a second and knew she was right, "Tell them all the truth, if they don't want to be part of it, let them leave." He asked trying to make sure he was on the same page as her.

"Exactly, we'll get who we can and work it out from there."

Then another flaw of the plan came into his head, "I know you don't want to hear this either," He said. "What about the Tower? How would you even get Hunter out, you don't just walk up to it, knock on the front door and say, 'hey I'm here to pick up Hunter after his playdate with Daman."

Hayley realised her plan was flawed but it didn't stop her from thinking about it, trying to fill in the gaps. "You're right, even if we did work out how to get Hunter, what about the chip? He'll just hit it and kill Hunter, then there's Callum, who knows where he has gone."

Minin thought Callum would be in less danger than Hunter was. "He's a traveller, he walks away from the camp all the time, that's the reason he's our lookout, he looks for any problems since he monitors every inch of the camp and island. It wouldn't surprise me if he went to the bunker for a few nights till everything cooled down," He said, trying to not get her to worry about him.

"It's not going to cool down for him, after what he did, there's going to be a huge bounty on his head. We're going to have to save him as well. You wanted to be a superhero," she said with a smile. "Now's your chance for that. All we have to do is *Save the lookout, save the island.*"

"Save the lookout, save the Island?" Minin asked.

"It's a start."

Tiffany began to moan in her sleep, both Minin and Hayley stood, they had completely forgotten about her. Hayley looked over her, "I think she's fine, but it was only a small amount of pain killers I gave her, depending on her resistance it might be wearing off," She said taking her best guess as to what was happening. "I don't see that it could be anything else."

"We don't have that much more left for her do we?" Minin asked already knowing the answer.

"Maybe a couple more doses, judging how quickly this lot wore off, maybe a couple of hours, but that's it. It's not going to be anywhere near enough for what she needs." Hayley explained, wiping Tiffany's forehead.

"How much do you think we need?" Minin asked hoping to get an answer to how serious this was.

"We are going to need at least a few more days worth and that's only a guess. And that depends on her pain threshold and how quickly she heals up."

Minin looked up, in a small opening through the trees he could see the one place where there would be plenty of everything she would need, The Tower. Hayley turned her head and looked at the same place. She closed her eyes, that was the last place she wanted to go, she only wanted to go there to get Hunter out. "He doesn't make deals, Screamer told us the last person that went to the Tower didn't return...." He hesitated, "Forget what I was thinking." He then had another thought, it was a long shot, but a better one than the alternative, "What about Screamer's group? they don't have any food, but they might have the pain killers we need."

Hayley thought about it for a second, it was a much better option than the other one, as much as she knew they might have to eventually go to the Tower, it wasn't yet time. Tiffany's moans were getting stronger, her pain getting worse, they had no choice, they had to take her now. "Ok, let's go visit the Coasties, but we can't move her much, it might only be her shoulder but I don't want to risk it."

14

All Minin could think, '*How do you move someone, without moving them much?*' At that moment, he wished Hunter were there, he would have thought of something to make quickly or already had something stored away that they could use. He tried to think of something, but his mind was blank. He began to stress, knowing he was wasting time, he needed an idea now. The stress of everything that had happened was making it almost impossible for his brain to work.

A hand and arm started to wave in front of him, pulling him out of his thoughts, he looked at the hand which belonged to Hayley. He shook his head to focus on her, "You zoned out there for a minute, you ok?" She asked.

He didn't sound so sure when he answered, "Uhhh yeah, no problem."

Hayley knew when he was lying, "Are you sure?" She questioned him forcefully.

"How do we minimise her movement?" He asked, frustrated with himself.

"You're only thinking about what you know we have, aren't you?"

"Yeah, of course," he replied.

"We're not all someone who can come up with an answer like that." She clicked her fingers together. "Think about what everyone else has, I know I don't have anything. I cleared out my last useful thing with my first aid kit. Go have a look in Hunter and Callum's huts, I'll stay here and watch her. I don't think there will be a problem, but it's best if I'm close by if there is."

Minin looked, nodding, not saying a thing. He didn't feel comfortable going into someone else's hut without first being invited but knew he didn't have a choice and walked off, towards Callum's hut. When he arrived, the door was slightly ajar, while none of the huts had locks, the rule of not entering someone else's hut worked on trust, but regardless the door being ajar felt out of place. Minin knew he couldn't think about that at the moment, so he opened the door and went in.

Minin had never been in Callum's hut before, he looked around, it looked like everyone else's and to his surprise, it was clean and tidy, not something he thought it would be like. There was a bed and a table with a partially unlit melted candle on one of the walls. There didn't appear to be anything that could be of any use.

Minin went over to the table hoping for something inside one of the drawers that could help, he opened it up, it was full of paper that looked like it had been folded at one point, and appeared blank until he lifted a sheet and turned it around. It appeared to be a fact sheet about Hunter, containing information on why he came to the island, including the drop date 06/07/2086 and why he came to the island. 'Where did Callum get this?' he wondered. He picked the next piece of paper, this time it was Hayley's information. Once again it all matched up to the story she had told everyone, except that she was a nurse, not a doctor, her drop date 17/04/2090.

Minin then realised that these were the processing information that they give to the guards before Prisoners are put on the dropships. He picked up the next piece of paper, it was Minin's. It was all here - convicted of possession of a firearm and intent to kill, the date of his drop – 27/02/2095.

Minin knew this was information, no-one on the island should have access to. Yet it was sitting here in a hut metres from his own, belonging to someone he called a friend, there was one last piece of paper in the drawer, it was more crumpled up than the rest, he picked it up since he had seen everyone else's he assumed it had to be Callum's. He was wrong, this one belonged to Daman, but he couldn't make out what was written on it since it was so crumpled up, the only thing he could see was the drop date – 01/12/2084, the date the island was first operational.

He put all the paper back into the drawer. Once they got back from the Coasties camp this was something he was going to have to show Hayley. Right now though, he needed to see if there was anything of use in the other drawer, he opened it up, it contained the magazine that Tiffany was featured in. '*How could this have been put in?* Minin thought to himself, they had not been anywhere close to going back to the huts since they found the magazine, before all the trouble started. '*He's been here since the shooting, but that was so recent, how did we not hear him?*'

Minin then noticed more paper lying in the drawer, '*I can find out more about the other islander's*' he thought, picking them up.

Hayley's voice called from the outside, "Are you ok in there? You're taking forever."

Minin didn't know what to say. Should he say what he found or keep it quiet until Tiffany was settled? He quickly decided to keep it quiet and have one less thing for Hayley to worry about, at least for the time being. "Yeah, I'm just going through the hut thoroughly," He said knowing that was only a partial truth. He put everything back, leaving the hut and began his journey to Hunter's Hut.

Once he arrived he tried opening the door, it was locked, this was more strange than Callum's hut being open, the only time the huts were locked, was when the camp would venture into the Freelands, and that was just in case someone that wasn't part of the camp might enter, otherwise everyone felt that there was enough security and trust that someone just wouldn't. The last thing before they enter the Freelands is to lock the doors and no-one had a chance to do that before Screamer came running to warn them.

The door didn't open, '*It must just be stuck or I must not be opening the door right*', he kept trying it but alas it didn't open. '*Screw this*' he thought in frustration. He took a run, ramming his shoulder hoping to dislodge what was blocking it or destroying the lock. This resulted in being knocked down to the ground and making his shoulder battered and bruised. Minin learnt his lesson from that and decided he wasn't going to enter by the door, the only other option he could think of was the window, but he didn't like his chances since the door wasn't open. He went to the window, trying to slide it open, once again no luck. *'This isn't what I need now, I can't waste time like this'* and decided to return to Hayley and tell her he couldn't get in. He turned around tripping over a rock, which gave him an idea. He picked the rock up and threw it, shattering the glass. He walked back to the window putting his arm carefully into the hole, unlatching the lock and opened the window. He lifted himself into the opening and pulled himself in.

The hut had walls of junk. Electronic boards, pieces of metal, plenty of stuff for Hunter to build anything he wanted, this was nothing like what the hut had looked like when they shared it when he first arrived. Minin was only in his own Hut for a couple of months, he was amazed that Hunter had collected so much in such little time. There was only enough room for a bed and a small path to the door.

Minin looked around hoping to find something of use, but quickly noticed a corner with a small red flashing light, he walked over to it and proceeded to pick up the source of the light. It looked to be a radio, there was a button on the top with what Minin believed to be a power symbol, he pressed it, the light turning from red to green but nothing but static playing. There was another dial on the radio, he moved it back and forth but just more static. *'He usually only showed us stuff he had made when it worked,'* he thought, *'Maybe this is one of those things that didn't, but didn't get rid of it. Maybe, just like the rafts at the beach, he hoped one day for it to work, then he would share it,'* He decided.

Minin put the radio back down into the junk pile but left it turned on. *'I need to hurry up, The others are waiting on me,'* he thought and began to scan the room. He then saw it, hanging up on the wall was a trolley. It was long, more than big enough to fit crates onto it, but another thought occurred, *'Why is he keeping something like this from us when it could help? Maybe he didn't want to take it into the Freelands since someone might steal it. But why not at least around the camp. Regardless this is perfect for what we need now.'*

Minin took the trolly off the hook on the wall, the hut only had enough room for it to be on its side. Minin slid it toward the door, unlocking it. The door opened and he pushed the trolley out onto the ground outside.

The static from the radio stopped, Minin inspected it. A green light was dimming, *'The batteries must be dying,'* He said to himself.

"Help us please, we are trapped inside a tower." A scared female voice came over the radio. The static then returned.

Minin looked at the radio in disbelief, he wasn't sure what he had just heard, *'It must have been my imagination'*, he thought. Minin left it at that, leaving the hut, taking the trolley to where Hayley and Tiffany were. Tiffany's condition had stayed the same, which Minin was glad about. "I found a trolley in Hunter's Hut, look at the size of it, I don't understand why he never brought it out for us."

Hayley looked at the trolley, "Maybe he never finished it? But for now, it'll do," she said. "You were gone for a while, I was starting to think you got lost."

"Hunter's Hut was locked, took me a while to get in. I ended up having to break in through the window."

"Why would it be locked?" Hayley asked wondering as well, knowing Minin wouldn't have the answer.

"His Hut was piled with junk, it was never like that when I was boarding with him, might have to change his name from Hunter to Hoarder," Minin replied trying to lighten the mood. "There was a radio inside as well."

"A radio?" Hayley asked, also thinking it was strange.

Minin then paused, he thought that maybe he should have saved that information for later, like the pieces of paper in Callum's hut. "Yeah, I think it was working, voices were coming out of it," he continued.

"You were probably just imagining it, we're in a pretty stressful situation," Hayley said trying to focus on the job at hand.

"It just felt so real, something out of a horror movie, one-minute static, the next voices coming from it and then the static again."

"Even if it was real, to be honest, that's the last thing I want to think about. We need to get her to the Coasties Camp," Hayley replied, trying to get them both on track for what they need to do.

"Ok, what do we do?"

"Get her on the trolley, you grab her legs, and when I count to three, we lift and place her on it," Hayley explained. He got into position. "Ok, I'll grab her shoulders." She paused for a moment and took a deep breath, "Ok, one...two...three...lift." The two of them lift her off the bench and shuffle over to the trolley placing her down gently.

Tiffany winced in pain but otherwise remained silent.

Minin went to the back of the Trolley where Tiffany's head was and grabbed the handle of the trolly, ready to push her out. "Ok, let's go."

"Just one more second, let me go over her, to make sure nothing is wrong," Hayley said as she began to look over her, the stitches had not come loose, which she took as a good sign. She then began to notice Tiffany's facial movements. She knew her pain killers were wearing off. "We have to get moving now," She commanded.

Minin agreed, he could see how much pain Tiffany was in, "How did it wear off so easily?" He asked as they began to push her away from the shed.

"Some people are different," She explained. "It wears off at different speeds for everyone, but this is so strange, I've never seen anyone have the painkiller wear off so quickly. Her tolerance for it must be high, even if the Coasties have more of it, I don't know how long it will last," She continued sounding more concerned with each word.

Minin began to push the Trolley quicker hoping to get to the Coasties area quicker than normal. He also noticed that the day was getting on, the sun would be setting sooner rather than later and neither one wanted to be on the Freelands when it was dark. "We better hurry it's getting late," He said.

Hayley stopped in front of her Hut, staring at the door, then she spoke. "I want to get changed before we leave." She then headed inside, "I'll be quick," came her voice from inside.

Minin just nodded his head, he didn't understand why she had to do this, Hayley didn't usually worry about the way she looked, and they didn't have the time for her to do that. *I'll keep pushing the trolley, she can catch up,'* He thought and began pushing it.

A couple of minutes later, Hayley had caught up to him, he was shocked at how quickly she got changed and could catch up. She was now wearing a white t-shirt and khaki pants, she also had a black backpack. "I just needed to get out of the clothes, they felt like they were blood-soaked," She explained but to Minin the clothes that she was wearing didn't have anything wrong with them. "I've also brought a change of clothes with us just in case we need them, to be honest, I don't know how long we are going to be away from the camp, did you want to get some yourself?"

Minin thought about this for a moment, he didn't think that they would be away from the camp for that long, "Nah, I should be alright, I don't think we will be gone that long." He replied hopefully.

They continued the journey, Minin pushed the trolley, it was smooth, didn't feel like they were pushing it along a dirt track, Minin was relieved. "It's so easy to push, I'm a little annoyed that Hunter kept this from us," he said.

Hayley just nodded her head in agreement. They soon arrived at the border of the camp, "Take one last look, it's going to be a while before we come back," She announced.

"It won't be that long, we'll just get the meds for Tiffany, then we'll be back, once that happens, we can figure out about Hunter and Callum," Minin replied.

They soon arrived in the Freelands, somehow it felt different. This was the first time Minin had been to the Freelands when they weren't either looking for crates or trading with others. It seemed so quiet but It was probably no quieter than normal but still, it felt off.

They continued walking for a few minutes in silence just enjoying the peace. Hayley then spoke, "Maybe Hunter wanted to put in a motor or something?"

"What?" Minin didn't quite know what she meant.

"The Trolley. Maybe Hunter wanted to motorise it or something. It works perfectly fine, I don't know why he didn't let us have it before," Hayley replied. "I don't think I've been in his hut before, I let him have his privacy, although I've been in everyone else's at least a few times for various reasons, just never Hunter's," she said, only just now realising it herself. She then smiled, "You didn't find anything weird in there did you?" She asked as she began to laugh.

"Mostly all junk, just stuff he must have collected over the years, I didn't really go through it all that much, the only other thing I found was the radio with the voices and static."

Hayley cut him off before he had time to continue, "Could be worse, you could have gotten your football teams score for that week and found they lost, that would have topped this day right off," She laughed a little more.

Minin began to laugh and started to mimic a sporting telecast, "In today's game the Dragons were beaten by the Slayers five hundred to zero, it was a slaughtering." He then laughed, "if that happened you would have heard me scream for sure." He continued to laugh for another moment. "I still don't know if I heard voices or not."

Hayley turned to him, she started to believe that the voices came from the radio more than Minin, "Wouldn't surprise me if you heard voices asking for help, there are other people out there."

"I think they said they were from the Tower," Minin continued.

With that, the happiness seemed to drain from Hayley's face. "It wouldn't surprise me if the Tower does have that kind of equipment," she paused for a moment, she didn't want to think about the horrors that communicating with the Tower would mean if Daman Biguy found out. "Next time you use it maybe we can change the channel?" She said half-hoping and half-joking, in an attempt to cheer herself up once more, "Maybe we can use it to order something?" The smile returned, "You know the one thing I would love to have here? An indoor heated shower with pressure, don't get me wrong I'm thankful for the one Hunter made us, the one near the beach but that's a trickle compared to the one that I used to have at home, I do love pressure in my showers."

"I thought I was the only one that thought it was crappy," Minin said with a smile forgetting about the radio for now.

The conversation between them made the journey quicker. It wasn't too long before they were at the entrance to the Coasties camp. A sandy pathway, torches on each side directing the way to the middle of the camp.

They continued to push the trolley over the entrance line, the wheel of the trolley then locked up. Minin tried pushing it a little hoping that whatever the cause would unlock itself. The trolley moved, but no longer smoothly but it was enough to do the job that was required for the short trip. They continued to move a few metres but with each step, the wheels locked more, till eventually no matter what Minin did it would not budge.

"I think I know why Hunter didn't give us the trolley yet," Hayley said. "He knew it wasn't going to last long, he liked building things, but hated repairing them." Hayley tried to take over, thinking that maybe Minin was becoming exhausted from all the pushing but the trolley just remained motionless.

"We have to walk and carry her," Minin announced, "The trolley isn't working."

"We can't." Hayley began to shake the trolley, hoping that whatever was wrong would fix itself. One thing about Hayley was she didn't like to feel like she was failing, it was one of her greatest fears that she didn't tell anyone. "Arghhh," she screamed, feeling frustrated.

She continued to shake the trolley, getting to the point where Minin began to think she had forgotten that Tiffany was still on it. He went to tell her to stop but as he did, a cracking sound could be heard, a wheel falls off, sending Tiffany to the ground.

"It hurts, it hurts," Tiffany said as she woke. "I can feel it so much!" Both Minin and Hayley realised her painkillers had worn off and the only thing stopping her from feeling the full amount of pain was that she was still waking up.

"It's all right, we are almost there," Minin said hoping to calm her down. "Once we get inside, we will find someone that can help." Tiffany looked at him, trying to smile, but the pain she was feeling made that near impossible.

Hayley leaned down, "I know it hurts," she said trying to also comfort her. "It can't be comfortable but believe me, we are trying to help, she said trying to sound calm.

Tiffany tried to speak but the pain made her struggle, "I know...... please be quick about it …. I think if I get up and walk, maybe it'll take my mind off it," she said, her words struggling to come through.

"Are you even able to walk?" Minin questioned, "You're in so much pain."

Hayley decided to answer, "We'll give her a chance, we won't know for sure, it's really fifty-fifty." The two of them try and lift Tiffany, trying not to put any pressure on the shoulder where the wound was. She got to her feet as they gently let go, ready to catch her if she was to fall. "How are you feeling standing up?" Hayley asked.

"I feel a little light-headed, my shoulder is still sore, but I should be able to walk."

"The painkillers seem to have almost completely worn off. We'll stay close, just in case you can't do it anymore," Hayley said as the sun began to set, "We better hurry."

The three of them began walking inside the Coasties camp area, Tiffany took a few steps and became too groggy as she slowly fell back to the ground. Minin knew they couldn't waste any more time. He lifted her into his arms and began walking the rest of the way.

15

The Coasties Camp was very similar looking to Minin's Camp, the only difference was the much larger size, this mostly being due to the larger population, which both Hayley and Minin thought to be about fifteen. The entrance was marked with torches that were on fire, each one representing a member of the camp, one on each side of the path. As they walked past, they noticed there were sixteen, but one was unlit.

"Another torch. Did you know they had another person come to the camp?" Hayley asked.

"Screamer didn't say anything to me, I take it he didn't say anything to you either?" Minin answered while looking at the unlit torch, "I'm more interested why the torch isn't burning anymore."

"It's probably run out of fuel, I've never understood why they would waste something so valuable to burn when everything is so limited."

"Everyone has their vices, this is theirs, I suppose," Minin replied.

The three arrived in the main area of the camp, slower than they normally would. Minin was beginning to think Tiffany was getting heavier by the second. The middle of the camp was larger but looked like a carbon copy of their own, the difference being tents rather than huts surrounding the campfire and many more of them. From here they could see the Tower much closer.

The camp looked deserted, no-one sitting around the fire, which was just smouldering coals, the tents were empty. To Minin and Hayley, this wouldn't have seemed to be out of place if it were during the middle of the day, but now it was getting closer to sunset and the temperature was lowering. The three of them wondered where any of them could be?

"Hello," Minin called out but there was no reply. "Hello," he called out once more but once again no answer.

"Why isn't there anyone here"? Tiffany asked in a groggy haze.

Hayley replied, "I have no idea Honey. We'll get you to rest here," She said as Minin set Tiffany to the ground.

Tiffany sat herself up, glad that she could rest. She knew she hadn't moved far after she had woken up, but to her, it felt like she had walked a hundred kilometres.

Hayley then looked at Minin, "Have a look around and see if you can find someone. I'll look after her." He began to look around, not exactly knowing where to go. Minin had been to this camp before, but this was the first time he would have to navigate around himself, suddenly there was a screaming noise coming from the beach. Both Hayley and Minin looked at the direction it came from, "Quick, go check it out!" Hayley instructed.

Minin bolted toward the beach, every single Coastie was there, they were all standing at the shoreline, looking at the ocean at a burning box that was drifting close to the shore. Minin slowed his run to a walk and had a closer look at what the burning box was. It soon dawned on him, the burning box was a casket, this was a Coasties funeral. The screaming noise was despair. He looked at the crowd, some were crying, some not even able to look at the casket, others just had their heads slightly bowed. Minin stopped and bowed his head in respect, although he didn't know who had died, he knew this was the right thing. He then understood who the unlit torch was for, the person that had died. He kept his distance at the back of the group, not knowing what to say.

"Let's have a moments silence, and remember all the good times we have had with Quinn," said a person at the front of the wall of people, who Minin recognised as Gin. Every person lowered their head, silence filled the air. Once the minute had passed everyone's head rose looking back at the Burning casket. "Thank you, everyone, Quinn would have liked that," Gin said finishing the ceremony.

Quinn had arrived on the island from the same dropship as Hayley. While she considered him her drop family, being in a different camp made it difficult for her to know him. All she knew was that he was smart like Hunter, he could do anything if he put his mind to it.

Everyone just stayed looking at the ocean, looking at the burning casket until finally, it burned enough that it broke apart and sunk into the water.

Screamer was the first to turn away from the ocean and noticed Minin standing there. "What are you doing here?" He asked shocked, not expecting to see anyone.

"I'm sorry for your loss, I didn't know Quinn all that much, this is going to be heartbreaking for Hayley since she was with him on their drop-day, What Happened?" Minin asked, knowing this wasn't the time to cash in his I.O.U.

The rest of the Coasties started to walk past. Each one putting their hand on Minin's shoulder as a thank you for coming and showing his respect. Minin knew it was a shame they were unaware it had happened and showing up was a coincidence. He knew Hayley would have wanted to be here if not for their own situation.

"You guys weren't the only ones to have trouble with him," Screamer said. "He came to our camp while I was getting supplies from you. He wanted Quinn to help with a project, he didn't say what it was. Quinn refused and ended up getting shot. Everyone thought it would be best to have his funeral and cremation on the beach as he loved it. They also wanted it to be as quick as possible. I got back to camp just as they were setting up. They chose sunset as Quinn loved looking at them, it was his peaceful time I think."

"I'm glad you chose something he would like," Minin said sympathetic, he knew he had to say why he was here before he would forget, he knew after what had happened to the Coasties no time would have been perfect. "I'm sorry but that's not why we are here, I know this isn't the best time for it, but we need to cash in our I.O.U."

Screamer was taken aback, he wasn't expecting to repay it so quickly, but knew it would eventually happen. "What do you need?" he asked.

"We need medical supplies, especially painkillers." Screamer's face dropped from the request, he wasn't so sure. Minin decided it would be best to tell him the whole story, hoping it would sway him, "...And that's when we knew Tiffany had been shot."

"We can't," Screamer told him bluntly. "I understand we had an I.O.U and that meant anything we had and when you needed it. It's not we can't give you any because we'll be in short supply. It's we can't give you any because we don't have any in the first place." Screamer turned, looking at the last remaining embers on the water. "Any we did have was used to try and save Quinn."

Even though Minin understood and wanted to try and be sympathetic, getting told a no still annoyed him but he tried to remain calm. "Seriously? You haven't got anything, we don't need much, just pain killers, she's doing well so we'll probably only need a small amount." Screamer just shook his head. Minin took one last chance trying to persuade him and make him feel guilty, "We didn't have anything ourselves, but we still managed to give you something."

Screamer just shook his head, "Believe me, I want to help you, but no-one here has anything like that."

Minin still sounded annoyed, it sounded to him as though Screamer was holding back, but asked one last time, "So, nothing at all?"

"Honestly nothing, everyone told me they used their last medical supplies, once I got back to camp, that's when I had to use mine."

Minin took a deep slow breath, he knew then there wasn't anything he could do. "Umm, thanks," the words sounding as though he was disappointed. "I better head back to Hayley," he then turned around, heading to the middle of the camp.

Once Minin arrived he saw five Coasties all surrounding and talking to both Hayley and Tiffany. While he couldn't hear what they were saying the movements of their heads told him it was about what happened, almost in unison the five Coasties nodded their head and moved away heading towards their tents.

Minin made it closer to Hayley, "What was that about?" He asked.

"Just watch," she replied with a smile and almost instantly the first Coastie, Lynette, a short skinny girl with dirty blond hair, a tattoo on her left shoulder and wearing a red dress with white spots, arrived back with a first aid kit and handed it to Hayley. Not too long after, another, Sam, a boy with a roundish head, bowl cut, brown hair, wearing blue board shorts, brought his first aid kit, this continued until all five were back.

Minin was now confused, no matter how hard Minin tried to get something to help Tiffany, Screamer had refused, now five of his camp had just made him out to be a liar. Minin was infuriated. Screamer came next to Minin to see what was happening, Minin turned his head, he wanted to know why he had been lied to but saw a look on Screamers face telling him he had no idea. Screamer looked back at Minin. "I didn't know," was all he could say for a moment. "They all told me they had tried everything, they had used everything they had and yet Quinn still died," He said with a tear in his eye. "I don't get it if they had even the littlest thing they could do to help they would have, why didn't they?" With that Minin wasn't angry with Screamer anymore, knowing he had been lied too.

"None of us has medical training," Lynette said trying to explain the situation to Screamer. "We don't know how to take a bullet out, or even where to start, we tried to take a guess but everything we did made it worse, Quinn died before we even had a chance to use any of this stuff before you even got back."

"Then why did you lie to me?" Screamer asked, his voice not hiding his annoyance.

"Everyone knew you would have wasted the first aid kits on something we had no chance to fix. I know it's harsh that he died when we barley tried to help, but we had to make a decision, he didn't have a chance." Lynette replied as a tear dropped from her cheek. "He was our friend too, I hate that this has happened, I hate that....." she then pointed toward the Tower, "…..That monster is killing us, and he won't give us anything to change that." She then stormed off.

"Wait," Screamer called after her before running to catch up.

Hayley looked in one of the first aid kits and saw a box of pills with a label that said 'painkiller' and gave one to Tiffany, she swallowed it without any hesitation, "try and close your eyes and relax, the pills will work in a second," she said to Tiffany. Hayley then looked up at Minin, "They told me the whole story. Once Quinn had been shot, no-one knew how to take the bullet out without making the situation worse, no-one had any medical training, not even a first aid course. Once he had been shot everyone started to freak out, they didn't even think of the basics, not even use painkillers to steady him, and they tried to get the bullet out right away." She began to cry, "I have no doubt it was the pain that killed him, he was my drop-family, and now he is dead." She began to sob, a few moments later, she reasoned, "At least he doesn't have to deal with this place anymore I suppose," trying to smile.

Gin, the leader of the Coasties, a man who arrived on the island about two years before Hayley, with black hair down to his shoulders and wrinkles under his brown eyes. He approached them, he had three bottles containing a brown liquid in his hand. "I'm sorry about Quinn," Minin said.

"It's fine, Quinn was never one to try and let things get him down, especially this place, he always tried to make the best of it." Gin replied as he handed a bottle each to Hayley and Minin, "Quinn liked to party and celebrate life, I think that's what we should do for him now, I had this bottle for your friend, but she doesn't look like she will be using it anytime soon, now let's party and remember our friend." With that, he walked off with a cheer with everyone else.

"A party suits Quinn perfectly," Hayley said to Minin with a smile. "When I was on the dropship, I was seated next to him, he never once worried about where we were going, he looked forward to it. Before I ended up in our camp with Hunter and after we left the Tower, he wanted to find a place we could find a drink and celebrate in what he considered his rebirth, his chance to start over and for that I admire him. It's actually where I got the idea for drop days." She lifted the bottle, "To Quinn," The two of them clinking the bottles together.

Four of the Coasties came over and inspected Tiffany, by this time she had fallen back to sleep. "We have a bed for her where she will be safe for the night, we can move her if you like?" Savanah, an older Coastie with short blonde hair, blue eyes and a gentle smile asked them. "It'll be better than you staying here and looking after her for the night, you two can party and relax for a bit." She stopped talking for a second, not sure if she had said the right thing.

"That would be good," Hayley replied with a smile.

The four took her to a tent, right in the middle of the camp. "At least she'll be easy to find if we need to check on her," Minin commented. "I might go have a look around."

"Go have some fun," Hayley said with a smile. She looked at the four Coasties that had just exited the tent, "I'm sure there is someone here that will like the story of when we arrived on the island." The Coasties smiled at the suggestion.

"I'm sure they will too," Minin said with a smile.

Time had passed, Minin had been making his way around the party, some were celebrating and partying to the life of Quinn and some had been mourning and crying over what had happened. In both situations, he could see that everyone loved Quinn in their special way. He eventually realised he had been away from both Tiffany and Hayley for a while, while he knew that either one would be ok, he thought it might be best if he went and checked in on them. He went to the tent that Tiffany was in, she was still sleeping, he checked her over to make sure that there wasn't any problem, she seemed Ok. He then quickly moved on to locate Hayley. He saw Gin who was sitting around the campfire with two girls, about the same age as Minin. One had red hair and one was brunette, both had piercing blue eyes, Minin looked closer and realised that they were identical except for the hair.

"Have you seen Hayley anywhere?" He asked them.

"Nah, man," Gin answered. "She could be anywhere just enjoying herself, she's probably got a drink and talking to someone. She's a smart girl she won't be anywhere she's not supposed to be."

Minin knew that he was right, but something inside was telling him to locate her just in case. He began to walk in the direction of the beach, Screamer walking in the opposite direction. "You didn't see Hayley when you were down there did you?" He asked as they passed each other.

"Yeah, I was just with her. I think she just enjoyed having the company and the sound of the ocean, we were talking for ages. Head down there, I'm sure she'll like having you around there too."

"Thanks," Minin replied continuing his walk. The beach was lit up by the moonlight, the last burning ashes of the now barely floating casket could be seen in the distance. The sound of a few quiet voices and the ocean could be heard. Hayley was sitting close to the shoreline on her own. Minin approached her, he looked down, she had been crying. "Are you ok?" He asked.

"I just keep thinking about Quinn," she told him. "I think I feel guilty after we were separated and not staying close. After we had left the Tower we started to search the island. Before you get here, all you hear is that you're on your own on the island, we started to think like that, we didn't know that some of the islanders had been making camps together. For a few days, we were on our own in the Freelands, we'd try to find places to keep warm at night, that was ok on the first night.

On the second night Freelander's attacked us, all I can remember was the green face paint they had on and they wore black, I couldn't see much else. We thought this was it, luckily we only suffered a few bruises and cuts, but lost everything we had collected, our food, any clothes we managed to find. The only things left were the clothes we were wearing. After that, we decided to move away from the Freelands and head into the forest. We found a path, which lead into the Coasties camp, at that time there was only six of them. They took us both in, we felt like we had found a home here, more so than anything, we were safe from the outside.

A couple of days later, Hunter had come into the camp to trade, I thought he was a Freelander that had attacked us. Since he was on his own I went up to him and blasted him for attacking us. It took almost all the Coasties that knew Hunter to explain that he wasn't a threat and he didn't classify himself as Freelander, he just lived on his own. I didn't fully believe them and needed to see his camp for myself, so he offered to take me. I asked if Quinn wanted to come, but he was happy to stay with the Coasties, so it ended up being just Hunter and myself.

We got to the camp, it was so much smaller than it is now, just one hut, one seat around a fire, one shed, just enough for one person. I felt sorry for him and asked, "Why do you live alone?" he told me, "I just do, it's not like I stop anyone else from staying here." It was then I decided that I wanted to stay with Hunter. So, I went back to the Coasties to tell them what was happening, I wanted Quinn to come too, but he was happy to stay where he was."

Minin sniggered a little, "I never heard the story of when you and Hunter first met."

"I guess you're right" Hayley replied with a smile. "I didn't worry that much about Quinn until now, he was safe here, every time we've had a chance to meet we've caught up, he is my drop-brother after all. I guess it must be like you and Ronald, you feel something for your drop-family that you don't feel with your camp." Hayley put her head on Minin's shoulder. "He was always happy, even in the scariest of times. Those first few days on the island he was always happy about it. I don't know what he did to end up here, he never told me, but whatever it was, he was happy that he was here. Even when the cargo doors on the dropship opened and he was sliding towards the opening he was looking at me and kept smiling, I knew when the doors opened we would be dropped onto the island and that scared the hell out of me, but with him smiling, I felt a bit of comfort and just for that he made me happy."

Minin replied, "I understand what you mean, on my drop-day, I was with Screamer. No-one knows how it feels except for those that drop with you, you always have that with them. I have that with Screamer, probably why I pushed so hard to give him something when he got to our camp and I was so annoyed he couldn't return the favour…well, that was until I found out he was lied to."

The two of them sat looking at the ocean for a moment until Hayley asked, "Do you know how Tiffany is doing?"

"I just looked in on her, she seemed fine," Minin replied.

"That's good. I may have lost a drop-family member today, but I at least still have my camp family, even if one is stuck in the Tower and another is MIA."

What she said meant a lot to Minin, "You didn't have the minute silence with us for Quinn when we first arrived when the funeral was on, did you want to do it now?" he asked.

"I would like that. Thank you," she replied as they just sat there in silence watching the last remaining embers of her drop-brother burn and sink into the ocean.

16

A cool breeze began to move over the beach, both Minin and Hayley thought they had only closed their eyes for a moment but soon realised, it may have been longer. Even though the beach had been quiet while they were enjoying each other's company, it was now completely deserted.

"Let's head back, it looks like the party has wound down for now," Hayley said, deciding they should both get back to the camp and closer to warmth for the night. They both got off the sandy ground and made their way to the middle of the camp.

The middle of the camp was quieter than when Minin had left to find Hayley, less than a handful of people were just lounging around talking. The party that once was, now just a memory.

"You don't know where we are sleeping for the night, do you?" Hayley asked. "I know we arranged for Tiffany to have somewhere to sleep but I don't think we even thought about ourselves."

"You're right," Minin paused for a moment, looking around at the few remaining people and spotted Gin still talking to one of the girls, the brunette but now they were getting closer with each other. "Hey Gin," He called. Gin glanced at him, slightly annoyed that he had been interrupted. "Hey sorry for interrupting you," Minin continued, "but we didn't work out where we're sleeping tonight, you can't help us can you?"

Gin's annoyance turned to a smile, realising this was only going to be a small conversation and he could get back to, 'getting to know the girl' better. "Yeah, you guys are in the same tent with Tiffany, Quinn's old tent just over there," pointing to the tent where Tiffany was. The girl whispered something into Gin's ear which Minin couldn't hear, which made Gin smile. "Yeah, we're about to head to bed ourselves, we'll see you guys in the morning," He said as they both made their way to his tent.

Minin and Hayley realise instantly that the tent wasn't designed for more than two people. Tonight, it was going to be a snug fit for the three of them. Minin unzipped the front of the tent, Tiffany was asleep on the left side, the pain meds that Hayley had given her were making an easy sleep for her. Two more sleeping bags were already positioned inside the tent, "At least they are prepared for us" Minin said, "Do you want the side or the middle?"

Hayley looked at the inside of the tent, there wasn't much difference between the two, "I'll take the side, that's if you are ok sleeping in the middle of two women?" She asked with a cheeky smile and moved inside and into her sleeping bag.

Minin moved inside, taking the remaining sleeping bag. This was the absolute maximum this tent was going to take, even rolling over in their sleep would prove difficult. Somehow Minin managed to lay down and got into his sleeping bag, Tiffany rolled over and put her arm around him.

"She's getting quite comfortable with you," Hayley said to him curtly.

"What do you mean by that?" He asked, confused by her words and tone.

"Nothing" She replied, in a friendlier tone. "Anyway, nighty night." With some degree of difficulty, Hayley rolled over and closed her eyes to sleep.

Minin just looked up at the roof of the tent with Tiffany's arm still over him, wondering what Hayley had meant. Was she joking or was she somewhat jealous that another girl that was completely asleep put her arms around him? Minin stayed looking at the roof for a few more minutes but knew this wasn't the time to worry about it. It had been a long day and worrying about something so little shouldn't cause a sleepless night so he closed his eyes.

Minin opened his eyes, it was now daylight, he must have fallen asleep almost instantly. He turned his head to where Hayley slept, she was no longer there. He then turned to Tiffany's side, the same thing, she was gone. *'How long have I been asleep?'* He thought to himself. He decided to stay in the sleeping bag for a little bit longer hoping to wake up more before he ventured out. To him it was nice just relaxing in the tent, especially now it had enough room to feel like you could move.

Time had passed and he began to wonder where his friends had gotten to. He decided to get out of the tent and go find them. He exited the tent but didn't have to travel far to find them, both they and Gin were sitting around the campfire.

"Good morning sleepyhead," Tiffany announced to him. She was looking much better than she had the night and day before.

"Morning, how are you feeling? Any better?"

"Much better thank you, that sleep did wonders. So did whatever was given to me, it only feels like a small cut now, not like I had been shot," She replied with a smile. "They'll have to do more than fire a bullet to finish me off, I'm back to take on the world," She finished proudly.

Minin was thrown off by her enthusiasm, he could see she was much healthier and feeling better, but this was over the top. He didn't think anyone could be that much different after what had happened.

Hayley began to laugh over what she had said. "How much did we give you? You should still be feeling some pain."

"Judging by how I feel, I'd say…. a lot." She announced proudly beginning to laugh.

"I think so. You might feel like it, but you're still not ready to take on the world, you still have to take it easy," Hayley told her.

"I thought you were being serious about being ready to take on the world there for a second," Minin said.

"Nope, just high off the meds," Tiffany said laughing, thinking what she had said was hilarious.

Minin looked around the camp area. He realised that they were the only people around. There was no sign of the rest of the Coasties, "Where is everyone? He asked.

Gin replied. "Everyone has the chores they do, we're really not that different from your camp, everyone has their part to play. I'll get to mine later, I figure I would be a good host to our guests and keep you company," He informed them hoping to give a good impression. "You missed breakfast, we had that a few hours ago, we figured it would be better to let you sleep after what you've been through in the last few days."

"Umm, thanks," Minin replied. "I feel a little better, I didn't realise that till now, come to think about it," Minin looked at both Tiffany and Hayley, they too looked like they were refreshed and looking better. "Did you two want to head back to our camp before lunch?"

Hayley looked back at him, "That was one thing we were talking about while you were still in the tent." Minin didn't like where this was heading, " I like staying in our own camp, in our own 'little world' away from everything that is happening on the outside, but we were thinking about staying here for a little bit."

"How long were you thinking?"

"Just a few days, nothing too major. I know Tiffany is looking good for the moment and the pain meds are holding, but I don't want to completely deplete what everyone around here has by us taking it all. I think if we were to only take a little bit it would be enough, but to be honest I just don't want to take that chance. It's a just in case thing," She told him with a smile. "I know I usually make the decisions for the camp but I want your input."

Tiffany smiled at him, "I like knowing there are other people outside of our camp, this is a good chance for us to get to know them." She said, hoping to convince him.

He smiled, staying quiet for a moment, weighing up his options. Another reason to stay came into his head, it would just be the three of them going to the camp, Hunter and Callum weren't going to be there. "I don't know if it will feel like home without them."

Hayley knew exactly who he meant but Tiffany asked, "You mean Hunter and Callum?"

"Yeah," He answered. The more he thought about it, the more in his head he didn't think it was right to go back without them as well. In his mind, if they had decided to walk away from the camp on their own this would have been a different situation, but that was their home as well. "We'll stay for a few days if our hosts are ok with it?" Knowing the resources were so light here, staying here permanently wasn't going to be a viable option either, "After that, we should head off." He told them.

Gin looked to Hayley, "I'm not trying to get you to leave but when you do, take as much of the meds as you need, everyone gave you what they had knowing they would be left without. They won't, or at least shouldn't argue with you taking them," He said with a smile.

She smiled in return, knowing that on the island giving useful resources away is a huge deal since you don't know when you'll be able to replace them. "After a few more days we'll know for sure exactly how she is doing, so thank you for your offer."

"If I didn't get myself shot, we wouldn't be in this situation," Tiffany said guiltily. "We'd still have our own meds."

The three turn and look at her, Hayley grabbing her hand. "This isn't your fault. You getting shot was an accident." She paused for a moment and thought, "I think you're the first person that I know of that's been shot, anyone else that has been attacked by that maniac was done by the kill chips, anyone without a kill chip only had a warning. You must be special." She smiled, trying to cheer her up.

They all began to laugh except Gin, "If you need to blame anyone, it's Callum, if he didn't try to be a hero, you wouldn't have been shot." He said seriously.

Everyone stopped laughing, staring at Gin. They couldn't believe what he had said. Minin knew he needed to say something to set the story straight and sternly told him, "We don't blame Callum, we blame Daman. He thinks he runs this place, he makes us live in a world of fear."

Gin cut him off. "You call it a world of fear. Well... fear is smart, fear doesn't get us killed......" He then pointed to Tiffany, ".....Doesn't get us shot......" He then began to point between himself and Hayley, ".....Doesn't get our kill chips activated."

Some of the Coasties had just returned and listened to what both were saying. Minin then cut him off in return, "If we didn't live with that fear we wouldn't have had to come here and use your Meds. We would have gotten them from the Tower, Stephanie wouldn't have gone missing looking for food for everyone. That fear you call smart stopped us from doing that, and that's just not fair. We should be able to go and get the meds he has, not just when Tiffany needs them but when anyone does. It's about time someone tells him we can't live like this."

The Coasties that listened to the speech began clapping and cheering. "But who would actually go and prove that to him?" Gin responded.

They all stayed quiet, Tiffany then spoke. She pointed to her bullet wound, "I can't go up against him anytime soon," She said, even though in reality this fact bothered her. "As much as I would like to, I'm still no use to you, even so, first it's this, next time I won't be so lucky."

"As much as I don't want to agree with Gin, we can't just walk up to the Tower," Hayley said. "We can't just knock on the door and say, "Hey, we need meds, can you give us some please? Stephanie proved that. The only way we could get supplies from the tower was if we were to steal them and without anyone in the Tower knowing, and I don't know about any of you but I don't know that way in."

Minin was happy to have Hayley on his side. As much as he hated the situation, he didn't have any ideas either.

A clapping noise came from the bushes behind Minin who didn't think anything of it, just assumed that it was one of the Coasties, hearing the end of the discussion. He turned around anyway.

Callum was standing in front of everyone, his clothes ripped and torn by what they could only assume were the bushes. Hayley stood up and ran over to hug him. Tiffany pulled herself up from her seat and proceeded to do the same. Once they broke apart Callum and Minin looked at each other, smiled, shook hands then hugged themselves.

Once it was over Callum looked at Gin, who had his arm out waiting to greet and shake it. Callum stood there with a look of disgust on his face and refused to shake it back. Gin didn't know what to make of it and tried again this time, speaking first, "Welcome to our camp." Once again he put his hand out.

Callum again chose not to shake it. Instead, he pointed to Gin, then closed his hand and proceeded to open it, he then pointed to Tiffany, then to himself and finishing off shaking his head.

"I don't understand," Gin said.

Minin answered for him, "It's simple, he must have heard what you said, blaming him for what had happened. Callum hides a lot, it doesn't surprise me that we didn't know he was here." Minin then turned to Callum, "Where have you been?"

Callum began making a digging motion with his hands.

"You were digging?" Hayley answered.

Callum nodded, he then moved his hand like he was throwing dice toward the ground.

"The.... the farmers?" Minin answered.

He smiled and nodded.

"How long were you there for?" Minin continued to question.

He put his hands together and pretended he was sleeping.

"You only slept there overnight? Why didn't you stay?" Hayley asked.

He then put his hand into his pocket and pulled out two pieces of paper and gave one to Minin to look over. He made sure that only Minin could see, blocking Gin's view.

It was a wanted poster with Callum's picture on it, the words wanted dead or alive, reward 3 supply crates if he is dead, 5 if he is alive. The last line, 'Bring him to the entrance of the tower for exchange'.

Minin went to Hayley showing her, "I've never seen anything like this before, have you?" He asked quietly, so no one else could hear.

"No posters or anything, I've been inside the tower before," She replied just as quietly. "I've never seen anything that could print anything out. Especially to make what I assume is mass quantities of something, but saying that I've only seen a few floors and that was enough for me to stay away. If Daman is making something like this, then he really wants Callum." She said with fear in her voice.

Callum then handed the other piece of paper to them. It was a handwritten note written by Chris, the leader of the Farmers.

'To whoever is reading this,

if you are reading this it means you have met up with Callum, we can't afford to let him stay with us as it is too risky. We have let him stay with us for one night but that was all we could afford as he has most likely now shown you there is now a bounty on his head. While we do not wish to give him up, we believe keeping him here with us would create havoc for ourselves, if someone were to tell the tower we were keeping him here. We are sorry but we need to protect ourselves, so please understand why we cannot let him stay with us.

If you allow him to stay with you, please keep him safe.

Chris.

"Well, at least that explains why they didn't let him stay," Hayley said quietly to Minin. "Have you been to any other camps?" She asked Callum trying to gauge how many people would have rejected him.

He shook his head, telling her he had been nowhere else.

"At least no-one knows where he is if they were going to give him up," Minin said just to Hayley.

"But there are only so many hiding places for him," Hayley replied worried.

"But if there are any hiding spots that no one else knows about, Callum will now have to use them. He's been around the island more than anyone, so that's an advantage for him."

"What did the papers say?" Gin asked curiously not knowing what was going on.

Neither Hayley or Minin knew what to say, as much as they wanted to trust the Coasties with the information, Callum didn't trust at least

Gin after what he had said about him and they both knew that. The Coasties as a group was in desperate need of supplies, and five crates for an alive body would be an extremely tempting deal for them. Minin replied, "It's from the farmers it's just a letter saying Callum wanted to find us and rather than Callum trying to speak to someone that didn't understand him, the letter explains what he needs."

The look of Gin's face said he didn't quite believe his explanation but he knew that he wasn't going to get another answer. "Fair enough," He replied annoyed and walked away.

Tiffany sat down for a moment. Minin looked at her, he could see that she was starting to feel the pain again, the meds were wearing off. Both Minin and Hayley went to make sure she was all right. Hayley looked over her, the pain was increasing but otherwise she was ok.

Callum began to wave his arms around to get the attention of the others. He made a look as though he was putting something into his mouth then looked like he had gotten a cup and was drinking out of it.

Hayley knew that he was asking if Tiffany had gotten any pain medication. "We should have enough for the time being, I thought we would be ok if we stayed here for a bit then headed back to the camp. But she had a top-up about an hour ago, now it's wearing off, she's going through it too quickly," Hayley informed everyone.

"It's been hurting for a while," Tiffany told her. "When you gave me the meds before it only numbed the pain slightly, I could still feel it even when I was high, now it's getting worse."

Minin became concerned that the meds were wearing off too quickly, or even not working as they should, "How long will she have pain?"

"I don't know, everyone is different," Hayley replied. "Every dose we give her only takes the pain away for an hour, I've now got my doubts whether we will have enough, even if we use what the Coasties give us," She conceded.

"I'm fine, it hurts…a lot, but I'll be fine," Tiffany told them trying to be brave.

A thought then occurred to Callum, he knew what needed to be done, he once again waved his arms to get everyone's attention. They looked at him, he pointed to Tiffany and made his fist look like it was screwing something then pointed towards the Tower then pointed to the ground, then made a shape of a door and finally put his fingers on his lips meaning to be quiet.

They all stood there for a moment trying to figure what he meant but no-one had even the slightest clue what he was saying. Minin took a guess, "You can fix Tiffany at the tower, down, at a door but we have to be quiet?" He didn't know what any of that meant. "That doesn't make any sense though."

Callum shook his head, the guess wasn't correct, he moved his hands around trying to figure out what else he could say, knowing he couldn't speak was beginning to frustrate him. He knew what he wanted to say, he did the same thing again hoping someone would pick up something that they missed the last time.

Tiffany then took a guess, "You can help me, but you have to go to the tower. At the bottom, there is a door but you have to be quiet while you are there?"

Callum nodded his head and put out the palm of his hand and shook it. She was close but didn't fully understand what he had tried to say to them.

"I'm going to get Tiffany some meds from the tent to help with the pain," Hayley said, walking to the tent to get what she needed, knowing she didn't have an answer and guessing was only wasting time.

Minin took another guess. "To help Tiffany, we have to go to the Tower, there's an entrance at the bottom but it's quiet." Minin thought for a second all of that made sense except the entrance is quiet, then it hit him. "…It's a secret… if we go to the tower there is a secret en-trance."

Callum nodded his head in excitement then hugged Minin, excited that someone had figured out what he had said.

"I didn't know there was another entrance," Minin said surprised.

Callum then shook his head and pointed a finger at himself.

"Are you sure you're the only one that knows of it? Do you think we can get in and out without anyone knowing?"

He nodded his head.

"How long have you known?"

Callum just shrugged his shoulders, he wasn't sure himself.

"Ok let's go get the meds," Minin announced.

Callum pointed to his head.

"Think about it?" Minin asked.

Callum nodded, knowing just walking up to the tower even if they go somewhere not popular was not a good idea.

"We need to think about a plan, don't we?" Minin asked. He paused for a moment, "I'll go get it myself, you're being hunted now, just tell me the way and I'll work it out from there."

Callum shook his head, he knew he had to go. If something happened to Minin inside he wouldn't be able to forgive himself. So, he pointed to Minin then himself.

"We both have to go, don't we?" Minin said, unsure that Callum should be attending with the bounty on his head.

Callum then pointed at Minin, Tiffany and himself then showed his palm, pointing at his thumb and two fingers. He then pointed to his fourth finger and the direction where Hayley had gone, then pointed to his fifth finger and the tower"

"You want to get Hunter while we are there?" Minin asked, hoping he was right.

Callum nodded again, telling him he was correct. He flipped his hand then began to tap his wrist.

Minin thought for a moment, he was stumped as to what that meant.

Tiffany then answered, "You need to pick the right time when there is less chance of being caught." She looked at Minin and smiled, "how is it that you've known him this long and I already know what he means better than you?"

Callum looked at her and smiled.

Hayley returned and injected a needle into Tiffany, "It'll be a few more minutes before it fully takes effect, but you'll feel better soon," she said. She then looked at Minin, "did you work it out? I was thinking that it might mean something about a secret entrance."

"Way ahead of you," he replied. "We were just finishing the plan." He then looked at Callum, "we should be able to get in and out with as many supplies as we can hold, priority is the meds. We just need to pick the right time to leave so fewer people are guarding the tower."

"What about drop-day?" She suggested. "Once the crates drop, there will be teams from the Tower looking for crates, it'll be your best chance."

"If we have a chance and I know it's almost impossible, we'll get Hunter out with us," Minin told her. "We already have one fugitive, we may as well have two," he added.

Hayley had a smile on her face that was almost impossible to remove, then a thought came into her head, removing it instantly. "Where will we go? Daman will hunt us down, we can't go back to our camp, that'll be the first place he will look."

Minin didn't know what else to say, he didn't think that far through. At that very moment, Gin returned, "I heard what you said about going into the tower, that's a pretty stupid move if you ask me, don't get me wrong, those meds are something we all need." He paused for a moment. "But to be completely honest I don't think you'll get out."

Minin knew the plan was stupid himself, but at that moment, didn't believe they had another choice. "I know it's stupid, but unless you have a better plan, it's either this or we clean you guys out."

"I don't have a better plan," Gin answered simply. He then turned to Callum, "I thought everything over, had time to calm down. I'm sorry for what I said."

Callum didn't know whether to believe him or not but he also knew to have an ally was good, so he decided to bury the hatchet and put out his hand, they shook.

Gin smiled at him, "Hayley and Tiffany can stay with us if they need too and if something happens, they can become one of us if they want. Under one condition."

The announcement surprised everyone. "Are you trying to make a deal?" Minin asked.

"Yes," he replied bluntly.

"This isn't the right time to make one," Minin said, annoyed that Gin would do something at that moment.

"Yes, it is, you need our camp to hide, we can do that."

Hayley came into the conversation and asked bluntly, "What is it?"

"We take control of your camp," he paused with a sly grin then continued to talk, trying to clarify what he had said. "More like we combine the two camps into one. Think of it as a joint camp in two areas." He continued talking but only looking at Minin, clearly attempting to block Hayley, "I'm sorry if it sounded bad, but I figured we are quite similar with rules and whatnot, and everyone in each group can come and go from either one however they like."

"He doesn't make the deals," Hayley told him furiously, "I do." She took a deep breath, "that one deal with Ronald, was a one-time deal, but this is much bigger," she said begrudgingly. "As much as you want to say you're combining the two camps, it's a takeover, plain and simple. I'm the leader, I make the final decision about anything and only after I talk to my camp but for this one, I won't make the deal, we'll stay here until we need to leave and that'll be it."

Gin was annoyed, he believed his deal was fair, "Are you sure?"

"Yes," she replied, sounding as though steam was coming from her ears. "We'll stay here until drop day, it's a bit longer than we thought but after that, we'll be back in our camp, and I don't think anyone else here has a problem with that." A small number of Coasties heard what she had just said and began to cheer, agreeing. Gin just looked annoyed

17

Drop day was here, the wait until this point wasn't something either Callum or Minin enjoyed. Waiting just made them think about things they normally wouldn't think about. Minin kept thinking he had discovered so much more about what Callum knew about the Tower then he thought possible. If anyone had known where a secret entrance to the Tower was it was Callum, he was always leaving the camp to explore the Island, leaving for days on end, just to return as though nothing had happened. Every time that he had done this, Minin wanted to ask what had happened or where he had gone, especially when he came back with the occasional bruises and scratches. Since Hayley and Hunter never asked and Callum never offered anything himself he assumed it was normal and he would mind his own business.

He wanted to ask about all the information Callum had inside his hut but didn't want to bring it up in front of anyone that didn't know about it. Being in a different camp, especially since its members were larger, making it almost impossible to bring it up without someone overhearing. So Minin decided the best course of action would be to ask as they were going to the Tower since it would only be the two of them.

Gin didn't like the idea that Hayley, Minin, Tiffany and Callum were staying with the Coasties at all now since his idea of 'merging the two' as he had called it had failed. Some of the Coasties tried to point out to him that it did sound like a take-over. He decided that it would be best to remain quiet about it as he knew that if the rest of the Coasties didn't agree with him and if they felt strongly enough about something, they could vote to have him banished out of the camp.

"Once they come back, we'll head back to our camp, and we'll be out of your hair." Hayley would say to Gin in a tone that sounded snarky but pleasant. She knew how he felt and she wanted to leave the camp as soon as she could and return home.

"It's ok, you can visit anytime once this is over." He would reply in the same tone as hers, hoping it didn't happen.

Minin and Callum were both given backpacks with a small number of supplies. Inside it contained rope, a first-aid kit and some food, which were all provided by members of the Coasties. While they didn't have much, they gave them what they could in the hope if they had returned they would receive something much larger for their generosity. Every member of the Coasties, as well as Hayley and Tiffany, came to see them off. While most of them didn't think what they were doing was possible, everyone had a hope they would be proved wrong and they would return.

"Ok you guys," Hayley reached out and hugged them, she had tears in her eyes. "Good luck, you know the plan, once the dropships come through, go to the Tower, they'll be distracted. Then it's up to you what happens next."

Tiffany came over and hugged them as well. Since the take over discussion, her wound had healed but the pain remained but not enough to require any medication, "Good luck, come back to us." She told them quietly.

"Good luck," Gin said trying to look supportive, but his voice didn't hide his lack of belief in their mission.

"Umm thanks," Minin replied.

The sun continued to rise as they waited for the dropships, usually, they would have heard something by this point. "What's taking so long?" Minin asked, "We can usually hear them by now."

"Don't you know anything?" Gin said. "You're usually the first place the dropships come over, we're covered by trees, which muffle the sound for longer. You guys are usually on the beach. If this plan has any hope of succeeding, you need to work on your patience," he continued annoyed.

Everyone continued to wait, a faint whooshing sound could now be heard in the distance, everyone turned in the direction of the sound, trying to catch a glimpse of the ship, but were unable to see past the trees. The sound soon became loud enough that Minin thought it was overhead but nothing could be seen. "We should be able to see it by now," he screamed impatiently, trying to get his voice over the noise.

"Now," Gin screamed, pointing directly at the dropship as it passed overhead.

The people that were connected to seats inside the Dropship fell out the back. A few seconds pass and some of the parachutes deploy. The others hurtle to the ground. "I wonder how many will make it this time?" A short young girl with straight black hair from the Coasties asked.

Minin and Callum continued to watch, "Go!" Hayley yelled. "Go now, once the dropship turns around and starts dropping crates, you'll be out of the Coasties and on your way," She told them. They both began running, hoping to get to the Tower quickly, "Good luck," She shouted to them. She then said to herself, "Please come back to us," in a worried tone, quiet enough that only she and Tiffany could hear.

Tiffany looked at her, putting her arm over her shoulder, "One way or another they will come back."

"I hope you are right," Hayley replied becoming even more worried as thoughts of what could happen inside the Tower flood her mind.

Minin and Callum arrived at the entrance of the Coasties camp. The dropship by this time had long passed overhead and had completed its first pass, it wouldn't be too long before it would be back, the two of them knew they needed to focus on getting there as fast as possible.

They were walking on a path Minin had never been on before, he didn't need to ask where it was going, he had never been to the Tower before and trusted Callum would get him there safely. The sound of the dropship returned, telling them that it was now making the return trip. The dropship flew overhead, the canopy of trees showing a small enough opening to get a glimpse of the return. Supply Crates began falling out of the back, hurtling towards the ground.

Callum looked exactly like he knew where he was going. This to Minin was comforting as he didn't want to be out for too long, knowing that people from the Tower would be on the lookout for any supplies, new people or even Callum. The two of them kept walking not hearing another soul, Minin then decided to ask what had been on his mind the past few months. "I need to ask you something about when Tiffany got shot."

Callum thought it was going to be about when he left for the night, so he turned his head smiling, but the question he expected did not arrive.

"I had to look for supplies from your hut, normally I wouldn't go in without your permission but it was an emergency. I hoped you wouldn't have a problem with me looking inside your hut. The point is, I found something I need to ask you about."

Callum's smile changed, he knew what was about to be asked of him, but he hoped that he would be wrong.

"I found some pieces of paper, they had information about everyone." He paused, not knowing how to word his question, "Well my question is…. What's the go with it?"

Callum smiled trying to figure out what to say or rather how to say it. Suddenly they could hear footsteps, without thinking he grabbed Minin's shirt taking him into a bush and got him to sit down. They stayed quiet, hoping the footsteps didn't belong to anyone from inside the Tower. They kept quiet, the footsteps became louder, then they saw who was making the footsteps between the foliage.

Four guards talking between themselves were walking by. "…Just keep to the plan, don't worry about anything else, find crates, people and take them back to the tower, if we see the bastard that got the girl shot, we take him in but he's not the priority today."

Another guard then asked, "How can he hide so much? The island isn't that big."

"Daman knows what he is doing, he'll get him sooner rather than later, trust me." The first guard replied.

Callum's hand was clenched in a fist, he wanted to show them what for. Minin grabbed his arm and held him down, just in case his anger took over, getting into a confrontation was the last thing either of them needed right now. Even though they had the element of surprise, they were outnumbered and they had people depending on them. The risk was too great, so keeping quiet and still, was the best option for the moment.

The guards walked off as quickly as they came. Once the noise of the footsteps and voices were gone, Minin and Callum returned to the path. Callum grabbed Minin and made a gesture with his hands conveying that they needed to go quicker. The two of them began to run, Minin staying just a bit behind so he could follow without having to ask directions. As they ran, Minin looked up at the tower, he had never been this close, never noticed its size before. In his life before the Island, he had seen skyscrapers and this Tower could have easily matched them in height and size but with its top looking more like a castle.

Callum began to slow down, "You starting to get tired?" Minin asked.

Callum just shook his head.

Minin, on the other hand, was beginning to get puffed out and was grateful he could slow down. The two of them stopped, Callum began to look around, "What are you looking for?" Minin asked.

Callum just shook his hands, telling him 'To be quiet and let him look.' He then saw a pile of shrubs, he moved them around, uncovering a metal grated door, attached to a pentagonal concrete pipe, just elevated off the ground, more than big enough for a person to be able to walk into if they crouched down.

Minin was shocked at the sight in front of him, "Does anyone else know about this?" Callum shook his head. '*This was the secret door he was talking* about,' Minin thought to himself.

Callum opened the grated door without any struggle, the door making a creaking sound. He jumped in, turned around and put his hand out to grab Minin. Minin took the hand and was pulled in. Minin looked further into the Tunnel, he couldn't see far. "Are you sure it's safe? How far down does it go?" Minin asked wondering if it was a good idea to continue.

Callum just smiled back and nodded, then put his thumb and index finger close together.

"Just a little bit," Minin translated with a sigh of relief. At this point, he was glad it was himself going with Callum and not someone else that didn't know how to communicate with him, otherwise, this would have been frustrating for them both.

Callum began to walk towards the darkness. Minin stared into the dark unknown, then back into the light and the opening he had come from. If he wanted to change his mind, this was the time to do it. He looked once more, towards the light, and then started to walk until he disappeared into the darkness.

Once Minin's eyes adjusted to the darkness, he could see a little bit. He wasn't sure if his voice would carry along the pipe and someone would be on the other side, so he remained silent. The silence also helped him to concentrate on looking where he was going. It wasn't long before he could see a light at the end of the tunnel, which was a relief.

They both arrived at the end, which once again was closed off by another metal grate. Callum went to open it right away, Minin stopped him, something in his stomach was telling him not to open it, he didn't know why though. Callum looked at him like he was acting strange or something, he put up his hands and shrugged his shoulders to ask, 'What's the problem?'

Minin didn't know what to say, all he could think in his head was the fact everyone up until now had told him to stay away from the Tower and now this was the complete opposite. "Let's have a look first," he said in the quietest voice he could. He went to the grate and looked as far out and to the sides as he could, it was empty and looked like it had been that way for a while. Minin decided that the fear he had was just his fear of the tower itself. "Ok, it's clear." Minin pushed the door open, it creaked, he stopped the second he heard it thinking he had given them away and people nearby would be coming into the room at any moment.

Callum was getting frustrated, he knew that there wasn't going to be anyone around and grabbed the door, pushing it all the way open. He stepped out and down to the damp muddy ground, the pipe was about a meter above, the fall creating a thud-splash noise. He looked back at the opening of the pipe waiting for Minin to come out.

Minin knew he was just above the edge and stepped down to the ground, also making the thud-splash noise. He looked around, it looked as though it was an elevator shaft. Two sides had what looked to be two rails rising to the sky, with thick metal chains connected. On one of the rails, there was a platform which was surrounded by a rickety, rusted, faded blue fence and a control panel on the side closest to the middle of the room. On the other side of the room, just another rail with empty crates placed underneath. Minin couldn't believe how easy getting into the tower was.

Callum began to walk towards the crates, looking around while Minin followed. "Freeze," came a voice from behind the crates.

So much for thinking it was easy to get in. A cold shiver went up Minin's spine, this was not what he wanted to hear.

"We've been waiting for you," said the same voice, Minin and Callum froze.

'How did they know we were coming?' Minin thought. 'Had someone betrayed them and told them what the plan was?'

The man had a white goatee with short white hair and brown eyes who looked too old to be sent to the Island, who was wearing the guard's uniform. He stepped out from behind the crates. "You took a little longer than we thought," he taunted. He then smiled at Callum, knowing that he had caught him.

Nine more guards revealed themselves, each one holding a gun with laser sights trained on Minin and Callum. They remained still and silent, facing the man with the goatee.

"Thanks for bringing Callum to us, it made it easier than us having to go out looking for him, although the wait for you to come here was annoying. None-the-less, you're here now." He then whispered in the ear of a guard standing next to him. Neither Callum or Minin could hear what he was saying, all they could hear was the last word, "Reward." Both guards looked down and glared at them, their facial expression then turned into a smile.

"Come onto the platform," The Goatee guard demanded.

Minin looked back at the pipe they had just arrived from, contemplating whether he should take the chance and try to get back inside and try to run, but it was just a quick thought, he knew the guns would fire before his feet even left the ground. The odds were too stacked against them.

Callum began to march onto the platform, Minin following almost instantly, the laser sights not once leaving. Five of the guards walk off the platform to make room as they walked past. The Goatee guard pressed a button on the control panel, the platform began to rise. The remaining guards staying at the bottom, still not taking their sights off them until they disappear. The guards with Callum and Minin remained still and say nothing. They all stared at Minin and Callum not once taking their eyes off their targets. Minin thought talking may distract them, so he tried to take his chance. "Hey, where are we going?" He asked but none of the guard's answer, "Tough crowd," he said to himself. He then looked over the side of the elevator, it had become dark, even if Minin was to take the chance and jump down, he didn't know how far it would be and even if it wasn't far, the remaining guards would either re-capture him or shoot on the spot. Minin then looked at the other side of the shaft, he could see the rail and thick metal chain moving in the middle, the other side was another elevator and it was moving as well. A few seconds later both elevators passed each other, the other side looking like a mirror reverse version of the platform they were on, heading towards the bottom, presumably, towards the other guards.

Time passed, then the elevator stopped. Minin looked above him, there was still plenty of room for the elevator to move. Metal doors in front of him open sideways revealing a hallway lit up with lights. "Time to go," The Goatee guard told them, they all start walking into the opening except for the Goatee Guard. The hallway is lined with red and white squared carpet. The walls were brick with painted pictures along, each picture a different landmark from all over the world. The Elevator doors close as they follow the hall around a corner. The end of the hallway had a Television on the top, but it was turned off. Minin wondered if they worked or just like the paintings, were just for decoration. The hallway looked familiar to him, then he remembered why they looked almost exactly like the halls of the office he used to work at before he came to the island.

'This wasn't what I was expecting, although there were days I thought my job was a prison,' Minin thought to himself. He always thought the Tower would be a horrible looking place with jail cells on each floor and maybe a level or two just for any guards and Daman to live in, which made him think that maybe this was one of the levels for the guards.

They were guided past a room, on the right with an open door, it had wooden desks with computers sitting on it. It once again reminded Minin of the workstations in his old office job. He wanted a chance to work out if the computers were just for show or connected to the outside world. He paused, trying to get a better look inside.

Minin felt a strong hit into his back, it was the end of a gun shaft from the guard walking behind him, "Continue walking," He ordered. Minin didn't try to argue, instead he turned his head and kept walking. At the end of the hall he noticed an open door, which shortly after they all enter.

More guards are waiting in the room that looked like the one they had just walked past, except in the middle computer servers with flashing lights which were protected by glass panelling. *'The lights must mean that the servers are at least turned on,'* Minin thought. As Minin and Callum walk in, the guards all aim their guns towards them, "You guys really don't want us to leave, do you?" Minin joked, trying to make light of the situation. Callum laughing slightly.

One of the guards lowered his gun and brought over a pair of handcuffs. He cuffed Callum's arms behind his back, while the remaining guards didn't budge. He then pulled out a second pair and did the same to Minin. Two guards then grabbed Callum dragging him into a door off to the side that Minin hadn't noticed before.

"Wait, let him go!" Minin screamed desperately but he was powerless. Now without his friend, he suddenly felt the danger around him. Two guards grabbed Minin by the arms and took him back through the doors they entered through and back towards the elevator. Minin was terrified and tried to squirm out of the guards' grasp but they held firm.

"Say goodbye to your friend," A guard taunted as they got to the elevator. The Guard with the Goatee was still waiting. The guards behind Minin push him onto the Elevator. The Goatee Guard pressed another button on the console, the elevator began to rise once more.

The Elevator ride seemed to take longer than the first time. His brain started running through the possibilities of what was going to happen to Callum. Was he still alive? Was he going to be put in a prison cell? Would he ever see him again? Minin had no idea.

The elevator stopped once again. The doors opened revealing what looked to be an open room that took the space of half the level. Timber frames in various locations held the roof in place, the walls were all made of glass, showing the east half of the island from any direction with the ocean framing it, the wall dividing the floor a huge mirror. In the middle of the room was a wooden desk with a high back chair, facing away from Minin towards one of the windows.

"Marvellous view. Isn't it?" Came a voice Minin knew too well. "You guards can go back into the elevator, I'll call you when I need you," he ordered as the chair swivelled around. Minin was now face-to-face with Daman.

18

Daman looked Minin up and down for a moment, he then turned back towards the view. "As I was saying, the view from here is amazing, isn't it? It kind of makes the rest of the room disappear wouldn't you say? I have no doubt that you didn't even notice the desk in the middle of the room at first, did you?" "You can see every groups area, group B or the Coasties as you people call them." He motioned with his hands toward the beach Minin and Callum left in what seemed like a lifetime ago but was only a few hours. He then motioned a little bit inland, "Group C or the Farmers to you. Oh yes, I know the different names you people call yourselves."

Minin was taken aback but he remained calm on the outside. Daman seemed calm too, which was strange to Minin, who almost expected to see steam coming out of his ears. Knowing his temper could switch with the slightest things, he decided to try to keep him calm as long as possible. "Yeah, the view is something else, the only time I've seen the view like this was when I arrived on the island. Since then, it's all been ground-view for me."

"That's quite a shame," Daman said looking at Minin disappointed. "If only you had a chance to come to the Tower one time, I could have taken you up here, we could have been friends you know?"

'Friends?' Minin thought, 'You're the reason one of my actual friends has been shot, another taken prisoner and a third ran away. You wanted to originally be friends?'

Daman continued, "I would like to be friends with everyone here, but someone needs to look over everyone else. That's why I am here in the Tower. Unfortunately, some people don't see that I should be in charge, so I must show that I am powerful to help them understand," He reasoned.

'You're insane! You clearly feed off the fear of everyone,' Minin thought.

Daman went quiet for a moment, he got out of his seat and walked over to Minin, put his hand on Minin's shoulder, "I'd like to thank you for bringing Callum to us, I would love to give you your supply crates so you can get what you need...., medicine for Tiffany, wasn't it?"

'How do you know that? Do you have spies in the Coasties camp?' Minin thought.

"But that is going to another since rather than easily giving him up, you instead kept Callum hidden. Don't fret, I'll give you something else though," Daman said changing to an angrier tone. "You hide him from me?! That's not how it works, anyone that betrays me needs to be punished." He continued as he began to walk away from Minin slowly.

Minin wanted to change his tone back to calm, but he had no idea how, so he tried removing his handcuffs just in case something were to happen.

Daman saw Minin's attempt, "Any sound out of the ordinary, you even so much as inhale too loudly and my guards will be back inside the room before you have a chance to do anything," He warned. "It would be much better if you had a kill chip but those things didn't have an unlimited supply as I wished." His tone changed back to calm. "Now, where was I?" He paused, seemingly trying to remember where the conversation left off, "Ahhh yes, anyone that betrays me needs to be punished, I proved that the first few weeks when I was on the island, did anyone ever tell you I was one of the first ten? Yeah, I've been on the island since it was first opened, have they told you how I first got on the island?"

Minin searched through his brain trying to remember if he had been told anything, "No, nothing, I don't think my camp knows much about that," He replied. *'And I was probably better off not knowing,'* he thought.

Daman began to chuckle to himself, "Anyone that gets dropped these days never knows anything, but I know that Hayley and Hunter know the story, oh they know the story too well. It's probably why they didn't want you or anyone else to come to the Tower and the reason why they actually have respect for me." Daman's eyes seemed to lose focus as he looked into the empty space before him, "I killed to get on the island, it wasn't an accident either, I killed because they didn't respect me then, but on the island, they respect me now."

"If you kill someone, they don't send you to the island, that's a high-class crime, that's a death sentence," Minin said unthinkingly. "The only time someone gets on the island for killing someone is if it's an accident...." He replied.

"Unless you happen to know someone important," Daman smiled. "I ended up here because of my brother, he saved me."

"How does anyone have that kind of power? Ending up on the island is through a closed court, your family would only know you ended up on the island once you've been sentenced to arrive here. I know my family wouldn't have known I was headed towards the island until long after I was on my way." Minin replied.

Daman took a breath sounding frustrated. "You calling me a liar? Before I was on the island, I worked for Polymon, as a 'debt collector', Anyone that owed Polymon, had to deal with me. My last collection was from Tony Bloom."

Minin knew that name well, his manager from Lens Corporation, Mathew Bloom, was the son of Tony, although he didn't like to tell Minin much about what had happened to his father, all Minin knew was that he had been murdered.

Daman continued his story, "He refused to give me the money that was owed, this wasn't the first person to say no, so I roughed him up a little, that usually was enough to show anyone that I was serious, I belted him, just short of knocking him out. I demanded the money but he kept saying no. Now that was a first, no-one said no after I did that, but he was just stupid and he wasn't showing me any respect!! I roughed him up more, maybe a little too much, I blacked out and kept going. Once everything was in focus, he was just on the ground not breathing, blood everywhere, I freaked out, I didn't know what to do."

Minin was shocked, he couldn't believe Daman would ever be scared or have any kind of regret or remorse.

Daman's voice then changed again, this time to anger, "The police soon arrived, someone had pressed a duress alarm, they came into the room and saw the blood on my knuckles and the body. When I was taken away they didn't have the close court system you have now." Daman looked at Minin with a smile, "Oh yes, I know how the world works off the island, I have my ways." He then continued his story, "In those days they get more witnesses to testify for you, you had lawyers to defend you. The case went on for months, anyway my boss Peter was made to testify over what had happened, most of the time he was trying to defend Polymon and what they did, saying it was only a debt collection agency and I was out of control. Before I had left my office to see Tony, Peter and myself had been in a fight, it turned out Peter had rung the police to find me, thinking something was going to happen on that collection. I have no doubt that Peter just wanted me arrested." Daman started to look Minin in the eye, "In the end, I was sentenced with Murder."

Minin was still confused. "With a murder conviction, how did you end up on the island?"

"I was getting to that, don't interrupt me again!" He roared, before continuing, "it's all got to do with Joseph Kahn, you know he came up with the idea of the island, don't you?"

"Yes," Minin answered, still very confused, trying to piece it all together. "Everyone knows he came up with the idea for the island."

"He's my brother, almost no-one knew. I was given up for adoption when I was born. A couple of years later Joseph was born, my deadbeat birthparents didn't bother to give him up, did they?" He seethed. "We grew up not knowing we were related. When Joseph was told about me, he went looking. During that time he had started his political career, he had dreams of helping the country as well as find his brother. By the time he did find me, I was already in jail for the murder of Tony, I was on death row, just waiting for the day that would be my last. He felt guilty over what my birth parents did and didn't want me to be killed, thinking my life may have been better if I had not been given away."

"That still doesn't explain how your sentence got changed," Minin replied, interrupting Daman.

The comment infuriated Daman, "If you continue to interrupt me, you can live without me telling you."

"Sorry about that," he mumbled.

Daman continued, "Joseph and I continued to talk, eventually we figured out his political power could be an advantage to saving me. He knew he could never get me released so we figured out another plan, somewhere else I could live. He located a group of islands with a very low population of natives, he convinced everyone that the islands were uninhabited, this was key to making his proposal a reality. The proposal was on its way but one thing had to happen. Joseph found a very skilled hacker, someone that could change sentences, the hacker didn't even need to break into the server, my brother already had the credentials, just not the skill to change my sentence from Murder to Bribery and Corruption."

Minin was shocked by the confession, he didn't think it was possible. He thought for a second, "Joseph was caught and sentenced to the island for changing your sentence, wasn't he?"

Daman looked at Minin, his eyes became blank. Minin could tell this was affecting him on a personal level. "No-one has ever wanted to know that part of the story."

Minin started to think he was getting through to Daman, enough to be able to use it to his own advantage, "After hearing that, you don't seem so bad..." He paused to find the correct words, "... just misunderstood."

"It's good to see you finally understand me," Daman thought for a moment, smiling. "During the early days of the island they didn't just randomly drop you onto the island like everyone believes. The drop-ships came to the tower, the roof retracted and the dropship lands in the middle of the tower and the prisoners then get processed. A lot of what was said was designed to be a scare tactic to those back home. In the early days, they had guards in the tower, who were allowed to go back home on a dropship when their contract was finished. If they determined that you had a minor sentence you ended up out on the island on your own but if they thought you were too dangerous they sent you to the cells, that's where they thought I should have been. Either way, they gave everyone a kill-chip, just in case. A few months had passed and I was sitting in my cell on the day more prisoners arrived. My cell opened, the guards were finally going to give me a cell-mate, they told me to stand facing my window and wait there while they put the new prisoner in. I heard one of the guards say, "put him in here, they can catch up." I turned around and standing in front of me was my brother. He told me what had happened, the hacker he hired turned all his information over to the police, showing them exactly what my brother had done, it was enough to get him arrested and sentenced to the island. Since the policy was to let the prisoners stay on the island they didn't bother to take me away, but still rot in those cells, now with my brother." Minin could see a tear in Daman's eye.

Minin was shocked that Daman seemed somewhat human. He needed to know more, "How did you get control of the island when the government still had control?"

Daman sighed, "Joseph and myself weren't allowed to ever exit our cells, except to shower. We heard a rumour from one of the guards, that it was some sort of revenge from the government for basically rorting the system and making fools of them, all based on lies and our personal gain."

"We talked a lot, coming up with a plan to take the island for ourselves. It all started during shower time. The guards had started to relax around the monotony of our day to day life. We had noticed that they had even stopped scanning our cells when they came to get us for our showers. I guess they figured, if we can't go anywhere, it would never be any different. They didn't even do body searches anymore. Anyway, the two guards took us to the showers and we started to strip off our clothes. We had managed to keep metal bars from our cell, hidden in our clothes. We hit a guard each in the back of the head at the same time, they were both knocked out. We then ran. Joseph knew the map of the Tower in his head, so he knew exactly where to go to find a computer that would be able to turn off the kill-chips without having to hack into it. We ran up a staircase which was deserted. We got about halfway up when the sirens went off. We bolted up the rest of the stairs and made it to this floor before we saw two guards, one had a kill-chip controller, he was about to press it but Joseph ran towards him, knocking him out just in time while I knocked the other guard out. We walked into this room, this very office," He smiled remembering. "On top of this very desk was the computer. He turned it on and found what he needed. A guard walked into the room with another controller, I looked at him. "Time's up," he said and pressed the button, I closed my eyes thinking that was it but Joseph had done it. He had managed to turn all the controllers off. The guard was confused and pressed the controller again, thinking it must have been faulty. I ran up to the guard aiming to just knock him out, but I kept hitting him and hitting him until it was over, I didn't stop until Joseph pulled me off him and stopped me. He got off me and walked over to a Microphone that was sitting on the desk next to the computer, turned it on and shouted through it, "Attention Prisoners, this is Joseph Kahn, the kill chips have been disabled and those of you that are in cells, they are now unlocked, that is all." He knew that would be all that was needed. The prisoners rioted. One of the guards must have got a message back to the Government on the mainland and they decided to keep the island opened, but this time, they were really going to use the 'set and forget' approach to the prisoners."

Minin couldn't believe what he was heard. Everything he 'knew' about the island's origins was a lie. He then asked the next thing on his mind, "Where's your brother?"

"Dead," Daman replied simply. "I killed him, he didn't respect me," He paused then smiled, "You probably want that story too, don't you?"

Minin nodded. Keeping Daman talking, kept him alive and may also help him learn more about his new 'home' and his enemy.

"A couple of months passed on the island," Daman said starting his story, "Joseph and I were now in charge, I wanted to rule over everyone, I wanted respect, a paradise-like it is now. My brother wanted something different, he wanted it exactly like the mainland, people voting for how things should be. He was crazy, this wasn't the mainland, this was my island and the prisoners needed to know it. Joseph thought he had the power like he did before he came to the island."

"It sounds to me like he wanted to do something good with the island," Minin said not thinking…. again.

"What? You and him are both wrong! You can't have a bunch of prisoners running the asylum." Daman's voice got angrier, "and this is my island, he just wanted to be popular, just to take over, put me in my place and I couldn't have that. He needed to be put in his place."

Minin needed to calm him again. "You're right," he replied. "Of course, a bunch of prisoners can't run an island."

He seemed appeased and continued, "One night I met my brother at the top of the roof of the Tower, I needed to find out his plan. He wanted each camp to have their say, have the Tower give supplies to those that needed it," Minin was starting to believe that Joesph had the correct idea. "But I knew better, all they need is for someone that has the power to make the right decisions for them, their decisions are what got them here in the first place. No matter what I did to tell Joseph that, he just didn't understand. He needed convincing, we started talking and I pushed him while telling him his idea of democracy didn't work. He pushed me back, we started to fight. We got to the edge, I was so angry that he couldn't understand my point that I threw a punch so hard that he was knocked out. This was my chance and I lifted my brother over the edge. If he wasn't going to see my side, it's what had to be done.

I ran back to this office, thinking what to do next, the first thing I found was a box containing all the kill chip controllers. I destroyed them, except one. I looked at it, it was marvellous, an idea then occurred to me, I went to the computer, and turned on the kill-chips. I would be the only one with the controller. I had the ultimate power, Power over life and death. I went to the microphone and turned it on and made my announcement, "This is Daman Biguy, my brother is dead, I've turned the kill chips on, and I've destroyed all the controllers except one, it is time you all learned to respect me."

'He was able to kill his brother just because, 'That's what needed to be done' for respect??' Minin thought. Even though Minin already knew Daman was unstable, he had never really thought about the extent to his heartlessness until this moment. This caused him to wonder, *what could he be doing to Callum?* "What happened to Callum?" He asked.

"Gin will be rewarded for his loyalty, now that's a man that knows how it all works," He replied. "Tiffany and Hayley are safe, Tiffany already paid for hiding Callum by getting herself shot and Hayley is a medic," Daman continued. "I'm not a barbarian to my people, my people need her, but they helped to hide Callum, so they won't be getting a damn thing as a reward."

Whatever lay ahead was bound to be horrible but knew to help Hayley and the camps at least one last time, he knew that the camps needed the meds. He had to find a way to convince him and the only way was by playing into what Daman believed, "Hayley will need those meds to be able to help your people, they don't have any." Daman didn't seem to be listening and didn't respond. That was the final straw, Minin's anger got the better of him, "Give them the supplies they need!"

Daman didn't like the tone he was using. "That is not how you talk to me, I let you live on this island in peace and you put in demands, how dare you?" He questioned.

"They need those meds, you say you have control of the island, but if you want Hayley to be the medic then she needs meds to help '*your people*,' and you're going to deny it to them?" He looked Daman in the eye with determination "What kind of sick freak are you?"

"I'm a sick freak?" He screamed back at Minin, "You hide the person I wanted from me, if you gave him to me, you would have gotten the meds, they all would have, but instead you showed loyalty to the wrong person!"

A knock came from the door, "He's ready."

"Bring him in," Daman called out calmly with a smile on his face. "Excellent! You want to know how much of a sick freak I am?"

The door opened, the Goatee Guard entered with Callum, who was wearing nothing but his underwear and chains all over his badly bruised body. His face was covered with a muzzle, with only his now blackened eyes visible.

Daman began to scream at Minin, "You disrespect me when I could have been lenient to you? Now you will see what I'm really capable of!"

Daman went to his desk and pressed a red button in the middle. A panel Minin hadn't noticed before, on the top of the desk opened. Inside were two folders, Daman opened one. Minin could just make out a picture of Callum inside. "Let's have a look shall we?" He looked down at the folder and then back up at Callum. He looked stunned. He glanced between the folder and Callum once more and he stopped. He stared, wide-eyed at Callum, "It can't be?" He all but mumbled. "Get him out of here!" he commanded the Goatee Guard.

"Sir?" the Goatee Guard said confused, "You didn't sentence him."

"Just get him out of here, take him to the Interrogation room, lock him in and I'll sentence him later," He stammered. If Minin didn't know any better, he'd say Daman looked afraid.

The Goatee guard then grabbed Callum, taking him back inside the Elevator with the door closing, both the guard and Callum disappearing with it.

Minin didn't know what was going on, he had seen Daman go from one emotion to another within seconds before but never seen fear on Daman's face. "What was in the folder?" He called out.

"Don't make demands, you're in enough trouble with me as it is." He replied trying to sound angry, but Minin could hear fear more than anger in his voice.

"You don't read everyone's information before they get on the island, do you?" Minin asked.

The fear in Daman's voice disappeared, "I told you you're in enough trouble," slamming his hands on the desk. He picked Minin's folder up and began to inspect it, a few moments passed and he then spoke. "You're here because you were trying to save your girlfriend in a fight?" He said calmly, the rage no longer there.

Minin, as much as he wanted to ask about Callum again, knew it would just enrage Daman. "Yes," he replied, trying to keep his answers short.

"That's very brave and noble of you and just now you tried to save your friend, I admire that bravery. But if I want something, I get it! I wanted Callum and you hid him from me, you need to be punished for that. I also can't let you go unpunished for trying to steal from me, normally stealing would be punishable by death, but I'm intrigued by your bravery and compassion for the people you love."

'He admires my bravery and is sparing my life?, somehow I don't think that's a compliment,' Minin thought to himself.

Daman sat at the desk and thought for a moment, he then looked at Minin and smiled, "The workers in the Tower need entertainment." He told Minin as his smile became larger, "I think you're the man to do it."

Minin didn't know what to make of the statement, "What do you want me to do?" He asked trying to be brave.

"I've got a deal for you," Daman replied.

Minin knew not to make a deal. "No, just give me my sentence," he replied calmly.

"You can't say no to the deal, it's part of your sentence," Daman replied.

Minin was confused, "What is it?"

"It's simple, you need medical supplies for not only Tiffany but the people you refer to as the Coasties, if you truly think you're the hero, you can fight for it."

"I don't think I was ever a hero," Minin responded.

"Nevertheless, I think it's a fair deal. If you really want those supplies, you will win."

Minin became very nervous, his mind whirring through the possibilities, each worse than the last. He wanted to know what Daman considered, 'entertainment'. Whatever it was, he was sure he wouldn't like it. He needed to do whatever it took for his friends though, even if he didn't make it out. His face took on a more determined look as he asked: "What is it?"

"You fight in the arena, against a fighter of my choice, the rules are simple, it's a fight to the death. You win, your friends will be given as many medical supplies as they could ever need. If your opponent wins, you die, it's as simple as that."

Minin considered this. He knew the odds would be against him. A fight against anyone wasn't going to be easy for Minin but he would do his best. He thought for a second before responding, "I want something else if I win."

"What do you want?" Daman asked curiously.

"Let me go!"

Daman was taken back by this demand, "I don't think that's an option."

"That isn't much of a deal then."

"You won't be leaving the tower," He said to Minin bluntly.

"So, I fight, kill a person of your choosing and won't be let go?"

"But your friends get the supplies they need. Take the deal or the second option, you'll run the gauntlet, one fight after another until you die and your friends get nothing."

Minin knew he didn't have a choice, he had little chance in the deal but it beat the alternative. Perhaps he could come up with a plan while Daman was getting the fight prepared. There had to be a way out of this. For now, he knew, it was best to play along though. "Fine, who am I fighting?"

Daman went quiet, smiling and just looking at Minin. He then called, "Guards!"

Two guards walked into the room. "Which one am I fighting?" Minin demanded, eyeing the guards. The guards grabbed Minin, who tried to fight them off with little luck. Minin was then pulled away into the Elevator. "Who am I fighting?!" He screamed out realising it wasn't the guards.

"Stop," Daman commanded, which the guards did immediately. Daman came face to face with Minin, looked him in the eyes and smiled. "Mark," he answered simply then flipped his hands at the guards, gesturing them to move along. The guards did as they were instructed and took Minin back into the Elevator, the door closing behind him.

Minin didn't know for sure but the only Mark he could think of was Mark Brockly. The fighter that accidentally killed his opponent in the ring. He didn't know what Mark looked like, but a professional fighter seemed like an impossible opponent for an ordinary person. Minin silently begged, *Please not him. Anyone but him*.

The Elevator began to lower, the lights around the elevator switched off. Moments later the elevator stopped. The doors open to reveal a hallway with grey stone floors which were very wet, there even appeared to be a few deep puddles. The walls, also made of grey stone blocks had green mossy patches. The wiring for the overhead lights was uncovered.

"Move," The guard warned Minin and pushed him into the hallway, Minin stalled, not wanting to enter the unknown. The same guard brought out a Taser from his pocket and nudged him with it as a warning. Minin took the hint and walked into the hallway, the elevator closing behind them. They made their way toward the end of the hallway, with the occasional puddle saturating their feet. They came upon more stone steps, leading down to a lower level. "Keep going," The guard told Minin, who was unaware that his feet had even stopped moving. The lower level looked the same, except with cells with closed metal doors. They reminded Minin of the jail block that he was in before he came to the Island. They kept walking to the middle where one of the metal doors was open, the guard pushing Minin inside before he closed and locked the door as he walked away.

19

The next morning Minin sat lying on the bed in the cell, he looked out the window at the trees nearby. The sound of rushing water filled the air. The cell itself didn't look that much different to the one that he was in before he arrived on the island. The sunshine was starting to inch in through the window as sunrise began.

Minin hadn't been able to sleep the whole night. Ideas kept swirling around inside his head on how to beat Mark, each idea more unlikely than the last. He wished he could go over old tapes or videos of Marks previous fights to help him create a game plan or fighting strategy against him.

"Ahhh," A feminine scream came from another cell, "Let me out of here!"

The scream had snapped Minin out of his relentless thought spiral. He called out, "Hey, who's there?" He briefly wondered if he'd get in trouble for talking from any of the guards that might be lurking around the cells but the fact he had been sentenced to a fight to the death the previous day was the kind of thing that made you shrug at the thought of, 'getting in trouble.'

"Wait… you can hear me?" The voice replied confused.

"Of course I can hear you," Minin replied, thinking that that was a strange comment.

"No-one has called out since I've been trapped here."

"How long have you been here?" asked Minin.

"Since I left my camp," the voice replied.

"When was that?" Minin asked, wondering if all his questions would have to be this specific.

"A couple of weeks I think." The female voice became quiet for a moment before asking, "When did you get here?"

"Uhhh…. last night," Minin said.

"So, only one night?"

"Yeah, I'm not going to be here long either."

"They never are. It's always someone else in that cell." The female voice began to laugh. "They've always got the same voice too, but you're different"

"What do you mean?" Minin asked.

"They always sound a bit like me, but they can't be me, they always think differently. Sometimes they can be really annoying, thinking that Daman is a good person." The female voice began to sound serious, "I think it's so they can get out of the cells and it works, they always get out first. Then there are others, they don't like him, they stay here much longer because of that."

"Have you tried telling the guards you think that Daman is a good person? It might help you get out of the cells," Minin suggested.

"I've tried, but the guards just get annoyed with me and hit my cell door, telling us to all quieten down. They never hit the other cells though, the other voices are the favourites, they get what they want."

"Do you know if there is anyone else down here?" Minin asked, beginning to wonder how many people were in the other cells.

"I'll call out, it always changes. Hey is there anyone out there?"

The two of them stay quiet hoping to hear a voice. There was silence.

"Who are you?" Minin asked.

"My name is Stephanie." The voice replied proudly. "Who are you?"

Minin began to wonder if this person was Stephanie from the Coasties, "My name is Minin, how long did you say you've been here again?"

The voice went silent for a moment then replied, "umm, a couple of weeks. I'm not sure, it's hard to work it out from here. I knocked on the front door asking for some supplies and they locked me in here."

Minin could understand the uncertainty about time. Most people that have been on the island don't exactly know how long they have been here. The only reason Minin and his camp knew was that they had been keeping count. He knew it would have been harder in here since there was no way to keep track. He wanted to get to know the girl more, she could be the last point of human connection he might have before he was beaten to death. "Where did you come from?"

"They call it the Coasties camp, have you heard of it?" Minin wished he could tell someone from the Coasties the good news that she was safe. Stephanie then continued, "Don't tell her anything, she'll tell the guards."

Minin was confused, he didn't understand what she meant.

"She's right, you don't want to tell the guards anything... The guards are good people though."

Minin became even more confused, "Umm, are you ok?"

"Of course I'm ok, why wouldn't I be?" Stephanie replied. "They finally brought more people to the cells," She called out, then a clapping noise could be heard from the same direction, "I'm going to talk to these people for a little bit, I'll talk to you later, ok?"

"Umm ok," Minin replied confused, he then started to understand what she had been saying before, there hadn't been anyone else in the cells near-by or if there had been they had been quiet and didn't respond, it had been Stephanie talking to herself.

For the next hour, Stephanie continued to talk to herself, Minin couldn't work out how many people she was speaking for. They all sounded the same, some spoke highly of Daman and the Tower, the others hated the place, the only person he could eventually work out was Stephanie herself when she 'spoke', her tone was ever so slightly different.

Eventually, a different voice spoke up. This time it was masculine and it was coming from the other direction. "Get her to shut up, it's hurting my head. I've been quiet, thinking it might shut her up if she couldn't hear anything."

"Wait there's someone else here?" Minin replied.

"Of course there is, I clearly have a different voice and I'm actually sane!" The voice replied.

"Maybe I'm the one that's sane and you're crazy!" Stephanie replied. "Have I been talking to the same person all this time?"

"Who are you, where are you from?" Minin asked the new voice.

"I'm Stephanie, I've been here for a few weeks, didn't I already tell you this?" Stephanie replied.

"No, not you," Minin replied annoyed. "How do I know I can trust you?"

"I only spoke up cause she was driving me insane, how do I know you're not someone trying to get more information out of me too?" The male voice replied.

Stephanie called out, "You're a mean voice, I'll get the others to drown you out….la la la la."

"I like to think myself a truthful voice," He replied. "Anyway, Minin isn't it?" The voice asked.

"Yeah… how do you know that?" Minin replied suspiciously.

"I know things, that's why I ended up being where we are. I know surprising things about the island."

"What kind of things?" Asked Minin.

"All sorts, I was arrested for trying to reveal them. I knew all about what they did to the island, how they got rid of the natives."

"Natives?" Minin asked cutting the voice off.

"That doesn't matter, they are not an issue. I was the person that revealed what Joseph Kahn did to put Daman on the island. It wasn't the hacker. The hacker eventually got arrested, funnily enough, he ended up on the island too, it's kinda sad that Quinn died though, I have no doubt, one day if Hunter and he teamed up they would have worked out a way off the island, I guess Daman will just have to get Hunter to do that."

Minin was shocked, he knew of a person named Charlie who was a protester that threatened to reveal all sorts of information. "Are you Charlie?" he called out.

"That's one name I did go by" The voice replied. "Now let me finish."

Minin was now more curious as to who this person was, but decided that interrupting him might cause him to shut him out.

The voice then continued, "I had everything ready, I was so close to showing everyone, I wanted to put it online on a social network website but I knew all that would happen was I'd get made out to be a crackpot, so I went to the World News Today building. I was going to show them all the information I had, let them tell the world what was going on with the island, try to get it shut down. But I was arrested in front of the news headquarters for it. The only breaking news was my own arrest and how the government changed the way the trial system was performed. Up until I was arrested you had a fair chance, you had lawyers, a chance to argue against what was said about you. When I was arrested, it all changed. Now it's you say your story, the other side says there's, then the jury decides. If you're innocent you go home by lunchtime. Everything designed so that if someone like me has information as I did, it has less chance of being leaked."

Minin knew that the system was changed, he just didn't know the reason, he always assumed before he got to the island that it was streamlined, knowing that if he had a chance to make a better case he might have been freed. 'Charlie' was probably right.

"Anyway, they sentenced you to a fight to the death, did they?" Charlie asked.

"Who are you?" Minin asked cutting Charlie off.

Charlie ignored the question, repeating his own. "They sentenced you to a fight to the death, did they?"

How did this voice know something like that? No-one knew what the sentence was except for Daman, so Minin gave an answer that wasn't the best, "Umm, I'm not sure."

"Common, I told you all sorts about me, let's talk about you." Charlie went quiet for a moment, "I guess I'm not supposed to know something like your sentence since it only happened last night, but I hear things, that's how I know all the things I knew that got me on the island in the first place." Charlie paused for another moment, "You probably don't trust me either do you? Well, how about I give you some information that might help. Jump to the left when he runs at you."

"Who runs at me?" Minin asked.

"Mark Brockly, Daman's personal bodyguard. He always starts his fights by charging forward and slightly to his right, once you jump out of the way you better capitalise and attack him. If he recovers, your chances of survival are slim to nil, also don't worry about the ground."

"How do you know that?" Minin asked curiously.

"I told you, I know things. Do you even know who Mark was before he was on the island?" The voice replied.

"I know he was a fighter, was sent to the island after he killed a man in a fight," Minin replied.

"It was ruled Manslaughter since the fight was professionally organised and his opponent was more than capable of defending himself. Personally, I blame the referee, he should have stopped the fight long before what had happened. The referee should have been the one to be charged." Charlie stopped for a moment then continued, "It was Marks big fight, the one for the championship, his opponent, Ted Freely had been undefeated for twenty-four fights, no-one thought he could be defeated and he'd retire pretty soon. This was Marks seventh fight, he was hungry, he wanted it. The bell rang and they both went in, the first round was close, as for the second, well, Mark started to show he could win. The third-round Ted showed he didn't want to give his championship up. Then it was the fourth and final round, both giving everything they had, Mark then hit the Temple of Ted knocking him back, he knew this was his chance and pounced, hitting him with everything he had. It became too much for Ted, who gave up his guard. That should have been the point the referee should have stopped the fight, but he let it go on. Mark kept attacking, Ted fell to the floor, it was only at that point the referee stopped the fight, but Ted was already dead. They arrested Mark and like you know, he ended up on the island."

Minin thought for a second, "How could someone that strong and capable of something like that work for Daman? Shouldn't it be the other way around?"

Charlie laughed, "Simple. The kill chip. Daman made sure Mark had a kill chip put in his head as soon as he landed on the island. Mark still wants to live, even if he's on the island because someone else screwed up."

"So, you're telling me if Mark didn't have a kill chip, I wouldn't be fighting him? And he'd probably be controlling the island?" Minin asked.

"Definitely not," Charlie replied, "If there wasn't kill chips, I don't think Mark would still be alive, Daman wouldn't want someone on the island that strong, he would have done something about him a long time ago."

Minin still wanted to know who 'Charlie' was, deciding to try and swing the conversation back. "So you know a few things about people, that still doesn't explain who you are?" Minin said again hoping this time to get an answer.

"Focus!" Charlie replied, "At the moment, who I am doesn't matter to you, you really need to focus on surviving the fight and getting back to your friends."

Minin decided to try and change his attitude towards the person talking, he started to think if he could make Charlie think he wasn't afraid of what was going to happen in the fight, that 'Charlie' might start to answer his question if there wasn't a need to be worried. "I don't need to focus on the fight, I'm going to win."

"Trying to change your story? Your lies don't impress me. I know in your voice when you are lying."

'How did he know?' Minin thought but didn't want to ask the question just in case he was someone working for Daman trying to get answers from him.

"You probably want to know for future reference," Charlie replied. "Your voice gives you away, it goes slightly higher, it's hard to hear, but it's there if you know what you're listening for."

Minin tried to change his voice, so his fear couldn't be detected, "It doesn't matter, I'm still going to win."

"Congratulations, your voice sounds closer to normal," Charlie replied. "Don't worry, I'm not going to tell them your secrets. I've got enough of my own." They could then hear two guards walking Toward the cells down the stone hallway, they were talking, but neither could understand what they were saying. Charlie then spoke again, "They don't believe the word of a crazy man."

'*Who said anything about being crazy?*' Minin wondered. He then asked Charlie, "A Crazy man doesn't think that they are crazy, why do you think you're crazy?"

The guards got closer as Charlie replied, "I had a bump to the head that made me crazy, or maybe I'm not?... They sent me to these cells cause I'm crazy...or maybe I'm not, maybe you're the crazy one, a normal person wouldn't want to be killed in the ring against someone." There was a squeak from a bedspring, Minin assumed Charlie got out of bed. "No, I'm the crazy one," then a noise that sounded like a padded brick hitting metal, "The blood on my forehead tells me that," he called out. "I have a physical scar on my head, and if I'm willing to hit my head on the metal bars of the cell to make it bleed, then surely what I know they can't possibly trust."

Minin then realised what 'Charlie' was doing, "You're not crazy, you just want everyone to think that you are, so they can't trust what you know." He said loud enough that Charlie could only hear.

"Exactly," Charlie replied.

A siren began to blare from outside Minin's cell. The noise was deafening. Minin put his hands over his ears and cowered down on the floor hoping it would stop. It took a minute, which Minin thought was more like an eternity. Two guards, wearing the white guards uniform were standing at the front of the cell which was now open, "Ok, time to go." One of them said. They grabbed Minin by the arms and lifted him forcibly off the ground, "Time to go," The same guard repeated then dragged him out of the cell.

Minin didn't put up a fight, walking with them, he knew any chance of getting away now, would be useless. Trying to fight Mark and winning would be his only chance of getting out of here. As he walked past the cells he could see Stephanie, a blond, slim girl, wearing a shirt that was a few sizes too big for her, her face looking exhausted was in the cell next to him.

The next cell belonged to Charlie. Minin was sure his mind was playing tricks on him though, Inside was Callum, not the mysterious Charlie, who had a gash on his forehead and two electrodes sticking out near his temple.

Callum was just smiling back at him, "Hey, let me talk to him one last time," he said looking at the guards.

The guards looked at each other, they both knew the fate that Minin had install for himself. "You have a minute," One of the guards replied.

"Well, you now know who I am," Callum said smiling at Minin.

"Why didn't you tell me it was you?" Minin asked, not knowing what else to say.

"I didn't want you worrying about me, I was trying to get you to focus on what was ahead of you. In fact, I didn't think you would see me as you went past." Callum stopped for a second. "Guess I don't know everything about the island then," he sniggered.

"Forty-five seconds, make it quick," The same guard continued.

"What did they do to you?" Minin asked, looking at the electrodes sticking out of his head.

"They managed to shock me enough so I got my voice back," He said, as his eyes twitched. "But they haven't done it properly, and other parts are having trouble working," He moved away from the cell bars, each step looked slow, and clumsy like he was having trouble trying to walk.

"Your brain isn't sending the signals is it?" Minin asked.

"You'll have to ask the nurse when you see her," He replied with a smile, "Just remember what I told you and it'll all come together."

"What do you mean it'll all come together?"

"That doesn't matter," Callum said shaking his head. "Just remember what I told you," his voice insisting, almost pleading.

"All right, times up for the reunion," The guard said and dragged Minin away from the cells. Minin was smiling knowing that Callum was safe, at least for the time being.

The guards took Minin to another Elevator. The doors opened and the guards press a couple of buttons on the console and the doors closed and the elevator began to rise. The elevator shaft was so dark that Minin couldn't see anything. The elevator stopped and the lights turned on, revealing a hallway, which looked like a copy of the other floor.

The three began to walk down the hallway, this one longer in length than the hall for the cells. As they walked, the light from the elevator became dim, eventually, till the point where the hallway was just darkness again. One of the guards let go of Minin, who knew he was there from only the sound of the guard's footsteps walking around him.

A panel lit up, its radiating light shone on the guard, the surrounding wall, and a door which Minin and the second Guard were standing in front of. The first guard put a code into the panel, the doors opened. The second guard shoved Minin inside and closed the door behind him.

20

Minin looked around the room in shock, it was a round-shaped double story arena. The first story, the one he was on, had a floor that was made of huge red stone pavers on an outer layer and the centre was wooden with the only other exit being a door opposite him. Minin looked above to the second story, it was open except for a viewing platform as wide as the red stone pavers surrounding the wall, a black railing being the only safe spot. The viewing platform looked to have a door in the centre of each quarter, except for one which had what appeared to be a throne in the spot where the door should be. A huge round gong was standing between 2 of the doors and speakers were placed throughout the room. Minin could only assume this room was for the guards to train before Daman took control of the Tower and the throne being probably placed after it had been taken over.

The gong began to sound and the doors on the top floor opened. People began walking through the open doors, finding a spot to stand at the railings. Minin scanned the faces of every person he could see but didn't recognise any of them, not that he really expected too. One thing he did notice was that none of them looked happy. They all had stone-faced expressions, void of emotion. Guards with their faces covered stood behind them holding guns. A few minutes pass as the platform filled with people. Soon the rush stopped but they all remained quiet. Suddenly they start cheering out of nowhere as though it was on command. Minin looked around trying to figure out why they all suddenly changed their attitude. Then he saw the reason, Daman walked from behind the throne and sat down, *'that must be the fourth door'* Minin thought.

Daman sat down, looked upon Minin and was smiling. The crowd cheering more, the smile on Daman's face became larger. Minin could only think to himself, *'is he happy they are cheering this? Does he even realise that the cheers are fake? Is this only a show for him?'* Daman put his hands up and started moving them down attempting to get the crowd to calm down. They continued their cheers not noticing at all. His face suddenly changed again, the crowd wasn't pleasing him anymore, he pointed to a guard on the left side of him. The guard shoving a few of the crowd into the guard rail, who went quiet but the rest of the crowd continued cheering. Daman became enraged, *"How dare they ignore Me!? He thought.* He pointed to another guard, who nodded and grabbed a small red-headed boy from the crowd, who looked barely old enough to be on the island and lifted him without any trouble, throwing him over the guard rail, causing the boy to fall onto the same level as Minin. The crowd went silent with a mixture of fear and worry evident on their faces. Daman smiled, glad the crowd had finally taken notice.

Minin ran to the boy on the floor, he knelt to check on him, "He isn't breathing!" Minin screamed out. Without hesitation, he tried what he could to resuscitate the boy. He kept trying for what felt like ages. Minin soon realised that there wasn't anything he could do and no one was coming to help and soon reluctantly stopped.

The crowd was shocked, they all look at Daman who was smiling. He began to clap and cheer over the dead boy. The crowd were quiet for a second looking worried at the boy, then in unison they looked at Daman and simultaneously began to cheer, copying Daman.

Minin couldn't believe what he was seeing, they were all cheering that a boy had been killed. He looked back at the crowd, his eyes stopping on one person, a brunette girl with hair down to her shoulders, about the same age as Minin. She had a fake smile but was cheering, then stopped for a moment, putting her hand over the back of her neck, fear clearly on her face and then continued to cheer. Minin realised they were all cheering because they were worried that something might happen to them if they didn't do what Daman was showing them.

Six guards enter from the opposite door that Minin had entered, they rush over to Minin and the fallen boy. They shove Minin out of the way with enough force that it made him fall to the ground then lift the boy, rushing him out of the room. The crowd beginning to hush.

Daman then put his hands up then down to tell the rest of the crowd to be quiet. This time the crowd do what they are told instantly, the room becoming so silent that Minin could hear some of the people breathing. "Welcome friends," Daman announced into the microphone, his voice amplified by the speakers, "Welcome to the fight." He paused and lifted his hands, the crowd cheering once more, "And without further ado, I present your challenger...."

'He's making this like it was a Televised fight,' Minin thought to himself.

"…. from the outside of the Tower, I present the criminal called Minin," The crowd began to boo. He allowed them to continue for a moment as he smiled, "….And, his opponent is our champion, whos record within the Tower stands at fifteen fights with fifteen wins, he is my personal Bodyguard," He took a deep breath and screamed out slowly, "Marrrrrkkkkkkkk Brockllllllyyyyyy."

The crowd erupted into an almost unstoppable cheer as a red light on the door directly opposite Minin turned on. Mark walked into the room wearing only boxer shorts. Somehow The crowd got louder the further he moved into the room. He had a look of determination on his face, the same look he had when he had looked Minin and Tiffany over, in what seemed like a lifetime ago now. He stared at Minin with such anger on his face, almost as though he was saying, *I'm going to kill you'.* He turned to the crowd and began to show off, doing shadow punches and kicking the air, finally raising his arms as though he had already been declared the winner, the crowd loving it even more.

Minin knew that this wasn't the right time to look scared, he stared right back at Mark, trying to convey a look of, *'just bring it'* to his opponent. He began to do his own showboating to the crowd, a few quick shadow punches of his own, then putting his arms in victory in the air, the crowd booing at his display. All except for the same girl, who Minin noticed before. She was smiling at him instead. Knowing that one person in the crowd was going to cheer him on gave Minin more confidence.

Daman stood up from his seat and used his hands to make the crowd quiet again. It worked, the crowd was even quieter than before. To Minin this was scarier than anything he had seen while inside the room, he didn't know what was going to happen in the silence, he just looked at Daman wondering what he was about to say. "Ladies and gentlemen, the rules for this fight are simple, it's a fight to the death." Enormous cheers erupting from the crowd. Daman once again getting the crowd to calm down until there was silence, "Only one person will make it out alive, both men know their rewards if they are victorious. Neither men will be allowed to use weapons of any kind unless it is the building or their own bodies. Blows below the belt will be frowned upon, but not stopped, the fight will continue until I call for it to stop," Daman took his seat again as the crowd once more began to cheer.

Minin understood the rules perfectly, he looked back where the woman in the crowd was but she had disappeared. Minin looked around the crowd searching frantically, trying to see if she had moved from her position. Just near Daman's entrance, he could see someone being taken against their will by two guards, Minin could only assume it was the girl, a rush of disappointment coming over him. He took a deep breath, knowing this wasn't the time to worry about her. Minin then looked back at his opponent. Mark began to psych himself up, belting his chest, tapping the sides of his head, jumping up and down on each leg, not once taking his eyes off Minin.

Minin began to shake his legs, trying to loosen up, he then shook his arms, he had never been in a fight like this before, only once with a guy from his office. It was against a short, chubby, older man with a roundish face by the name of Ramsey Nash, who was known as the office bully. He wanted to be the boss badly and would do everything he could to make it so. One day Ramsey was talking to Minin's Boss, Mathew Bloom, spouting all kinds of lies that were making Minin out to be a bad employee. Minin could overhear what was being said about him and called him up on it later. Ramsey kept denying any of it but Minin wasn't backing down. Ramsey had had enough and threw a punch at Minin. Minin retaliated knocking Ramsey onto the floor, every co-worker around grabbed Minin and Ramsey and broke them apart. Ramsey was dismissed from the job for starting the fight, Minin was given a warning.

Minin was snapped out of the memory with the lights in the room being switched off. Minin instantly covered his head for protection. The lights then turned on for the level where Minin and Mark stood. The crowd looking cloaked in darkness. Mark was still standing where he was before, looking like he was ready to rush at Minin at that very moment but something was holding him back. Minin then noticed red dots from laser sights on himself and guessed that he was meant to stay put until it was time.

A beeping noise then sounding through the speakers, Mark began his jumping on the spot once again. The red dots disappeared and Minin realised that it was almost time. His heart began hammering in his chest, his palms sweating but he knew he must not show fear, his friends counting on him. A second beep and Mark stopped jumping, looking like he was ready to run at any moment, his face once again with a determination to take Minin down. Finally, a third longer, louder beep is heard and Mark sprints towards Minin. With the faces of his friends firmly in his mind, Minin braced himself. This was it.

Mark was sprinting as fast as he could towards the other end of the room. All Minin could do was just look at him, he was frozen, the sprint towards him looking as though it was in slow motion, then suddenly he remembered what Callum had told him, *'Jump to the left.'* He waited until the last possible moment before leaping out of the way causing Mark to slam into the door head first. The crowd began to boo at the display.

Mark was dazed, he turned and composed himself. He reached up at his forehead, feeling a gash and looked at his fingers which were bloody. He couldn't believe that Minin had made him bleed first, without even touching him. He looked around trying to locate where Minin had gotten to. He saw him to his left, in the middle of the room, he quickly began to charge, this time in a powerwalk, not repeating the same mistake that he just did.

'Ok so, jumping out of the way isn't going to be an option anymore', Minin mentally noted. *What to do, what to do?* He kept looking at Mark charging towards him while trying to think. He quickly came up with a plan as he spotted the gash on Mark's head, which was bleeding profusely. *'I'm just going to have to hit around there and bust him open, after each hit I'll run out of the way, maybe he'll pass out from blood loss?'* Minin thought.

Mark quickly reached Minin, throwing a punch, causing Minin to land on the ground hard. The crowd was cheering. Mark ran, charging again, this time Minin not having a chance to move out of the way, meeting a flurry of punches. Minin covered his face, trying to protect himself, punch after punch, he continued to keep his cover. He soon noticed that none of the punches were actually hurting, but couldn't understand why.

Mark picked Minin up, lifting him off the ground, then threw him back down as though Minin weighed like a feather, *'He certainly is strong'*, Minin thought. He landed in the middle of the room, the landing was soft like there was a spring underneath. *'Also don't worry about the ground.'* Callum's words, once again coming back to Minin.

Mark once again raising his arms in victory, this time screaming out, the crowd erupting once more. He quickly ran towards Minin and jumped up intending to throw a punch as he came down but missed his target and hit the ground around him, bloodying his fist. He looked at his fist, the crowd quickly 'booing'. Marks face suddenly looked more enraged.

Minin took the opportunity to get himself off the floor and back onto his feet, throwing a punch at Mark hitting his face where the gash was, he then threw another, once again it connected with his target, then he threw another.

Mark used his forearm and shoved Minin away from him, getting up from the floor, setting his sights upon Minin once more.

Minin ran back at Mark, his confidence increasing, he threw another punch that Mark was unable to block in time, the gash opening more. Minin threw another punch but this time Mark countered, pulling Minin's arm behind his head. Mark then put his arm around Minin's neck, Minin not feeling any pain but was unable to escape either.

Minin tried desperately to move out of the situation, attempting to move to his left then right. He then tried to lift Mark off his feet, trying to unbalance him but nothing worked.

Mark then spoke to Minin quiet enough that only he could hear, "Look like you're in a sleeper hold." The crowd cheering again, thinking Mark was in the final stages of victory. Minin tried to make a sound, attempting to reply. "Don't talk back, they'll see, just do as I say," Mark commanded. "Look like the sleeper hold is working."

Minin didn't know what to make of all this but knew he didn't have a choice, he had no chance of getting out of the situation, doing as he was told, pretending he was fading.

"Good. He can't see me talking to you since I'm behind you. I hate that bastard," Mark said as he swung Minin's body so that he was in Daman's direction. "I need to bring him down," The crowd getting louder, thinking this was the final point of the fight. "I'll get you out of here, you go and help your friends but I need you to work out how to stop the kill chips." He let Minin out of the hold, throwing him forward.

'This is a setup?' Minin thought to himself.

Mark charged at Minin, spearing him into the wooden part of the floor, a cracking noise quickly sounded below them. Mark throwing more punches that once again Minin hardly felt as Mark leaned in, "I would have got us out of here before the lights came on, before the start the fight but then he would have used the kill switch on me, like everyone else in here, I'm trapped."

'His own personal bodyguard, wants to be free too?' Minin thought. 'Is there anyone that wants to work for him, or are they all scared that they will be killed if they don't do what they are commanded as well?'

"Give me a few more seconds and I'll get you out of here," Mark said still hitting him. He lifted his arm, further than before, the crowd going crazy thinking these would be the final blows.

Minin was unsure whether to believe him or not. '*What if this has all been a trick to get me to stop hitting him?*' The punch came down with immense force, missing Minin and hitting the floor below him, it began to crack more.

Minin looked at Mark, who winked at Minin, "It's time, help your friends, then help me." Crack... Crack... Crack, the floor gave in, taking both men through it. Mark grabbed hold of Minin, "Lift your head up and fall on your back, get up and run." He told him as he let go.

Minin did as he was instructed and hit the floor with a thud he had never felt before, this floor was not made of the same wood designed to take the impact of the falls. It wouldn't have surprised Minin if his back was broken from the impact. He looked over to his side, Mark was lying face-first on the ground, Minin had no idea whether he was alive or dead. Around him was nothing but broken pieces of wood, above him a hole much larger than both would have made. This was his time to escape.

21

Minin tried to lift himself but he felt nearly unbearable pain. It was a struggle, every muscle in his body felt like it was on fire. Somehow he managed through determination and lifted himself off the ground. He had another look around the room and saw nothing but wooden shrapnel lying all over the place. Above him, the edges of the hole looked as though they could collapse at any moment. Mark's body was still lying on the floor not moving, Minin unsure whether he was alive or not. *'Get up and run,'* those words pop into his head, he decided to listen and make his way out of the room.

On his way out he spotted a lone bag in the corner. Minin was drawn to it, despite the fact he needed to hurry, he just had to know what was inside. He lifted the bag, looking inside. He could not believe his eyes, it was the meds. Daman had collected and put the meds together in a bag in the unlikely chance he had won. "He thought I had a chance And he kept his word?" He said to himself confused as he looked at the hole in the roof.

The lights turned on above, shining through the hole, *'They'll be looking through the hole any moment,'* Minin realised. He searched the room for a way to get out without being caught. The room was made of brick, no windows, just a door. He looked once more at Mark's lifeless form lying on the floor, before walking over to the door, which was locked. Minin looked around again hoping to see some other exit. The only other possibility was the hole in the roof, *'That's definitely not an option,'* he thought. *'I need to get out of here now.'*

Crack…crack…crack, the sound came from the roof as people were walking on top, more rubble began to fall into the room and all over Marks body. Crack…crack…Snap!' A huge timber frame falling on top of Mark, splitting in two. *'If he wasn't dead before, he is now'.* Minin concluded.

The sound of clapping came from the hole in the roof, standing around the hole, looking down was Daman and four guards, "Congratulations, somehow you managed to do it, he's dead, you win." Daman said with disappointment.

Mark began to groan as his body began to move, "How the hell?" Minin said shockingly, quiet enough that only he could hear.

"I guess you didn't win," Daman said happily. "Now would be a good time to take your chance to finish off the job." he sneered.

Minin just looked around, first at Mark who was barely moving, then at the door. He took a deep breath, the door wasn't going to open, he had no choice, he began a slow walk towards Mark, picking one of the broken pieces of timber, knowing what he needed to do. Then he heard a click sound coming from the door. He turned his head to look at what it was as it began to open. Minin stopped in his tracks, looked up at Daman. "I'm not your slave," he yelled before running as fast as he could toward the opening door. He entered through the door, just as gunfire began in the room he had just left.

Minin entered what appeared to be a hall, made of more stone with no sign of whoever opened the door for him. There were two other doors in the hall. One on his left and one on his right, situated at either end of the hall. Directly opposite Minin was a giant window through which another room could be seen. He walked to the window getting a better look of the room, seeing a stainless-steel platform with metal railings along each wall. Floating in the middle of the room was something that Minin recognised instantly, a Dropship! Minin's face dropped in disbelief. *'How the hell did he get one of those?'* Minin wondered. He knew that the dropships were programmed to only drop supplies and people to the island then return to it's Homebase. Surely someone would have noticed if one never returned.

Minin stared at the dropship a while longer before a siren began to wale, forcing him to snap out of his daze. He had to move now! Every guard inside the tower will be on the lookout for him and this floor is going to be the first place they look. The door to his right opened and he could see someone standing just inside it. Minin was unable to make out who it was and he wasn't going to wait around in case it was a guard, more would probably be on their way through the door at any moment.

He sprinted towards the door on the left, getting halfway down the hall when it opened and guards began pouring in. Minin came to a skidding halt. The guards aimed their guns at him, Minin looked back at the other door, it still only had one person just standing there. *'More guards could come through the door at any moment,'* He thought to himself. *'One verse many. Screw it, I'm going the other way, I can barrel him over,'* He ran towards the person on their own.

Minin was running straight at the person guarding the door bracing for a fight, becoming vaguely aware that the person was waving him down. The pain that he was feeling from the fall and fight, no longer existed. Adrenaline was pumping through his body, all he could think was, *'I'm going to get out of* here.' He looked at the person guarding the door, eyes fixed on them. He was a few metres from the door and the person moved out of the way, making a clear way through. Minin was thankful as he knew to barrel the person over would have only slowed him down and he needed all the time he could get.

He went through the door and onto an outside balcony. He crashed into a wall which was half white brick and half glass window. The wall knocked him backwards and caused him to fall to the ground. The door he came through slammed shut. A person wearing a hood stood over him, trying to pull Kinin to his feet. Minin tried to see who was under the hood but was unable to see their face, *'I'm not taking any chances, just in case this is Daman wanting to beat me up himself.'* He thought to himself and began throwing punches in the air.

The masked man dodged the punches, pushing Minin away from him, "What are you doing? I'm trying to help you!" A voice that was instantly familiar to Minin. The person removed his hood, it was Hunter.

Minin stopped throwing punches and shock overwhelmed him and he fell to the ground. He just couldn't believe his friend was standing there in front of him. Once Minin regained his thoughts he said, "We came for the meds to help Tiffany and anyone else that needs them." Somehow feeling as though he needed to explain why he was there.

"What happened to Tiffany?" Hunter asked in concern.

"She got shot and we ran out of meds to help her," Minin replied.

Hunter looked around nervously, knowing he couldn't sit around listening to the full story, "Ok, that's enough, we haven't got time for the rest." He said looking around, putting his hand out to lift Minin back to his feet.

Minin looked around the Balcony, trying to figure out where he could go from here to escape, the only options were the same door he came from which had a control panel next to it, another door or jumping over the ledge. "We have to get out of here. The guards were right behind me," he said frantically as he grabbed Hunter and tried to drag him to the second door.

"I know, why do you think I locked the door behind us?" Hunter smugly asked, raising an eyebrow as he stood there as if Minin tugging on his arm was no more than a child's attempt. "But I'm not coming with you," he announced.

"Are you kidding me?" Minin said annoyed.

"No, I can't leave, once he figures that I'm gone, I'm dead." Hunter pointed to his kill chip "Besides there is a lot more for me to do," Hunter declared.

"What do you mean?" Minin asked shocked as to what could be more important than leaving the Tower. "I lost Callum, I'm not losing you as well."

"I can't tell you what it is, but trust me you've seen more than anyone else."

"You mean the dropship?" Minin asked.

"I can't tell you anymore…yet," Hunter replied, looking around.

Bang…bang…bang. A loud knocking noise came from the door that Minin and Hunter entered from.

"They're coming, you need to go now, the door is locked, I don't know how much longer it will last," Hunter said trying to hurry Minin.

There was more banging on the door, this time much louder, Bang…it stops, then a louder bang which stops again. Then one last louder still, bang. Then silence from it.

"They've stopped, we're fine," Minin said relieved.

"You think they've stopped? They're working on something else," Hunter replied.

At that moment, a gun began firing at the door.

"See I told you they are coming through, it's time for you to go."

Minin realised he didn't have a choice, "Where's the door lead too?" He asked looking at the remaining door.

"You're not taking the door, that's how I'm getting out of here," Hunter informed him.

Minin knew what the other option was, he didn't like it. "Wait, you want me to jump?"

"It's that or you're meeting the guards," Hunter replied as he went over to the control panel, pressed a few buttons and the glass panels over the balcony began to lower into the wall as a strong breeze began to blow over them. "You're not going to survive inside for much longer."

Minin looked over the edge, which was a huge drop. The breeze rushing against his face made the drop seem even further. He looked down at the descent, at the bottom was a river. "How deep is it?"

"Deep enough to survive the fall. Just jump out, away from the tower and you'll survive."

Minin lifted himself onto the ledge, his fear of heights began to surface, a familiar sensation kicked in, the ground trying to suck him in. "It's too high," He said as he jumped back onto the balcony. "How do you know it's not shallow?"

"I found a schematic of the tower and the surrounds, it's pretty deep. The river goes down as far as the tower, about twenty metres," Hunter replied trying to assure him. "So plenty of room to land."

Guns began firing at the door again, this time it sounded different, as though a different type of gun was being used as the door was starting to break and give way. Minin went back onto the ledge, he closed his eyes not looking down. The gunfire ringing through his head from the door. He looked back at Hunter, "You'll have to tell me about a radio I found, in your room," Minin said with a petrified smile, trying not to think about what he was about to do.

"Trust me this isn't the last time we'll meet," Hunter replied with his smile, "But you need to go now." With that, he pushed Minin over the edge causing him to fall, a part of him knowing Minin would not have been able to do it on his own. Hunter running into the other door without a second look.

Minin looked back at where he was pushed. Guards came and look over the ledge, just staring at Minin as he descended. Air rushed past Minin as he turned back to the ground, he closed his eyes, he didn't want to look at the wall of water that was rushing towards him.

Minin crashed into the water. He fell deep, the water was ice cold, he quickly composed himself and swam upwards, for what felt like ages before his head broke the surface of the water and he could take a deep breath. He looked back up at the tower, no longer seeing the floor from which he came, nor the guards. He was finally free.

22

Minin began to float on his back, *'I'm enemy number one now, there's no doubt about that,'* He thought to himself and let the current take him downstream. The current wasn't very strong, just enough to gently move Minin away from the Tower, the only thing Minin having to do was stay afloat.

Minin continued to float down the stream, taking in the sights, the area was all new to him. He thought he knew the island well, not as well as what Callum did, but enough that if he got into a situation where he was lost he would be able to work out where he was and how to get home, but this wasn't the case, he didn't even know where the stream was taking him. *'Eventually, I'll see something that I'll recognise... soon...I hope,'* he thought. *'Wait, I've never been on the other side of the Tower, what if I'm being pulled that way?'* He began to think and worry.

He quickly calmed himself down, figuring that worrying about that now would be the worst thing he could do, the best thing was to try to relax. Besides, even if this was the side of the island he had known about, it wasn't going to be any safer for him now since he was on the run.

Once he had submitted himself to wherever the water took him, he would look curiously at the bank of the river to see as much of the Island from the river as he could. It was quite a nice view, especially here, with nothing but trees on either side, it was somewhat peaceful to him. Unfortunately, he hadn't seen any beaches or clearings to make his way out of the water if he wished, yet. Only low cliffs, that had forest backdrops as far as Minin could see. He was exhausted and knew getting up the cliffs would be a challenge.

More time passed then another thought came into his head, *'How long will Tiffany's meds last if I don't get to her?'* He thought for a second, deciding that they would only last a few more days, so she should be fine until he found her. Feeling more content, he just floated along the river knowing there was no urgency.

He closed his eyes trying to relax, trying to clear his mind of any worries he had, just making sure he kept his head above the water and not fall asleep. *'No doubt someone from the Tower would have worked out where the river went,'* he thought. He wouldn't want to be found, asleep on the water. He was so tired though that he decided, *'That's for future Minin to worry about'*.

Minin continued to float downstream for a while before he heard the cracking noise of a branch breaking. He looked around worried, *'This is it, no more relaxing,'* and lowered himself into the water just enough to keep his eyes and nose above the surface, hoping that those around him would think he was a rock. He looked around trying to work out where exactly the noise came from. He was unable to locate anyone nearby, just a flock of birds flying away, *'They must have broken the branch and flew away,'* He thought, calming himself once again.

He closed his eyes and continued the journey downstream. Time passed and the stream was beginning to move quicker, Minin opened his eyes but was unable to see anything from his position, so he tried launching himself out of the water to get more height and a better field of view but produced nothing out of the ordinary. *'I think it's time for me to finish my trip downstream,'* he thought to himself. He looked to the edge of the water, hoping to find something to make it out of the water, but there were still only cliffs on either side.

The flow began to quicken. Minin was frantically searching for a way out of the river. Suddenly, he saw it, an opening to a small beach. *'This is it,'* he thought to himself and began to swim towards it. The current had now become strong. Even though he was trying to swim across the river, it was near impossible to change his path.

The opening became clearer, two girls were standing on the edge who were wearing white dresses with long jet black hair down to the middle of their backs. They were staring at Minin as if in a trance as he floated by. One was a head taller than the other. The shorter girl looked too young to be allowed onto the island. Minin had never seen them before, not knowing whether to call out for help or not.

The current continued to gain force, Minin was worried what would happen if he didn't make his way out very soon. In his head, he imagined he was being pulled towards the only waterfall that he knew of on the Island, Deadly Falls. Deadly Falls was a huge waterfall in the middle of the Island. The image of himself going over, falling onto the jagged rocks below, killing him instantly, replayed in his brain, Minin knew he must take his chance and called out to the girls, "Help me!"

The girls snap out of the trance, looking directly at him. They began talking to each other, not loud enough so that Minin could hear though. All Minin could see was their movements, one shakes her head looking worried, the other looks around worried, but ultimately starts to nod her head. The first still looking worried, began to nod her head slowly, still unsure. They soon look around, Minin didn't know whether they didn't know how to help him or whether they were going to even try. The girls continued to talk to each other. Once they finished, the shorter one ran into the forest behind them. The taller girl started waving her arms trying to get Minin's attention, he looked at her, and she pointed further downstream furiously. It was obvious she knew what was coming up and it was something to be worried about.

Minin looked to where the girl was pointing, seeing rocks, lots of them, pointing out of the water. Minin then knew his exact location, 'The Rapids.' He knew if he didn't get out of the water now, it was going to be a rough ride, and even worse, what was waiting for him afterwards, 'Deadly Falls'.

He started to swim as hard as he could toward the beach. The girl standing by was waving her arms trying to encourage Minin. He kicked his legs and moved his arms, but it was no use, the current was just too strong for him. The second girl returned from the forest, she was holding a long stick, she threw one end into the water, "Grab it," she called out.

Minin could barely understand her, but he did as he was told, grabbing it as hard as he could, while both girls held the other end. Minin was now stalled in the one spot. The girls tried to pull Minin towards them but it was no use, they didn't have the strength to pull Minin's weight, plus the pulling current. Minin just stayed in the one spot, he then came up with an idea, "Can you hold the stick straight?" He yelled at the girls.

The girls nod. Minin began to pull himself along the stick, he got halfway, *This is it, I'm going to be out of the water,* He thought. Then, Crack, the stick began to break halfway between himself and the girls. The stick cracked once more, snapping in two, taking Minin once again towards the Rapids, Minin looked at the girls who had a look of shock on their faces.

The flow of the river was becoming stronger. Minin looked back at the girls, who had now run off into the forest. It wasn't long before Minin was at the Rapids, he crashed into a rock, he grabbed it and hung on, hoping the girls would come back. The water was trying to suck him away from his rock, and it wasn't long before it had it's wish and took him away to the next rock, which he managed to grip onto for a short while before once again, the current took him. This war between the current and Minin's grip continued, each time Minin held onto the next rock harder than the last, hoping it would be enough but each time he lost his hold, eventually becoming too much for him, he no longer had the strength to keep holding himself onto the rocks, just to end up being swept back into the waters flow. He just wished it would stop, each time he hit a rock, pain rushed through his body. He didn't know if this was worse than falling through the floor inside the Tower or if each time the blow of the rocks was just making the original pain worse than it was.

He hit one last rock and as he swept passed it, Minin realised he was now free of the rapids, he took a couple of deep breaths to recover, looked around, and realised he was now on the same side of the river as the girls, but as the first part of the river, there wasn't an opening or a beach for him to make his way out and to make it worse the cliffs were now higher than before.

The flow of the water didn't subside. Minin looked ahead, trying to figure out how far before 'Deadly Falls' was upon him. He couldn't see ahead due to a wall of mist, but the roar of the water told him that it wasn't going to be long before he went over that edge. Minin looked around hoping that the girls would make a reappearance somehow, but soon realised, *'It's up to me,'* and was desperately racking his brain for a plan to get out before the time was up. The mist suddenly surrounded him, blocking whatever remaining visibility he had had. It was thick, so he had to rely on the roar of the river to gauge how far away the edge was, Guessing that it wasn't far at all.

The mist soon cleared and Minin could see the edge, the reality of what was coming up began to sink in. Minin started looking for any-thing that he could hold onto until either help arrived or he could work out another plan. There was nothing he could see in front of him. On the cliff to his side, a few roots from the above trees were sticking out of the cliff. They didn't look strong but since he was running out of op-tions, he grabbed onto them. They were very weak, and each one he held broke, but it did slow his progress down the river.

Minin was frantically searching for another option and saw a branch from a tree, hanging right over the edge of the waterfall, *'The roots don't look like they can hold me, but I have no other choice, if this doesn't work, then at least I tried,'* He thought. He made his way to the edge and gripped the branch with both hands. It swung wildly, back and forth, but to Minin's surprise it was strong enough to hold his weight and he didn't go over the edge. He swung in the air above the waterfall, get-ting his bearings and looked over. He could see most of the east side of the island, with its green rolling hills in the Freelands, the outskirts of the Coastie and Farmers camps, a mound that Minin could only assume was the Bunker and the forest entrance to his own camp. 'This view is amazing,' he thought to himself, but then he made the mistake of looking down at the drop. Just as he suspected, there were jagged rocks, barely visible from the mist of the waterfall. He couldn't even concentrate on them because he was suddenly taken over by the same sucking feeling he had at the Tower. Once he looked back up, the feeling disappeared.

Minin looked at the end of his lifeline. It was part of a fallen tree, it's roots still stuck firmly in the ground on the cliff. Taking a guess, he didn't think the tree was going to go anywhere though.

There was a faint crunching noise coming from the direction of the end of the fallen tree. Minin looked in the direction of the sound, 'Please be those girls,' he pleadingly thought, not wanting to be saved at the last moment just to be taken by someone from the Tower. The girls move into his line of sight, with smiles on their faces. More girls who were wearing the same white dresses come and have a look at what was happening. 'The girls must have gone and tried to get help,' Minin thought relieved.

The two original girls were carrying ropes, the shorter one ties one of the ends around to make a lasso, she swung it around, throwing it towards Minin but missed. She pulled it back to her, swung it around once more then threw it again, this time making it to Minin. He put the lasso around himself with one arm, but as he did, he quickly realised he was exhausted, losing his grip of the branch, falling over into the waterfall, he fell a metre and stopped, swinging in the air, the rope saving him. He looked into the open, relieved that he didn't fall any further.

It wasn't long before Minin could feel himself being pulled up, towards the girls in the white dresses, they pulled him out of the water and into safety. Minin looked up at his saviours, "Thank you," he said to them exhausted. He tried to pull himself off the ground, he looked at the girl that made the lasso, he smiled at her as his vision became blurry, then becoming lightheaded, he then collapsed.

23

Minin opened his eyes, his vision was blurry, his head felt as though it had been hit with a baseball bat. He tried to put his palm to where the pain in his head was coming from but his arm was so heavy it felt like he was trying to lift a jumbo jet. He tried lifting himself but the pain from his back made it quite difficult. Minin couldn't understand why his pain was so intense.

Minin looked around the room as his vision came into a better focus. He was somewhere he didn't recognise, inside a room. In front of the bed he was in, was a table sitting underneath the window which had lacy curtains. There was a door next to it, which Minin could only assume was to the outside. Above him was another window, matching the previous one, the only other thing, a table next to the bed. Minin tried to remember how he could have gotten here, but all he could remember were flashes of the waterfall, then the girls in white, and now waking up here.

Minin laid back on the bed, it was comfortable considering the pain he was in. There was a grinding noise, coming from the outside of the door, which suddenly opened. Minin stared at it, fear began to strike him, not knowing who was going to walk into the room. He relaxed a little when he saw it was another girl wearing the same type of white dress that the girls that had saved Minin from the waterfall had on. He didn't recognize her though. Unlike the other girls, he could get a better look at her. She had long blonde hair down to the middle of her back and dark brown eyes. She looked nervous. He glanced at her hands and saw that she held a damp cloth and a bowl of water.

"Umm, hi," Minin said to her, not knowing what else to say. He still couldn't be sure that these girls didn't work for the Tower, but he hoped not.

The girl went from nervous to shocked. She put the bowl and cloth down on the table near the window and walked out of the room, not saying a thing. Minin just laid there not knowing whether he said anything wrong or if he had offended her in any way.

Minin could feel his headache getting stronger each second he was awake. He didn't know if he should close his eyes again and try to fall back to sleep. He didn't know if they'd be coming back again soon or not. Instead, he just kept looking over himself surprised that nothing else was wrong, considering what he had been through.

The door opened again, this time Hayley walked in. She stood there looking at Minin, her smile from ear to ear, she had never been so excited to see him as she was at that moment. "He really is awake!" She shouted out to the door and went over and hugged him, the movement and slight crushing of the hug sent pain through Minin's body, but at that moment he didn't care, he was glad to have that from her. She let go still smiling.

Tiffany walked into the room, she ran over, hugging harder than Hayley, the pain was greater and made Minin wince, Tiffany heard his slight cry and let go as quickly as she held on. "Looks like you'll need those meds you got us yourself," She told him.

"I think I do," Minin replied, smiling, happy that they were both safe.

"There's plenty to go around now," Hayley said smiling. "How'd you end up like this? I had a quick look at you, I don't think you've got any broken bones or anything, you're basically just one big bruise."

Tiffany started to laugh, "What did you do, go twelve rounds with Daman's Bodyguard?" She said sarcastically.

"It wasn't twelve rounds," Minin replied with a slight laugh, "But I did end up against him."

Tiffany stopped laughing, "Wait...what?"

Both of his friends' faces were in shock.

"You're serious? You went against his bodyguard ....and you're alive?" Hayley questioned him in disbelief.

Minin then went on to tell them what had happened in the fight. ".... I don't know if Mark, that's his bodyguards' name, by the way, knew that the floor was weak or if someone was helping him to collapse it, but I'm here."

Both Hayley and Tiffany stood there in shock, they couldn't believe what he had told them. Hayley then had a look on her face trying to figure out something, "What about Callum, did he make it out with you, was he part of the fight?" She asked frantically.

"He's still in the tower," Minin replied disappointed. "Daman knew that we were coming, he was tipped off, he didn't get out with me.... they did something to him, I don't know what it was, but he can talk now."

Hayley once again couldn't believe what she was being told, "Callum can't talk, he's never been able to talk, you're delirious from the pain."

"I saw him before I got into the fight, they did something to his head, he could talk, but he wasn't like himself, I think it might be a charade, but he can talk none-the-less," he explained. "The Tower thinks he knows things.... things people aren't supposed to know about either the Tower or the island, and they want to get it out of him."

Minin tried to once again to lift himself out of the bed, the pain was still intense, he could only manage to lift himself into a seated position.

"Wait...wait...wait.... Careful," Hayley instructed to him. "Take it easy, after what you've been through, I'm honestly surprised you're not still asleep."

Minin looked at her, "I don't want to just sit here, I don't want to feel like I'm wasting time lying in bed," he told her.

Hayley looked back at him and smiled, "Well judging by the way you tried to get up, the pain is going to make you stay down even if you do try."

Minin stared at her, as much as he wanted to get out of the bed, what she told him was the truth, every time he did move he felt pain, "you're right," he said defeated.

"I'm glad everyone is safe," Hayley said as a knock came from the door.

"Come in," Tiffany shouted toward the door.

Minin looked at her confused, not sure if that should be his call or not, considering this was his room.

A woman in an off-colour white dress walked into the room. She looked older than the other girls, her hair was black, and just like the other girls, down to her shoulder. Her eyes were an electric blue colour, her face looked gentle and caring. She was holding a tray with a mug, steam pouring out, she placed it on the table next to Minin's bed, "How is our patient doing?" She asked.

"I'm in a lot of pain, it feels like I got hit by a bus, but I think I'll be alright, thanks," Minin replied, peering inside the mug. He was shocked and delighted to see it contained coffee."

"Your friends told me how much you like coffee, so we made you some to try to make you feel welcome," The woman replied.

"Thank you," Minin replied. "I used to drink way too much of it before I got to the island, coming here is one way to detox someone. It's been ages since I've had one considering our camp doesn't have any." Minin lifted his arms to try and lift the mug, the pain still surged through him, but he managed.

"You're welcome," The woman in white replied, "I'm Simone by the way, Welcome to our camp, which everyone has dubbed 'All-girls'.

Minin now knew instantly why he didn't recognise anyone. Beside the Tower, this had been the one group on the island he had been involved with the least. It wasn't because they were considered a danger or anything, he just didn't need to.

Simone didn't know what to say at this point, "Well I'll let you go for now so you can rest and be with your friends," she then proceeded to make her way to the door.

"Wait," Minin said to her, "I need to know a few things."

She turned back around smiling, "Yes, what is it?"

"I need to know what happened to me after I came out of the river."

"What was the last thing you remember?" She questioned him.

"I was hanging on the branch at the waterfall, you all pulled me out, then not much after that, just waking up here."

Simone smiled then spoke, "Once you collapsed we brought you here into our own camp, to be honest, you're in one of our cells, we didn't know who you are or if you're working for the Tower or not, so forgive us for that," She admitted, looking embarrassed.

Minin looked around the room one more time, "If this is a cell, I'd like to see your actual houses or whatever you have," He replied with a smile. "It's nice in here."

"We didn't know what to do with you," Simone continued. "If you did work for the tower, we would have kept you locked up, but as you don't, you will be let go once you're ok." She paused for a moment, realising she was going off track. "Anyway, a few days before we found you, we had Ellie go to make a trade with the Coasties. She was told of the plan of you and Callum going to the tower to get meds. She stayed overnight, by that time you should have returned. Ellie came back to the camp the next day and told us about what you were doing, none of us thought it was possible, but then she and Mel went for a walk along the river. They saw your body floating down the river, they didn't know if you were alive or not so they kept looking trying to figure it out. It wasn't until you called out to them that they figured out you were alive, so Mel quickly ran to find something to get you out with. Once that failed, they both rushed back to camp to find whoever they could to help pull you out. They decided the best course of action was to get to the waterfall and follow it back until they found you, but you got to the waterfall quicker than they thought. Luckily you can hold onto things. Anyway, we got you out of the river that's when you collapsed and we brought you back here. Ellie put one and one together and rushed back to the Coasties to find Hayley and Tiffany."

"I'll take over for a bit," Hayley then said to Simone. "When Ellie got to the camp she found Tiffany and me around the campfire talking to

Gin. She blurted out that they thought they had found you. Gin looked nervous right away, like he didn't know what to do and just ran, leaving the camp. We didn't know why. Anyway, we came right here with Ellie, we had to know for ourselves if it was you," She ended with a smile.

"I know why Gin ran. He is the one that dobbed me and Callum in. Anyway, it's a good thing you did find me," Minin said smiling. "How long was I out for?"

"About a day and a half since we got here," Tiffany answered, "It's been about four days since you left for the Tower."

This was all a lot of information for Minin to take in, in his current condition. He wasn't sure if he had absorbed it all. Some of it seemed to just go in one ear and out the other, but he hoped, if he had a chance to let it sink in, he would remember it all.

Simone looked at Minin, "You didn't get all of that, did you?" She asked him.

"I'll be honest, no."

"Don't worry about it, I'm not going to be offended if you have to ask me about it again?" Simone said with a smile.

"I need to thank those girls that found me," Minin said hoping he could meet them.

"They aren't in the camp at the moment, but once they get back, I don't see why they can't meet you."

"Thanks."

Simone then looked at Minin seriously and took a deep breath then sternly said, "Once you're healed, I'm going to have to ask you to leave."

Tiffany looked at her with wonder, "Why? He hasn't done anything to you," Tiffany asked her, although Minin and Hayley knew exactly why.

"We have rules in our camp, rules that we can't break, one of them is men aren't allowed to stay here, they are only allowed within the camp boundaries if they are here to trade, never to stay. It's also partially why you're staying in a cell, and the second reason is you're too much of a risk."

Minin was taken back by this, "What do you mean, too much of a risk?"

Hayley looked at Tiffany, then looked at Minin, "This is the question we hoped you didn't ask. The day you got out, Daman sent a raiding party to the Coasties camp, we didn't know why. He instructed the guards to take the place apart, the place was destroyed. Every single guard was shouting at everyone, "where is he? No one had any idea who they were talking about. We figured out it was you once we knew you had escaped."

Simone interrupted her, "They might have come here too, if it wasn't for our rule, that rule keeps us safe. They won't expect you to be here, but I can't guarantee how long that will last until they decide to try and look around."

Tiffany then spoke up, "You are number 1 on his list, he didn't put this much effort into finding Callum. You must have pissed him off something fierce!"

"Anyway, I have a few things I need to do around the camp, get better soon," Simone told Minin with a smile as though nothing was wrong and walked out of the room.

Minin's head was pounding, he hadn't noticed while he was talking to everyone, but as Simone left the pain made itself known again. "You don't have anything for a headache by any chance? My head's killing me."

"We actually do," Hayley announced. "The backpack you had with you, had tons of meds we can use, I'll go get it," She said and walked out of the room, hurryingly.

"I'm glad your back," Tiffany told him. "Hayley has been worried sick about you. I've tried to calm her down, but she was just too worried about you."

"She's probably worried about all three of us," He replied, trying to dissuade any ideas she may be getting. "Anyway, how have you been? You look a lot better."

"I'm definitely a lot better," she announced proudly. "I haven't needed to use any meds in ages, probably even before you left, so I kinda feel guilty about you going," she admitted.

"There's nothing to feel guilty about, even if you didn't need the meds, there are plenty of others that do," he replied trying to lessen her guilt.

"That's what Hayley told me."

"I told you, what?" Hayley interrupted as she came into the door.

"About Minin and Callum leaving for the tower, and me feeling guilty for them getting the meds."

"We still needed them regardless, not just for you, but everyone else," Hayley said, handing Minin a tablet and glass of water. "Even people that went and got the meds," She paused for a moment and directed her words toward Minin, "As you can see our OLD," She emphasised the word, "Patient is much better. Now I have another to look after."

"What happened to Hunter?" Tiffany asked. "You said you found him, but then Simone came into the room."

"I found Hunter," Minin continued his story. ".... I wanted him to come with me, but he said he had other things to do and refused to come with me, that's when he helped me out and into the river, if they found out about it, he hasn't got much chance either."

"So, his time is numbered in there?" Hayley asked concerned.

"He is fine, at least for now. Whatever they wanted to do with him, they needed him, if not they would have killed him or wouldn't have even taken him. So, while they need him he will be fine. It has something to do with a dropship, he didn't want to tell me what it was."

"How can it have something to do with the dropships?" Tiffany inquired.

"I saw one. It was just floating inside the tower, going nowhere." Minin thought about the answer a little longer, "I think Hunter has found a way off the island, once he can work how to control them."

"How can there be a drop ship?" Hayley asked confused.

"I don't know how it got onto the island," Minin replied. "But it's there."

"Is it ready to be used?" Tiffany asked.

"I don't know," Minin replied. "I don't know anything about it, all I know is that it's there and I think Hunter is doing something with it."

There was a knock at the door, Tiffany walked over to the door and opened it, Simone walked in. "There's a guard from the Tower at the perimeter of our camp," She paused and looked annoyed. "So much for not suspecting us, the guard hasn't come into our area, and we think he is alone, but he is here, I think he's just observing if Minin is here or not, but I thought I would warn you just in case."

"Ahhh…. Thanks," Tiffany said to her, not sure what else she could say. She turned back to Hayley and looked nervous, Hayley looked back at her, nervous as well.

"What is it?" Simone said, noticing them looking at each other, "You're hiding something, aren't you?"

Tiffany reached into her pocket and brought out a piece of paper and handed it to Minin. It was a wanted poster, just like the one of Callum, but with Minin's information on it. The reward was ten crates of supplies, dead or alive. "We don't know who has seen it, we're hoping no-one here has, but we don't know for sure. We don't know what kind of price people will sell us out for."

"We're not going to," Simone announced. "We hate him! In the end, you're one of us, just from a different camp." She said trying to comfort them. She looked and pointed at Minin then smiled, "him, not so much," She continued, attempting a joke.

"Whether it's you that turns me in or someone else from the camp, that reward would be tempting," He said honestly to her. "Who's to say that guard isn't there just to make sure I'm not moving and someone has already said where I am?"

"My girls don't do that," Simone said to him forcefully. "We want him brought down, and if someone from my camp did snitch, they know the punishment they would receive if I found out what they did."

Hayley looked shocked at the announcement, "What punishment?"

"It doesn't matter, that's for us to know," Simone said simply.

"If you want him brought down, we have to take the kill chip remote off him." Minin announced, changing the subject. "Even his own body-guard doesn't want to work with him, and that's the only thing holding him back from taking control of the island himself."

Hayley, Tiffany and Simone were looking at him, they were contemplating what Minin had said. They moved in closer to each other, and began to talk quietly to each other. Quiet enough so that Minin was unable to hear.

"We need to hide you and lie about it, you're the only one that can get the chip since the rest of us aren't being hunted," Hayley said adding to the plan that Minin didn't know was happening. "You might be able to get close enough if we can all hide you and get you into the tower."

"What are you talking about?" Minin asked, unsure what was happening. "I don't know anything about the Tower, I went to different levels and got lucky to get out."

"It's crazy, but it might work," Simone said to him, "As long as everyone can help us, it should work, as long as we can hide you."

"Wait a second" Minin interrupted her, still unsure what was going on. "The last person that 'helped us' ended up turning two of us in, which resulted in Callum probably being tortured in the Tower." His voice started to get stronger, "So forgive me for thinking getting every-one to help us is a bad idea. Besides I have no idea what is happening."

"That won't happen again," Hayley replied.

"And how can you be so sure?"

"Gin made a run for it, so we don't have to worry about him screw-ing you over like that," Hayley answered. "We have to fight back, I'm no longer going to live in fear, I've said it before, and I'm going to make damn sure we have as many people fighting with us when we need to! This is our best chance."

Minin sat and took what she said in. He took a guess at what they were thinking, they wanted him to get the killchip controller from Daman, but everything in him said it was a horrible idea but no-mat-ter-what he could say, when Hayley was convinced of something, there was no way she could have her mind changed.

Tiffany looked at Simone and Hayley, she thought of an idea of why the plan wasn't ready. "Stop, we can't do this.... Well not yet anyway, you want to go in all guns blazing, and by the sound of it, you want to do it now. Here's a flaw in your plan, Minin isn't anywhere near ready, we shouldn't move him unless we need to. For the time being, let him rest. If the guard does something, then we'll decide something in return, but for now, we hold off until everyone is ready." Hayley and Simone looked at her, they thought to make the plan right away was the smartest thing.

"She's right, you need to wait," Minin said, backing Tiffany. "We're not ready, you said the guard is on the lookout? Just don't move me and act like everything is normal." He paused for a moment, "Someone probably told the Tower Hayley and Tiffany were heading this way and had someone follow them, thinking they will lead the Tower to me. As long as you act normal, there's no proof I'm here," Minin could tell from the look on their faces that Hayley and Simone were starting to come around to the idea of waiting, at least for the time being. "Let's relax for now, if something happens, we will figure it out then."

24

Minin woke up the next morning after what must have been the worst night sleep since he had arrived on the island, he kept tossing and turning, the memories of the fight, then the memory of almost going over the waterfall kept flooding his dreams. He must have woken up at least twenty times throughout the night. Tiffany suddenly burst into the room unannounced, her smile reaching from ear to ear. Minin couldn't understand what she was so ecstatic about, "Why are you so happy?" He asked.

"It's a great day to be alive and I've decided to stop feeling sorry for myself about being shot, I'm going to stay positive if I can," She replied. "After being able to tell Hayley and Simone to calm down, I feel like I'm a part of the team, that my opinions matter and not just some little scared girl that just arrived on the island."

Minin had another idea as to why she was so peppy. Tiffany's eyes were glazed over, "You had some meds this morning and they were a bit strong?"

"Maybe a little bit? Hayley still wants me to take some, although I told her I'm fine," She said smiling. "But I've finally acknowledged our situation here and have accepted it, so I'm making the best of it," She insisted again.

"I'm impressed with your upbeat attitude and your ability to make the best of it. We were abandoned here with a crazed lunatic who can kill half of us with a press of a button." Minin replied explaining the situation of the island.

Tiffany didn't agree with him, "We have to make the best of what we have. They've started a plan to take him down but if it doesn't work, then we will have to find some sort of happiness."

"Finding any kind of happiness here is an achievement," Minin replied. He rose out of the bed, the pain had subsided but was still present. He was making progress because unlike the previous day, he could now get out, make it to his feet, walk over to Tiffany, grabbed her arms and looked into her eyes. "But you shouldn't have to live like this, none of us should live like this, all of us have only done petty crimes, and we've ended up in hell with a dictator for a leader," He said annoyed.

She just stared back at him, "I know, but I've been broken on the island, now I'm repairing myself," she said seriously. She then continued, "Also you didn't have to add '-tator' to his description," She said chuckling to herself.

Minin chuckled lightly as well, he admired this part of her, even when she had realised this was something that had to be taken seriously, she was still able to smile. He felt most people would have been broken and not been able to repair themselves so much or even as quickly but she was different.

Tiffany sat down on the bed, her forehead was beading with sweat, "Is it really hot in this room or is it just me?" she asked.

Minin joined her, he hadn't taken notice of the heat until now, but his room was hotter than normal, the island usually had the same temperature range all year round, so once anyone was used to it, it always felt the same but this was different, "Yeah, it is a bit warm in here, isn't it?"

"I'll just take this off." She proceeded to remove her shirt, once again in her underwear. "Hopefully this cools me down a little," Then created a fan with her shirt to circulate the air.

Minin was once again taken aback by how comfortable Tiffany was showing her body around someone reasonably new. It made him remember Amber before he came on the island, she was completely the opposite. Amber hated going even to the beach, she hated how her body looked, even though Minin thought she was beautiful, nothing he could tell her would change her mind.

There was a knock on the door, which took Minin away from his memories, "Hey, are you awake?" Came a question from the outside.

"Yeah, we're awake. Come on in," Minin replied.

Hayley walked into the room and saw Tiffany sitting on the bed. Her face was unable to hide the look of surprise and jealousy. Minin instantly noticed the look on her face, "Nothing's happening," he said sharply. It was at that very second, he realised with an answer like that, there would be no doubt Hayley would have assumed that something was.

Hayley just shook her head. She wasn't convinced at all. "It's not like we're together, you're free to be with other people," She said annoyed.

"Don't worry there isn't anything going on?" Tiffany said with a smile, realising how the situation looked.

"It doesn't matter," Hayley replied sharply. She closed her eyes for a moment and took a deep breath, "Can you walk?" She asked Minin in her normal tone.

"I think so, I'm a bit sore, but…."

She cut him off, "Good, I've been talking to a few more people and they are on board with the plan to take down the Tower, but we need you to speak with us, you've gotten out of the tower, so we need your input."

Minin was shocked, he was under the impression that everyone was going to wait until later to go forward with the plan to take down the Tower, then he realised this was Hayley, and if she had an idea that she wanted to go ahead with, she would do it. Minin began to limp toward the door, he was slow, but he was just grateful to be moving at all.

Tiffany followed him, he looked back at her, "Aren't you going to put on your shirt again?" He questioned her.

"Why? It's not like this camp hasn't seen a girl before or anything," She responded smiling, trying to attempt a joke.

Hayley answered her coldly, "Even so, they are letting us stay here, maybe just until they get used to you, you could consider wearing something more than your underwear?" She then walked out the door.

"Umm, ok?" Tiffany replied, confused, and put her shirt back on.

The camp looked different to the ones Minin had seen before. In the other camps, most of the accommodation surrounded a campfire. This was different, they had what looked to be white houses, a little bigger than the huts from Minin's home camp. Twelve Houses, all lined up parallel next to each other, behind them, six more houses with enough room for another six to be built. He kept walking, there were a lot of women, dressed in the same white dresses as the others, all of whom were looking at Minin, everyone had the same look of mistrust and annoyance. He had two guesses as to why that was, either since he was number one on the Towers list or they didn't like any men inside their camp boundaries. As he walked around the camp, he could see it was surrounded by a forest. Rushing water could be heard from one side. On the opposite side, toward the area where they were heading, the forest had been cleared out to form a circle. The tower from this camp looked huge, it wouldn't be far if they ever needed to walk there. Inside of the circled area was a podium with six rows of carved wooden chairs looking upon it. Minin couldn't understand how this camp could look so different. Normally a meeting area was the campfire, but this camp didn't appear to even have one. The girls in white started to fill the area, taking a seat where they could find one. Minin, Hayley and Tiffany took a seat at the front near the podium.

"Is that all the people in this camp?" Minin asked Hayley quietly.

"No, there are still a few people being lookouts. From what I've been told, the lookout from the Tower is still there, he is still on his own though, and hasn't even tried to make a move towards the camp or back to the tower. Simone has guessed that he isn't to do anything unless he sees you. We're also guessing that guards are being posted outside the other camps too."

"I'm not sure, I'm still thinking it's because I'm here and you two arriving at the camp trigger some sort of guess that I might be here?"

"Yes and no. Seeing us come here might be the reason the guard isn't leaving, but it's not completely strange for women from other camps to come and settle here. We're two women whose camp has been practically abandoned, that's all we will need to say if the tower raids the camp and ask us why we are here. If he doesn't move soon, we'll wear the white dresses, at least for the time being to make them think we've joined."

Tiffany then asked a question, "Why do they wear the white dresses?"

Hayley answered, "Simone was the first one in the camp, in fact she was part of the first few dropships. She kept getting attacked when she was in the Freelands. She found the area and it was safe, probably because it's so close to the Tower. She settled here and made it her own, but because of her problems with getting attacked, she made sure that it was only women or girls that stayed here. She found a crate one day, containing nothing but the same white dresses. She decided to make it the camps uniform, to show everyone else where they are from. Ever since then, they haven't had any trouble from any other camp, except maybe from the Tower, but that's it." Hayley then looked at Minin, "They probably look at you with distrust thinking you might attack them. Simone tells a lot of stories from her beginnings on the island. Whenever they have someone new come into the island, the new person doesn't know any different. You add a couple of people that have a similar story, then the new person believes anything you want if they don't know or don't want to know anything different."

Minin started to think that ideology could have been how Hayley and Hunter felt about the Tower, that was if he didn't see what Daman could do and what he was like himself. "Makes sense to me," he said.

Simone was standing at the front of the podium. "Is that everyone that needs to be here, there isn't anyone missing, is there?" She asked the people sitting on the chairs. They all started to nod. No-one seemed to be out of place, "So we're all good to start the camp meeting?"

"Wow," Minin said to himself, this was all so different from how it was in his own camp. In his own camp, they didn't need to hold a meeting, anything they needed to say as a group, was always said over Dinner in front of the campfire.

Simone began to talk, "Everyone knows why we are here?" She asked. There was a resounding yes from the crowd. "I'm glad word got around to everyone, and just like we agreed, I hope it stayed in the camp," She said, although the tone in her voice made it clear that it wasn't a confirmation but sounding more closer to a command.

Minin knew with an announcement like that, she was worried about the safety of everyone if Daman knew what they were planning or that they were hiding Minin.

"We want to revolt," She continued. "We're no longer going to live like this, we are going to revolt, pure and simple. But this is your choice. If you choose not to, I do not blame you and there won't be any repercussions, it is your choice. All I ask is that you keep what we plan a secret. For the rest of us, this is your chance to be part of the island's history." A resounding cheer went up, "We can't do this on our own though, we need the other groups." The cheering went quiet almost instantly, the distrust they had for the other groups was still strong.

A short woman in the row behind Minin stood up. She had blonde hair, down to her shoulders, she looked about the same age as Minin. "How can we trust the other groups? The others have broken promises before and this happened," She pointed to Minin, indicating his injuries, "How can we be sure this won't happen again?" She sat back down annoyed.

The crowd started to make noises in agreement; they all knew she was right. Minin, Hayley and Tiffany also knew.

Another girl, much taller than the last, but much younger with black hair, stood, "What if those groups start attacking us, what if they want to take our supplies?" She sat back down looking worried.

The crowd was cheering again, except for Minin, Hayley and Tiffany, who knew the comment was only made from fear.

Simone started to move her hands around to get the group's attention and to quiet them. It took about a minute, but they all came to a hush once more. "I'm going to be honest with everyone. We can't, it's as simple as that, we can only hope." The crowd began to make noise again, they were no longer so enthusiastic about the plan. "But do you really want to stay like this or do you want to take the chance to save ourselves?" She asked them. "If there is a problem just remember, we've fought off the other groups before if they ever started trouble."

The crowd was silent for a moment before another blonde girl stood, she had sat a few rows behind Minin, her height roughly between the two previous stood up. To Minin she looked like she wasn't old enough to be on the island. "We fight back and try to be free, it's better than living in fear, if we fail, I'd rather die knowing I tried, than live and know I didn't!"

"What about if the other groups attack us?" Asked the girl that originally stood up.

Tiffany became annoyed from how little the camp thought about the others and stood up, "They won't." She paused for a second, thinking about how she could word what she needed to say so that the camp would listen. "They'll be too distracted taking on the Tower to even want to attack you," She smiled. "I'm sure if they do though, you'll have no problem sending them back where they came from." The crowd rose with cheers. Tiffany sat down.

Minin then asked her, "You don't honestly think that another camp will attack them?"

"No, but everyone here does and we need them to help. Sometimes you need to play into their fears. Hopefully, if they work with them they will see that most of them aren't so bad."

"Ok, ok," Simone said trying to get everyone to calm down. "At this stage, it's all hypothetical. If we did this, it won't be easy and it IS dangerous," She emphasised. "Out of everyone that has gone to the Tower, I've never known anyone to break out. That was until a few days ago." She signalled Minin to come up to the podium, "that's why I want to bring Minin up here so he can explain, what kind of dangers we are dealing with."

Minin looked confused, he didn't know he was going to make a speech, he didn't want to say anything, speeches were never his strong suit, in the past, he would do everything he could to avoid being in front of a crowd. He looked at Hayley, hoping she would rescue him somehow, "go," she whispered forcefully. Minin looked at the crowd, they looked back eagerly. Minin went from his seat and stood at the podium, he had never been in front of this many people before. Anytime during the past that he had to do a speech, it had only been in front of a small group. He was nervous. He stood there and just looked at everyone staring back at him.

Simone could see his nerves wanted to get the best of him. "There's no need to be nervous," she said trying to calm him down. "Maybe just tell us what happened in the Tower, just to begin with," She suggested.

Minin opened his mouth, "Umm," He said, shutting it as quickly, he couldn't believe how hard even saying this was. He closed his eyes and tried to speak once more, "err... Hunter told me to wait, he needed more time," was all he could manage.

The crowd started to look confused, Minin wasn't sure if it was because it was too hard to speak about or if he was annoying them since he wasn't saying anything.

Simone decided to take a different route, "Don't look at them just speak with me." She said hoping just focusing on her would get a better answer each time, she then asked him a question, "What does he want you to wait for?".

Minin turned in Simone's direction concentrating only on her. It calmed him down, "He needs us to wait as he is doing something. I think if we wait at least until the next supply drop before we do anything, he would have worked it out." He didn't want to say anything about the dropship, thinking it would create a panic somehow.

Simone smiled encouragingly, "Anything else?" she prompted.

"No, I can't even really tell you about the Tower," He said thinking about it. "I didn't see enough of anything before I was caught," He thought about it for a second longer. "Umm, there's an elevator shaft in the middle, that could help everyone...." He paused again for a moment then blurted out without thinking to continue the secret. "Oh yeah, there's a working dropship in there too," he declared to everyone.

Everyone sat in stunned silence. Minin himself, couldn't believe he just blurted that out. His plan was just to keep that quiet and only tell the people he trusted the most.

Suddenly there was a crunching noise of leaves on the ground, footsteps were rushing towards the meeting area, everyone looked at where it was coming from. Three girls were running in quickly. "Run, run now!" They were screaming, "Run, run now." Everyone got up out of their seats and did as they were told, scrambling in every direction possible.

25

The place was suddenly a movement of mayhem. No-one had been prepared for something like this. Everyone was knocking into each other, some falling to the ground, only a few knew they needed to cover their heads, to protect themselves while they were down.

Minin and Hayley stood up and looked at the chaos around them. Tiffany, on the other hand, was looking around trying to figure out which way would be the safest to flee. "Look there," she said as she pointed toward an exit which seemed to be the less crowded of the options. It looked like it would only be big enough to allow one person to go through at a time.

A wall of fire came from the centre of the camp. Minin stared at it in horror, he couldn't take his eyes off it, trying to figure out where it was coming from. He then saw what was causing the wall of fire, guards with flamethrowers, torching the camp. "They must have found out I was here," He told Hayley and Tiffany. Everyone that was running toward that direction turned around, heading to the same exit that Tiffany had pointed out earlier.

"We've got to move now," Hayley commanded as she grabbed Minin's hand, who then grabbed Tiffany's and they ran toward the exit. The exit was too small to allow the number of bodies trying to get through it. Everyone came to a complete halt waiting for the person in front to make their way through. The wall of flames getting closer as each second passed. Minin could begin to feel the heat as it was getting nearer to himself. The flow of people going through the exit seemed to be slower than the wall of fire coming closer to them.

The people trying to get through the exit started to move quicker, everyone had realised they needed to work together to make it go easier and safer for everyone. If someone was coming in from the side they were no longer being blocked and having to try to fight their way in, they were given a spot to get to safety. Even with this improved system the flames were still getting closer and was making people panic even more. Minin, Hayley and Tiffany were in the middle of the crowd, they could feel themselves getting burnt, they didn't want to think how bad it must be for anyone behind them especially someone right at the back.

"Ahhhh." A scream came from the back of the line, the flames had reached the back of the queue, it had now turned deadly. Minin, Hayley and Tiffany, could almost touch the exit, but as they got through, they could hear two more screams. They made it to the exit, Tiffany went through first, then Minin, then Hayley, neither one letting go of each other's hands, making sure whomever they were attached too, made it to safety.

They were soon through to a more open area, anyone in front or behind them spread out in all directions, making their way to where ever they could feel safe. Another person screamed. Minin stopped, causing Hayley and Tiffany to stop with him, they all turned around as those behind them passed quickly. They looked at the camp, which appeared to be nothing more than fire and smoke rising into the air. Soon there was another scream as the last person made it out of the exit. Minin could see their shirt was burnt as she ran past, just as the exit had flames coming through it. The girl dived onto the ground, rolling around, attempting to put the flames out.

Tiffany began pulling Minin, "We have to go," she told him desperately with tears in her eyes.

Hayley agreed, "She's right. We have to go," And pulled Minin, who just stood there, staring at the girls camp which was now nothing but flames and smoke. They kept pulling him, he eventually realised what they were trying to do and started to run with them.

They all kept running in silence. Their minds just replaying what had happened. Minin feeling worse than anyone else. He was convinced this happened because of him, *'Everyone of that camp just lost their home because of me'*. He looked at both Tiffany and Hayley who he could see were also shocked, so he kept this worry to himself, *'They clearly have enough to think about themselves,'* He thought.

Minin watched those from the girls camp as they just wandered around until they found someone they knew. They would talk for a second, then move onto someone else, then some would look at Minin and smile. He could not understand the reaction since he felt their home was destroyed because of him. Others would look at Minin and shake their head, a reaction which made much more sense.

Tiffany stopped moving after a while, forcing Hayley and Minin to do the same, "Where are we going?" She asked. "I've been watching the girls and they don't seem to have any direction either. I don't think they know where they are going and I don't think they were prepared for this."

"This is my fault. I should have just turned myself in," Minin said disappointed with himself.

"What are you talking about?" Hayley asked.

"We talk about a revolution, and people lose their homes, people have died, if I turned myself in, this wouldn't have happened," Minin replied.

"And if you turned yourself in, it would have gotten much worse. We're telling him we are no longer going to be controlled by him, isn't that better in the end?" Hayley replied.

"I hope you're right," Minin said, not so sure.

"You can't say this happened because of you," Tiffany told him. "We don't know if someone turned you in, and this was what Daman did as punishment, or whether this was a warning to the other groups of what will happen if you don't get turned in, we just don't know yet," She said trying to comfort Minin. "Either way we need to work out where to go, staying in the open is the worst thing to do."

Hayley turned to Tiffany, "I don't have the slightest clue on where to go," She admitted. "I was hoping to follow the girls and see if they lead us somewhere."

"What if we go home?" Tiffany asked.

"I would love too, but there's going to be guards from the Tower there waiting for Minin, I don't even need someone to tell us that," Hayley replied.

"What about the Coasties?" Tiffany asked making another suggestion.

Minin looked up at her, "If there's a chance that Gin is there, I don't want to be. I don't want to be in another fight this week," he said angrily.

"Ummm," Tiffany hesitated not knowing many other groups on the Island, "The Farmers?"

"They rejected Callum to protect themselves, they won't turn us in, but also wouldn't take us in," Hayley replied, finding a flaw in her plan.

"But we need to get the farmers on board with what we are doing," A voice said behind them. All three turn around, Simone was standing there, "I'm instructing all my girls to head there, Chris owes me an IOU, it's a big one, he'll take us in."

"But is it big enough to take me in?" Minin questioned her.

"You let me deal with that," Simone replied, she then smiled. "We need this revolution to happen, so they'd better let you in."

Minin looked at her, not entirely sure if she would be able to pull that much of an IOU or not. Hayley then replied, smiling, "Ok, we'll see how it goes."

"Get there as soon as you can," Simone Instructed, "I'll fill you in on everything, once we are safe," She said as she walked away.

"Well it's settled then, we're off to the Farmers," Tiffany announced. She looked around, the girls in white were still moving in a somewhat nonsensical direction, "Which way do we go?"

Hayley pointed to a man-made pine forest with one dirt track in the middle, "It's a bit of a distance to walk, but if we start now, we'll get there soon enough." The three of them began walking, Hayley noticed that the girls were not going in the same direction. She smiled, thinking that she knew what was happening. "They've been told not to go to the same areas, it's something they've been taught to survive, not have everyone in the same area unless it was their own camp," She smiled some more. "I think the scrambling and looking confused might be part of it, I think they were told to do that until Simone or someone came up with a plan. They were told to try to look helpless, but believe me, they can look after themselves. Simone makes the girls learn self-defence when they became part of the camp, she never wanted what happened to her to happen to any of them. But against flame throwers, the training would never have worked, and I think the tower knew that."

Minin started to think back at what he had seen, "The girls were never far from each other were they? More than enough to be able to see anyone if they were in trouble."

"And then talking to each other must have been to see if they heard what the new plan was," Tiffany added in.

Knowing that the confusion was a charade cheered Minin up a little and made him feel a little less guilty. Minin looked around, this was another part of the island he had never ventured into. The dirt track had a downward slope and was very rocky and damp from the shade of the trees. "How long do you think it will take?"

"Maybe a couple of hours, but to be honest I'm not sure, I've never been around this part of the island that much," Hayley admitted.

They all started walking towards the Farmers camp. "I didn't think I would see this much of the Island this quickly," Tiffany admitted.

"I've been here like six months and have seen more of the island in the last few weeks than the entire time I've been here," Minin replied, "What has been your favourite bit?"

"Our camp," Tiffany said with a smile. "That short time in our camp before all this happened."

"Since this all started, I agree," Minin didn't know what else to say, as they continued their journey to the new camp.

Minin and Tiffany continued just with small talk, neither one knew what to say, they just knew that saying something would make the journey go quicker. Hayley, on the other hand, just remained quiet, the look on her face suggesting that she was deep in thought. She then suddenly spoke up, "It had to have come from the Coasties."

"What do you mean?" Tiffany asked.

"There was no way could the Tower have known for sure that you were inside that camp. It had to have been when Ellie was at the Coasties, someone must have heard that you were at the Girls camp and told the Tower."

"We don't know that for sure," Tiffany replied. "We don't know what had happened, it might have just been a warning since the Girls camp is close to the Tower."

"No, the Girls keep to themselves, they try not to associate with any other group unless they have too, they would have left the girls alone, unless they suspected Minin was there."

"We'll work out what happened," Tiffany told her. "We can't just continue to accuse everyone of everything, we are all stuck on this Island together." She thought for a moment trying to figure out how to get her mind off it and focus on what was ahead of them.

Minin could only see two girls from the girls camp remain in front of him, for a while the number looked quite large, that started to worry him. "The number of girls has gone down, are you sure this is the way to the Farmers?" He asked Hayley, thinking that she might have made a mistake.

"I'm positive" She replied. "Remember Simone would have sent fewer girls to the farmer's camp than we thought."

"Maybe it's a trap. Maybe Simone has done a deal to turn us in?" Tiffany said sarcastically and began to laugh. "Aren't we supposed to be suspicious of everyone else except ourselves?" Both Minin and Hayley looked at her disapprovingly, they didn't see the funny side to what she said. "Sorry, if I get nervous, depending on how bad it is, I either break down or start making bad jokes," She said trying to justify what she had just said. She then smiled knowing this had taken Hayley's mind off what she was thinking.

Minin smiled back, thinking her smile was her attempt at part of the apology, "It's fine, probably just laugh before you say it?"

"I'm sorry," She apologised again. "I just don't understand how everyone can be so suspicious of everyone else when we are in such close proximity to each other. Also, I just can't imagine how it would be like being captured by the Tower."

"It's horrible," Hayley answered. "When I got here, they made sure you were put inside the Tower, made sure you feared the consequences of being here, you're in a better situation being dropped off all over the island, no-one has ever been able to work out why it changed, but it happened about the same time as when they ran out of kill-chips."

"It's not the Tower that scares me, it's Daman," Minin said. "You don't know what mood he is in when you're in front of him, it's so unpredictable."

They continued walking, Tiffany could see someone, they weren't wearing white, standing on a ledge in the distance. "Who's that?" She asked pointing at the person.

"I have no idea," Hayley replied, "It's got to be a Freelander. They must be trying to get something to eat." She glared at them with a sense of fear, a part of her just wanted to run at that exact moment.

"Maybe they want to help us?" Tiffany suggested and began shouting out, "Hello."

The Freelander looked at her, shook her head and ran off.

Both Minin and Hayley stopped her from saying anything else, covering her mouth. "Are you crazy, the Freelander's have no association with anyone, we don't know them, ten crates is an insane amount for any camp, for a Freelander, it's a fortune," Minin told her in a forceful tone.

"And what if she doesn't turn on us and would like to help? What if she has had trouble with Daman and the Tower before?" Tiffany questioned back.

"I don't want their help," Hayley said sternly.

Minin thought about what Tiffany had said for a moment, "As much as you don't want their help, we could use all the help we can." He said to Hayley seeing Tiffany's point.

Hayley thought for a moment, "If we need it, we'll get them, if we don't, we'll leave them." She replied coldly then began to walk ahead of them.

"What's up with her?" Tiffany asked Minin quietly.

"After her first few weeks outside the Tower, she's never liked any of the Freelander's," Minin Replied. "Me on the other hand, if I've come across one, they've seemed alright, most just want to be loners and survive the island on their own, but she's gotten it in her head they are dangerous, I've always just left it."

Before Tiffany had a chance to reply, she saw Hayley stopped in her path, they both walked up to her, they could see why she had stopped, they had made it. They were at the outside of the Farmers camp. The only boundary with wooden fences, behind those looked to be paddocks with crops, in the middle was a walkway, the area always reminded Minin of the towns from wild west movies except for the tents, behind the tents was only one house, it made itself stand out. "We're here" Hayley announced proudly, forgetting the annoyance she just had and continued to walk into the walkway.

26

They all walked into the middle of the camp, which was fenced off paddocks surrounded a wall of tents, something Minin was never able to understand. Anyone living here could make those fences but never bothered to make their own living quarters more than something so temporary.

The camp looked empty, hardly anyone was around, "I'm starting to think that maybe they didn't send the girls here," Tiffany suggested.

Minin thought she was right, the number of people the camp had was already at a minimum, for a place that was supposed to be the meeting area, this was too little. Minin had been to this camp a few times in the past and he was positive he had seen more. "Even without the girls, there should be more people, I don't understand."

"We'll just keep looking around, with everything that had happened in the last few days, it wouldn't surprise me if everyone has gone into hiding," Hayley said.

They all kept looking around, the first person they found was Simone, not someone they were expecting to see first, a member of the Farmers. As they continued to walk around they saw, not the members of the Farmers camp, but rather the leaders of the various other camps just walking around. "I was expecting more of the camps own people," Hayley said slightly confused.

"Who are all these people?" Tiffany asked, trying to understand what she meant.

"They're the 'leaders' of the camps," Minin explained. "I don't know why they would all be in the one area, they meet up every now and then, to trade and whatnot, but never this many maybe two or three at the most."

"Bout time you got here," came from a tall young man with blonde hair down to his shoulders with grey eyes. He wore ripped muddy coloured shorts with a black ripped shirt.

"This is Stephen," Hayley introduced. "He's from the 'Lake camp,' either they or the Coasties are the Closest to our home camp. If nothing happened, you probably would have met them soonish regardless. We trade with them about the same as the Coasties since they are so close."

"Don't take too long, I'll see you soon?" Stephen said as he wandered off.

"What did he mean? 'Don't take too long'," Minin asked curiously.

"I have no idea. Like you, I didn't expect to see anyone here, only the Farmers and the girls," Hayley replied just as confused.

"Don't take too long walking around, the meetings about to start." Said another voice, this time belonging to a woman." Standing in front of them was a short woman, with very tanned skinned, piercing grey eyes. Her black hair past her shoulders while wearing black lycra leggings and a black lycra shirt.

"This is Michelle," Hayley once again introduced, "She's from the Rocky Isles, it's the furthest inhabited point from our camp, I've only been there once," Hayley paused for a second. "She's been on the island longer than most, she was on the fifth dropship."

"Yeah, Daman had already managed to take over by then though," Michelle explained.

"What's this meeting?" Hayley asked, "why are all the leaders here?"

"You were already on your way," Michelle shrugged not knowing what else to say. "I'll show you where we're having it," Michelle continued and began to walk in the same direction as Stephen.

Hayley felt betrayed, Minin and Tiffany could see she was unhappy about something like this happening without her knowledge. "Should we follow?" Tiffany asked.

"I've known every one of them enough to know, if they are all here then something is wrong, it's never happened before. I just wish they had told me beforehand," Hayley said. "I'll join them, you guys just keep yourselves busy for the time being since it's the leaders. Just don't get caught."

"Sorry for overhearing," came a male voice with a strong accent. "They need to come too."

Hayley and Minin didn't need to know who the voice came from, the accent giving it away. "Tiffany, meet George," Minin said to her as they walked around.

Standing in front of them was an average height man with patchy grey facial hair and brown eyes. He was beginning to bald, what hair remained was grey, he wore no shirt but long pants, which Minin could never understand since the island was always so warm. "How is ya doing?" He said to her, putting out his hand to shake. "I'm from...well, they dubbed us the 'Fishers' it's probably pretty obvious what we do."

Tiffany shook back, "That accent sounds strange, I don't think I know it."

George smiled at her, "Doesn't matter, a war destroyed my country. I was a refugee, which caused me to end up here." He shrugged his shoulders, trying to not let that thought bother him. "Either way, this is home now. Common, they're all gathering around," George then began walking in the same direction.

"Do you know where it was?" Tiffany asked Hayley and Minin.

"Nope, no-one knows," Minin replied. "He won't say."

"Might have to ask Callum, if we ever see him again. He might have seen his prisoner sheet," Hayley mentioned. "Except for Chris, you've now met every camp 'leader'," Hayley had an impressed smile. "In less than a month too, that's impressive, still doesn't explain why they are all here though."

"Chris is the Farmer's leader?" Tiffany asked, taking an educated guess.

"Yep," Minin answered.

"Probably be someone else from the Coasties though," Hayley pointed out.

"You're probably right……" Minin said. It was at that moment he saw the one person he didn't expect. Gin walking in the same direction as the rest of the 'leaders'. A fiery rage overcame him, Minin ran, he clenched his fist, all he could think to himself, *What the hell is he doing here?* He caught up to Gin, grabbed him by the shoulder and forced him to turn in his direction, then threw a punch, knocking Gin to the ground. Gin covered up his head as Minin continued his onslaught of punches. Minin couldn't stop if he wanted, everything inside telling him to attack and not stop.

Stephen, Michelle, George, ran toward the commotion, grabbed Minin and pulled him off Gin, Simone screamed at Minin, "He isn't hitting you, stop it, I know you want to hit him, believe me, I do and I don't blame you, but for now, stop it."

Minin tried to do what he could in his rage to push toward Gin, he didn't want to calm down, all he could think about was trying to get his revenge again, no matter how much he tried to push ahead, the people holding him back succeeded. "How can we trust him?" He pointed to Gin, "He screwed us over once before, we have to get out of here before they come here," he screamed, attempting to get his point across.

Hayley knew that something must have happened if they were trusting Gin again and in such a short time, although she knew that Gin did turn Minin and Callum into the Tower, and she still felt betrayed, not being told about the meeting, she knew they wouldn't have done it without a reason. "Take a few deep breaths," Hayley commanded. "Listen to them."

Minin stopped fighting, he took a couple of deep breaths, his hands were still shaking, he never took his glaring eyes off Gin. "Ok, I'm calm," He declared. Everyone including himself knew that it was a lie, but he was calmer than he had been.

"Ok, now we'll continue," Simone said. "He made a mistake, but he is a key for us overthrowing Daman. He is the only one Daman trusts to give information like where you are, we can use that trust to our advantage."

"And you honestly think he isn't going to screw us over like he did last time?" Minin asked, annoyed that Gin had not yet been banished again.

"I made a mistake, alright," Gin said to Minin. "You have every right to bash my head in, If I was in the same situation, I'd be in the same spot as you being held back, I was only trying to do what I thought was right for my camp."

"The right thing almost got me killed, it got Callum captured," Minin replied, not feeling sympathetic.

"We didn't want to bring Gin in on this after what he did," Simone admitted. "but the more we talked about it, the more we realised if Gin wants redemption, this is what he can do for us."

Minin didn't understand what she meant, "What do you mean?"

"We're fighting back, it's what you said to Screamer. He kept sending the message to the camps, if those people ended up in another camp they sent on the message, that's what you wanted to do and that's what we're doing," Simone explained.

"Still doesn't explain why he's here," Minin said glaring at Gin.

"As word spread of what we wanted to do, all the 'leaders' kept sending messages trying to decide a plan. Without being suspicious, we'd send the message about the plan in a letter, everything was written in code, only the leaders understood." Minin had never heard of a code the leaders used, but a quick glance at Hayley showed that she knew about it. Simone continued, "It was the best we had without whoever was taking the message to another camp knowing about it, as much as we trust our own people there was still a chance they would tell the tower. As the plan started to grow, we knew we had to have someone that Daman trusted to send him fake information."

Gin then spoke up, "None of the camps trusted me after they heard what I did, every time I went to a camp to get something to eat or try to join, they didn't want anything to do with me. I kept telling them it was a mistake and it shouldn't have happened, I was exiled, I was a Freelander."

Simone then continued, "Once we realised that Gin was the person Daman trusted, we knew we didn't have a choice but to get his help, honestly we tried to think of anyone else, but we all kept coming up with too many problems with the other choices. Daman would have been suspicious with anyone else trying to tell him suddenly what was happening in such a short time. So, we chose Gin."

Hayley was confused, "Why was I only told about some of the plan? I thought it was only the girls and the Farmers that are onboard."

"You're too close to Minin. We thought about telling you everything, but we thought that if Minin was still hiding, Daman might want you caught, luring Minin to give himself up," Simone explained.

Hayley wasn't happy with what she had been told, "So we started to come up with a plan, then you take over until you needed us?"

Simone sighed, "From that point of view, yes."

Hayley became quiet, she was thinking over what had been said to her. Minin still wasn't happy, he continued to glare at Gin, all he could think, *This man could turn on them at any moment.* He then looked at Hayley, who looked back at him, she didn't need to say anything verbally, her eyes did it all, *We need to trust them.*

Minin then looked back at Gin, no matter what was being said, he didn't want to trust him. Steam began to come out of his ears, he looked back at Hayley her eyes still saying the same as before, he then turned to Tiffany and quietly said, "What do you think?"

"Honestly, I don't know," she paused for a moment. "All I can think is why would Hayley believe them? if it was the other 'leaders' then I'd say don't trust what's going on, Hayley has our best interests, surely, she must be thinking why would they put us through everything, just to turn their back on us?"

Minin thought about what she said for a moment then announced, "I don't trust him, I'll keep my cool, but the first second he steps out of line, I won't be so cool anymore. I'm not going to hesitate to smash his head in," Minin said bluntly.

"You're stubborn aren't you," Gin remarked.

"Only when I don't trust people," Minin replied coldly.

"Ok...ok...ok," Hayley interrupted them, trying to defuse the situation. "I think it's time for that meeting, maybe we can get you two to think about something else. Let's go to the meeting."

Everyone walked to Chris's House, the only solid housing in the camp. It was huge, it contained a lounge room and a bedroom to one side, on another side was a kitchen, this looked to Minin to be the only modern looking house on the island, except for the Tower. "I thought you said our camp had the best accommodation, this is the second camp I've seen that's had something that resembles something other than a tent," Tiffany said to Hayley.

"We did, they must have upgraded, it's been a fair while since we've been here," Hayley answered, not knowing any other reason why the house would look so nice. Everyone sat down on seats, made from carved logs, at one end of the room was a fireplace that wasn't lit.

A man with long brown hair just past his shoulders and brown eyes, he was wearing a cowboy hat, leather pants, a white shirt overlaid with a vest sat near a window. Minin knew who he was, he looked as though he fitted in perfectly for how the camp appeared. "Good, now everyone's here. For those of you that don't know me, I'm Chris," He said directing his look at Tiffany. "Let's get this meeting started."

Everyone just sat in silence, just looked around waiting for someone else to be the first person to say something, Minin kept looking around also, each time he would scan past Gin he would become agitated again, still not convinced he should have a place at this meeting, he eventually spoke up. "This silence is deafening, I can't handle it." He pointed to Chris, "Do you have anything to say?" He asked, "This is your home after all."

"My problem is, I don't really know where to start," He answered. "As far as I know, unless someone else has come up with something, all we've worked out is we agree we want to take down the Tower, and we need Gin to send misinformation."

"I was in the process of telling my camp we were working on something when all hell broke loose," Simone announced. "Did anyone tell the Tower that Minin was with us?" She began to sound more distrusting of everyone in the room.

"No, we were talking about that before you got here. We're sorry about your camp," Chris replied sincerely.

Silence returned over the room, everyone just stared at everyone else, they all had the same thought that someone in the room could have told the Tower where Minin was.

Tiffany then spoke up, "We can't keep secrets here, it's why you don't trust each other, it's why you only came up with a near non-existent plan, it's why you all think the attack on the girl's camp was caused by someone in this room. Who's to say he only attacked that camp as a warning because it's the closest to the river that Minin went down or that Hayley and I were there. We need to speak up, we can't have secrets and distrust in this room if we want to take down the Tower."

Most of the people inside the room smiled at her speech except for Chris, "Why are you here?" He said annoyed, "This meeting is supposed to be for the 'leaders' of the camp, you're only new, you're not a leader, you shouldn't be here."

"Seriously?" Hayley answered him astonished. "Thirty seconds ago you introduced yourself to her in the room, now you're asking why she's even here?"

"I'm serious," Chris replied. "Minin wouldn't be here if it wasn't for the fact he has seen the inside of the tower most recently, and we need what he has seen. She is just a member of your camp. As for introducing myself, it's just plain manners."

Minin replied, coming to Tiffany's defence, "If she's not here, neither am I."

Hayley then interrupted him, "And neither will I," She said, snapping at Chris.

Everyone in the room began to argue, bringing up any problems they had with any other group, it continued for some time. Minin glanced at Tiffany who was smiling, "Why are you smiling?"

"This is what they need to get started talking, get it out in the open, they'll argue, get everything out of the way," She answered. "Then they'll be able to construct something workable, I've done it a few times myself in modelling shoots with stuff I didn't want to do, or the photographer didn't like, although here, it's a little more than if I'm posing on a beach or the grass or what pose they want me in."

Minin smiled back at her, the idea felt brilliant to him, it also made his head clearer, focusing on the plan rather than his distrust of Gin being in the room.

Over the arguments, Minin could hear a comment from Michelle directed at Chris, "You wouldn't attack, all you're going to do is sit around and smoke and 'chill.' As for this cowboy façade, it's just an act."

He replied, "We're able to chill, 'cause' we have weapons to defend ourselves, what happens with you, you just run and hide in those rocks. As for this 'façade? I'm more cowboy than you'll ever be."

Minin then commented to Tiffany, "We need those weapons."

Michelle then screamed loud enough everyone in the room to listen to her, "Once we fight back we're going to be cut off from our homes if we lose, we're losing more than you."

"Take the bunker for all we care, no-one lives there," Simone said quietly. She went even quieter so that no-one else was able to hear. "All you do is say how bad you have it anyway."

"We don't want to live in the bunker, we want to live in our home, so we can't lose," Michelle said trying to convey how serious they were.

Everyone went silent again, Tiffany then spoke up, "What does everyone have that we can use? Who has weapons in their camp? Be honest."

Chris put up his hand knowing he had already answered, everyone else looked around sheepishly, Tiffany put up her hand revealing her own camps stash, Minin and Hayley looked at her annoyed, she just stared back at them waiting for them to raise their arms, they eventually gave in and did so. They then looked at everyone else in the room, one by one they raised, all showing they had some sort of stash of weapons that no other camp knew of.

"Good," Tiffany said. "Once again no secrets, now does anyone have an idea on how to take down the Tower, just spit it out, doesn't matter how stupid it is, just say it."

George then spoke up, "We march to the tower with the weapons and attack."

Michelle then interrupted, "That's stupid, anyone with a kill-chip will be wiped out instantly."

The room went silent, they all knew the idea was flawed.

Hayley then spoke, "One way or another we need to attack the Tower, kill-chips or not."

"Even if we use everyone that doesn't have a kill-chip, he's just going to swarm every guard to protect where we attack, they're going to be wiped out," Stephen said, creating another problem.

"Ok, so we have found some problems. These are pretty much the problems that have stopped us fighting back in the past," Hayley said gathering a reason why no-one has tried to take the island before. "We have weapons, what else do we have?"

"I don't know about you," Chris said. "But other than weapons we don't have much we can use to attack and that's not me trying to hide anything, that's the truth."

Everyone around the room nodded agreeing. More ideas came forth from different people but nothing that could be used. Minin just sat there listening to the ideas going back and forth, all he could think was that nothing was coming together, everyone just kept saying they didn't have the resources to be able to fight back. "No-one has actually said what we do have," he announced. "All I've heard was that not one camp has the resources to march on the Tower."

Tiffany knew from that comment she needed to bring the plan into another direction, "What about people, who's going to fight?"

"All my girls will," Simone announced. The same type of answer came from everyone else, anyone that was part of a camp was going to help one way or another.

An idea popped into Minin's head, "we have the weapons and people to fight back. What if we just do one attack on the Tower that looks like an attack. We send a message," Minin said.

Everyone looked at Minin for a moment. Michelle then asked, "Why would we have an attack that only looks like an attack? I'm not losing my camp, just to send a message."

Minin went quiet for a moment thinking more about his plan, "We all agreed to not keep secrets in this meeting," Minin said. "If you haven't been told already, there's a dropship in the Tower, it looks like it's working, maybe we don't take control of the tower, what if we take the dropship and just leave the island? If Daman wants the island, let him have it."

Every person in the room, beside Hayley and Tiffany, were shocked by the announcement. They all started to look annoyed at Minin. Michelle then spoke "Why didn't you tell us about this before? We weren't going to keep secrets, and this isn't something you just forget."

Minin looked back at her directly in the eye, "I didn't think it was the time, besides the girl's camp already knew, it wasn't exactly a secret, I'm surprised Simone didn't tell anyone."

Michelle went quiet, knowing Minin was telling the truth.

"I never had a chance too," Simone admitted.

"Maybe part of it was I didn't know it could be used as part of the plan," Minin announced, but I don't think we have another choice."

The room went back to being quiet everyone started to think of a plan they could use, except for Hayley, her mind had drifted back to thinking about what had happened to the Girls camp with the flame throwers and burning the camp to the ground. "Why wasn't the kill chips used at the Girls Camp?" She asked suddenly.

Everyone's train of thought became broken by the question.

"She's right," Tiffany said. "It doesn't make sense if he's used kill-chips in the past to scare people, why didn't he do it then, burning down a camp, potentially killing everyone, when we don't even know if he knew Minin was there doesn't make sense. Surely just using one kill-chip on someone would have scared someone enough to give Minin up."

"The kill-chip's probably low range," Minin said coming up with a guess, "Probably didn't want to leave the Tower waiting for my return"

"Pfft," Chris scoffed. "There's probably enough range from the top of the Tower to cover the whole Island. Besides wiping out a whole camp, even those without a kill-chip is going to scare more people."

"I agree," Michelle said.

"So do I," Simone replied.

The whole room agreed with Chris, except for Minin, Hayley and Tiffany, something in the back of their mind was telling them that it was something else.

"Anyway, how do we get the dropship?" Simone asked trying to get everyone back on track.

"We still have to work out how to look like we are attacking the tower, just long enough to get to the dropship, take it and get out of the Tower," Minin replied.

"And where do we take the dropship after that?" Simone asked thinking that the plan was getting harder and more likely not able to succeed.

"To be honest, I don't know" Minin replied.

"I would like to go home, but we can't do that," George said disappointed.

The room went quiet again, no-one had an idea of where to go. Tiffany then spoke up. "We're criminals, well at least to the government we are, I don't know what the rest of your stories are as to why you're here, but I was only in the wrong place at the wrong time, either way, if we try to go home, we'll be hunted and arrested again, they'll probably send us back here, charging us with escaping the island or something and this time we won't have a way off."

"She's right," Hayley said. "I don't see the point of leaving the island and then having to come back here shortly after, it'll be a nice holiday but I want something more permanent, and that's if they don't shoot the drop ship out of the sky before we even land, we're going to need to find another island."

Minin then remembered something before he arrived on the island when he was being processed before coming on his dropship. "I remember something the guards said when I was being processed to come to the island, they mentioned other islands. If I heard right, there's at least another island close by, they might have not even inhabited some."

A few people in the room started to cheer, they liked the idea, they all wanted their own peaceful island, away from Daman and the Tower. They knew if they couldn't take control of this island, they needed to find an island of their own.

"So, what do we have now?" Tiffany asked trying to gather all the information they had.

Minin answered, "People willing to fight with weapons, which is just a distraction. and instead of the island to take control of, we take the dropship and leave."

"That's easy," Gin said. Everyone became a little shocked, they realised up until this point he hadn't said a word to help with the plan. "We arm people with weapons, we send those people to look like they're attacking the Tower. While another smaller group, to be honest, it's got to be tiny, maybe three or four people, find another way into the tower to get the dropship."

"Who's going after the dropship?" Hayley asked.

"I will," Gin told her.

"No, I will," Minin told him sternly. "I still don't trust you to be honest. I'll admit it's a nice plan, but you're not going to get the dropship."

Gin didn't like what had been said to him, he just stared at Minin, but knew that this wasn't the time to create an argument, after what he had done he was on thin-ice with not only Minin but everyone in the room. "You're right, you've been inside the Tower, you've seen the dropship, you're the right person to go. But you can't do it on your own," he said hoping that that statement would mean he would also be able to join.

"We'll find someone else to go with him," Hayley said knowing what he was getting too. Gin knew his plan was foiled. Hayley continued. "Your part is sending Daman the wrong information when we need you too, don't screw that up," She said to him bluntly.

Gin glared at Hayley, "You still need to train people for the weapons, they're not all going to know how to use them."

George then answered, "In my old country I was trained to use weapons, I'll help train anyone that doesn't know how."

'It was a plan, it was rough and wasn't much of it but it was some sort of a plan,' Minin thought. He looked around the room, everyone was smiling that there was finally progress, the only person who wasn't, was Gin, still upset that he didn't get his way. Minin looked at him, it made him a little uneasy knowing that the person that betrayed him before had essentially come up with the basis of the plan and will play a pivotal part of it when it came together.

Hayley looked at him, she could tell how he was feeling and put her hand on his shoulder, "I don't fully trust him either, but we need him," She told him reassuringly.

He looked back at her and gave a fake smile. Another thought occurred to him, "I can't stay near anyone else, not until everyone else is trained up and the plan is ready to go. I don't want to risk what happened before."

Hayley thought for a moment, "The only safe spot for you would be the bunker, it can be locked from the inside, it's the only place." She looked at the ground worried, "I don't want to lose you again. If only we could go home."

Minin looked at her and smiled, "It'll only be temporary, then we'll get the ship and it'll be over."

27

"Are you sure you want to do this?" Hayley and Tiffany kept asking Minin the whole morning.

"Of course I do, we need to do this, I'll be careful, The lookouts haven't seen any guards hanging around there, if there are guards, then we'll figure something out, we'll make sure we're hidden," Minin replied.

"Ok, but if we do see a guard, you need to hide and do anything else you can to come back here," Hayley replied, worried about what the consequence would be if any of them would be seen.

"I know, we'll get our weapons from home….." Minin replied, he thought for a second then realised that was the first time he had called his own camp home. "……Then combine what we have with everyone else's, then back here to safety."

The bunker was completely different to anything else any of them had been in since they arrived on the island. The room where they were staying had bunk beds, it contained Twenty beds, ten on each side. The walls were completely made of cement, no windows, not that putting them in would make a difference as they were underground. It was designed for any bomb threats the island may have, although that has never happened since the island became operational.

They began to walk out of the room and into a hallway which once again was made from cement. As they walked down they passed more rooms, seven in total, all containing another of the same looking twenty bunk beds, in the same room designed as their own. The room they slept in that night was the furthest one down the hall. They made their way to the end of the hall into the main quarters, inside were lounges in front of televisions, which only displayed static. Connected was a dining area which contained dining tables with dining chairs and a large open kitchen, doors sprouted off leading to the different areas of the bunker, although none of them had time to explore where the various paths lead too, except for the one path they had entered from the day before.

Once they were inside the main area Minin asked, "Should we eat before we leave?" Inside the kitchen were preparation tables and more ovens and burners than they would ever need if they were to stay here permanently. The door directly across from that was the storage room, which had rows of tinned food on either side sitting on shelves, the labels had long fallen off or faded, so much that it made it almost impossible to know what it contained.

"I'll grab something, but I want to eat it on the way," Hayley told him and walked into the storage room, picked up a can with no label, hoping that it was something at least edible. "The sooner we can get what we need from home, and go back into hiding, the better."

"Yeah, I'll get something too," Tiffany said, grabbing another faded label can.

Minin also grabbed a can. He found a can opener lying closeby and proceeded to open the can, which had baked beans inside. He passed the can opener to the others, Hayley's containing tinned spaghetti and Tiffany's had baked beans and meatballs.

They continued their way through to the outside, the path quickly changed from flat to a somewhat steep gradient with steps in the middle, a ramp on either side, which was wide enough to bring a small truck through without issue. They all walked up, what felt like hundreds of metres. They arrived at the top, seeing the blast doors which were rusty and stubborn to open. It took some force to unlock, which made them feel safe knowing that if they were attacked, the chance of someone breaking in was near impossible. That was except for Tiffany, "First thing I'm looking for is something we can use to loosen the doors a little, I don't want to feel like I'm trapped if we're staying there for a while," She said.

"Just remember, if it's hard for us, it's hard for anyone in the Tower to open as well," Hayley said, "Especially if it's locked and we're inside and they're outside."

Minin could see both points to the argument but knew now wasn't the time to think about it, he wanted to focus on the job at hand. "Let's just focus on getting the weapons." He reminded them.

"And get back here before sunset," Tiffany continued, "So let's not take too long."

"You're definitely not the scared girl you were when you came here," Minin said to her with a smile.

"And I won't be a scared girl when I get to the new island either, the time for being scared is over," she replied proudly.

All three felt uplifted and empowered over the thought they were going home if only being a short time.

"So, what will you guys do once we get to the new island?" Tiffany asked.

"Relax and not have to worry for once," Hayley told them with a smile.

They all thought about what that would mean for them. For Tiffany, it meant hopefully getting Hunter to make a shower of some sort and she could use it and just relax. Hayley and Minin had the same thought, even though they didn't want to say it, relaxing with each other somewhere private. They continued walking, enjoying the thoughts of what could be.

Quickly it was all over. Tiffany then grabbed both Hayley and Minin, forcing them out of their daydream, "Look," She said to them in shock.

The area where their camp once stood was now a pile of burning smouldering ash, smoke rising from what little remained. Minin looked at it, everything he thought was his home was gone, shock and fear poured over him filling his insides, he didn't know what to do, all he could do was stare at it. His only thought apart from the shock was that this must have been how the girls felt when their camp was destroyed.

Hayley dropped to the ground, in a ball on her knees, her hands shaking, fists clenched over her eyes, whatever fear and anger she held inside, now boiling to the surface. She let out a scream, "Ahhh." She began to punch the ground in anger, tears rolling down her face.

Minin went to her level, attempting to hug her, but every time he got close she just pushed him away. He knew just to let her go. He lifted himself from the ground and went to Tiffany, her eyes filled with tears. "What…what happened?" Tiffany asked confused and shocked.

"We thought that there was a chance that they were going to hide here waiting for us, they didn't want to wait," Minin said trying to be calm, but his voice was rocky. "We shouldn't have come here, we knew the dangers, we should have sent someone else, this is the first place they would have come to, this was just a warning for when we came back," He continued as a tear rolled down his face. He looked around for a moment and saw the path that would lead to the camp. Something inside told him to go inside and have a look. He walked in, heading into what would have been the middle of the camp, covered by a wall of smoke.

Tiffany did what she could to hold onto him but she soon let go. Hayley looked up, seeing Minin enter into the smoke, "What are you doing?" She screamed out through her tears.

"I'm going to have a look if there is anything else left," His voice said desperately.

"There's nothing left," Hayley responded angrily through her sobs, thinking he was a fool for trying.

"Look after her," Minin directed Tiffany as he continued to make his way into the smoky wall.

Tiffany nodded at him, not knowing what else to do. The smoke was thick, he covered his face with his shirt, hoping it would stop some of the smoke coming into his lungs, just leaving his eyes uncovered which caused them to sting. The shirt covering his mouth did little to slow the flow, he could still taste every little bit that was coming into his mouth, but he kept moving along the path, which he could never remember being that long before.

The wall of smoke began to clear, he looked up hoping to get some sort of sign telling him that he was close, it was then that he could see the sky open, showing blue. *I'm close to the middle of the camp,'* he thought to himself and kept walking, the smoke cleared enough for him to remove his shirt. He was now in the middle of the camp.

The camp was in ashes, the huts were still standing, but barely with flames coming out. It was obvious that it wouldn't be long till they collapsed into ash, joining the rest of the camp. The crops were long burnt. Minin walked past Hunter's Hut to where the animal pen would have been, the pen was in flames but had been opened. *'It was to send a message, he at least let them out,'* Minin thought to himself relieved the animals would have had a chance at surviving.

Minin kept looking and staring at the burning and the ashes of what once was. He looked hoping to find something, anything he could take back, there was nothing. He didn't want to give up and continued to look, but ultimately, he conceded defeat and began his return to Hayley and Tiffany. That was when he saw two pieces of what looked to be paper moving on the ground, one near Callum's Hut, it was a photo that didn't look as though it had been in the middle of a fire, it was of Tiffany standing with another girl on the beach, it looked as though it was from a modelling shoot. The girl was slightly taller than Tiffany with a slim frame and long blonde hair. The other piece of paper was near Hayley's hut. It was another photo, this one had its edges burnt, it was a picture of Hayley in her blue nurse's scrubs standing next to a building, she was smiling and looked much younger than she did on the Island. *'I didn't think anyone else had photos of their old lives here,'* Minin thought to himself.

He looked around the camp one last time, then toward the smoke wall, which he thought was getting thicker. Minin didn't think there was a reason to stay any longer and began his journey out. Scraping along the ground was another photo, he picked it up, it was his own, his photo of Amber and himself that he was able to sneak onto the island, the inscription on the back was still clear, *'never let them get to you.'* He thought about what that meant for a moment and he knew he wasn't going to let the Tower or Daman get to him over this either. And ran toward the wall of smoke, trying to get to the other side.

Tiffany and Hayley were still on the other side sitting on the ground waiting for Minin to return. He came running out of the smoke and stopped just in front of them. "There wasn't anything there, was there?" Hayley asked through her angry sobs, thinking she knew the answer.

"Not much left at all," he admitted. "But I had to see for myself, had to make sure the camp was gone, not just the opening," he explained as he handed the photos he found to them. "This is all I could find,"

They both looked at the photos. Tiffany looked confused then spoke, "This is Kellie, we started our careers together, she was my best friend, but I never brought a photo like this to the Island."

"And this is one of my first days as a nurse," Hayley said. "I don't know how it ended up in our camp..." She scrunched up the photo, throwing it towards the fire. "….and it doesn't matter," She said sharply, looking at the camp.

Minin had two guesses as to why the photos were at the camp. The first was that it was part of the message that Daman and the tower were sending to them if they had returned. The other that it was part of what Callum had and Minin didn't see it when he had looked before.

"We need to go back to the farmers and tell them what had happened," Hayley said no longer sobbing, but it was clear she was angry, more so than she had ever been before. She picked herself up from the ground and began to walk in a huff.

Minin picked up the photo that Hayley had just thrown, unscrunched it, placing it in his pocket. He attempted to catch up to her, hoping he could talk to her about it, Tiffany grabbed his leg and pulled herself up, looked at Minin desperately, "She just lost her home." She said, hoping he would understand.

He did understand but the comment annoyed him, "Our home." He said to her sharply.

Tiffany instantly knew she hadn't chosen her words correctly, she needed to say something otherwise it was going to be a quiet walk back to the Farmer's camp, "I'm sorry, what I said came out wrong."

Minin took a deep breath, "It's fine," he replied, knowing that this had been stressful on everyone.

The walk to the Farmer's camp was quiet, even though Tiffany thought apologising wouldn't make it so. They eventually arrived at the camp, it seemed like they were later than everyone else, it was void of most people. Minin saw Simone and walked up to her, "Where is everyone?"

"Everyone that went and got their weapons have already left, we were starting to get worried about you, to be honest, we thought you got nabbed." Simone then looked at Hayley, she could tell that she wasn't herself. "What happened?"

"Our camp was burnt out just like yours, I don't think it was all that long ago, we always knew that they were waiting, I think they waited long enough," Hayley replied with a voice so close that her tears were returning.

"Are you sure you are alright? Some of my girls are in shock pretty badly still." Simone asked concerned.

"It's fine," Hayley said sniffling.

Tiffany piped in, "Hayley is taking it harder than the rest of us, but she'll be fine, she just needs time," She said hoping it will be enough for everyone to leave Hayley alone.

"I hope so," Simone replied.

Michelle came up to Minin. "What happened to your weapons? I didn't see you bring them in."

"Our camp got torched, we don't have anything left," He replied.

"I'll go tell everyone, make sure they understand, not everyone is here though," Michelle said trying to tell him everything would be fine.

The word spread quickly around the leaders, they were understanding over the situation, except for one. "They probably think this is my fault somehow," Gin said snarky, as he walked past Minin and Tiffany.

Tiffany was unable to keep her mouth shut, "Sometimes it's not about you…jerk." She screamed out as she marched toward him.

A shirtless man with a muscly body in cargo shorts and a scruffy brown beard, his hair was short, but looked as though he had cut it himself, stopped her. "Whoa…whoa, calm down, he's an ass I get that, but we need to be on the same page for now."

Michelle quickly walked over again, "Meet Lukas," She introduced them.

"I recognise most of the people here, but I don't recognise you," Minin said putting his hand out to shake it.

Lukas shook back, "I'm not exactly part of any 'group' as you would call it."

"You're a Freelander, aren't you?" Tiffany asked with a confused smile, happy she was able to meet one, but not sure if she should after what Hayley told her about the past.

"If that's what you want to call it, then yes…. yes, I am," Lukas said calmly.

"Great," Hayley said sarcastically still looking sad, her distrust of the Freelander's hadn't changed over what had recently happened.

Michelle continued her introduction. "He's going to help us, we were talking to him when he came to trade today and said he has had problems with Daman as well."

"I'll explain," Lukas said. "Every time he finds a 'Freelander' he would rough us up, thinking we know something about some 'Natives.' He thinks they are dangerous or something, wants them destroyed and since he can't find any of them he keeps punishing us, we can't give him anything about them since we don't know anything." Lukas turned around showing scars covering his back, "And this is what happens if we can't give them answers."

"The Natives are probably some sort of paranoid delusion he has," Tiffany said.

"Callum said, when I spoke to him, they aren't anything to worry about. I think he meant they are dead, probably all gone, since the government had taken over." Minin said trying to tell them what he knew.

Lukas then spoke once more, "so anyone that's on their own has been torched because of Ghosts? I'm even more glad to help and leave this place, he can find these Ghosts on his own. Anyway....." he paused for a moment to change the subject. ".....I was part of the army before I came on the island, it's why I'm on my own, I can survive off the land easily, I'm trained in weapons, heard you guys could use some help."

Simone interrupted him before he could continue, "Ok, it's time to show you how much we have collected, come with me." They all followed her, "As you know, our group couldn't contribute, just like yourselves, but I've been talking with the other leaders, we still think we have plenty." She brought them to a shed, that was full of homemade weapons, "This is everything we have, I don't think anyone held back to be honest." Minin and Tiffany were amazed by how much they had. Until recently they didn't feel like the other camps were stockpiling any weapons unlike themselves, but this proved them different. Hayley tried to smile over it, she knew it was a good thing, but what had happened to her still clouded her thoughts.

Chris walked up behind them, "It's a lot isn't it, we have one more thing to show you as well. Follow me." They all walk with him, they didn't think anything else could surprise them at this moment, but standing in front of them was a cannon, "It's beautiful, isn't it?" The Cannon was made of rusted steel with old wooden wheels at the bottom. It looked as though it could fall apart at any moment.

"Where did a Cannon come from?" Minin asked confused.

"We were storing it," Chris said proudly.

Hayley then asked, also confused, "What would a bunch of farmers need with a Cannon?"

"We don't really need it, we made it, like everyone else with what we could find from the leftover from the supply drops and this is what we came up with. I only think it will work once, we could use it on the door and then go rushing in, 'guns blazing'" He explained.

Minin was smiling, he was amazed at what they had done. "How did you make it? no offence or anything but your skill sets from what I understand before you came to the island, was growing certain crops, not building weapons that can take down doors and walls."

"Crops take a long time to grow, had to do something in the meantime, took a bit of thinking and planning, not everyone is like Quinn or Hunter, where they can just make something out of thin air."

Hayley interrupted them, next to the cannon was a small wooden box, she opened it, revealing paper sheets that were covering grenades, "What about these?" She said with no emotion.

"They were from our camp," Gin admitted. "We found these in some supply crate months ago, they aren't food or clothing that's for sure, but we weren't going to trade them unless it was the absolute final straw." He paused for a moment, "You can't really blame me for hiding them, everyone else had weapons they made. Like the cannon, I don't know if they work, it's not like we have tested them out or anything."

Everyone was silent for a moment. Minin started to trust Gin for a second, grenades were invaluable, for him to give them up to fight with everyone, must have meant he wanted to be trusted. Minin put out his hand, they shook, "I still don't fully trust you, but this means a lot." Minin said. "But believe me, you screw any of us over again and I'll make sure you won't, ever again." Putting out a warning.

Tiffany then spoke, "we can't hide any of this here, it's too open," She explained. "Every single weapon, the cannon, the grenades, all in one place. It's hard enough when we need to hide one person, who can move on their own but we can't move any of this if there's a raid. If that happens the Tower takes it all and we have nothing. I don't want to even think about how he would punish us.

"It has to go to the bunker with me," Minin announced. "We have a hard enough time opening the door ourselves from the inside, it'll be near impossible to open it from the outside."

Chris then spoke, "That's all good and well but moving the cannon would be better if it wasn't moved at all, I think it should stay here. I don't want to be repairing it if it breaks down on the way there. It's going to be bad enough if it does on the way to the Tower."

"But everything else goes?" Minin asked, making sure he understood. Chris nodded.

Everyone began to think for a second, trying to come up with a better solution, one that would be beneficial to their own camp, but none had a better answer. Gin then spoke for everyone, "I don't have a better solution or place. I don't know about anyone else."

"Then it's settled, it'll come with me till we need to use them," Minin said, making sure no-one else wanted to disagree. Everyone stayed quiet.

Lukas then walked up to Minin, "I have something that might be able to help you." He brought out a piece of paper.

They were plans for building something, but Minin wasn't sure what they were, "What are they?" He asked.

"They're designs for a paraglider," Lukas replied. "Before I came to the island I liked to paraglide but I haven't been able too here. I wanted to make one but surviving with everything that has happened, has made it near- impossible, now I get that chance. I wanted to make this and glide off the island, I've been trying to find a high enough ledge to do that but the only high enough place is the tower, I found one drop-off that's reasonably high, but not high enough for me to go far enough past the island. If this plan goes through I won't have to go that high.

"You're talking about Deadly Falls, aren't you?" Minin replied, amazed at what he was still looking at.

"I'm not sure what it's called but if it is the right one, it'll be enough to get to about the middle of the Tower."

Minin started to think, ideas were popping into his head, "I've got it," He announced. "We are going to use the cannon as a distraction so we can get into the Tower via the paraglide."

Lukas looked confused, "The paraglide isn't built yet, it's going to take time."

"How hard is it to build?"

"It shouldn't be that hard, although I admit I've never built one, I'm a drawer, not a builder. The paraglides I had were pre-made," Lukas replied. "It's just getting the supplies to make it."

"We'll give you what you need" Minin replied.

The leaders of the groups didn't look annoyed that someone had spoken for them like they normally would, this time they were more than happy to oblige.

Minin turned to Gin, "You're still talking to Daman, right?"

"Yeah, but I don't want too after he screwed us over," he replied annoyed, thinking about it.

Minin didn't say anything to the comment, "You keep talking to him, just before the day we do it, you tell him about the cannon, but not the paraglide."

"Why?" Gin asked. "Wouldn't telling him about the Cannon be stupid, he's going to be expecting it."

"But he's not going to be expecting the Paraglide, and that's what we need to make it into the Tower."

Gin thought for a moment, "I'll do it."

Hayley suddenly grabbed Minin and pulled him to the side, "I'm worried about the plan."

"You told me to trust Gin, and that's what I'm doing," Minin replied.

"It's not that. Everyone is going in guns blazing to take down the Tower. We have friends still in there, Hunter can try to show that he is still needed for whatever plan they have. Callum, on the other hand, is a prisoner, he'll be the first to be killed, if he hasn't been already, the only thing keeping him alive is that they think he knows all that stuff."

"If he knows stuff and hasn't told, he'll still be alive" Minin replied, trying to calm her. A thought then occurred, which worried him. "And if he has said everything, his chances are pretty slim already."

Tiffany overheard the conversation, "I know this is bad, but we can't think about that now, we can't have a distraction like that hanging over our heads, I only knew Callum for a short time, but I know he would want this as much as the rest of us," she said to them trying to get them to focus. "Where about are the cells," She asked.

"I was inside, I have no idea."

"Think," Tiffany encouraged him.

Minin closed his eyes trying to remember what it was like inside the cell, "In the morning, I could see trees outside, there was a stream of water close by that I could hear, there was a rumbling sometimes like a door or something opening."

"That's probably the main door," Tiffany said with a smile. "If there's a stream of water nearby and some windows, I'm willing to bet that's where you were kept."

Minin smiled at her, knowing what she was thinking, "We make it look like a break-in, but it's really a breakout."

"Exactly, all we need is someone to get close enough to the Tower to be able to see if we are correct, otherwise we don't have a choice and must make it a break-in. Either way, I know Callum enough to know he would agree that this is the best situation," Tiffany said. She turned to Hayley, "You're our leader, what do you think?"

Hayley still looked worried, she thought about it for a moment, "That's what we have to do."

Minin then went and spoke to the leaders, "We have a plan," he announced. "Gin and a couple of Coasties have to go visit the Tower a couple of times beforehand, get Daman to trust them for sure. While they are doing that, they need to work out if there are cells or not on the lower levels. If there are, we aim for the cells, if not, we aim for the door with the Cannon, either way, creating a hole into the tower, anyone that wants to fight and go into the raid will need to use a weapon, anyone that doesn't find somewhere to hide," he warned. "Until that time anyone that wants to be trained in using the weapons needs to talk to Lukas and Chris, they'll tell you what you need to know."

Tiffany then asked, "Is there anyone that is going to hide?"

The crowd went silent, except for Simone, "I've spoken to all my girls, they are going to fight."

"So is my Camp," said Gin.

"and mine," said Chris.

Every leader had the same answer, there wasn't anyone that wasn't going to fight.

Minin then continued, "Either way, once the cannon has fired everyone rush to the tower. If they are wearing guards uniforms they are your targets, if they aren't, try not to attack them, get anyone that isn't wearing a guard uniform out into safety."

"What about you?" Gin asked.

"I'm going with Lukas and gliding onto a higher level, we will get the dropship, once we have it, we'll come to get everyone," Minin replied. "You need to tell him I'll be in the crowd fighting"

"Isn't he looking for you?" Gin replied.

"If he thinks I'm coming towards him, he'll let up the search a bit, he's paranoid but he's not dumb. I don't think he'll use resources and guards all over the place if he doesn't have too. He'll use those guards to protect the Tower."

"I want to use a paraglide too and help get the dropship," Tiffany said.

"No," Minin said swiftly. "Daman has to focus on the attack on the ground if there are too many things flying in the air he'll get suspicious. If there's just one, I'm hoping he'll think it's a Freelander and leave them alone."

"What if it starts to get too much?" asked Simone.

"If you can't handle it, run. I'm not holding it against you if you do, I'm not going to hold anything against anyone, this island was created to be every man for themselves and we proved that wrong, but if you run then so be it," Minin said calmly.

"When's it all happening?" Chris asked.

"Once we are ready," Minin announced.

28

Two weeks had passed since the plan had been made. Each day until this Minin would go up to Gin trying to find out if he could confirm if he believed the Cells were near the front doors of the tower or not. "I don't know yet," was the only reply Gin would give. Eventually, Gin began to get annoyed with being asked the same question day in, day out and added, "It's not like I can go up to Daman and ask if that's where the cells are. I need time."With that answer, Minin decided not to ask again, even though he needed to know as it was the final piece of the evolution of the plan.

Once a day Minin would come to the Farmers camp to speak to everyone, find out how they were coming along and if they were ready for what was to come. Everyone he asked sounded enthusiastic even though deep down they were nervous thinking about what the consequence of failing would be.

"They're coming, they're coming." A voice screamed toward the group that kept repeating. It was Jacob, a young boy with black hair with a bowl cut, he was short and chubby, who had only recently arrived on the island and made his home with the Farmers.

"Who's coming?" Tiffany asked.

"Guards from the Tower, I think they are doing a raid," replied Jacob who was huffing.

Minin looked at Gin, he wasn't happy. "You said you would warn us if you knew about any raids happening."

Gin looked as confused over what happened as everyone else, "I would have warned you about this…" he paused for a second still trying to think, "…If I had known about it."

This had been the fourth time that a raid had happened in the area since the plan had been made, each raiding party had been small, just enough to show that the Tower was trying to send a message that they will never be free of the Tower. But as Minin had suspected they were not the normal size, they only contained three or four people at a time. They would come into the camps, look around, throw a few items around, admit they couldn't find anything and walk away. The three times before this raid Minin had been warned and was always hiding inside the bunker, away from everyone else.

"How big is the raiding party?" Tiffany asked.

"Bigger than the last time, I counted six," Jacob replied. "But it was only a quick count, could be more."

"And we don't have time to send Minin back to the Bunker," Tiffany said, thinking everything could become unravelled at any moment. "Go back and keep a lookout, try not to make yourself seem suspicious," She told Jacob and he ran back to his post.

"Do you think they are keeping me out of the loop cause they know I'm working with you?" Gin asked everyone.

'More like you spilt your guts,' Minin thought to himself. "Let's hope not," he then replied trying to show solidarity with everyone.

No-one said anything but everyone thought the same thing as Tiffany, without a chance to hide Minin, the plan was going to unfold, Minin would be caught. Minin thought for a moment trying to figure out what a second plan would be, "Let them capture me," Minin spoke out to everyone. "The plan goes ahead, but someone else needs to go on the paraglide though."

"Are you sure, you can't do that, we need you, you know what you're looking for," Tiffany replied.

"We need this plan to work, end of the story," Minin said knowing they didn't have a choice otherwise. "I'm only going in because I've been there before, I barely have an idea of where to go."

Everyone thought the plan through and began to nod in agreement, even though they didn't fully agree. Jacob then came walking back, "False alarm," he called out.

A feeling of relief came over everyone, except for Gin, "What do you mean False alarm?" He asked.

"They came to the boundary of the camp lined up, looking like they were going to enter, stopped for a minute then walked off," Jacob said thinking it was strange.

Confusion then came over everyone, it also sounded strange to them, if anyone from the Tower was to surround a camp they always came into it, they didn't just leave once they lined up. Tiffany then looked at Gin, she had worked out what had happened and smiled "You haven't told them about Minin have you?"

"I told you, I haven't." Gin replied gritting his teeth.

Tiffany kept smiling, everyone just looked at her as though she had lost her mind, they didn't think this was the time to be smiling. "They're trying a new strategy, they were never coming into the camp, they wanted to see how we would look if it was unannounced, or not mentioned it to Gin, if everyone started to look nervous, they would have thought something was up," She then looked at Jacob. "They left cause you didn't act any different to normal. I'm going to take a guess that you normally send your lookout to warn you if anyone is near your camp that normally isn't supposed to be?"

Chris then replied, "It's true so that we can hide anything that shouldn't be out. I'd be surprised if the rest of you don't."

"They walked away because they didn't think there was anything out of the ordinary, if you had a hundred-people suddenly scrambling around they would have known and started the raid," Tiffany replied, she then turned to Gin. "They're not going to tell you anything anymore," She said firmly to him. "They've probably noticed you aren't near your camp that much, or that you keep coming here, even though we're trying to act normal, they're starting to think something is up."

Minin then spoke to him with a forceful tone. "We can't wait any longer, do you think that the cells are near the door?"

"I told you, I don't know for sure."

Tiffany then asked, this time with a voice that demanded an answer. "Do you think that the cells are near the door? Yes or no."

"You're not the leader of a camp." He said to her annoyed. "We agreed we speak to the leaders or Minin and they send that info to their camps."

"Hayley still isn't herself at the moment," Tiffany snapped in return. "Until she is, I'm taking her place," She announced.

"Whoa" Minin replied shocked at her announcement.

"Anyway," Tiffany continued even more forceful than before, "Yes or no?"

Gin knew he couldn't argue with her, "Yes, I think the cells are near the front but I don't know for sure, it's a waste of the cannon if I'm wrong."

"Then we waste it," Minin replied. "Get the leaders around, it's time to start," he announced.

Word got out quickly and everyone met at Chris's Hut. Everyone took their seat, Lukas was asked to join, he sat in the front row with Tiffany and Minin. "Your other friend isn't going to come to this, I thought she was the leader of your camp?" He asked, wondering where Hayley was.

"She's not been feeling the best in the last few weeks, ever since our camp was burnt down, she's been feeling pretty low," Minin replied telling him the truth of the situation.

"I can understand, I've never lost my home unless you count when I was brought here, but as for my home getting destroyed it's never happened, it must have been horrible for her."

"I think she holds onto the memories of it too much and it's just taken its toll on her," Tiffany said, telling him what she thought about it. "Once we are off this island and we have some sort of normality when we find a new home, I think she'll be alright."

Chris stood up once everyone was settled. "Ok, Is everyone here?" He looked at Lukas. "Honestly tell us, are the ones you have been training, ready to go?"

Lukas stood up, "They are at the best I can get them for the time being, I know we were short on time, you give me another six months and I can turn them into an army capable of taking the Tower no problem, but we don't have that much time. This is all we need to create a bit of a distraction," He announced.

Simone looked at him and nodded her head, her face could tell you this wasn't the answer she was looking for, but she, like the other leaders understood. "We have to go with what we have then," She said.

Minin then spoke up "The raid is only a distraction while we get the dropship. If no-one gets killed it'll be a better success than we could imagine."

"You honestly don't think anyone is not going to be killed," Hayley said angrily from the door. "I've spent the last few days going over everything in my head, we're dead in the water." Everyone in the house became nervous, knowing that the odds were against them. They all looked at each other seeing everyone else worried, some more so than others.

Gin didn't look nervous, "then we die trying," he said simply. "It's as simple as that, we die or we live in fear, I'm not living in fear anymore." Everyone heard what he said, it was what they needed to keep going.

Hayley walked away from the house. Minin got out of his chair, trying to get up to chase after her, Lukas grabbed him and pulled him back on the chair, "We need you here."

Tiffany looked at Lukas annoyed, "If we were leaving right now, I'd agree with you." She looked at Minin, "Go help her," She said.

Minin got from his chair and began to chase after Hayley. He stopped suddenly, hearing a dropship in the distance. *It can't be,'* he thought. *It's no-where near the right time for that'.* He looked back at everyone in the house, wondering if he was the only one that could hear the noise, all the leaders were making their way out, looking around up at the sky, he wasn't the only one.

Everyone began to walk toward where the noise was coming from, the west, the same direction as the Tower. This was even more peculiar to them, as any dropships usually came from the east. The sound was coming from a completely different direction to normal, as though it was making a return trip after it had dropped people and was ready to drop the supplies.

The noise was getting louder, more so than normal, "Shouldn't it be overhead by now, it's so loud," said Simone, who was screaming, but was being muffled by the sound.

Minin had a look of shock on his face, thinking he knew what was happening. He looked at Tiffany, as soon as she saw his face, she thought the same thing. "They've launched the Dropship, and it's headed this way," She shouted out to everyone.

A look of worry came over everyone, they started to think the same thing, the plan took too long, they failed to get the dropship as a gust of air swept toward everyone.

"I've never felt something like this, it's close, it must be flying low," Minin said to Tiffany.

Six guards from the tower ran past the camp looking at the sky. Not one glances toward the camp, not taking their eyes off the sky, trying to get a glimpse of the dropship. Tiffany saw them and grabbed Minin pulling him behind the other leaders hoping to shield their vision. The guards still took no notice and continue to make their way toward the Tower.

Then they saw it, a Dropship, but this was not like any they had seen before, it was smaller, although the same shape as a larger one, flying lower and faster, metallic in colour. Everyone was more confused than before. They've never seen a dropship like that.

"Was that the dropship?" Simone screamed to Minin, meaning the one he had seen in the Tower.

He could barely hear her, not even making out some of the words, but he heard enough to think he knew what she had said, "No, I don't think so," he screamed back, his own words muffled. "But I didn't see the bottom, only from the side, it's too small, I don't think this one is it."

The new dropship stopped mid-flight, floating above everyone, the sound of the engine lowered, almost to the point where it was silent, the only way they knew it was still operational was the gust of air hitting their faces. Everyone stared at the floating, in-audible object above them. Trap doors open from the bottom, small crates, much smaller than from a normal dropship began floating down to the people below. Twenty crates are released after which the trap doors once again close. Everyone was expecting the drop-ship to move off but it just continued to float in the air.

Minin then thought for a second, "This is the distraction we need," he screamed out. "Get everyone, we go now." His words now easily heard.

The new dropship's engines then began to become once again deafening, the air between it and the ground blowing a cyclone. The dropship then rushed off away from the island.

"We agreed, not on a drop day," Tiffany said with a confused look on her face, telling him that he should know that.

"This isn't a normal drop-day, we didn't expect this, I don't think Daman would have either. This is the distraction we need, he's going to send people out for those crates, we fight back now," Minin replied as everyone around them nodded. "Go and get everyone and tell them it's time, it's time to grab the dropship and time to get off this hell-hole he created."

Everyone began to run off to where they needed to be while Minin went and searched for Lukas. Bodies were rushing around in every direction Minin looked, all he could see were bodies scrambling around heading to where they were needed. The only person Minin couldn't find was Lukas. He found Hayley who was sitting in a house by herself watching all the commotion out of a window. Minin decided to go in and see how she was doing. He knocked on the door, "Come in," Hayley's voice replied. He opened the door, Hayley was standing, looking like she was getting ready to be part of the raid.

"I didn't think you were going to be taking part," He said to her confused.

"I did some thinking when the dropship came. I'm a part of this, I need to help somehow, if I can find Callum or Hunter and get them out, you have no idea how happy it'll make me. I still think it's madness taking part but something inside me is telling me to do so. I still don't feel like myself though." She explained.

"When we had the meeting, you didn't look like you were in a good place."

"I'm not in a good place, I hate it, I hate that I can't turn it off like normal, seeing our home like that was the final straw, it was just too much," Hayley confessed.

"It'll take time, once this is all over, once we leave this place, it'll be over," Minin said, trying to reassure her.

"You really think it'll be all over, Don't you?" Hayley said trying to smile.

While Minin realised he had doubts, telling her wasn't going to help, "I do," he told her, showing a smile.

"I can do this," Hayley announced to him bravely with a smile taking a deep breath.

"Damn right you can," Minin said with a smile.

A voice called from outside the room. "Minin, where are you?" It was Lukas.

"That'll be my call," Minin said. "Let's get off this island." He then began to walk away from her.

Hayley grabbed Minin's arm, she looked him in the eye, she paused, looked down, then looked up, "Umm…. good luck," She told him and then let go.

Minin smiled and nodded, they both knew now wasn't the time, he walked out of the room and saw Lukas a bit further down from the house, who was still searching for Minin, "Lukas," He called out.

Lukas turned around and saw Minin, coming toward him. Hayley walked out of the door just as Lukas got to Minin, she smiled at Minin and brushed her fingers along his arm as she walked past.

"Where did you go?" Minin questioned.

"I went to get the Paraglide," he said, as he showed him the blue backpack he was wearing.

"Ok, let's go," Minin said and they both began to run in a different direction to everyone else. Masses of people were running towards the Tower, Minin and Lukas did everything they could to make their way through the wall of people coming toward them. They soon saw the four people pushing the Cannon, who were struggling to move it from the weight and rickety wheels.

"Give us some time, we'll launch when we hear the cannon," Minin said.

The four-people pushing the cannon nod their heads as they continued to walk.

"Are we even going to be able to hear the cannon over the waterfall?" Lukas asked.

"I hope so," Minin replied, not realising that may not be even an option.

They ran in the direction of the Girls camp, through the woods and up the grassy hills, knowing if they stop they might miss their chance. Once they arrived at the outskirts of the burnt-out remains of the camp, Minin's mind raced back to what happened to his camp, he shook it off, knowing now wasn't the right time to think about what had happened, he needed to focus on what was ahead of him, distractions couldn't be accepted, time was precious.

They turn left and follow the path, eventually arriving at the waterfall. Minin looked around then over the edge, he felt like it was sucking him over, he pulled himself back, the memories of almost falling over the edge into the waterfall take over. He stopped for a moment and took a few deep breaths to compose himself. Minin looked around the area which was full of trees, none of which had been affected by the flame throwers, there also wasn't much of a clear area for them to launch out. "Are we going to have enough room to launch?" He asked.

"We only need it wide enough for the paraglide to fit," Lukas replied as he put the bag on the ground, open it, and began to take pieces' out. The paraglide was in five pieces, "All we need to do is click them into place."

The pieces locked in together, it looked as though it may barely fit through the opening, or even strong enough to stay together. The wings were made of old blue tarp, the skeleton looked as though it was made from any piece of metal that could fit and the straps made from old car seat belts.

"Are you sure this will work?" Minin asked Lukas as he began to have doubts.

"About ninety-nine per cent sure," Lukas replied with a smile. "I haven't had a chance to test it out."

"And the other one per cent?" Minin queried.

"We'll launch over the waterfall and the paraglide breaks apart, let's hope the water is deep enough for us to survive," Lukas said, smiling as he put himself into the straps that would hold him to the paraglide.

Minin didn't know whether to laugh or be frightened by what he said, he wasn't sure if the waterfall was survivable last time, he certainly didn't want to risk it this time either.

"Hurry up it's time to strap in, they will sound the cannon anytime soon," Lukas said in a more serious tone.

"That's If we hear the cannon," Minin said, as he strapped himself in next to Lukas. They align themselves to go over the waterfall waiting to go, Minin's heart began to race, and he began to think about what was about to happen, he realised he was not ready for it. "I'm not so sure about this," he admitted.

"What's wrong?"

"I'm starting to think too much about it, about everything that could go wrong. I've never been good with heights, you know."

"What could go wrong?" Lukas asked wondering what the problem was.

Minin closed his eyes to think, "Well, what if the paraglide doesn't work and we crash as you said? What if the straps don't hold us in?" A booming sound is heard from afar, "Wait, is that it?" Minin asked not sure what sound the cannon would make.

"That'll be it, let's do this" Lukas said and got ready to run.

Minin closed his eyes, "umm…. Ok, let's go," He said still with doubts.

They both ran toward the edge, eventually, Minin was running on air, he didn't open his eyes, if they were falling to their deaths he didn't want to look.

"Open your eyes," Lukas told him, "Have a look at the view, she's beautiful."

Minin still didn't want to but could feel they were both being pushed higher, he eventually opened his eyes. They were high enough to see everything from deadly fall onwards, all the camps, the forests, the beaches. "This is amazing," he said, thinking the same as Lukas.

"If only it would last a bit longer, but we got work to do," Lukas said, as he turned the paraglide around in the direction of the Tower. "The currents will keep lifting us, just need to hope it's high enough to get to the roof of the Tower."

Minin looked below him, he could see a mass of people heading toward the Tower. He looked ahead, the group that had been surrounding the cannon before it had gone off were all scrambling toward the Tower, ahead of the group behind them. The front door of the Tower opened with an influx of guards, who rushed toward the people heading to the Tower.

"They need my help. I should have gotten someone else to help you," Lukas said, thinking he had selected the wrong part of the plan. "I should be down there with them." Minin turned his head and saw Lukas' annoyance that he had thought he picked the wrong part to take.

"There isn't anyone else that can help me with this, I don't know how to operate it on my own," Minin replied, trying to convince him that he had picked the right task.

"I could have done so much more down there," Lukas said still annoyed.

Gunfire began to take over below them, both sides trying to not let the other take over. Minin tried to think what he could say to try and get Lukas to forget his regret, he couldn't think of anything, knowing if he did, he would just look down and remember it right away. Minin pointed to the side of the Tower, a hole more than big enough for any-one to get in or out, "Look they did some damage on their own without you." People not wearing guard's uniforms were running out toward the people attacking the Tower. Minin instantly wondered if one of them was Callum or Hunter.

Seeing that the attacking group was able to do what they have done pleased Lukas. He could see that they didn't need him. He started to concentrate on the paraglide once more, "We're not going any higher," Lukas announced, noticing they were no longer reaching any height, "We're not going get to the roof like this."

Minin noticed the problem himself, "You're right, what are we go-ing to do? We can't pull out now."

"We need a plan B, what about that balcony you said you stood on before you jumped from the Tower, isn't there any more of them?"

"I'll look," Minin replied. He began to scan the Tower, every level looked like it only had the occasional window attached. He kept scan-ning, eventually finding one. "Look over there," he said pointing to his slightly lower right.

Lukas saw where Minin was pointing, "I see it, it's not that big though."

Minin knew this was the only chance they had, "Doesn't matter, get us close to the ledge, I'll disengage, drop down and as we glide past, come back around and disconnect yourself. We'll lose the paraglide, but we only have one chance at this, we have to go for it."

Lukas wasn't sure about the plan, "Are you even confident about jumping down, you didn't like it when we left the ground the first time, now your volunteering to jump."

"No," Minin admitted. "I don't like the idea at all but unless you have another plan, this is it."

The people fighting below were starting to lose ground, they kept firing back at the guards from the Tower, but the guards were begin-ning to overpower them.

Minin and Lukas got close enough to the Tower lining themselves. Minin breathed quickly trying to psyche himself up. He closed his eyes for a few seconds and told himself, *'You can do this.'* He kept repeating it over as they got closer, his breathing got heavier.

"Open your eyes," Lukas screamed. "You have to look where you're going." The balcony was now close enough to jump on to. "Go... go... go...." He screamed out again.

Minin disconnected himself from the harness, he flung himself at the balcony and began to fall, everything felt like it was in slow-motion. He made it onto the ledge, barely missing the barrier although it was close enough to feel it as he went passed. He hit the ground, rolling until he hit a wall. His breath was sharp and quick, it took a second to realise he had made it. He lifted himself from the floor, "I did it," he told himself relieved. He then checked himself over, there were only a few scratches that he could see, other than that he was perfectly fine.

As Lukas glided the paraglide away from the Tower for his return, Minin looked around the balcony. It was almost exactly like the last one he jumped from, except that this had only one door. Minin was still in shock that he had actually made it. He walked over the barrier waiting for Lukas to make his return.

He looked over the edge, the fight was continuing, the people fighting were losing even more ground. It was obvious that it won't be long before it's all over. It was already too much for some people who were running back to safety, leaving the remaining an even harder job.

Lukas began to line the paraglide up once again. He began to unhook his harness, but it was jammed, he kept pulling it as hard as he could, but there was nothing he could do, it wouldn't budge. He was now close to the balcony, he gave up and screamed, "I can't get out, you're on your own," steering away from the Tower.

Minin just stood there trying to process what had happened, realising he was once again on his own to navigate the Tower.

29

Minin kept staring at the sky, watching the paraglide sail further away, he wasn't sure what to do, doing this on his own wasn't part of the plan but he also knew that getting onto the balcony wasn't part of it either. He looked over the balcony again, the people fighting were falling back at greater numbers, barely anyone was staying, most had now left and made a retreat. Those that remained were doing anything to hide while firing their weapons toward the guards, the guards doing the same. Minin then scanned around, looking over to the left, he saw the river, it looked like it was close to the same height as the last balcony.

He turned his head and took one last look at the battle, the last of those that remained were now pulling back, the guards had now taken complete control of the battle, and he would need to hurry before the distraction would be completely over. He went to the door, it didn't have a keypad or even a lock and opened it slowly. He peeked through making sure it was empty, no-one was there, so he walked through quietly and pulled the door slow enough behind himself that when it closed it just made a barely audible clicking sound.

Inside the room there was silence, Minin tried to concentrate on hearing, what noise he could hear of the battle outside was now gone. A light turned on, Minin put his hands up in a fighting position. The light revealed an empty corridor, 'W*hy did the light turn on?*' Minin thought to himself. He scanned the corridor, turning back to the door and saw a sensor, *'It must turn the light on for some time once the door has been opened and closed,'* he thought to himself.

"Hello," Minin called out to the empty corridor, as soon as he said that he realised how stupid of an idea that it was. *'This isn't the time to get anyone's attention,'* He thought unless it was Hunter or Callum but the chances for them to appear were almost zero. The emptiness didn't bring a reply from which Minin was appreciative about. *'It's now or never,'* Minin thought and began the walk up the corridor, all Minin could hear was the sound of his shoes on the metal grated floor, Clink…. clink…. Clink. A minute passed and Minin could see the door at the end of the corridor, in front was a cardboard box.

The box was larger than himself, sealed with packing tape, he took the knife he had on him and opened the box and looked inside, it was empty. *'Why would a box be in here, in the middle of nowhere?'* Minin thought to himself, *'I can't be too surprised, this place does have a working dropship.'*

Minin heard a squeaking sound, it was the door being opened, Minin looked for somewhere to hide. The only thing was the box, he jumped in, crouched down, closed the lid over him and stayed as still as he could. The only thing that might have revealed Minin was his breath, which seemed much louder than usual.

Minin heard the door closing, then the sound of footsteps walking toward the box, he held his knife ready, in case his cover was blown. The footsteps came closer, "What's that?" A male voice questioned. The footsteps got louder, Minin gripped the knife even harder. He held his breath in case the guard could hear, trying to hide that little bit more. "It's just a box," The voice said surprised. "Must have set the sensor for the light off," The voice paused for a moment then shouted out in the direction of the door, "Hey, what's a box doing in here?"

Minin readied himself more, thinking this could reveal him, "It's nothing, I lost a box when I was sorting out supplies the other month, I must have put it in there by accident, I'll pick it up later," a second guard called out. Minin became calmer, thinking that the box wasn't going to be opened. "Hurry up and take your position, they need someone to be a sniper," The second voice called out, I'll close the door for you."

The door closed but Minin knew he needed to do something otherwise anyone that had not retreated yet would be taken out. He thought for a moment, *I'll take him out when he starts walking to the other door.'*

The first guard waited till the door was closed then said quiet enough that he thought no one else would have heard. "They're still going to be there in a minute, I'll have a smoke first."

'I have to do this, Minin thought.

The guards lighter kept failing as he flicked it. "First thing I'm doing when we get off this rock is get a better lighter," He said. "This plan of the boss's better hurry up, the damn vultures are getting restless, the sooner we leave them, the better. They can fend for themselves," he began to sound annoyed. "We do so much for them and now they're attacking us, they would have been killed on the mainland, now they want to fight us?"

Minin took a deep breath as quietly as he could while hearing the guard, *'He thinks Daman is the good guy?'* He then launched out of the box as he held his knife, throwing a punch in the direction where he thought the guard was and connected in the corner of his chin. The guard fell to the ground as quickly as Minin got out of the box, he was out cold. Minin stopped and froze, thinking the sounds could have been heard by another guard. Time passed, *'I'm good'* Minin thought relieved. He began to examine the guard's body, who looked as though he was the same size and height as Minin, which gave him an idea, *'If I wear the guard's clothes I can just walk around until I find the dropship'.*

As Minin began to strip the guard of his clothes, the guard woke and grabbed Minin's arm, the guard looked at Minin with anger in his eyes, without thinking Minin threw a punch, once again knocking him out. Minin finished stripping the guard then lifted him into the cardboard box. Minin then stripped himself and put on the guard's clothes. He was now wearing black pants and a long black sleeve shirt, a balaclava covering his face with a gun and gun holster on the side. The smell of cigarettes was strong, which made him want to cough, *'This isn't the first time he went on a smoke break,'* Minin thought. He then put his own clothes into the box with the guard and closed the lid.

Minin went to the door, opened it, then tried to walk around casually. In the room were guards who were walking around looking like they were on edge, but none took notice of Minin. On the other side of the room was the glass panel, Minin could see the dropship still inside floating mid-air. Next to the panel was a door, Minin walked to the door and tried to open it but it was locked, attached to the door was a keypad.

Minin kept staring at the keypad, wondering what the combination could be, he became nervous, thinking that the guards around him might get suspicious that he didn't know what to press. At that very second, the door opened from the inside, out came a man wearing a white lab coat, whose hair was short and greying and about the same height as Minin, he was looking at the ground, shaking his head. Minin could only assume he was some sort of scientist working on the dropship. The scientist looked up at Minin then back directly at the floor, as if he would be punished for looking at the guards and made a mistake then continued to walk forward in a hurry leaving the door open.

The door began to close, Minin grabbed the door and walked inside. The room was huge, more so than what it seemed from the outside, a metal grate walkway surrounded the dropship. Below him went into a dark unknown. Above him, the roof was closed but could be open at any moment. He then put his hand out, the dropship was close enough to touch, *'It's real, it's actually real,'* he thought to himself with a smile. The room and the dropship seemed so surreal.

"Hey, stop touching that," A man's voice said from behind. "How many times do I have to tell you to not touch it. It's not ready."

A shockwave went through Minin's body. *It's not ready, but we raided the Tower, it has to be ready now. The last piece to the plan and it's not ready?'* He thought. He just stood there for a moment not sure what to do, he needed the dropship. He kept staring, trying to think of something he could do, his arms knocking against the gun in the side holster, *'I have to take it anyway,'* He thought and began to pull the gun out. He turned around and aimed it at the person who instantly put his hands up to surrender. "You're a big man, aiming a gun at me, you know your friends on the other side of the panel aren't going to do anything to stop you, they want me shot anyway, they think I'm islander scum." Minin then realised who was standing in front of him, it was Hunter, and put his gun back into its holster, "It's me, I thought you were someone else."

Hunter was confused, he thought he could recognise the voice, but all he could see in front of him was a guard, "Me, who?" He asked.

"Me...Minin," And proceeded to pull the balaclava up.

"Wait...don't do it," Hunter warned. "They'll see you."

Minin knew he was right, doing it was as stupid as calling out, 'Hello' from the corridor.

Hunter just stood in front of him, "I honestly didn't think I would see you again," He said. "What are you doing here? You were free of this place."

Minin then began to recap what had happened to him since he had left the Tower the last time. ".... And then we made the plan to come after the dropship, I'm here since he's going to be expecting me to be in the crowd somewhere."

"Whoa, that's a lot of information to take in," Hunter said surprised. "I didn't think he would hunt you down."

"Wait...what...you didn't?" Minin said surprised. "You've seen what he is capable of though, you of all people know how dangerous he is."

"He's different in the tower, he's actually somewhat fair to the people that help him, I thought he would have let you go for winning the fight."

"It was a fight to the death, the last I saw Mark Brockly was still alive," Minin replied.

"But you survived, to me that's a win."

"I can't believe you're sympathetic to him now," Minin said annoyed and began to get more confused over what Hunter was saying. "Why are you defending him? he's probably only nice cause he needs those people, you want out of this island more than anyone."

Hunter tried to defend what he had said, "I'm not trying to be sympathetic, I do want out, believe me, I do, but it is a bit different in here." He began to realise what he said, "You're probably right it's only because he needs me."

Minin shook his head, surprised that someone that once hated Daman so much could change their attitude, but was relieved that he had changed his mind, "I thought he brainwashed you or something."

"Maybe I'm suffering from a bit of Stockholm syndrome," Hunter said as he shrugged his shoulders, guessing as to what was happening.

"Doesn't matter?" Minin said. "We need to take the ship now," he demanded.

"I don't know how to fully control it," Hunter replied. "That's why I told you it wasn't ready." He paused for a moment and began to walk away, "Common, I'll show you what I've got so far," he said hoping that Minin would believe him.

At the back of the dropship, Hunter pressed a button on the side, a ramp began to lower creating a walkway. They both walk into the dropship, it was slightly different from the one Minin had arrived on. Eight seats, four on each side with a few crates scattered all over are the only things occupying an empty area. They walk to the end which has a door and another keypad, Hunter presses a combination and the door opened revealing the cockpit, a window that could see in all directions in front, underneath the control panel which was covered in buttons, more than Minin could ever understand the use for. Between the window and the control panel were three computer screens, one on the left, one on the right and one in the middle. Two seats ready for anyone to use.

"Dropships don't have cockpits, what's going on?" Minin asked as he took his balaclava off, thinking he was safe from being seen.

"As I've been working I've found all sorts of information," Hunter explained. "When I first got to the island the Dropships were all controlled manually, I knew that already, some time afterwards they were changed to being an automated service. I didn't know when. Now from the information, I found there was an attempted hi-jacking on one of the dropships. It was this dropship. The guards, pilots and whatnot, had an escape pod they could leave on. Its why I or anyone else didn't know what happened."

Minin was still confused, "That doesn't explain why the dropship is here."

"If a Dropship detects that an escape pod is used, it'll go into an automated mode and find a repair station and wait till it has been told that it's functional, I've looked over everything I can find, there's nothing wrong with the dropship, I just don't know how to tell it that it's functional, once I can do that the dropship will operate, no problem," Hunter continued to explain.

"But why did they change from manual dropships too automated?" Minin asked.

"The official story is that the government thought it was too much of a risk to send anyone with the dropships that didn't need to be on board, so the whole fleet was changed to an automated service. The real story is that whoever sponsors the government needed a cost-cutting exercise, but whoever that is, has made themselves hidden."

"So they fly, they drop and they leave, no Humans needed," Minin said trying to fully understand why it would be done like that.

"It's the old saying, 'set and forget," Hunter replied. "I found something else, I haven't told anyone."

"What?" Minin asked curiously.

"The parachutes, they're not all designed to open. It's a lottery as to which ones will."

"Why would they only open some and not the others, or even just not open any?" Minin asked once again.

"I don't know." Hunter went to the control panel and brought up a computer keyboard, he pressed a button and the screen in front began to light up. "This is what I have been working with. It's got so much information on it, everything the Towers servers have. It's how I was able to know the river would be deep enough for you to jump into and survive." As Hunter began to show Minin everything, he began to light up inside. "It's constantly updating the information it has, I haven't had a chance to get to the Towers computers though. I'm sure the Tower servers have access to the outside world. But at the moment I can only access a fraction of what it contains."

"What sort of information do you think it has?" Minin asked curiously.

"Like I said I've only begun to cover the surface, there could be more on this than I could ever imagine."

"What about the people on the island?"

"To be honest, I don't see why it wouldn't." Hunter paused for a second, the question sounded odd, "Why would you think that?"

"Callum had information on people, me, you, Hayley, everyone. It was all in his hut. I think I know how he got it, I think he knew where the computers were in the Tower and every time he disappeared he went and got the information off the Tower's computers."

"It wouldn't surprise me, all I need is a username and password, the tower won't give me one, they use another person for that, but I'll get it, it's just going to take time." Hunter stopped for a second and smiled. "You know that drop ship that came today?"

"Yeah."

"I sent it. I figured out how to send a call to the mainland to send supply dropships whenever they are needed. We never needed to starve except no one else knew how that worked."

"If you knew something like that, then why can't we leave? Surely you've worked out how to control the thing?" Minin asked becoming overwhelmed by the information that Hunter was telling him.

"The dropships control panel is another beast entirely. The system is saying that the dropship is fine but it's like someone has managed to change the programming to not operate until the right log-in credentials for the dropship are entered. I've been working on getting control but even if I wasn't doing anything else like getting all the information off the Towers servers, it's a slow process, whoever changed the log-in credentials to take control doesn't want it to be taken over. I will get in but it's going to take time?"

"How much time?" Minin asked sounding slightly impatient.

"I'm close, I can get certain parts to work but as for launching the engines that's still some time off."

Minin was disappointed by the answer, "We need it now though."

"There isn't anything I can do. I wish there was," Hunter said disappointingly.

Minin knew there was no chance it could suddenly work and somehow would have to come back for it when it was ready. "How will we know when to come for it, we can't send someone to the Tower each day and just ask, 'Hey is the dropship ready for us to take from you'?"

"Daman is going to want more supply drops sent, now that he knows it can be done. I can program the supplies to drop near the Tower until then and when the dropship is ready I can send it to the Bunker?"

"Won't Daman notice one of his supply drops is in the wrong spot?"

"He still thinks there are problems, I'll tell them it's an error in the system, he won't know any different," Hunter replied. "How are you going to get everyone to the Tower this time, I don't think you're going to stand a chance raiding the Tower again."

"It'll be a small group. I have no idea how we will get inside," Minin admitted. "Or how we'll get to the Dropship, but we'll do it."

"Yes you will," Hunter reassured him. "You better get going, what are you going to tell everyone about the Dropship."

"I'm going to tell them the truth, it's not ready and we have to wait, I have no doubt it's not going to go over well with any of them but it's all I got."

"They're going to riot you know. All that work for the raid and the end result is Daman is even more pissed."

"They knew what they were getting into," Minin replied as he put his balaclava back on. He saw a walkie-talkie on the control panel, which reminded him, "One more question, in your room when we were looking for the trolley, I found a radio." He paused for a moment, "It was working, there were people on the other end asking for help."

Hunter smiled, "I think there are some people inside the Tower that want to leave, they've been sending out messages hoping someone from the outside could hear their calls. I didn't tell anyone about it since I was working on trying to reply, but I didn't get to make a microphone."

Minin smiled, "I knew you were waiting till it was done before you told us about it," He said. He then put his hand out to shake, "Next time we take the ship."

Hunter put his out and they shook, "Next time we take the ship," He repeated.

As their hands connected, a siren from just outside the dropship blasts, it was so loud that they both had to cover their ears.

30

"What the hell is that?" Minin screamed, barely being able to hear himself.

"It's an alarm, I don't know what it's about though, I didn't think we did anything wrong," Hunter answered. "If I had to take a guess, it's about what's going on outside but there was already a call over the speaker system for it, I guess there weren't enough people and they need more?"

"But I thought everyone was falling back," Minin replied.

"Either way, this is your best chance to leave, everyone will probably head that way, you can exit with everyone without getting caught," Hunter suggested. "I'll signal you when you should come back."

Minin nodded his head and began to walk to the back of the dropship, as he did an explosion hit the side, forcing Minin to fall to the ground. *Wait this isn't part of the plan, they're not supposed to get to the dropship, just fall back after a while,'* Minin thought to himself, believing that those from the outside had made it inside.

Minin looked back into the cockpit, the glass windows at the front of the dropship were closed, metal blast doors now covering them. He saw Hunter lying on the floor, who kept waving Minin off, "I'm fine, find out what happened."

Minin picked himself off the ground and continued to walk out of the dropship, he got back on the metal walkway, another explosion hit the dropship, this time from the front. Minin looked around and was unable to see anyone, he pulled out his gun from the holster and slowly snuck around toward the front, hoping to not get seen by who was attacking the dropship. He saw four guards holding grenades aiming for the dropship. *'They are trying to destroy the dropship, I can't let them do that,'* Minin thought as he hid behind the back then aimed at the guard closest to him and fired the gun, it hit him in the shoulder, the guard began to have a fit as though he had been electrocuted, the guard then collapsed to the ground.

Minin looked at the gun thinking what happened was strange, he then figured out the bullets and guns were the same as law enforcement had on the mainland. The bullets were designed to be more of a taser than a bullet, designed not to be as deadly depending where you aim the bullet, instead, sending electric shocks all over the body, they were named taser-bullets.

The guards instantly noticed what Minin had done, turning toward him. Minin fired another bullet at the next closest guard, once again hitting them. This time piercing their chest, the guard instantly began to have convulsions and fell to the ground. The other guards took cover behind what little they could, dropping the grenades and pulled their guns out of their holsters and began to fire at Minin.

Minin hid back behind the dropship, the bullets were close enough that he could feel the air being cut around him as the bullet pass, one getting close enough that it cuts Minins neck. Minin fired back, unable to hit either guard. The guards' fire back, this continued until click...click...click, Minin's gun had run empty.

"We have you now, traitor," one of the guards shouted out and tried to fire back. Click...click...click, their gun now had run empty. "Screw this," The same guard screamed out and both guards threw their pistols toward Minin. Minin did the same, his pistol hitting both mid-air, taking all three off their trajectories. The guards got out of there covering position and began to run toward Minin, "You're gonna get it now," the same guard screamed out.

Minin didn't know what to do. If It had been just one guard, he might have been able to fight them off but with two, the numbers were too much for him. *'I have no choice,'* he thought to himself, putting a defensive stance with his hands, getting ready for the fight.

A door opened behind Minin, "What the hell are you doing?" A voice too familiar to Minin, which sent chills down his spine. The voice belonged to Daman Biguy.

Minin knew his time was up, putting up a fight against two was going to be too much, three, absolutely no chance. He put his arms up in surrender not turning around. He didn't want to know whether it was just Daman or if there were escorts with him.

"What the hell are you doing? Answer me," Daman screamed. "Look at me when I'm talking to you," he commanded. Minin turned around knowing he had no choice, his hands still in the air. Daman was on his own, he walked up to Minin, looked him up and down, "put your arms down," he commanded. "Not you, those two idiots there," his look passed through Minin, glaring at the guards. Minin put down his arms, "Good." Daman then stormed past Minin toward the other guards screaming at them. "What are you doing? How stupid can you be?"

Relief came over Minin, his disguise had worked, Daman didn't recognise him at least not for the short time. *'This is my perfect time to leave,'* he thought and began to slowly walk away, hoping to not be heard.

"You, wait there," Daman screamed at Minin. Minin froze, knowing that he would have to wait for his escape. Daman kept screaming at the guards, "What are you doing, you know the plan, you don't attack the ship unless it's in danger, it's not in danger."

Daman stopped speaking for a moment, one of the guards had a chance to answer. "They're attacking the Tower sir," they replied angrily.

"Yes, the Tower, not the dropship. If you had been paying attention, we are drawing them back and there is going to be hell to pay, my little spy told me about the attack, Minin was in the group somewhere, it's why we haven't just taken them out, when we find him, they will pay."

"Why?" The second guard asked nervously, "…..Why don't we just kill him and get it over and done with?"

"I'll decide that," said Daman as his voice then calmed down. "I want my fight between him and Mark and that's what I will have." He then walked over to Minin and put his hands on his shoulder.

'How would he feel, knowing that the person he is touching was Me?' Minin thought.

"At least one of you knows and understands the plan, your shooting is rubbish but at least you follow orders," Daman told Minin. He then looked over the two guards on the floor and looked back at the remaining guards, "It's your lucky day, I need all the guards I can get at the moment, take your friends to medical and get out of my sight." Both the guards scrambled to get the unconscious guards away from Daman before he changed his mind and ran as quickly as possible.

Daman stood in front of Minin, who looked him up and down, there were no weapons on him, just the kill chip controller protruding out of his pocket slightly. Minin thought this would be the perfect time to kill him on his own. Suddenly two guards came out of the same door Daman had entered from, Minin's chance had vanished.

"They are retreating sir, they did get some of the prisoners out though," One of the guards told him with a slight sound of disappointment in his voice.

"What about Minin?" Daman asked, hoping they had found their number one priority.

"No-one claims to have seen him I'm afraid," The Guard reported.

Daman began to sound frustrated, "How can he hide so well?" He then calmed down and looked at Minin. "I want you to see someone," he told one of the guards that had walked in. "He defended the dropship when no-one else was able to" Minin just stood there silent. Daman continued, "he did good today, he needs more training though, should have been able to hit the guards that disobeyed commands."

"Yes sir," the guard answered.

Daman continued, "make sure he gets trained up. I want him on my personal protection team with Mark. As for the rest of your guards, I want loyalty and at least basic listening from people like he did today."

'This man likes my loyalty? I want nothing more than to put a bullet between his eyes,' Minin thought.

Daman then looked at Minin and smiled, "Take off your balaclava and show them who you are."

Minin froze with fear from the request, *'until now I was fine but now it's over,'* he thought. He knew he had no choice and began to slowly lift the balaclava over his face. He looked at the guards and noticed they were close together, *'if I run towards them, I can knock them down then get to the door, open it and escape'.* He got ready to run.

Daman interrupted him, "Don't worry about it, we haven't got time for this now."

Relief came over Minin, for once he was grateful at how much Daman changed his mind.

"I need to make sure the dropship is all right," Daman continued as he put his hand on Minin's shoulder. "Come with me inside the ship, I want to make sure those idiots haven't damaged anything and put us further behind, it's taking forever for my team to get control of it, the last thing I want is for them to be behind even more." Minin nodded, thinking this would be the only way he might be able to make it out without revealing himself and began to walk up the ramp, Daman following. "Guard the exit, I don't want anyone in or out until I leave," Daman commanded the other Guards. "You ever been inside the dropship?" He directed his attention back to Minin, "I meant this one, not the one you came on." Minin just shook his head to answer but kept quiet none-the-less. "You're a man of few words, I like that," Daman said with a smile. "You do what you have to do and you don't answer back, a lot of people on the island would be smart if they took lessons off you," He thought for a second. "Callum would have been the perfect example if he was still mute.... if he knew which side was the correct one." He paused again, "Anyway, do you know how we got the dropship?"

Minin shook his head again, lying since he already knew. "It's how I knew Mark Brockly was someone that shouldn't have been messed with. He's strong, extremely strong. He managed to break the restraints that were holding him in his seat in the dropship. He went on a rampage, killing anyone inside, Prisoners, guards, anyone, it didn't matter to him. The newspapers and any information you can find will tell you that the guards and pilots escaped, but it was a lie. He didn't want to come to the Island, once there wasn't anyone else in the dropship, he tried to take control, he might be strong but he can't take over a dropship, all the information the dropship needed to arrive on the island was already entered, there was nothing he could do to change it. He went on another rampage destroying the inside. The dropship landed inside the Tower in need of repair. It had been a long time since a dropship had landed inside the Tower, so my guards and I went to investigate. The tailgate dropped and standing there was Mark with bloody bodies lying around him, it looked like a warzone. I never thought it was possible to escape the restraints, so it would have been unwise not to take him in but I had to give him a kill chip, I had to make sure he could be controlled. It took six taser bullets to take him down, I've never seen anyone else last more than two and that's if they were on a rampage themselves. We had him on the table giving him his chip, he woke up mid-operation, started to attack my doctors. My guards laid another three bullets into him, finally giving him the chip. That many should have killed him." Daman paused for a moment, "Do you have a chip?" he asked. Minin turned around, revealing the scar from the taser-bullet, Daman looked at it, "hmm interesting, the chip is out," Daman thought for a moment. "How did that happen?" I knew I was having trouble with the chips, but it should have exploded when it got taken out. It's why I didn't kill those that rebelled that have them."

Minin turned around looking at Daman, interested as to what he meant. "Don't worry about it," He answered, knowing he had said too much. "I'll ask one of the eggheads when I see them," He opened his vest revealing he held a pistol.

Minin then thought, 'I couldn't have attacked him anyway, I couldn't see the weapon, he would have fired back if I missed.'

"Always must have a backup plan," Daman explained, then quickly changed to an annoyed voice. "Besides not everyone has a chip on themselves." He then calmed down again. "Have you had the plan explained to you?" Minin shook his head and began to worry that Daman might think he was stupid. "They don't tell you anything, do they? Must have been why those idiots attacked the dropship," He sounded once again annoyed. "The way it works, I give people the plan and they pass it on, then so on and so forth, till everyone gets it," He thought for a second, "Do me a favour, make sure you pass it on to the guards."

Minin nodded in agreeance, this was his chance to find out from the source what was happening. *'I'll tell everyone. It just won't be the people you want me to tell,'* He thought to himself.

"We're taking over," Daman declared. "Not this island, oh no, definitely not this island, I've already done that. Besides they're a bunch of criminals here, they'll stay where they belong. I'm talking about the mainland. I'm taking this ship and destroying the government that made me come here." Minin knew for an instant Daman was crazy, he knew that if he even tried, it would be suicide. "You're probably thinking that's suicide, aren't you? Minin nodded his head. "It's quite simple, all we need to do is fly the dropship to D.A.G.S. or Dropship Air Guidance Systems," Daman explained. Minin didn't know where that was, he had never heard of the place before. Daman continued, "It's where the commands for the automatic dropships are programmed on the mainland. Once we get there, we destroy it, making any automatic dropships useless. Since all defence mechanisms run automatically, they'll be scrambling to save themselves."

Minin didn't know how the plan would work, how it would even be possible for the drop ship to be able to destroy D.A.G.S quick enough so that none of the automatic dropships would be rendered useless. "After that, it's as simple as a few more attacks in certain places and they'll give up, giving me the power and they'll all pay for sending me here."

'If Daman does know how to make the automatic dropships useless, he can't have that kind of power,' Minin thought. He knew now it was more important than ever to take control of the dropship, not only to save his friends on the island but everyone else as well.

"In the meantime, I wish those savages would just give up Minin," Daman admitted frustrated. "I sent them such a strong message, destroying the girls camp, destroying his camp and instead of giving him up, they try to attack the Tower." He sighed, "It didn't have to be like this, it really didn't, one way or another I'll show them that he has to be given up."

Daman started looking around the cabin. They walk to the door for the cockpit, it was closed. Daman pressed the combination on the keypad, Minin made sure this time he took notice, 6-7-1-9-8-6, the door opened. Inside Hunter was sitting on a seat, a computer screen was in front of him, a model of the dropship was displayed, it was separated into sections, most areas were green while three were red, two at the front, one on the side.

"What are you doing here?" Daman questioned Hunter.

"My job of trying to get this up in the air, then your idiot goons attack, now I'm trying to work out what they've damaged, it would have only taken five minutes, but now it's taking me more," Hunter replied annoyed.

"You're not wrong about them being idiots. Do you know what's wrong with the controller?" Daman then showed him the kill chip controller.

Hunter examined it, to him it looked in perfect condition. "What do you mean, what's wrong with it?' He answered.

"It's not working properly, I can only track people with it, if it doesn't work then it's no use to me," Daman became frustrated. "If they think it's working, then they fear it. Fear makes them a slave, my slaves, but they just attacked the Tower, and I haven't used the Controller on anyone, they are going to think something is up with it. Get it fixed,"

"I have no idea what's wrong with it. I haven't gotten any information about the controller to work with," Hunter replied, knowing this wasn't going to make Daman pleased.

"Fine," Daman replied. Minin noticed the tone in which they were talking to each other, almost as if they were friends, maybe this was why Hunter didn't seem to have as much hatred towards Daman when he and Minin last met. "How much damage did the dropship take?" Daman asked, now being serious.

"It looks like it's just damage to the outside, nothing actually damaged that needs to work," Hunter responded. "But until I can test it for sure I just don't know if the computer is lying to me or not. If I had full access I could get it done quicker."

"Excellent," Daman said smiling again ignoring the request. "If they think the kill-chip controller is broken, we need something else. I think it's time to test the weapon," Daman said sternly.

"Where do you want me to aim?" Hunter asked worriedly.

"The farmers camp. I need your friends to back off and show them I mean business."

"You can shoot anywhere to show how powerful the weapon is, why the Farmers camp?" Hunter gulped, replying with fear in his voice, knowing what he meant.

"That's where the last sighting for Minin was. Now aim it," Daman commanded.

"You said, if I helped you they wouldn't get hurt," Hunter replied concerned. "That was the deal, besides I thought you didn't want Minin dead if possible."

"He won't be there, they're hiding him, besides our agreement didn't include them attacking my Tower. They attack, I destroy. Aim the damn weapon at them," Daman said frustrated and began to scream at him. "Stop hesitating and do it," Daman grabbed the pistol from his jacket and aimed it at his head, "Do it now."

Hunter knew he was in a difficult situation, he didn't want to use the weapons, but it was getting obvious he had no other choice, he didn't want to kill his friends. Hunter knew that it was Minin inside the

Guards uniform, not some random Guard that worked for Daman, he looked at Minin trying to get a sign of what he should do.

Minin looked back, he knew they didn't have a choice, even if Hunter didn't do as he was told, eventually, Daman would do it himself anyway. A tear-filled his eye. He nodded his head slightly, telling him to do it.

Hunter pressed a button on the screen, a video feed coming from a satellite, displayed on the screen, it showed the outside of the Tower, the video was live, it showed in perfect resolution anyone moving away from the Tower. It also showed released Prisoners with them.

"They're falling back, I don't have to do this to them," Hunter said, in one last attempt. "It looks like all they were doing was trying to rescue the prisoners."

"You don't have to, but you will. This isn't about punishment. This is about sending them a message. They're not going to mess with me if they know what kind of power I have, my peace will be restored."

"What about Minin?" Hunter asked trying to think of anything that might be an answer to stopping the attack.

"It'll also send the message. With this kind of power, it would be wise to give him up."

Minin heard everything and thought to himself, 'This isn't peace, its annihilation. They'll have no choice but to bow down, if he can kill so many in such a quick time, the kill chips will look like a water gun compared to what I think this thing can do. I'll give myself up, it'll save everyone.'

Hunter could see what Minin was thinking, he looked at him and shook his head, *Don't do it. They need you,* He tried to say.

Daman started to pull the trigger of his pistol, "I can replace you, you know that, fire the damn weapon."

Hunter closed his eyes, a tear came from one, he hated doing it, but had no choice. He couldn't give up Minin, if they had a chance of getting off the island, they needed Minin. He pressed a button on the computer, the roof above the dropship opened, revealing the outside.

Hunter pressed another button, opening a map of the island on the screen. Everything he was doing, felt as though it was in slow motion.

Daman pushed Hunter out of the seat he was in, "I'll do it," and pressed the Farmers area on the screen. A huge green light blast from out of the front of the ship, firing upwards into the sky.

Minin knew right then, that this was how Daman intended to destroy D.A.G.S.

Sparks then began flying out of a part of the console, followed by smoke. "What happened?" Daman demanded.

"Your goons must have hit the weapon from the outside. I told you, I didn't know for sure if the computer was telling me what was wrong," Hunter explained as the diagnostics screen of the dropship flashes another section red, exactly where the weapons had fired from.

Daman didn't listen, "Did it hit though?"

Hunter brought up another screen, pressed a few buttons, bringing up the satellite feed once more, displaying the Farmer's area. Everything looked as though it was the same, except for the outskirts which looked to be scorched, nothing could have survived.

"Guidance and aiming are off too, it's going to take time to fix it," Hunter announced with a bit of relief knowing what a direct hit could have done. "You wanted a warning shot, there you have it," he said sternly.

Daman was smiling over what he had just seen, "They at least know what I'm capable of, fix it quickly." He looked at Minin, "You can keep him company for a while, make sure he doesn't do anything funny," then walked off out of the cockpit leaving Minin and Hunter alone.

Once Daman was out of the cockpit, the door closed behind him. "How'd you do that?" Minin asked, thinking he deliberately set it off course.

"I didn't, I almost killed them." Hunter began to go pale with fear, knowing what had happened and being as lucky as he was that he didn't kill anyone, provided they weren't just outside of the Farmers camp.

Minin knew why he had gone pale, "Keep it together," He said to him strongly. "You need to find out how to control the ship, you need to find it now, we need to get out of here and when we do, fire at the Tower when he's inside."

"No," Hunter said bluntly, refusing to kill anyone else. "There are too many innocents inside, we'll leave the Island like the plan, he can rot here with anyone that doesn't want to come." He paused for a minute still thinking about what had happened, "You need to find out if anyone survived." He composed himself, knowing he couldn't break down and that everyone was relying on him to get control of the drop-ship. He then pulled up a video stream of the outside of the Tower where everyone had been fighting, it was empty. "You can't go that way now, they'll realise something is up if you go that way on your own. You're going to need to jump and escape again."

Minin hated that idea, he hated the drop the last time, he didn't want to do it, "Isn't there an alternative?"

"leave through the front, get killed, it's really your choice."

"Fine" Minin said, accepting his fate.

"I'll come with you, if anyone asks, I'll say you're accompanying me for some air.

"You don't think they'll get suspicious?"

"You're Daman's number one guard now, you're the golden child," Hunter replied as he got out of his seat and began to guide Minin to the same balcony which he left the Tower the previous time.

They arrived at the balcony and Minin looked over the edge, memories rushed back of when he was here last, "Are you sure about this?" He asked one last time.

"You better hurry," Hunter replied.

Minin lifted himself on the ledge and looked toward the horizon, a storm looking as though it was coming toward the Island, he closed his eyes, put his arms out and gently fell forward.

31

Minin landed in the water, just as he had done the previous time and began to float, once again drifting toward the waterfall. For the time being, he knew that the only thing to worry about was seeing anyone from the Tower. As he relaxed, he started to think about what he had seen, *'That weapon was crazy, and it's functional.'* Thoughts about who the weapon might have hit began to flood his head. The two he was most worried about were Hayley and Tiffany, *'I don't know where they were.'* He tried to calm himself down, *'They couldn't have been near the farmers camp, they were out fighting near the Tower.'* This was able to calm him for a moment until more thoughts began to flood his head, *'Did something happen to them during the raid or had they retreated before then and got hit by the weapon?'* He tried to breathe in and out slowly trying to calm himself, *'I know I'm being irrational. Everything is a 'what-if,' at the moment, I need to calm down.'* So he began to look around the river and look at the banks doing what he could to take his mind off it. *'I'll figure out a way to get from the river first, this time I'm not going to end up near-deadly falls.'* He then remembered the beach area. *'I'll swim towards the edge and keep myself there until I get near the beach.'*

Swimming toward the edge was easier this time, whether the flow of the water was weaker or the exhaustion from the fight from last time was making a difference, Minin didn't know and he didn't care, all he knew was that this time he stood a better chance of getting out on his own.

He kept looking around, 'The beach is going to be coming up soon. I hope it comes up soon.' He thought and began to worry that something might be wrong with this river. 'What if there wasn't a beach area and I hallucinated it last time?' With that thought, his breathing began to get stronger, he was worried. He then noticed movement from the river banks, he didn't know what or who was creating it, he bobbed down into the water just enough to keep his eyes and nose above and just looked at what was above him.

The answer came close to the river bank. A young boy and a young girl dressed in what looked to be the same type of clothes the Coasties wore. They looked similar, enough that Minin could tell they were related, they both had black hair, the girl's longer than the boys' with dark eyes. The boy was taller than the girl, they were both very slim and young enough that they would have only just gotten to the island recently. They kept looking over the river banks staring into it as though they were trying to look for something.

Minin didn't know what to make of them, he wasn't sure why there would be two Coasties walking along the river banks, he was told everyone was helping with the raid. He began to think, *This has to be a trick. Daman must have found out that I haven't been part of the raiding group and made it into the Tower and got a couple of guards to run down the river to find me, I need to stay low, they won't see me this way.*' The two-people walked slowly along the river bank, looking carefully over the water, they knew something was in there, all they needed to do was find it. Minin tried to lower his head to the lowest he could while still being able to breathe, *'My name isn't Wally, they're not going to find me,*' he hoped.

The boy nudged the girl and pointed to Minin. Minin knew he had been seen, "Hey" The boy called out. Minin didn't answer, still unsure if they were friends or not. "Hey," He called out again, still not receiving an answer. He called out again, "You're not dead, are you?"

The girl began to tie a rope around herself, picked up a thick stick from the ground and then dived in and began to swim toward Minin.

Minin continued to play dead, hoping that once she had examined him, she would leave quickly. She stayed close, she wasn't sure if he was alive or not, *'I have to know for sure,'* She thought and put her finger and thumb over his nose, her palm cupping his mouth, closing Minin's airway.

Minin tried holding his breath, eventually, it became too much and started to move and fight to try to breathe once more. "Tower scum," She shouted and began to swing the stick toward Minin's head, trying to knock him out.

As soon as she had said, 'Tower scum,' Minin realised he was still wearing the guard's uniform. They weren't enemy's in friendly clothes, he was a friend in the enemy's clothes. Minin began to do everything to could to take off the balaclava he was wearing while trying to avoid the stick. He got hit a couple of times in the process, the depth of the wetness and with Minin doing what he could to float, slowing the revealing process down significantly. The balaclava eventually slid off his face, showing who he was. The girl continued to swing the stick at Minin, she hadn't noticed who had been revealed, "Stop it," Minin yelled at her.

She stopped for a second and looked at Minin, realising who he was. "Sorry…sorry…sorry," She kept repeating over and over, knowing she had made a mistake. She looked at the boy on the bank waiting for her to return. "Grab onto me and we'll take you to shore."

Minin grabbed onto the woman, the boy then began to pull them to the edge, "It's going to be too heavy with two of you, one at a time," The boy called out.

Minin held onto the edge as the girl was pulled up, once she made it to the top, the rope was lowered once more, Minin then tied himself into it and was pulled onto dry land. Minin tried to catch his breath as the person that attacked him once again apologised, "Once again, I'm sorry, I really didn't realise it was you."

"It's fine," Minin assured her.

"Yeah, after that attack that hit the farmers land, we said we would take revenge on someone from the Tower," The girl explained.

"I saw the attack, it wasn't good, it was horrible seeing it from where I was," Minin replied. "You weren't at the raid?" He asked them, thinking it would have been almost impossible for them to make it to where they were if that had fought.

"Gin told some of us to stay back, I don't know why, I wanted to help but he said for us to just leave it,' The girl replied. "Once that weapon fired, we couldn't just stand back anymore, we had to do something."

"He told me that everyone was going to help, all the camps said the same thing," Minin told them, confused over why they didn't help either. "Who are you anyway?" He asked, trying to change the subject.

"I'm Emmitt and this is Emily" The boy explained.

"What happened up there," Emily asked.

"They've weaponised the dropship, I didn't know about it until I saw it for myself, long story short but the ship isn't ready to be taken yet. Daman has plans for the dropship as well, once he can use it," Minin explained. "I know it doesn't help, but the weapons are damaged and can't be used at the moment, but that will only be for a short time".

"So, we didn't get the ship?" Emily asked disappointed.

"No, it wasn't ready to be taken, there wasn't anything we could do," Minin replied. "Have you actually seen the damage it's done?"

"No, we only saw a huge green light come from the Tower and then a huge explosion when it landed. That was enough for us to know we had to do something," Emmitt said.

"I'm going to go see what it's done," Minin announced. "It's up to you if you want to come with me or not, but I have to see what happened for myself."

"Umm, we'll come," Emmitt said confused. "We didn't think anyone would head towards what had happened."

"As I said, you don't have to come," Minin said one more time as he began walking toward the damage.

Both Emmitt and Emily looked at each other for a second and nodded to each other. "We're coming with you," Emily called out.

Emily and Emmitt kept asking how the inside of the Tower was, it was obvious that neither one had been inside and they were curious.

Minin told them all he could, thinking after Gin had told Emily and Emmitt to stay back in camp and not help, Gin might have not been the best at telling anyone in his camp much information. Eventually, as they continued walking, Minin noticed that they were the only ones on the path, not that he expected it to be a bustling city but he did expect to see someone, whether they were from the Tower or an Islander would be another question.

All three arrived where the weapon had hit. It was completely black, burnt out, chard, no-one could have survived. The burnt-out area was a perfect circle, not a single char mark out of place. Everything inside the circle was burnt to a crisp, trees, rocks, grass, ground, all burnt but not a single shape that even looked like a body. Everything outside of the circle looked perfect as though nothing out of the ordinary had happened, still green and alive, behind, the Farmers camp was still in a perfect condition.

All three scanned the area trying to find signs of life from anyone that could have been caught up in the blast, there wasn't a single body anywhere. Even where the Farmers camp boundary where the weapon didn't hit was void of anyone.

"Did any of you hear how many?" Minin asked beginning to worry.

"How many what"? Emmitt replied.

"How many people did it hit? How many were killed?" Minin asked with a stressed voice.

"We don't know, honestly, we weren't anywhere near here or seen anyone that would have run away from it," Emily replied calmly.

"Honestly I don't think it would be that many people," Emmitt said, trying to be positive. "As far as we know everyone was at the Tower fighting when it all happened."

"They were all getting pushed back, some were already running away when this all happened," Minin said with a tear in his eyes, he was starting to think that everyone that was part of the raid may have met in the area and had been hit.

"Why are you so worried?" Emmitt asked, not understanding why Minin was so worried. "You saw from the tower where and when they hit, you must have known if there were people there or not."

"It didn't hit the same place as where it was aimed," Minin explained. "I didn't see the video feed of who or what got destroyed."

"The explosion we heard coming from the Tower was deafening. It was so loud that at first, we thought it was being destroyed, everyone else would have heard the same thing, surely they would have run to safety if they thought they were going to get hit by whatever was coming towards them," Emily suggested.

A feeling of relief came over Minin, he knew they would be right. He then thought about what they said, "It was deafening? I didn't hear anything from inside the dropship when it got fired."

"Wait, you didn't say you were inside the dropship when it got fired," Emmitt said with an instant suspicion as his voice changed to anger, "Did you fire the weapon on them?" His fist clenched, ready to attack.

"No," Minin said out flatly. "It was Daman, I was hidden in the guard's uniform but I did see it happen."

"So, you had a chance to stop it"? Emily said annoyed.

"If I stopped it, he would have known who I was, he would have killed Hunter as well, then he would have fired the weapon anyway," Minin said trying to justify his actions.

They both looked back at him and shook their heads, Emmitt looked him in the eye, "You better hope, no-one died," He warned in disgust, thinking Minin could have still stopped the weapon.

Silence fell over the three of them for minutes, they just kept staring at the burnt-out ground then at the farm. "Where are they?" Emily asked breaking the silence. "If that many people did get hit, there would have to be some sort of remains left behind, they couldn't have all been in this one area but there's nothing, it doesn't make any sense, they have to be somewhere else."

"Ok, so let's go into the camp then," Emmitt suggested. "They might be inside hiding."

Minin stood quietly thinking it over. "They haven't gone to any of the camps, they needed somewhere safer, with a weapon like that, something that can destroy a whole camp without leaving the tower, it doesn't matter which camp they go to, it's just going to target them."

"Then where have they gone"? Emily asked.

"Everywhere is exposed," Emmitt added.

"They've gone to the bunker," Minin announced.

"What's the Bunker?" Emmitt asked curiously.

"Yeah, we've never heard of this 'Bunker' before," Emily said backing his question, thinking Minin was making it up.

"How do you not know what it is?" Minin replied, surprised they didn't know what it was.

"We don't leave our camp much, only when we needed too," Emily answered. "Gin always told us it was too dangerous, too many people that wanted to do us harm outside the camp."

Emmitt continued, "Whenever someone came to the camp, we were told not to say much too them, keep to ourselves, we weren't meant to hide or anything but 'Be careful of any outsiders,' he'd tell us."

Minin felt a little confused, he only thought that the girls camp had a leader that tried to sway her people away from the other camps and not explore the island. He began to feel sorry for them since they had gotten to the island their world became so small. While Minin was in his camp he had the chance to explore the island as much as he wanted but chose not to. "The island was designed for Criminals. You're scared of what they could do to you? You know it's only ever low-level crimes, nothing too dangerous?" Minin was curious as to why they didn't just leave and explore anyway.

"Oh, we're not criminals," Emily said seriously.

"No-one ever is," Minin said with a smile, thinking she was joking.

"No, it's true," Emmitt replied. "We were kidnapped, we tried to do whatever we could to not end up here. We hated the stories that got told to us, everyone killing each other, you have to fight for survival. When we got to the Island, Gin told us that's exactly what happens on the island and being inside our camp was one of the only safe places there was and we were lucky to be there. He'd make sure only certain people left the camp, ones he determined were able to survive outside."

"We've had basic martial arts training, enough to hold our own, but he still wouldn't let us out of the camp," commented Emily. "If you ever wanted to leave the camp he'd punish you. After leaving the camp I'm starting to think the only dangerous place is the Tower and he just didn't want anyone to leave."

"There are still other dangerous places," Minin warned but not as bad as you think, if you are prepared, you'll survive." He paused, "Who kidnapped you?" He asked, changing the subject thinking what they were saying sounded peculiar.

"We don't know," Emily replied. "There were a few small news articles I read, saying this kind of thing was happening, that people were getting kidnapped then sent away to another island, but it wasn't the prisoner's island. If I had to take a guess I think it was all meant to be kept quiet."

"There's always been a theory about it. It's never been one hundred per cent confirmed, but everyone knows there is," Emmitt continued.

"When I first came to the island, I overheard the guards saying take me to island A, I didn't know for sure but after they said that, I always thought there was more than one island," Minin told them.

A cold breeze began to blow, Emmitt started to rub his body to try and get a bit warmer, "We should start walking to get to this Bunker."

Emily thought the same thing, "You're right, the sooner we get there, the sooner we can get warmer." They then began the walk toward the bunker. "What's this Bunker like?" She asked.

"It's pretty big, until a few weeks ago, I'd never been inside, there's definitely enough room in there for everyone to fit." Minin began to think what he had just said, he wasn't sure if his memories were clouded and he just thought the Bunker was big enough. "I hope."

"The Island is so much different to what I thought it would be," Emily said with a smile. "I've only seen this when we landed, I didn't realise how much we're missing."

"Once this is all over we're never staying trapped with Gin again," Emmitt announced.

"You can stay with our camp, I'm sure you'll always be welcome. Where ever that'll be," Minin said, knowing that everyone else wouldn't have a problem with it.

The Bunker was now in sight. The outside was quiet, void of people. Looking around it didn't seem as though anyone had ever travelled there, especially in the last few hours. "It can't be, they have to be here," Minin said shocked.

"Are you sure this is where they would go?" Emily asked thinking Minin must have gotten the location wrong.

"It has to be. That many people don't suddenly disappear, this is the only place that could take that many people."

"Maybe something did happen to them," Emmitt said thinking the worst. "That weapon did do some incredible damage."

"No," Minin said bluntly, "I refuse to believe that, they're somewhere." He looked at the direction of the Tower, he knew that was the only other place where a mass amount of people like that could vanish. He kept shaking his head knowing it couldn't possibly be the answer.

Emily began looking around the outside of the bunker, trying to see if she could find a sign telling them where everyone had gone. When she got to the door she put her ear against it, hoping to hear something or someone inside.

"You're not going to hear anything," Emmitt said. "There's no-one there," he continued, convinced they had gone to the wrong place.

Emily made a swishing motion with her hand toward him, trying to get him to be quiet, she heard a faint sound which she thought was talking but was unable to understand it. She kept her ear against the door, knowing what she might have heard was nothing. She could hear the same noise again, "Quick come here, there is something in here," She shouted to them both. Minin and Emmitt came running, "There's movement or at least someone talking inside."

"It's probably just a rat," Emmitt said thinking he had solved it.

"Rats don't talk," Emily replied, annoyed that he didn't believe her.

'I have seen a few gangster movies though,' Minin thought to himself smiling. He then looked at the left corner of the door, he saw a security camera, a red-light flashed above it "If there isn't anyone in here, we need to go now," He said, calmly but persuasive.

A creaking noise came from inside the door, it was being unlocked. Minin, Emmitt and Emily made fists, they were not sure if they should fight or shake hands with whoever was coming out of the door. They knew hiding was not an option, they had been seen. The door opened, two men with homemade guns, the same that the camps owned came out aiming at them. They said nothing, just aiming at the three. The three kept their fists clenched.

32

"It's all right," a voice came from behind the armed men. A voice that Minin knew well. Tiffany walked in front of the armed men, she turned to face them, "All right, you can go," she commanded. She then turned to Minin, walked up to him, hugged him, held it for a few seconds then let go. "You didn't bring the dropship?" She asked, knowing the answer.

"No, not yet," Minin replied, sounding slightly disappointed with his own answer, even though he knew it wasn't over yet, "I'll explain later."

"Either way, I'm so glad you're all right, you have no idea how worried I've been, that blast they did to the Farmers area was *his* way of telling us the raid was over." She then smiled and grabbed his hand, "Quick, I have to show you something," and pulled Minin inside. Emmitt and Emily followed quickly and the door was shut behind them with a final metal sounding bang, the creaking noise followed as the door was locked. They kept running further down the Main tunnel, the only thing providing light now was the occasional light on the roof that was still working. They both got to the end of the hall and arrive at another blast door with a light above it. The door looked like a smaller version of the outside door and once again was locked, Minin could hear people inside, lots of people. Tiffany just banged on the door. The door unlocked and opened, revealing a huge room. "We just discovered that there was another blast door near the main area," Tiffany explained.

The people inside the room became quiet and stared at Minin, he wasn't sure whether they were happy to see him or wished to kill him after what had happened, he let go of Tiffany's hand and stared back at them, not knowing what to say. They continued to stare back.

"Common, let's keep going," Tiffany said and grabbed Minin's hand once more and began to rush down another tunnel. "I didn't think this place would be big enough to hold everyone," She told him. They arrived at a T-intersection, they then went left, to a room with another closed door. Tiffany knocked on the door, "This place has everything," She announced happily. The door opened, Hayley, wearing a white lab coat, answered the door, "Look who I found," Tiffany told her, moving out of the way revealing Minin.

Hayley still had a slight look of sadness on her face, until she saw Minin and she lit up, running over and hugging him harder than she had ever done before, Minin returned the favour, they both felt as though they did not want to let go.

"Hey Doc," a voice from inside the room called, "You want to finish up with lover-boy and help us, you'll have plenty of time to hold each other once this is done."

Hayley let go, Minin did the same, she turned back into the room, "It's a few seconds' worth of work, I liked you a lot better when you were mute," She said annoyed.

Minin walked into the room, sitting on a bed was Callum, beaten, bruised, with a scar over his cheek. "Welcome to Medical," He said to Minin with a smile.

Hearing his voice still threw Minin off, even though he was the first of his camp to hear him, it was still something he didn't believe.

"I still can't believe you can talk," Minin said not knowing what else to say.

"Well it's true, Now I can talk all I want since these lovely ladies were able to save me," Callum replied winking towards Tiffany, "Don't have to beat any more pots and pans to get your attention"

"I'll beat you with a pot and pan," Tiffany said smiling back sarcastically.

"Guess some people aren't fans of my type," Callum said, shrugging his shoulders.

"Some people really aren't fans of your type," Tiffany said still smiling.

Hayley cut them both off, "What happened to you, why don't you have the dropship?

Minin then began to recap what had happened. "I got in…. I met Hunter…. He's disabled the kill-chips…. There was a fight…. I almost got revealed by Daman…. he launched the Weapon," He told them in great detail. Everyone else in the room listened, taking everything they had heard in.

"So, we can still get the dropship?" Tiffany asked.

"Eventually yes but we need to wait. How long that is, I don't know but the longer it takes, the more the Tower will realise we are here," Minin conceded.

"And the Kill-chips don't work?" Hayley asked with a smile, needing one last confirmation.

"They're still active but the controller doesn't, so you don't have to worry about it," Minin told her with a smile. "What Happened when he launched the Weapon? What happened on the ground? Why did everyone end up here, how did everyone rush here so quickly?" Minin asked, wanting to know what had happened to them in the meantime.

Hayley's eyes went blank like she had seen a ghost. Tiffany spoke for her, "She saw it all when the Weapon hit, she was waiting outside of the Farmers camp. I hadn't made it back to camp by this time, I was on my way, I saw a huge green light fly right over me, I knew it wasn't something normal, then I heard this huge bang-crash of noise, everyone around me rushed to where the noise had come from. We got there and there was just…." She paused, she started to look the same as Hayley but was able to continue, "Everything was burnt out, destroyed, everyone looked at it, then looked at the Tower, not knowing what had happened, they didn't want to take any chance and everyone just started running. I just screamed out, "Go to the bunker, go to the bunker." Those that heard me started running in that direction, everyone else must have started to follow them, that's when I looked up and saw Hayley just looking at what had been hit. She was in shock, I don't blame her, I grabbed her and ran to the Bunker with everyone else. It was open, everyone was just rushing in, once the rush of people died, they closed and locked the doors behind everyone. I took Hayley straight to the medical room, sitting on the beds were Stephanie and Callum. Someone must have put them here, hoping they'd get checked out. Once Hayley saw Callum, she snapped out of whatever it was."

"I've been checking on every one since then, Callum had the most problems, nothing life-threatening just needed stitches, so I've been taking my time with him," Hayley said still smiling. "I'm not a hundred per cent but I'm better than I was."

"I can see that," Minin said happy for her. He thought for a second, then turned his direction to Callum, "I need to know what happened to you."

"What do you mean?" Callum replied not knowing what he was on about.

"Everything, why you can't talk, what happened to you in the Tower, why you know so much. I just need to know," Minin said, taking a huge breath after.

"Where do you want me to begin?"

"How'd you get to the Island?" Hayley asked before anyone else has a chance to answer.

Callum took a deep breath then began to speak, "My name isn't Callum, It's Charlie Pallum, I won't have a problem if you keep calling me Callum since you're so used to it. Anyway, before I got to the Island I was a journalist working for Roaming World News. Usually, I wrote small stories, happy things about dogs and cats getting new owners after being impounded for months, it was nice stuff but I wanted, 'THE,' news story, one that would put me on the map, make people know I was a real journalist. One day I had a package delivered to me, it contained all this classified information about the Island. It said that the Government had no control of the island, Prisoners were just dropped out of the dropship instead of being processed, some of those weren't even given a chance and their parachutes wouldn't even open, stuff that would have horrified everyone, stuff that should have made the Island shutdown. At first, I thought it was fake but as I looked into it, more information looked to be authentic. I went to my editor and asked him if I could run the story, he agreed, said it shouldn't be hidden from anyone. The next day I was arrested, charged with having the property of the government and that it was treasonable material. Normally that would mean that you'd have a death sentence placed upon you but the judge said it would be much more fitting that I should be sent to the Island. That's how I ended up here."

"Wow," Hayley said, not expecting to hear what Callum had said.

Everyone else was silent, no-one else knew what to say it was so much to take in.

"What else do you want to know?" Callum asked.

Everyone was thrown back that Callum wanted to be asked more questions, anytime anyone else said about their past life, it affected them, not to the point of completely shutting down but enough that they were brought down a little. Callum was completely different, he wanted to be asked more.

"Umm, why couldn't you talk until now," Tiffany asked.

"I like a girl that asks the next logical question to the story," Callum said with a cheeky smile. Tiffany just sighed but remained quiet. "Anyway, after I was sentenced I wasn't placed in a jail cell to wait to go onto the Island like the rest of you. I was taken to some sort of research facility, two men in white lab coats came into the room, they tied me down to a bench. "What are you going to do to me?" I asked them. "You're never going to speak out again," They told me as they connected these things that looked like heart rate monitors to my temple, I didn't know what they were. If this was a part of the conspiracy, it wasn't in the information I had. They pressed a button," Tears came from Callum's eyes, he was beginning to feel affected as he told the story. "I don't know what it was, I think it was the electricity they sent to my head but I started to have a fit, the weird thing was I knew I was having it, it lasted a couple of minutes, then they stopped. "How are you feeling," One of the lab coats asked me with a smile. I tried to tell him I hated it but nothing came out. They both started to laugh at me. I was taken off the bench and dragged immediately to a waiting dropship. It was smaller than a normal dropship, only had four seats. I was placed in my seat and strapped in but I was the only one on this dropship. I was taken to the Island and dropped, It was at night. I thought I was going to be dropped without the parachute opening, but it did luckily. I landed somewhere between our camp and the lake. I didn't know what to do, I was on my own. I just started walking towards our camp, if I had gone the other way I probably would have ended up being part of the Lake camp. I eventually made it to our camp, that's when Hayley and Hunter found me."

"And you've been one of us ever since," Hayley said proudly, hugging him.

Callum looked at Minin and smiled, "Your question is going to be, what happened to me in the Tower?"

"No"

"No?" Callum asked confused.

"How do you know how to enter the Tower without getting caught, even before we both went?" He asked. "Why did you have information on everyone in your hut? I don't think that would have been part of the information that was posted to you."

"It wasn't," Callum said shaking his head. "Our camp lets us travel and leave and come back whenever we want. I used that opportunity to explore the Island. The first time I got into the Tower was by accident, I found the same pipe we entered into when we were caught and decided to follow it down, got to the end and had a look around, it was empty. I knew I should have left, but I wanted to keep looking. I knew it was the Tower instantly when I first got inside, I just knew it. I got onto an elevator and went up a floor, there's an abandoned office, it was covered in dust, I knew no-one had been there in a long, long time. There was a computer, I turned it on. I didn't know what I would find, for some strange reason it was unlocked, it contained everything about the Island, and I mean everything, All the prisoner's information and anything you can think of about the Tower. Unless they have the right login I don't think they have full access, no matter what they believe. They've got access to the Prisoner files and bits and pieces but not full control, probably explains why they can't control the dropship yet. Since I had full access I created my own login." Callum looked around, on top of the desk was a pen and a stack of junk paper, "Hand me the pen and paper over there." He asked.

Hayley went to the desk, "Why didn't you tell us this?" She asked as she handed him the paper and pen.

Callum began to write on the paper, "I was mute. If I had to say we were being raided by the Tower I'd have to hit pots and pans together sometimes, trying to explain I found a secret computer that contained all the information anyone could ever want about the Island, probably would have sounded crazy the first time I found it."

Minin then spoke, "You're probably right, but what about later on?"

Callum looked around unsure, "Honestly, I didn't think about it, maybe it was my secret that I wanted for myself?" He shrugged his shoulders, "I don't know."

"Wait a second," Tiffany interrupted. "What if Daman or someone from the Tower found out about the computer?"

"Don't worry, I already thought about that, I made sure it was locked down when I left. But it wouldn't surprise me if all the computers inside were linked up to the same server, they all just needed to be locked down. I just don't think anyone in the Tower has been able to get in."

"Hunters in the process," Minin replied. "But as you said, it's pretty locked down."

"If anyone can get in, it's Hunter," Callum said. "I'm just glad it's him not anyone else, I have no doubt anyone else would talk as soon as they are done. It's not going to matter once we have the dropship anyway." He handed Minin the piece of paper, "If Hunter can't do it then this will let him."

Minin looked at the piece of paper, on it was written U- 8246831 P-4876877. He placed it in his pocket, "I don't even know how we would even get it to him." He said.

Callum paused for a moment, "Knowing this information is why Daman wanted to torcher me. He knows I know about the island, he wanted to know how I know everything. His goons hooked me up to whatever they could to get me to say what I knew, they'd whip me, beat me. Since I was mute, it made it impossible to say anything, then they decided to electrocute me. They hooked my temple up to a defibrillator and got it to start, once they did, I was able to speak again, making their job a lot easier and mine a lot harder. I did everything I could to keep quiet, eventually, they sent me to the cell where I met Minin and Stephanie. Once Minin had been taken to fight Mark, they took me again, each day doing the same thing over and over, hoping I would talk. I decided to tell them the information that I was given, hoping they would believe that's all I knew but I made sure not to tell him about the computers, or give him anything else that could be useful. That just kept happening until they wanted to know about a raid on the Tower that was going to happen, that was one thing I was honest about not knowing."

"At least we know Gin kept his part of the deal," Minin said. "I'm sorry that they did that to you."

"It doesn't matter, they were doing it regardless, they just had another reason, either way, I'm out and we're making a difference to everyone," Callum replied.

"What do we do now?" Hayley asked. "If we raid against the Tower again, he'll fire another 'warning shot' at everyone, we lost our chance," Hayley said, her voice sounding frustrated while being realistic. "He's going to be looking at the ground, at the sky, at the pipe. We can't go under, over or through."

Minin didn't know what to say, his mind was locked to the idea that all he needed to do was wait for the signal and that would be it, knowing that every way to the Tower was being monitored just made it impossible.

"There's always a chance," Callum said to everyone smiling, "I know one other way into the Tower and It's connected to the Bunker."

"Wait...What?" Minin said surprised, not expecting anyone to have an answer.

"There is a problem though. If he or anyone else knows about it, he's going to send guards down here. That's if or when he finds out everyone is here," Callum sighed, knowing it was not the best answer.

"What if he doesn't know about it?" Tiffany said, trying to focus on the positives from his reveal. "Where is it?"

"The door that's connected to the inside of the Tower has an alarm to it, so anytime I've been in the Tower I've never used that door. When that alarm goes off, it's not going to be a situation of 'take your time' making sure you don't get caught. It's a run like hell till you get to the dropship and hope you haven't been caught until then," Callum said seriously. "Honestly, it's too dangerous."

"We're doing it," Hayley announced without hesitation. Callum and Minin looked at her. They expected she would think about the consequences, this time she just announced they would do it. "We're getting that dropship, we're getting off this Island."

"You're getting us caught," Callum said seriously, "I told you the dangers, you've seen the weapons he has, he'll start firing at the Bunker if he needs too. As much as the Bunker is a safe space, I don't think it will be a match against the weapon."

Hayley then replied, "I need to get away from him, to start a new." Her voice had the passion that had been missing for weeks.

"I told you what happened to me in the tower, that'll happen to you too," Callum said, still trying to warn her."

"You don't have to help, I can't be truly sympathetic to what happened to you, cause I don't know how it feels, but we're taking the ship, stay here if you want, I don't care," Hayley replied, her attitude not waining.

"Is that what you honestly think? That I don't want to come?" Callum replied.

"You've been trying to make it clear that you didn't want to go back to the Tower again," Minin replied, trying to be sympathetic to both sides.

Callum stopped for a second, he closed his eyes and took a deep breath, "I didn't say that. I've only been trying to warn you, you only got a minor piece of what went down in the Tower. I'm coming with you to see the end," He said, trying to rectify what he meant before.

Hayley then spoke up, "I'm not waiting any longer, I'm taking that dropship now. We have a way of controlling the ship and I'm using it."

"We can't yet," Minin said trying to remind her, "We have to wait till we get the dropship signal from Hunter, I'm not going back and having to return again, it's just not happening. Even with the piece of paper, he's not going to be expecting us. I'm not going to sit in the dropship waiting for Hunter to work out how everything works, while all hell rains on us from the outside."

"Fine," She conceded and took a seat in a corner.

"This is crap, I hate having to sit around," Tiffany said wanting to go, she then began to think. "Why don't we make a plan on how we are going to do it," Tiffany said, hoping this would bring people on the same page and not begin to fight.

"Every plan we've had so far has had to change. No more plans," Hayley declared.

"We need something, how many of us are going?" Tiffany said again, trying to make Hayley think her way.

"The smaller the better," Minin replied. "Just enough to get to the Dropship, take it and run, if there is a bigger group it'll probably just slow us down."

"Let's work out the team then," Tiffany said with a smile. "We also need a way of telling Hunter about the piece of paper, how do we do that?"

"I don't want anyone else to know unless they are on the team," Hayley suggested. "We've failed so many times, each time we fail, it brings us down more," She said. *'Or at least it does for me,'* She thought.

There was a banging noise on the door, Tiffany went to open it. Minin could not see who was on the other side but could hear what the announcement was. "You guys have to come and see this. It's another dropship," The messenger explained.

33

——

"He can't be ready, I was expecting weeks," Minin thought. "There is no way could Hunter be sending one now, I know he is good at what he does, but not this good," Minin announced, thinking this was too good to be true. Everyone left the medical centre and rushed through the bunker, most people had already left to go outside, anyone that was still inside was making their way to the top to see what was going on. They all arrived outside, floating above the Bunker was another dropship, it looked exactly like the one that had dropped off supplies to the Farmers camp. A siren sounded from the dropship as the tailgate began to open. People began to fall from the back, more people than a normal drop, none were sitting on a chair, their parachute's all strapped to their backs.

Minin counted the people as they dropped ".... eighteen, nineteen, twenty." Each one got to a certain height and their parachute opened.

"That's never happened before," Callum said confused, "It should be a lottery."

"They're just going to make it to the island and we're going to take them away from it," Minin said, knowing this was a bad time for anyone to be arriving on the island.

"That's not the problem right now," Callum informed him. "If Daman does know about all the dropships coming to the island, he'll know about this one. If he didn't know about anyone in the Bunker, he can see where the dropship is dropping everyone." He paused for a moment, thinking about that consequence, his eyes widened in horror. "The damn ship just revealed our location."

"We go now!" Tiffany shouted.

Hayley looked at her bewildered. She began to think Tiffany was trying to take her spot as leader. She was the leader, she didn't want someone else taking that from her, "What?" She asked annoyed.

"We go now to the Tower. We end it now, with or without Hunter being ready, we go now," Tiffany replied not knowing that Hayley was annoyed with her.

"And what if you're wrong and it's the wrong time and we all get killed for it? You need to make the best decision for everyone," Hayley replied, trying to pull back control.

Callum and Minin looked at each other, they knew that this was the completely wrong time for a fight between them both. "You two shut up, this isn't the right time. You can have your little catfight after. We need to do something now," Minin shouted at them, trying to get then to snap out of it. Hayley glared at him disgusted, thinking he was taking Tiffany's side. Tiffany looked at him confused wondering what she had said. "Hunter said he'll send a dropship to the bunker when he was ready, I don't think he's this quick at fixing it, but we don't have a choice, besides we have the user name and password," he said. He then turned to Hayley, "You might not like it, but this is the best plan we have right now, you wanted to go and get the dropship before, now you've changed your mind hoping it's for the best for us?" He paused, hoping what he was thinking wouldn't come out of his mouth but it did, "Our camp never officially had a leader, it was all of us." He paused again looking shocked, he knew what that role meant to Hayley.

Hayley looked at him with a look that could kill. She was furious, angry that she had been put in her spot. She was also angry that she knew deep down that this was the truth, "Fine," She said with a slow deep breath, trying to remain calm. "What do you think we should do then?" She continued angrily but quiet enough that she wasn't screaming.

Callum then spoke up, "We're going to the Tower now, we're grabbing who we said was coming and going to the Tower." He then began walking back into the Bunker.

Hayley just stood there in shock, there was a slight tear in her eye that she quickly got rid of and composed herself. Tiffany grabbed her arm, smiling, hoping the situation was defused for at least the time being and followed Callum.

Minin followed them swiftly, "Who do we get? You know about everyone that comes to the island," He asked Callum.

"There's already four of us, it's our camp, we go together," He announced. "Go find Emily and Emmitt, they might be naive about the island but they can handle themselves. Get Lukas, he's good with weapons. Also both Screamer and Simone, they will do what we need of them without question, that's the kind of thing we need right now and as much as she had annoyed me in the Tower.... Stephanie, I promised her I'd make sure she was away from Daman as quickly as possible."

"You really know about people on the island, don't you?" Tiffany asked.

"I probably know more about the island than anyone, including Daman," he replied proudly. "I just never had a chance to use it, probably why he wanted all the information from me and wanted it for himself."

"Anything else we need to know before we go?" Minin asked.

"There's a small supply of weapons on the second level, we might be able to use those."

"What about the Tunnel, where is that?" Hayley asked, knowing it wasn't the time to be angry now and just listen to the commands from someone else.

"Next to the medical room," He said with a smile. "If the Tower broke into the Bunker via that tunnel we would have known it."

"Ok, Minin you go get..." Hayley called out. She then stopped knowing she was just about to take over again.

Everyone stopped and looked at her. They all smiled, knowing what she had done was a natural reaction, Tiffany went to her and hugged her. "It's ok, we are all the leader," She said with a smile, "Callum just had his turn and now it's yours."

Hayley smiled in return, having this chance to be the leader made her feel like herself, her energy returning. "Minin you go get Emily and Emmitt, Callum you get Lukas and Simone, Tiffany you get Stephanie and Screamer."

Tiffany cut her off, "…. And you get the guns." She smiled, "now I've had my turn."

"Fine…" Hayley said, gritting her teeth with a smile, knowing she was joking.

They all ran off to where they needed to go, except for Minin who was trying to think where Emily and Emmitt might be. His mind was blank, he knew he couldn't just stand around, he was beside the common room, and went inside. The last time he was in here, it was flooded with people, it now contained five, all of whom weren't either one he was after, "Has anyone seen Emily or Emmitt?" He asked.

They all looked at him with blank stares except for one, an older man with grey hair, dark eyes, wrinkles underneath, he looked as though he should have been too old to be on the island, even if he had arrived with one of the first dropships, he was also someone who Minin had never recognised before. "They're not here, they went outside to see what all the commotion was about."

"All right, thanks," Minin said and began to make his way back to the entrance. He wanted to ask who the man was and why he looked as though he shouldn't have been old enough to be on the Island but knew he couldn't waste time.

Minin walked up the Tunnel toward the entrance, as he did Emily and Emmitt were making their way inside walking toward Minin. "I thought you would have been outside finding out what was going on," Emmitt said.

"Yeah, I was," he paused. "Something else came up, we need your help, you need to come with me."

Emily smiled, "Ok, we'll do it." She said speaking for them both. They then followed Minin toward the Medical room. "What are we doing?" she asked, not sure what was going on.

"You're helping us get the Dropship back," Minin announced.

Minin, Emily and Emmitt arrived at the Medical room first and waited till everyone arrived. The wait was short as Hayley then arrived with four guns, only what she could hold. They were not the same type of homemade guns that had been inside the camps but rather the same type the police had when they arrested Minin before he arrived on the island, the very same that could be loaded with Taser-bullets. Not long after Callum arrived with Lukas and Simone, finally Tiffany with Stephanie and Screamer.

"Follow me and I'll show everyone where we need to go," Callum announced. Everyone exited the medical room and turned left, then took a short walk down to the end of the corridor, standing in front of them was a brick wall without a door.

"Where's this door?" Tiffany asked Callum, thinking he had taken them to the wrong place. "If Hunter did send the dropship, I don't think he wants to wait around any more."

"Right here," Callum replied pointing to a wall.

"Umm, there's nothing there," Minin pointed out.

"Wait…you can't see the door?" Callum asked sarcastically with a smile, trying to make the others think he was hallucinating. He walked over to the wall, felt the edge and began to slide the wall to the left, revealing the door. "One time I was down here on my own, I put that there, just in case someone from the Tower found out about the entrance, I'd hope they'd be dumb enough not to try to touch it and think it was sealed over."

Minin smiled, "Well it worked for me."

Callum grabbed the handle of the door and began to move it, it barely budged as though it had not been used for years. Callum continued to struggle, Minin joined him, grabbing another part of the handle, and used his weight to push down. The handle began to move more freely but was still a struggle even with the two of them. Eventually, the door handle could move enough so that only Callum was able to move it himself. He opened the door, inside was dark, damp, all anyone could see was a naturally made tunnel and that it was clear that it had barely been touched. "Ok guys, this is it," he announced. "By any chance, you didn't happen to bring any torches or anything with you when you got the guns?" Callum asked Hayley, remembering he didn't ask her.

"No, I didn't think about it," Hayley replied. "But there were some in the medical centre, not enough that everyone could have one, maybe one per two people, I'll go get them." she then walked off in the direction of the medical centre.

"Leave one for the people in the Bunker, they might need one," Tiffany called out.

Hayley sighed, she still wasn't over the fight from last time, still not liking that she wasn't the leader of the camp like she thought, she left, remaining silent, knowing it might cause a bust-up.

Minin walked over to Tiffany, "You need to stop taking over in an instant."

"I know I do, that's the worst part, but I can't help it. I've always had to take charge, ever since I began modelling. If the photographer couldn't come up with an idea or something I would make it up and tell them what I wanted," She explained. "Taking charge is just a natural instinct for me."

"But you're going to try?" Minin asked. "Hayley needs to get used to it as well. You obviously realised it a while ago, she hasn't, it's going to take time for her."

Tiffany smiled, "I'm going to try, but you can't expect either one of us to just change right away. But I will try."

Minin returned the smile, "That's all I ask."

Hayley returned with 4 torches, "I left one for everyone else," She announced.

"I'm sorry, I should have let you make that decision," Tiffany said, trying to make it up to her.

Hayley just looked at her, she didn't know whether to be annoyed by the comment or be happy that she was realising she was trying to take over.

"I'll go in last so I can lock the door," Callum announced to everyone, holding the door.

Minin was first to go through as he was the closest, "Good luck, see you on the other side," He said as he walked through.

"Same to you," Callum replied.

Everyone walked through one after another, till eventually, Callum entered, closing the door behind himself.

The tunnel was incredibly dark that no one could see anything in front of them, the only clue that anyone was close was the sound of everyone else's breathing. The walls began to glow a green colour, showing how long the Tunnel would be. "It's the glow worms, it's amazing how many of them there are," Callum explained. Hayley turned her torch on first, the light from the glow-worms disappeared. Anyone else with a torch began turning theirs on as well.

"Let's get going," Callum announce, "I don't remember exactly how long the Tunnel is."

They all began to walk down the Tunnel, not a single word was spoken, everyone amazed that there was a tunnel that went under the Island and no-one knew about it. They all looked along the perfect created tunnel, wondering how long it had been there and why exactly it was between the two buildings.

Minin looked intensely at one part, he saw something move. It looked as though they were eyes looking at the group as they were making their way through, judging them with every step. Minin shined the torch at the eyes, they belonged to a rat. "Did anyone see that rat?" He asked thinking it might have been his imagination.

"I didn't think the Island had rats," Tiffany replied.

"Neither did I," Hayley said backing her up. "I've been here for so long and have never seen one."

"They were all exterminated when the government took over the island," Callum explained. "The survivors must have gone underground."

Everyone continued walking in silence, Minin began to think that it was taking too long, "This tunnel seems to be taking forever to get through. Would it have taken this long to get to the Tower if we had gone on the surface?" He asked Callum.

"This is definitely the right way," Callum answered. "I have no doubt about it."

"Probably just feels longer since we can't see the end," Tiffany suggested.

Everyone kept walking further along, "What's that?" Screamer asked, pointing in front of them.

"I can't see anything," Minin answered, thinking he was hallucinating.

"No, turn your light off, you'll see it," Screamer instructed.

Everyone did as he said and turned their lights off. In front of them was a faint light, the type you could only see if there wasn't any light pollution to overpower it.

"It's the light at the end of the Tunnel," Callum announced. "I hope this doesn't mean we're dead," He continued, trying to make a joke.

Emmitt and Emily gave a light laugh, the rest didn't know how to take what was said, except for Minin who joked back, "Doesn't sound like a train coming either." He then began to laugh. He quickly composed himself, "It's got to be the door."

Everyone turned their torches back on and ran towards the end of the tunnel, as they got closer to the door, the brightness was clear even with the light from the torches. They arrived at the end, but it wasn't a door but rather a wall with cracks where the light was able to shine through.

Callum arrived then felt around the border, hoping that it was fake just like the inside of the Bunker. "It must have been boarded up at some point, we have to open it."

"How do we do that?" Hayley asked. "I brought a few pistols and a couple of lights, not sledge-hammers. The pistols and lights aren't designed to destroy brick."

"They're better than nothing," Tiffany said and began to fire at the wall, once again taking charge. A few more cracks began to appear but not enough to break the wall.

Everyone except Callum grabbed her. Minin took the gun away as Hayley tackled her to the ground, "You're going to get us killed, what if someone heard it?" Minin said annoyed.

Hayley looked at her directly in the face. "You need to think, don't just take charge all the time," she said forcefully, her hands shaking in anger.

Tiffany looked at her surprised then realised that she had made a mistake. "I'm sorry," she said disappointed at herself. "I just didn't know what to do. We needed to do something."

Callum kept looking at the door, he had his gun raised waiting for someone to come near but everything was quiet. "The coast is clear, no one is coming," he informed.

Minin began to inspect the wall with Callum, he noticed the hole made from the gunfire was big enough for his hand to fit. He looked in and was unable to see anyone on the other side, He put his hand through the hole and reached around and felt a handle, he pressed down, it made a clicking sound and the wall began to move toward them slightly. "It's a door," Minin announced. He pulled the door more, enough to be able to walk through. Minin walked through first, he knew exactly where he was, the bottom of the Elevator shaft, only this time he was looking at the pipe he had come through last time.

"Where are we?" Lukas asked.

"Not where I thought we would be," Callum announced. Memories began to flood his mind of what happened the last time he was here. "We're in the Elevator shaft, where I and Minin got caught last time."

Minin felt overwhelmed as well. All he could think was that it felt like Deja Vu, and any minute guards were going to make themselves noticed and the plan would be over, no doubt that Daman would be with them this time. He waited, not a single guard made their way out. The shaft was eerily quiet without guards appearing, commanding everyone to give themselves up. Minin looked around the room trying to locate the Elevators, only one was down on their level, the one that Minin and Callum didn't use the last time. Where the other elevator was would be anyone's guess. Everyone except Callum and Minin was staring up at the shaft looking into its eventual darkness.

"How high do you think it goes up, how high is this Tower?" asked Hayley.

"If I had to take a guess, all the way to the top, maybe even the roof" replied Minin, who was still nervous over the thoughts about the last time he was here. "You don't know do you?" He asked Callum.

"One hundred and forty – two stories. As for how high the Elevator goes, I have no idea, I've never been on all the floors, I barely used it and only if I knew I was going to a safe floor," Callum replied.

Tiffany, who was still looking at the darkness then asked. "Where do we go from here?"

Callum answered, "Don't know, it wasn't much of a plan to get here, we're pretty much doing this as we go, all I know is that the Dropship isn't at the top and not the bottom. There's that room with the computer, it's only a floor above us, a couple of floors above that is the Cells. You have Daman's office, maybe a few levels below the roof. Somewhere in the middle is the Guards quarters. You know, I never really studied the layout of the Tower," he sniggered to himself, "You'd think I would have memorised that, wouldn't you?"

Minin had another idea, he started to think back to when he had glided and landed on the floor with the Dropship, he pictured the Tower in his head moving towards it, there was about a quarter to go till the roof. "We need to go about three-quarters of the way up," He announced.

"I don't like this," Hayley said annoyed. "I don't like taking guesses. I like to know what my next move is, I need to have some sort of control."

"We all need to control something in our lives," Tiffany said, agreeing with her. "But at the moment, the only thing we can control is what's right in front of us, going up about three quarters is the best guess we have unless someone else can think of anything different."

"None of us even knew there was a dropship in here," Stephanie said in a voice that sounded as though she was still unsure, "What do we have to lose?" She continued trying to agree with the plan.

"Everything, if we get caught," Emmitt replied, also not sure about the plan.

Tiffany walked onto the elevator, Callum followed her, the rest were weary to follow, having their doubts about the plan, but eventually, one after another followed. Minin was last to get on, there was just enough room for them all to fit.

Hayley was standing at the control panel with Callum, she looked at it. "Which one do I press?" She asked.

"Like I said it's a guess," Callum replied. Hayley thought for a brief moment then pressed a button. It made a beeping sound and a red-light flashed.

"You're rushing it a bit don't you think, aren't you the one that usually thinks about it?" Tiffany said.

She shook her head, "I'm trying something different. At the moment, the only thing we can control is what's right in front of us," She replied smiling at Tiffany.

Tiffany smiled in return, "Ok let's get to the floor."

Hayley pressed another button, once again the control panel beeped and flashed red, she looked at the control panel confused as to why it wasn't working.

"Why isn't it working?" Callum asked her.

"I don't know. The control panel has all these buttons with numbers, I figured it meant they were floors." Hayley answered.

"That's what I thought it meant too," Callum replied.

"Maybe it's got a password?" Tiffany guessed.

Minin stood there thinking, trying to figure out what was happening. He began to remember what had happened the last time he was on the Elevator. "They dragged us onto the elevator, pulled and closed the gates, pressed the button and we went up," He thought out loud.

Simone looked around as Minin spoke, figuring out the missing part, "This elevator doesn't have a gate."

"It's got to be some sort a failsafe," Hayley said and began to look at the console again trying to figure out how to get the gates to lift and close.

"She's right," Callum agreed. "If the gates don't close, it must not run."

"There's no button here to lift the gate," Hayley shouted out.

Everyone began to check the side to see if it had fallen off, Minin then saw a slot on the floor, big enough for something to slide out of, just inside was a rounded piece of metal. "That must be it, it's got to be broken or something." He put his hand inside and tried to lift, but wasn't strong enough and was unable to get enough of a grip. Callum and Tiffany help and lift the rounded piece of metal, which revealed the gate. They lift till they heard a clicking noise and let go, the gate stayed in place. "Ok, hit the button again," Minin called out.

Hayley pressed the same button as before, the console beeped, the red-light turned off and the elevator began to rise. "The gate must be broken that's why it's down here, they must have left it, till they can fix it,"

"I don't think they were going to fix it," Minin replied.

"It was down here last time" Callum added.

"They've probably got more important things to fix at the moment and while they still have another elevator they're not going to fix it," Minin said.

The Elevator continued to rise until it was encased in darkness, the only thing that could be seen was the console radiating with light and anything that light radiated onto. Everyone was silent waiting for the elevator to finish its journey. The elevator stopped, the console made another beep and a door opened, the gate stayed in the spot. It showed a stone hallway.

Callum looked at the hallway that had been revealed, he knew exactly where it lead, the torcher rooms. Memories about what had happened at the end of the hallway flood his thoughts, he was petrified. "No, no, no, not this one," He turned to the console and pressed a button and it beeped, the door closed and the elevator rose higher.

34

The door revealed a room packed with crates stacked all over, not someone that they thought would be waiting for them. At the end of the room was another brick hallway with stairs leading up.

"Are you sure you didn't press the button?" Minin asked Hayley, still expecting someone to be waiting there if she had.

"Positive, I don't know why we ended up here," She replied.

"Ok. I don't know about the rest of you but I'm confused. How did we end up in this room?" Minin asked still thinking the elevator taking itself to a level was peculiar.

"I'll have a look?" Screamer announced and unlocked the gate of the elevator, sending it to crash back down the gap. He moved into the room, glanced at every visible spot thinking someone might have been hiding, "It's empty," he announced.

Everyone followed him into the room slowly, holding their pistol tightly, peaking around the corners thinking he missed a spot and that someone might be hiding. Once again no one was there. "There's no one here," Stephanie said confused.

The sound of footsteps came from the stairs, everyone looked in that direction. *This must be it,* they all thought and simultaneously aim their pistols at the hallway. The steps got louder, everyone's hands began to shake, waiting for that final moment when they could pull the trigger. Tiffany saw a shadow moving in the hall and pulled her trigger, everyone else followed suit and fired their own, they all fired five shots then stop, hoping that this was enough to stop whoever was making their way down.

"Don't shoot," a voice screamed out from the stairs. The person at the stairs came down into the room with their hands above their head, it was Hunter. Everyone was relieved to see him, Hayley ran towards him and hugged. Tiffany, Callum and Minin following, The others joining. "You guys are really on edge, aren't you?" Hunter said, "It's fine, no-one is around this room or hallway at the moment." With that announcement, everyone put their pistols away.

"It's good to see you," Callum said to Hunter with a smile.

Hunter looked back at him, smiling, "So the legends are true, you can speak" He said with a voice that didn't seem sure. His eyes kept ever so slightly moving around.

Minin looked at Hunter's eyes and heard the sound of his voice, he could tell something wasn't right, that something just didn't add up, "What is it?"

"I don't think Daman trusts me anymore, I don't know why, I thought I was doing a good job of keeping my cover, I almost fired the weapon, surely that must have made him believe I'm on his side."

"He's paranoid," Minin replied.

"Yeah, but more so than usual. It's only been a few hours and there is a huge change in him. Anyone that he thinks is lying to him he just shoots. He's not worried about trying the kill-chip Controller anymore."

"What do you think has caused it?" Hayley asked curiously.

"He wants the weapon back online. He knows you've all gone to the Bunker, He's become impatient, I don't know for sure but I think he's going to fire the weapon at the Bunker."

Everyone gasps. "That'll kill everyone inside," Emily said aloud, with her hand over her mouth.

"Only those near the top," Callum told her. "The underground part of the Bunker is designed to survive a nuclear blast."

"No-one else knows about the other exit, do they?" Minin asked.

"I didn't tell anyone else, I don't know if any of you did," Callum replied, "Everyone else will be trapped inside, they'll eventually die out if he can get the weapon online."

"He wants the weapon back online quicker than what I can do on my own, so he sent Newton to help me, almost as soon as you left," Hunter said and paused for a moment. "You have no idea how lucky you were that you didn't get seen by Newton."

"What do you mean?"

"I brought you to this level," Hunter replied. "I saw you on the security cameras inside the dropship when I was trying to recalibrate the engines, Newton had left the dropship to go get something to eat, only a couple of minutes before. All hell would have broken out if he was still in the cockpit looking at the security cameras." He then paused for a moment beginning to look confused, "What are you guys doing here?"

"You sent a dropship to the Bunker" Hayley replied to him also confused, "You said that would be the sign."

"No, I didn't" Hunter replied nervously and paused for a moment knowing exactly what happened. "It was Newton, he's been trying to figure out how everything on the computers works, trying to get everything up to speed. The first thing he figured out was how to targeting system worked. He must have worked out how to send the other dropships and sent a new one to the Bunker as a test for when he gets the weapon fixed." He sighed, "I'm definitely not ready for any of you guys to be here yet," Hunter announced with a slow deep breath.

"We can't go back, this is a onetime only deal," Minin said. "We can't go back, we need the ship and we need it now. Especially if he's planning to target the Bunker at the first chance he gets." Minin gave Hunter the piece of paper that Callum gave to him from his pocket, "This will give you full access."

Hunter looked at the paper for a moment. "Where did you get this? Are you sure it will work." He asked unsure about it.

"It'll work, trust me, it's what I've used to access the computers inside the Tower," Callum explained.

Hunter thought for a second, "If it doesn't work, we are screwed."

"We have to take it," Minin said, knowing there was no turning back.

"Follow me," Hunter announced. They all follow him up a flight of stairs, damp brick walls covering each side. A flat level with a door appeared telling that they had arrived one level above where they were. "Not this floor," Hunter informed them. "It's a few more levels up, but taking the stairs has less chance of the guards seeing us. Best if everyone stays quiet." The staircase continued with the damp brick walls, they arrive at another level and continue, repeating three more times. They arrived at the final level and Hunter stopped, everyone froze in their steps. "I'll see if the coast is clear," He told them and walked through the door. He came back a minute later, "Coast is clear." Everyone remained quiet, as they walked through the door.

Minin realised the second he entered, which door it was, the same one that Daman had come in when he had his shoot out with the Guards the last time he was here, "We're lucky we didn't see Daman."

"Very lucky, he prefers to take the stairs, he could have come this way, but trust me the chances were a lot slimmer of getting caught by anyone than another way," Hunter said quietly knowing of the risks. Everyone else just stood there, looking at the dropship floating in mid-air in front of them. They all knew that it had to be here, otherwise they wouldn't have come, but the fact they could see it and it was their key to get off the island was still unbelievable to them.

Minin noticed the cockpit's window was now covered with a metal sheet, "Why is it closed like that?" he wondered.

"I didn't want to take a chance that if the dropship was attacked again, that the window would get broken, I still don't trust the guards," Hunter replied. "Don't worry it'll open when I tell it too."

"I've been to the Tower so many times without being caught before and I didn't even hear a Rumour about a dropship being here," Callum said still in shock at what was floating in front of him.

"Yeah, I don't think most of the people inside the Tower know either, I think Daman wanted this to be a huge secret, the only people that know are those in his innermost circle and those he needs. Anyone that does know still believe they will be punished if they said anything to anyone else," Hunter replied. "Anyway we can't really keep holding back like this, I don't know how long until the guards will come back."

Everyone began to walk to the back of the dropship, the ramp was down, they walk in, everyone's spirits were high, they knew they were so close to getting the dropship. More crates had been placed in the middle. "Doesn't a dropship have ten seats for the prisoners?" Hayley said remembering when she arrived on the island, "There's only eight here."

"Two were so damaged that they had to be removed," Hunter replied. "It'll be ok, a couple of people will have to stand, just hang on while the dropship lifts. Once it's moving it'll be less turbulent, everyone should be able to stand then."

Minin saw a rope on the ground laid out in front of the seats, "What's this?"

Hunter examined it, "I don't know." He thought for a moment, "If turbulence gets too much for whoever is standing can hold that," He continued, sounding positive. "Minin can come with me to the cockpit."

They both walk toward the cockpit door, everyone else took a seat, except Lukas and Callum who decided to stand. "I'm going to be a gentleman and let the ladies have a seat," Callum said winking at both Tiffany and Hayley who were both seated next to each other.

Hayley smiled at the gesture, Tiffany on the other hand, quietly said to Hayley, "I preferred him when he was mute and not a jerk."

Hunter and Minin opened the cockpit door. Newton, a young boy with curly blonde haired with round glasses and a lab coat that looked a bit too small for him was sitting on a seat, looking at the computer but doesn't look back. "That was a long coffee break," He said to Hunter sounding annoyed.

"I found a few friends that I was talking to," Hunter replied smiling at Minin.

"Don't make that a permanent thing, Daman wants the Weapon ready and this thing in the air as soon as possible remember, socialising is only going to slow us down, I want my reward for helping him."

Minin then bent down beside him, so that his head was level with Newton, "He's not going to reward you."

Newton, not recognising the voice, turned his head looking directly at Minin. He knew exactly who he was from the wanted posters. "Wait," he said, not knowing what was going on, "How did you get in here?" He got out of the chair the opposite way to Minin and stood up and looked at Hunter, becoming more confused.

"I told you, I was talking to a few friends," Hunter replied. "Decided to give them a guided tour."

Newton kept looking at them both nervously, then ran out of the cockpit, he stopped in the Cargo area, saw everyone seated then saw Callum, fear overcame him and ran out of the dropship completely.

"Well that was easy," Minin said with a smile.

"It is now, but he's going to find someone to tell."

"Well, Let's hope this password works," Minin said, knowing what would happen if it doesn't.

Hunter sat down and began to type on the computer, he closed everything that was displayed until a screen that asked for a username and password was displayed. He inputted the username and password that Callum had provided. A welcome screen displayed. Hunter began to check through everything, seeing what he now had access too, "This is insane," He said. Minin couldn't keep up with what was being displayed, only managing glimpses of everything before a new screen popped up. A screen displayed with a map of Islands which were all green, except for one which was flashing red. "I have access, I have full access," Hunter said smiling and shocked. He looked at Minin, "we're getting off the Island." He pressed the Island that was flashing red. A beeping noise came from the console. Hunter had a confused look on his face and pressed the Island again. A notice displayed, he read it. *This location cannot be chosen as it is too close to your current vicinity, please choose another. Please note too many close vicinity choices will activate the self-destruct mechanism.* Hunter sighed knowing that freedom wasn't going to be that easy, "I need to pick another island to go to first," He informed Minin.

Minin looked at him confused, "What about the Bunker? We need to go their first and pick everyone up."

"We can't," Hunter announced.

"We have too, we can't let them all stay there. Daman is going to know we have the dropship. He'll send guards."

"The system won't let me, it has a failsafe, it has to go to another island, otherwise it tries to self-destruct, thinking it's being taken over," Hunter explained. "As soon as we get to the other island, I'll turn the dropship around and send it to pick everyone up from the Bunker, I promise."

"Everyone in that Bunker will be in danger as soon as he knows we've taken the dropship, he'll raid it as punishment, they will be slaughtered."

"I know," Hunter conceded. "But the dropship will go quick enough there and back that we can defend them before it becomes a problem. We have his precious weapon."

Minin took a deep breath, "Are you sure?"

"We don't have a choice," Hunter explained. "The old pilots were only on the dropships to make sure they arrived, nothing was manually controlled, I'm surprised the dropships were never automatic from the first day."

"Pick the closest one you can, get us there and get us back as quickly as you can," Minin said frustrated.

Hunter pressed one of the Islands that was green, the display had a green background with the letter C and the words, *'press here to confirm'.* He pressed the confirmation. He turned his head into the other area and could see the tailgate rise.

Minin could hear the same engine start-up sound as he heard from the dropship that brought him to the Island, he knew they had control of the dropship, "Let's get out of here," He said to Hunter, with a slight sound of relief in his voice.

A siren then began to blare from the outside of the dropship. The platform surrounding the dropship felt like it had instantly filled with guards, each one taking the position and aiming their guns at the dropship. "Give up the dropship, come out slowly," came a voice from a loudspeaker.

Hunter and Minin looked at each other, they knew that was not an option. Hunter began to press buttons on the console, which displayed a security feed from the outside of the dropship. "It must be every guard that knows about the Dropship," Hunter said. "I've never seen them all at once."

"If we start to move and they fire, will the dropship handle it?" Minin asked.

"I don't know with all the damage it suffered last time. It's only been a few hours since the panels were patched up," Hunter answered. He thought for a few seconds, then began to press a few buttons on the console, "Screw it, we're dead anyway. If they are going to destroy the Dropship, at least he won't have it."

The drawbridge at the back began to rise, this was enough to tell the guards that they would not be giving up the Dropship. The guards began to fire into the closing space, but not at the Dropship itself.

"Go out there and help them, if they're strapped down they don't have a chance against the bullets coming in," Hunter commanded.

Minin rushed out of his seat and into the cabin. To Minin's surprise, everyone was out of their seats and were hiding behind the metal crates. Minin rushed behind the closest one to the cockpit's door, Callum was also hiding behind it. "I unstrapped everyone once the alarm went off, didn't know what it meant," Callum explained. Bullets kept hailing into the cabin, the drawbridge was still rising but slowly, "They've hit something just inside the drawbridge, it was going up at a normal speed until then."

Minin looked at the drawbridge sparks were coming out of a little black box just inside, "We'll just have to wait it out," he replied.

Increasingly more bullets kept coming into the cabin as the drawbridge rose. It eventually made it to the halfway point and the bullets stopped.

"That's it," Callum announced to everyone.

Everyone came out from behind the crate they were hiding behind. They look at the drawbridge slowly closing. Bang, bang. There was a knock on the drawbridge as though something big had made contact multiple times. Everyone looked at the drawbridge wondering what it was. They then saw four pairs of arms reaching over the gap, the guards were climbing into the dropship for one last attempt to take back possession.

"Go back behind the crates," Hayley and Tiffany both shouted at the same time.

Everyone inside the cabin didn't argue and moved back into position as quickly as possible. Without even being told, everyone took their guns out and held them tightly, knowing that it would be the last thing to save them if needed.

The guards climbed the drawbridge and fell to the ground, feet first as it continued to close. Everyone hiding behind the crates was silent, hoping to not get caught. The guards look at each other and made sure their weapons were loaded and began to slowly move around hoping to find whoever was hiding. They check the crates closest to where they entered, but no one was there. One of the guards then taps another on the shoulder and pointed at the crates toward the cockpit. During this Hayley was peering around the corner of the crate she was behind, she knew the crate the guard had pointed to belonged to Callum and Minin. She pulled out her gun and fired at the guards, hitting one in the ankle sending him to the floor in pain, the other guard retreated as quickly as possible behind the crates they first searched.

The guard that was hit was writhing in pain on the floor, he started to scream, "Ahhh." The other guards try to pull him to safety but were unable to reach him from their location. He continued to scream. The screaming became too much for a guard, who decided he had heard enough and fired his own gun at the guard, the taser-bullet sending a huge shock, killing him.

Everyone began firing at the guards, who intern began to fire back. Bullets launch back and forth all over the cabin, another guard was hit in the shoulder forcing him out of his cover. "Two to go," Hayley screamed out, although no-one was able to hear her over the sound of the bullets being fired. They kept firing, the last two guards do a better job of protecting themselves. They fire two bullets then return into hiding, wait for a few seconds then fire two more and repeat. Each bullet narrowly missing whoever they were aiming for.

Minin noticed the guards firing pattern, each time they came out of hiding it was in the same spot, he waited and kept looking to make sure, but the pattern never changed. The guards go behind into cover again, Minin aimed his gun, waiting for a guard to come out. The guards come out, Minin fired his gun and a third guard was hit this time in the stomach.

The fourth guard knew he did not stand a chance and threw his weapon away into the middle of the cabin, everyone knew he had signalled that he had given up and stopped firing at him. The guard put his hands up above his head and came out of the crates where he was hiding. "I give up," He called out, walking to the middle of the room.

Everyone came out of hiding themselves, except for Tiffany. Minin, Callum and Hayley storm toward the guard. Hayley put her hand into a fist and took a swing at the guard's face, which connected, knocking him back.

Callum grabbed Hayley before she could do it once more, "Cool it," he told her.

"This asshole tried to kill us," She screamed at the guard.

"Yeah, but not now," Callum said, struggling to contain her. Hayley tried to compose herself but she was struggling. "You two," Callum said to Lukas and Stephanie, "Take her for a bit." They both came over, taking her to her seat.

While all this happened Minin was just staring at the guard making sure he didn't move, the guard stared back trying to not look intimidated. Callum soon came over. "What do we do with him?" Minin asked Callum, "We can't take him with us."

The Guard then spoke, "You'll never be able to defeat us, Daman will lead us to glory, everyone else has given up on us, but he will never let us down." He shakes his head in disappointment then spits in Minin and Callum's faces. "Why would you not allow him to give you a better life? All you have done is disappoint him."

Minin and Callum roll their eyes at what he was saying, they couldn't believe any of this was true. "He treats us horribly outside the Tower," Minin explained.

"The Tower is for the true believers," The guard replied. "If you believed in him from the start he would have chosen you and saved you."

"That's crap," Hayley told the guard, "He treats us like animals out there. There is no way would we believe in him."

"He treats you like family and you disappoint him."

Hunter walked into the room as the guard was speaking, "The only reason you think like that is that you've only seen how he is in the Tower, it's completely different out there."

The guard shook his head looking disgusted at Hunter. "You're the worst one, he gave you a chance to redeem yourself from the rest of this scum and you turned your back on him."

Hayley had heard enough and stormed to the closed drawbridge, she took a guess and pressed a button on the black box that was still sparking. The drawbridge lowered, she pressed it again, it stopped just wide enough that someone would be able to fit through. She stormed toward the guard, grabbed him by the arm and the back of the neck and marched him to the opening, "If you're so loyal to Daman, you can tell him yourself." Then tossed the guard through the opening.

The guard screamed as he went through the opening, thinking he would fall through the gap to his death between the platform and the dropship. A metal knocking sound could then be heard, the guard had made it to the platform and the screaming stopped.

Minin ran to the guard that got hit in the stomach, picked him up and did the same to the surviving guard. Then once again to the guard that was hit in the shoulder. They both make the same knocking on metal sound when they landed. Minin then returned to the dead guard. "What about this one?"

"Help me lift him," Callum replied. "They can bury him. He was only doing what he was told. He deserves that at least."

They both lift the lifeless body off the ground from the arms and legs, Minin taking one side, Callum taking the other and make their way toward the drawbridge. They start swinging the body, "One," they both say to each other as they swing. "Two.... Three," then throw the body back into the open. Callum then pressed the button near the drawbridge and it began to close, sealing itself back up.

"Let's get out of here," Minin said annoyed, wishing what was happening to be over and began to walk back to the cockpit.

Minin and Hunter arrived at the cockpit door when Haley called out, "Where's Tiffany?"

Everyone then realised, they had not seen her since they were all hidden behind the crates when the guards came into the cabin. "Hey, Tiff, it's fine to come out," Callum called, but there was no answer.

Minin had seen which crate she had hidden behind. He walked to it, there was a trickle of blood coming out from behind, Minin knew this wasn't a good sign. "Hayley.... I need you," he screamed out thinking the worst.

Hayley rushed over to see what the problem was, laying on the ground was Tiffany, barely able to breathe, a wound of blood on her chest, she had been hit during the confrontation. Hayley rushed over and compressed the wound. Tiffany's breathing was shallow, she looked up at Hayley and smiled, who smiled back. Tiffany then closed her eyes.

Hayley looked up at Minin, she had tears in her eyes, she shook her head. Callum and Hunter arrive just as she did this. Her face told them Tiffany's fate, there wasn't anything she could do for her, the bleeding was too much nor did she have the equipment if she could.

Tiffany opened her eyes and looked at the four people who found her on the island. The look on their faces told her what was happening.

She began to talk to them slowly, "I'm glad you all found me." She then smiled, "You have to beat him." She then closed her eyes and took her last breath.

35

Minin, Hayley, Callum and Hunter could not believe what had just happened. Plenty of people around the island had died, some that they were close too, even their drop family. But until this point, it was never someone that was part of their camp, this felt different from the others. A rush of anger overcame Hayley, she was now determined to finish this sooner rather than later. Hunter was in shock, a tear shed from Callum's eye. Minin's emotions were a selection of all three. '*You have to beat him*', those words kept swirling inside his head. "We have to keep going," Minin told those around him, "I'm not going to let her die in vain."

They all look at him and knew that he was right. Hunter walked Haley back to her seat, her face was red, she had a look that could cut through steel. He was worried about her, he had never seen her this angry before, he then returned. "I've never seen her like this, I've seen her angry but this is something else. She looks like she wants to kill the first person she sees."

"She wants revenge, I don't blame her," Minin replied.

"Keep a lookout for her, if she's this bad she might make a mistake and it'll be horrible for all of us," Hunter told Callum. "Anyway, let's get this dropship," He replied, focusing on the job at hand.

Everyone else in the cabin started to make their way over to see what had happened. They could see by the way Hayley looked that something bad had happened and they wanted to know for themselves. Callum let them look a little but made sure they all kept their distance.

He let them for a few seconds' morn in their own way. They all said their goodbyes then returned to their seats, they also wanted this to end now as well.

Minin's feelings kept changing from sadness and remorse to anger and determination for it to end. The look on his face showed he wasn't to be messed with. He stormed toward the cockpit, "Get this thing in the air, now." He commanded Hunter forcefully.

Hunter followed Minin to the cockpit and they both sat down. He began to put commands into the system then turned to Minin, "Make sure everyone else is sitting, it's time."

Everyone was now seated in the available seats except for Callum who didn't want to leave Tiffany's body on her own. He didn't think it would be right, Minin went to him. Callum was cradling Tiffany's body, the realisation of what had happened was sinking in. He began to talk to her softly, "I'm sorry, this didn't have to happen to you."

"We need you to take a seat," Minin realised right away he needed to say something else and placed his hand on Callum's shoulder. "It's hard losing a loved one. When I lost Amber before I came to the island it was a horrible feeling, I don't know how your feeling but I want this to end, not only for ourselves but now for her."

Callum looked back at Minin and smiled, "I needed that."

Hayley, who heard what Minin had said, she too needed to hear those words, called out to Callum, "Come here." She had begun to calm down. She stood up and hugged him, "We will all miss her."

Minin gave him a slight tap on the back, Callum turned back smiling as he walked past. "Thank you," He told him softly.

Minin then made his way back to the cockpit taking his seat. He turned to Hunter, "Do it, let's get out of here."

Hunter pressed a few keys on the keyboard of the on-board computer, but nothing happened. He pressed the same combination, once again, nothing. A screen then displayed in the cargo area, which was flashing red with a message, *'unseated passengers detected.'*

"Oh no," Hunter said.

"What's *'oh no,'* Minin asked, wondering what it could be?

"I can't go, they all have to be seated, the cabin area has sensors in it. It won't allow me to go with someone not taking a seat, I'm sorry but its saying Tiffany's body and Callum need a seat as well."

Minin looked at him with disbelief. "You can't be serious, there aren't enough seats, and it's not like we can just get people to leave the ship, there are guards surrounding us, there's probably even more coming as we speak, why didn't we know this before?"

"I told you, I didn't know if this plan would work a hundred per cent," Hunter replied in disbelief himself. They just sat in silence, neither had an idea of what to do.

"What do we do?" Minin asked, breaking the silence.

"I don't have a choice in this, I can't change the programming, at least not in the short time," Hunter replied, annoyed with his answer.

The silence between them returned, they both just stared into space, both thinking of a solution. They both knew the only way to get the ship to move was for someone to leave the ship with Tiffany's body, but neither one wanted to admit it.

More guards could be seen on the security monitor coming around the ship, all taking aim at the ship but not attacking. The guards stare at the dropship, as though they were waiting to be told when to fire. "Why aren't they firing at us? They look like they are ready to pounce the first chance they get," Hunter couldn't understand.

"Probably after the last lot of guards were firing at the ship, they probably don't want to take the chance that they will damage the ship again. They're probably waiting to get given the word when to fire."

Hunter looked at Minin, "Why don't you get into your guards' uniform again, go out of the ship and see your best friend Daman and get him to leave the ship to us," He said sarcastically.

"Sure, and we'll all have a party with cake afterwards."

Hunter suddenly had a look as though he had thought of another plan and began looking at the computer, bringing up a schematic of the ship, hoping to figure out a different answer. He looked over it for a few seconds, he then pointed to what looked to be a door. "This looks like some stairs, it goes down to the lower level, the level where the supplies would drop down from. If someone takes Tiffany's body and goes down, we can leave that way, the sensors don't work there. I can't believe I didn't see this before."

Minin got out of his seat, tapped Hunter on the shoulder and walked out of the cockpit and closed the door behind him. He walked over to Hayley and Callum and started to explain the situation.

Callum, without saying anything, walked toward Tiffany's body, lifted her, then proceeded to the door. Minin followed and tried to unlock it but it did not budge. He kept trying then realised that it was locked from the other side. He screamed at it in frustration, began hitting it, then charging at it with his shoulder but he knew it was no use. He turned to Callum, "It won't open." He told him defeated, "We have to do it the other way."

Callum didn't want to hear that, he didn't want to give up Tiffany's body to the tower. "Anything? anything else we can do?" He asked in desperation.

"No." He then began to talk loud enough that everyone in the room could hear him. "Someone has to go with her, I'll open the drawbridge then take her." He then walked toward the drawbridge.

"No," Callum replied, stopping Minin. "I got you all into this. I should have never taken you into the tower, should have never attacked when they took Hunter. I'm taking her."

Hayley stood up, Callum hugged her and he quietly told her, "Don't stop me, it's my choice. You two are perfect for each other. Take care of Hunter as well." He lifted Tiffany's body and looked at Minin, "We have to do this quickly."

Minin hugged Callum, then nodded his head agreeing, he knew that there was nothing he could say to convince him otherwise. He then walked to the end of the dropship and pressed the button to lower the drawbridge. It lowered but this time quickly. Quick enough that it was fully open before anyone knew what had happened. Minin hid behind a crate, Callum ran with Tiffany's body to hide next to Minin. There were no gunshots, the guards just waiting outside, knowing what had happened last time.

Minin and Callum just sat there not knowing what to do, they knew they could not hide behind the crates forever. Callum held Tiffany tightly not letting her go, "Close the drawbridge when I leave. They see you as an inspiration, don't waste it."

A call came over what sounded to be a P.A system in the room, Hunter's voice came through. "Guys whatever you are doing, do it now, I know this isn't fair, but more guards are lining up, they look ready to fire the guns now."

Minin looked around on the wall there was another microphone for the P.A system and pressed the button to respond to the call, "Give us a second."

Callum just looked at Minin, smiling once more, stood and ran out the back of the dropship. "Hit that damn button," He commanded as he left.

"No," Minin said desperately, not wanting to lose another friend, but it was too late, Callum was gone. Minin looked in horror realising his friend had just sacrificed himself. He had a tear in his eye. He did everything he could do to control himself from breaking, in a matter of minutes he had lost two, not only friends but family. Minin took a few deep breaths in the seconds that passed and composed himself, he knew what he had to do and pressed the button to bring the drawbridge back, it rose as quickly as it opened. He collapsed to the floor hating himself, even though he knew it had to be done.

A deafening rattling noise of gunfire came from the outside of the ship and then silence. Minin looked at Hayley with a look of sorrow, she stared back at him, they both knew that no matter how much they could wish or hope, there was simply no way could Callum have survived.

36

Minin walked over to Hayley, she was emotionless, two of the people she called family were now taken from them and in a matter of moments. Minin tried to hug her, she pulled away, not wanting to be touched. She looked at Minin, her eyes filled with tears. She wanted nothing more than this nightmare to be over with.

Minin knew there was nothing he could do, he looked at her one last time. "I'm so sorry," he whispered to her. He wanted nothing more than to cry. He then looked at the cockpit, storming toward it, he was more determined than ever to get the dropship into the air. He sat down at his seat and nodded in silence for Hunter to get the Dropship off the ground and get away from the Island once and for all.

"Did you see anything?" Minin asked Hunter softly, he was close to breaking.

"Nothing" he replied, his voice was shaky. "There isn't a security camera working on that side of the ship. To be honest, I'm glad I didn't see anything, I don't want to see anything like that, seeing a friend sacrifice themself like that, I.... I just couldn't." Hunter looked back at the keyboard and pressed a few buttons on the console, a loud humming sound began then the ship began to shutter. 'Crack', something snapped from the outside, both Hunter and Minin knew that the dropship was breaking away from the platform.

Hunter and Minin look at the video feed of the outside, the platform began to dismantle, some parts were still connected by a thread to the dropship, the rest had fallen taking some of the guards with it. The remaining guards made it to safety, away from the platform, once they were safe they began to shoot at the dropship, doing what little they could to stop it from moving.

Hunter looked at Minin, he was smiling. "It's floating... we're on our way out.... we're finally on our way off the island." Hunter began to laugh, he pumped his hand and arm in the air, got out of his seat and shook his hand in celebration, "I'm finally off this rock, away from that asshole," he declared. He had ever been this happy before.

Minin, on the other hand, sat on his seat silently, he was smiling but was still depressed, what Hunter had just said lifted his spirits, but at the same time, he was still mourning for his two lost friends.

Hunter's celebration was short-lived, he sat back on his seat, looked up at the roof of the Tower which was still closed. He knew that getting the ship to hover on its own without being connected to the platforms was only a small portion of what he had to do. His next job was to open the roof and get the ship into the open air, "I need you to press the button that says 'open hatch' on that console there," He said to Minin, pointing to a button he was sitting next too. Minin was still in his own world with his own thoughts and was barely able to hear him. "Hey, did you hear me?" Hunter called out.

Minin turned, realising that Hunter was talking to him, "Wait. What?"

"We're almost free, I need you to pay attention." He looked behind himself slightly, "they need you to pay attention, I know that's hard, but we need to focus," Hunter explained. He pressed a combination on the console and the metal blocking their view of the outside began to retract into the sides on the dropship. "Lookup. That's what we need to open."

Minin looked up and saw the roof of the Tower, having a current purpose snapped him out of his slump and pressed the button. The roof began to part in two, Minin and Hunter could see the sky which was bright, blue and cloudless.

Hunter looked back down at the console and began to press more buttons, "All I have to do is press this and this and...." He pressed the button, the dropship began to rise toward the opening. "…Once we're out, we're free," He declared. The dropship rose slowly, almost as if it was barely moving.

"Why is it taking so long?" Minin asked, thinking something was wrong.

"My guess is that it must be sensing how narrow the Tower is and doesn't want to hit itself and get damaged, other than that I have no idea.

Minin turned his head toward the Cargo area, he wanted to check on Hayley and see how she was doing, "Can we get out of our seats or is the sensor still on?"

Hunter knew without being told that he wanted to check on Hayley, "I'm not sure, I'll give it a try, He replied as he got off his own seat and walked about the cockpit himself with the ship still rising, not even slightly slowing down. "See it's fine. I'll call you if I need you."

Minin got out of his seat and made his way into the cargo area, he spotted Hayley just sitting there, staring into space, she looked more defeated than ever. He knew this wasn't a good sign and rushed over to her.

"She's getting worse," said Emily, who was seated across from Hayley.

"I can't turn it off, I need to turn it off," Hayley said to Minin, her breathing became quick and shallow, tears rolling down her cheeks.

"You can't keep turning your emotions off, it can't be good for you," Minin replied as he hugged her. He felt helpless.

She held him as tightly as she could, "I can't help this way, I can't do anything this way." She replied sobbing into his shoulder.

"You don't need to do anything now, we're almost free," Minin said to her softly. "The dropship is rising, once we're out of the Tower that's it, It's over."

Hayley pulled away, her breathing slowly became normal, those were the words she needed, just to know that everyone else was safe and smiled back. She returned to the hug, "Thank you." She said softly.

After a minute they broke away, "I'm going to go back and see if Hunter needs me." He looked at Emily, "Look after her." Emily nodded.

"Ok," Hayley replied just before she grabbed him for one last hug before she let go.

Minin looked through the cockpit window as the dropship began to leave the Tower. He looked out the window, the sky was clearer than he had ever seen it before. The Dropship made a violent jerk forward as the Dropship began to move away from the Tower, gaining speed. He smiled knowing it was over and continued to look through the cockpit window, taking in the blue sky.

Suddenly there was a crashing noise coming from the level below them. Minin asked Hunter, "What's that?"

"No idea," Hunter replied, confused as much as Minin was.

A loud banging of metal on metal came from the door to the lower level, so loud that it could be heard clearly from the cockpit. The noise got louder and more violent.

"There's someone down there and they want to get out!" Minin replied, worried about who it could be.

Hunter tried bringing up information on the computer. "I can't find information for that level, I don't know who or what it is," He announced, worried himself.

There was more scraping noise coming from the door, Minin knew whoever was trying to get in must be close. He shouted to Hunter, "You're going to need to fly this on your own for a while." He then pressed a button on the cockpit door, locking it from the inside.

There was another scraping noise, it stopped. The door then began to open slowly.

37

A wall of dust fell from the cracks of the door, which had not been opened in a long time. Everyone sitting in the cargo area got out of their seats, got whatever weapons they have ready and scattered and hid behind the furthest crate from the door.

"They have to be guards. There can't be another answer, they must have figured out another way to get on," Stephanie said, guessing who it was.

"I hope you're wrong," Minin replied. He looked at Hayley, her face was in disbelief, wondering, '*What could possibly happen next?*' Minin looked back at everyone else, they were all ready. "Everyone, stay vigilant, we can't let whoever this is, take this Dropship. We've come so far to lose it now."

The dust settled, which showed a silhouette of a huge mountain of a person and what appeared to be slightly more people below them. Everyone hiding was unsure if they should shoot now and take the guess that they were enemies, or not shoot and hope they were friends and allies, who somehow made it on board.

The dust settled more, the silhouettes had become clearer. These were not friends, the mountain of a person was Mark Brockly who had bruises and cuts all over his face, behind him were guards. Hayley's hands were shaking uncontrollably, she took the first shot, she missed Mark but managed to hit another guard standing on his left in the shoulder, he stumbled back, eventually falling down the stairs they were climbing.

The first shot was enough to tell everyone to begin shooting at the doorway, "Fall back, fall back," a voice called from the lower level. The guards and Mark began to pull back until they were no longer seen.

"Hold your fire," screamed Minin.

The rattling of the guns went silent. The doorway was empty but everyone kept their aim knowing what was on the other side. They all had the same thoughts. How many of them? What kind of weapons do they have? Will they be able to fight them?

A small metal container came flying into the room and landed in the middle. Without thinking, Screamer, Stephanie, Simone and Emmitt took aim and began shooting at it, an unknown gas began spurting out. The room quickly became covered, but no one had any ill effects. They soon realised it was only a distraction, all retaking aim at the door and began firing. No-one wanted to take the risk for anyone to run through the doorway, they all just fired into the gas.

The gas began to clear as more bullets were fired. Minin noticed a silhouette of someone who made it through the gas and ran toward where Hayley had taken her cover. He fired his gun at the person but the gun miss fired, he pulled the trigger once more but again it failed, he was out of bullets. "Crap, not now," he said to himself angrily.

As the gas cleared, more guards made their way out of the doorway and stairs and took cover behind other crates closest to the door. Eventually, anyone that was originally in the cargo area began to run out of bullets. The guards came out from their positions, their guns aiming at the crates where the others were taking cover. There were seven guards, all waiting for their chance to shoot at the first person that they could.

"You're all out of bullets," Mark called out. "There's no use hiding, everyone come out now," He demanded. Everyone hiding stayed still. "We know where you are, don't make this any harder than it has to be," He commanded again. Not a single person budged.

A guard to the right of Mark had enough of waiting and decided to give a warning shot of his own, he pulled the trigger, there was a clicking sound without a fired bullet, the guard was also out of bullets.

"We're not coming out," shouted Minin, who knew just like everyone else, this was now a standoff. "I think I can take you hand to hand if I need too, you got nothing," He continued, trying to sell himself as braver than what he really was.

There was silence from both sides. Two new guards appeared from the doorway and stairs, two guards swapping with them, making their way back down. One of the new guards fired a bullet in the air to show that at least both the new guard's guns were full.

"We've got plenty of bullets spare…you got nothing," Mark declared, mocking what Minin had said. This was no longer the standoff everyone was hoping. The odds were now clearly not in their favour but no one came out of hiding. "Out…. Now!" Mark commanded in a strong forceful tone, his patience growing thin. The guards that went back in the door returned while another group of two went down to reload.

"This swapping the guards out for new ammo is a scare tactic, they didn't reload, you're bluffing," Minin shouted back. The first set of guards that had left the room then returned, aimed and fired at where at Minin's voice but both missed.

"Any other bright ideas?" Mark replied. "Out now! I'm warning you."

Everyone stood still while the next group of two guards return as the final three left to reload. Minin could see through a hole in the crate exactly what was happening. "There's more of us, how about we just charge at you?" He shouted as the fear in his voice was beginning to appear.

Every person hiding looked at him with a look of wonder and disbelief as to why he would even say that. They knew that even though they had the number of people, they clearly didn't have the weapons to be able to do it. They knew that they would be slaughtered the second they tried. Even Mark knew he couldn't be serious, "We have all the weapons. I don't like your chances."

One of the groups of three guards walked back into the room and took his position while The other two fail to return. Another person came out of the doorway, not wearing a guard's uniform, it was Daman. Everyone hiding that could see through or around the crates could see him standing there, he was smiling. He walked to the middle of the room, between the guards and everyone else and dropped nine clips of ammo on the floor in random places and returned to the guards. "You don't want to give up, that's fine but you're out of ammunition and we have plenty. I'm a fair man just ask my followers." The guards around him began to nod. "So I'll share some with you, all you have to do is come out of hiding and make a run for it. It's as simple as that," he told them calmly. The guards were still aiming at the hiding spots.

No one came out, they all knew that it was a trap. A standoff ensued, they all just stayed in their position weighing up their options, the longer they thought, the longer they knew it was not in their favour. Screamer slid his gun out from hiding, looked at Minin and mouthed to him, "I'm sorry." He then put his hands up and shouted, "Don't shoot." A couple of guards aim their sights at him but don't shoot. Screamer stood up with his hands in the air and walked over to the guards and gave himself up.

Daman came to Screamer smiling. The fear of what Daman might do overwhelmed him, he then began to shiver in fear. "Well done, you did the right thing," Daman said patting Screamer on the shoulder. He then called out calmly to everyone else hiding. "Take a note from your friend and come out." He then nodded his head, two guards grabbed Screamer harshly by the arms and shoulders, "Strap him into the seat and make sure he can't get out," Daman commanded. The guards do as they are told and slammed Screamer into the seat and made sure the straps were done as tightly as possible to the point he could barely move.

Everyone that was still hiding did not know what to do. Eventually, Emily threw her hands up, stood out from hiding and walked over to the guards. She stopped where the ammunition clips were and threw herself to the ground, scattering the ammunition toward those that were hiding. Emily tried to lift herself from the floor as the guards all began to fire at her, almost instantly she fell back to the ground, she had been hit but no one knew to what toll.

"Stop shooting!" Daman commanded. The room went quiet. He shook his head, "Silly, silly girl, that was a very stupid move by that girl," He screamed. "Don't be stupid like her, come out and give yourself up. I'm willing to be lenient on everyone, I don't want any of you, I just want the ship. Come out, don't be a hero and you won't be hurt."

The Guards pick up Emily's body and place her in a seat harshly. The movements taking their toll on her, she was still bleeding. Emmit had a look of shock on his face unsure if he should reveal himself. He looked down, there was a clip of ammo at his feet but the thoughts of what happened to Emily overcame him, instantly he put his hands up.

Stephanie looked at those around her, she shook her head in defeat, "I'm sorry," She said placing her hands above her head and came out. They were both grabbed and taken to their seats then strapped in as hard as possible.

Lukas was looking at the ammo then back at the guards, he was weighing up his options. Lukas finally looked at Minin, "it's over," He said quietly and put his arms up, moving out of the cover.

Simone shook her head disappointed, "He's right," she called out, a tear going down her cheek knowing they had been defeated as she revealed herself. The same fate occurring to them like the others.

Hayley sat curled up, she knew it was over, she looked at Minin and was about to tell him, when she noticed a button above Minin's head. It was red and had a sign above saying, 'Emergency Exit'. She knew it was their chance, she shouted out in Minin's direction loud enough so that everyone could hear, "We don't have a choice, it's over, he has the ship. We tried but he has it now." Minin looked at her and she pointed directly at the button, Minin turned around to see what she was indicating, he saw the button, next to the Emergency Exit sign was a small picture of the open tailgate with the seats falling away. He turned back, looked at Hayley, she was nodding, he knew exactly what she meant. Hayley continued to nod as she put her hands up and like everyone else then came out of hiding. The guards then grabbed her.

Daman walked over to her, he smiled. Hayley at that moment wanted to cry, "It's good seeing leaders showing the way," Daman said to her. "If he has any intelligence at all he will come out and give himself up."

"It's done sir," One of the guards announced. "There are no other seats for him."

"Good," Daman replied, he then directed his voice at Minin. "If he doesn't want to come out......" He paused for a moment, "....then execute them." All the guards make their way to the seats and aim their guns at point-blank range.

"Do it!" Hayley screamed out.

Minin jumped from where he was, hit the button, then landed behind another crate. The guards turn toward him and they fire their guns but miss. The cargo doors break off the back of the dropship, revealing the dropship was still flying above the Island. A huge gust of air fills the cargo area. All the seats began to disengage quickly, there was no delay unlike when Minin came to the island. They were all dragged towards the opening at a speed which they didn't think was possible.

The crates began to move like a tornado from the air currents. Everyone not connected to a seat ran to the sides, grabbing what they could. Minin grabbed the door to the cockpit and held on tightly, closed his eyes, hoping it would be over quickly. He could hear the crashing noise of the crates and the screams of those the crates were knocking into.

The noise soon subsided, Minin took a sigh of relief as he let go and looked at the cargo area. All the guards were gone but he was not alone, Mark and Daman had survived.

A siren began to sound, the lights in the cargo area turned off, only emergency lighting and light from the outside was visible, a flashing red light began to blink. The plane dipped slightly to the left, forcing Minin, Daman and Mark toward the side of the dropship. The plane then realigned itself as the lights turned back to normal, Minin made it to his feet and shouted out towards the cockpit, "What was that?" Even though he didn't know if Hunter would have been able to hear it or not.

Hunters voice came over the Dropships P.A. "I don't know what happened, the ship just turned its self around, it's not going to leave the island, give me a couple of minutes to figure it out."

Daman began to laugh at the announcement, "It doesn't want to leave the island, it knows who its master is." Both Daman and Mark aim their guns at Minin. Minin just stood there, staring at the two of them. He eventually put his hands up, knowing that there was nothing he could do. "Get to the middle of the room," Daman commanded.

Minin could barely hear him from the rush of air. He knew he had no choice, they would shoot him if he didn't comply and began to walk. "What are you going to do with me?" He asked. Both his captors remain quiet, frustrating Minin. "What are you going to do to me?" He screamed, demanding to know. Suddenly Daman and Mark threw their guns out the back of the dropship. Minin went from frustrated to confused. "What are you going to do with me?"

"You didn't finish the last fight when you were with us the last time?" Daman replied. "You're going to finish it," he paused for a moment thinking. "Let's call this round two but what the winner receives has changed. You don't get any meds, the winner gets the ship."

Minin didn't want to fight, he knew he was lucky the last time. This time wouldn't be so lucky. If he was a cat, he would have surely had lost eight of his nine lives, he wasn't going to survive this fight.

Mark looked at Minin and smiled, "What do you say?" He said, has as he cracked his knuckles, "It's this or you roll over and we just take the ship."

Minin couldn't allow that to happen either. He tried to be tough, he lifted his head to make himself slightly taller and also cracked his knuckles. "This ship is mine," he replied in a voice that tried to sound brave but could easily hear the fear. "You aren't taking it," he proceeded to run toward Mark, trying to spear tackle him. Mark with his fast reflexes moved out of the way and sent Minin into the wall hard, knocking him to the ground.

Daman then moved to the side waiting for the result to be decided, "This shouldn't take too long," he said proudly. He then told Mark coldly, "Check a mirror if you want a reminder of what happens if you fail me and if that's not good enough…." He took the controller out of his pocket and began to wave it.

Mark turned and ran after Minin, crashing into his body holding him tightly. "Got to put on one last show for his amusement before I get rid of him," He told Minin. "Once I get the controller, he won't be so amused."

That's when Minin remembered about the kill-chip controller being deactivated, "It doesn't…" Mark cut him off before he had a chance to finish his sentence, putting Minin into a chokehold making it impossible to speak.

"That's right, send him to sleep before you throw him off," Daman shouted, cheering and clapping with joy that Mark looked as though he was winning.

Mark then released Minin, throwing him onto the floor in the middle of the room. He then ran and jumped, landing on top of Minin, as he landed he threw a punch connecting in his chest.

"The floor won't break here to save you, " Daman commented.

'These punches are harder than the last time' Minin thought, thinking one of his ribs had been broken from the punch, he then realised what was going on. 'He's putting on a show to stop Daman from being suspicious, but is also trying to kill me.' Mark tried to throw another punch, Minin moved out of the way and got to his feet and threw one in return. Mark did not feel it, he just shook his head, frustrated that his own punch did not finish Minin. "The kill chip…." Minin tried saying again as Mark connected with another punch to the stomach, winding Minin. Mark quickly jabbed Minin in the chest, sending him to the ground. He then jumped on top pummelling him with more punches.

Daman began to get frustrated with how long everything was taking, "Just get rid of him already!" he commanded. The dropship then began shaking and rocking as it hit rough turbulence, sending Mark and Minin into opposite sides of the dropship. Daman held onto the side. The turbulence had paused the fight but to Daman the fight had already gone on too long, causing him to become even more frustrated.

"Don't showboat, finish him off," he screamed. "Get up from the ground and fight him." He began to wave the kill chip controller and aimed it at Mark, "You know what I'll do it myself." He pressed it as hard as he could.

Mark saw the controller being pressed and had a look of fear on his face, he knew what that meant. One of the only things he feared happening to him on the island was happening. He just looked at Daman waiting for what was to come, thinking that there was nothing he could do, that it was over.

Minin could see what was happening and screamed out, "It doesn't work, that's what I've been trying to tell you, it doesn't work."

Daman continued to press the trigger, hoping for something to work. He eventually gave up, throwing the trigger at Mark, hitting him on the chest.

Mark knew he was free of having to worry about the trigger being pulled. His emotions turned from fear to anger. He lifted himself from the ground staring at Daman with determination, then charged at him as fast as he could.

Daman saw the man rushing towards him and jumped out of the way, causing Mark to hit a wall. Daman ran toward the cockpit door, the furthest point away from the man that was hunting him. He tried everything to could to open it, trying to get further away, but it was still sealed shut, no matter what he did it would not budge. Minin saw something that he had never seen until that point, pure fear from Daman. Mark brushed himself off, looked around and saw his prey and charged once again at Daman, this time colliding with him and the door.

Hunter turned his head away from the computer and windscreen, looking at what happened behind him and saw the unconscious body of Daman lying there. He then saw Mark, lying down behind him, trying to get up. Hunter turned back to the computer and began frantically typing into it.

Mark lifted himself off the floor, saw Daman lying on the ground, picked up his body and threw him toward the opening at the back of the ship, "I'm free of you." He said, looking like he was about to charge again. "Your rule of power is over, it's mine now," he then charged at Daman again landing on top of his body, throwing punches.

Minin looked over what was happening, the last sentence, *'It's mine now,'* ran through his head. He lifted himself from the ground and ran toward Mark, tackling him off his opponent and slamming both himself and Mark into the wall. The knock affected Minin as he fell to the ground.

Mark lifted Minin off the ground and threw him to the other side of the room, more forceful than any other time. "I'll destroy the both of you," Mark screamed out and turned his attention to Daman, "This is my island, not yours." He then pointed to Minin, "Not yours either…mine."

Minin slowly lifted himself, he knew what Marks idea was. He didn't want to just bring down Daman, he wanted to take control of the island for himself, Minin couldn't let that happen. "No…it's everyone's," he said struggling, still hurting from being slammed into the wall. He made it to his feet and put out his arm and indicated for him to come and get him. "Just bring it."

Mark took notice and rushed toward him, Minin jumped out of the way, sending him crashing into the wall. He recovered quickly, lifting himself but Minin was quicker and spear tackled him from behind, a piece of broken crate had lodged itself in the wall and was sticking out, creating a wound on his side.

Minin saw the wound and for a split second, he was impressed, *'He does bleed.'* He then threw a punch to Mark's face, who then threw one back. They go back and forth until Minin managed to duck under one, causing Mark to lose his balance and stagger to the middle of the Cargo area. Minin ran toward Mark and started to throw punches again, who returned what was given to him.

Hunter came out of the cockpit, walking over the fallen door, wearing a parachute on his back. He shouted out to the two men fighting, "Hey." Neither one heard him, he shouted out again, "Hey."

Mark connected a punch into Minin's face, which knocked Minin off-balance and backwards. He turned his head slightly and could see Hunter, trying to get his attention. Mark looked at what he was looking at. Hunter saw that he had their attention, he looked directly at Mark, "You're not taking the ship, you're not taking the island." He then as hard as he could hit a button on the panel that would open the lock for the cockpit, destroying it.

An announcement came over the P.A. system from a pre-recorded message, "Due to no location set and damage to the internal systems this dropship will self-destruct in *One Hundred and Twenty Seconds.*" A siren began to turn on and off, with each passing second.

Hunter ran toward the back of the Dropship as fast as he could, he threw the parachute that he was holding toward Minin but it fell short, landing closer to the middle of the cargo area. Mark ignored what was thrown, thinking that Hunter had the only parachute and chased after him attempting to catch the equipment he needed to get to safety.

Daman began to stir, looking at everything that was happening around. He was groggy but he slowly tried to get upright.

Minin knew his friend wouldn't be anywhere near quick enough to outrun his chaser and ran toward Mark. He barely caught up and put out his arm and pushed, just enough to put him off balance and enough for Hunter to get a bit more distance.

Hunter was unaware that this happened as he arrived at the opening and without slowing down he glanced back in the Dropship, hoping that he could see Minin getting the spare parachute. In his quick glanced he wasn't able to see what he had hoped, but still dived out head first without hesitation, he floated down, back at the island, soon disappearing.

Minin remembered the spare parachute and made his way toward it, thinking this was his chance at escape and began to attach it to his back.

Mark was furious, thinking that Hunter had the only parachute to get himself to safety. He saw a gun on the ground located near him and picked it up. He began a scan of the area looking for Minin. He located him and saw that he was wearing the spare parachute, *'I have a chance,'* He thought and aimed the gun at Minin. "Take it off," He warned in a cold voice "Hand it over."

Minin turned around and saw the gun aimed at him, unsure if it had bullets or not. He doesn't take the chance and put his hands above his head. He did not know what to do, give up the parachute and go with the Dropship or take his chance that the gun was empty.

"Ninety Seconds." The pre-recorded voice shouts over the P.A. System.

Minin began to think that if either Daman or Mark got the parachute and escaped the Dropship, his friends would have to deal with either one trying to take back control of the island. Minin couldn't allow that, "No." He replied looking him square in the eye and put his arms down, "I'm not giving it to you," He said, knowing that even if he got killed with the explosion so would they. All he needed to do was last until the count ran out.

"I'm not going to ask nicely," Mark said forcefully but calmly, his voice then turned to a scream. "Now take it off and give it to me."

"No," Minin replied as his lip trembled.

Mark pulled the trigger down slightly, getting ready to fire the gun, "I'm not joking, do it now."

"No," came the reply one more time. "Take it from me," Minin taunted his enemy nervously.

Mark had enough and pulled the trigger all the way down, the gun fired a bullet, missing Minin. "That was a warning shot." Minin jumped slightly. His breath was slow and began to move around, hoping that the movement would put Mark off. Mark followed the movement, "Stop moving, we both know the gun is loaded." He commanded.

Minin moved a little bit more, his feet knocked into something, he looked down, just enough not to take his eyes fully off Mark. He saw another gun and thought for a second, *'If I take the parachute off and throw it away, it'll give me enough time to get the gun and shoot him.'* He took a deep breath, "Fine," He said pretending to sound like he had no other choice then removed the parachute and threw it into the middle of the room.

"You made a smart choice, I'll tell them about it," Mark said smiling, walking toward the parachute.

Minin took his chance and picked the gun up and aimed it at Mark, "I wouldn't put it on too quickly," he said.

Mark turned and saw that Minin now had a gun aimed toward him. He quickly re-aimed his gun at Minin. "Smart," he said knowing the odds had evened up.

Minin knew he could not hesitate any longer. He pressed the trigger. It made a clicking noise but the chamber was empty.

Mark smiled, he knew he had won, he kept his gun aimed at Minin and began to walk back toward the opening. "You were smart but smart doesn't give you luck," He said.

Suddenly, the butt of a gun cracked Mark over the head, it was Daman, who had enough of the two men fighting and wanted to save himself. The hit forced Mark to the ground. "It's been fun," Daman said smiling. "But these people need their ruler, if I can't have the dropship at least I'll have the Island. " Daman walked back, toward the opening, aiming his gun between Mark and Minin. "Those that opposed me, will never have had such punishment."

"Sixty Seconds," A call came from the P.A.

Minin then thought, *'This is the last chance I'm going to get, to get the parachute back off Daman, even if I get shot, I have to take it.'* He then ran toward him as fast as he could. Daman began firing the gun, bullets narrowly miss with each shot.

Turbulence overcame the Dropship, it was too strong to fight, both men lost their footing and began to stumble. Minin falling to the side of the dropship and hitting a wall, Daman toward the other side, during which he lost both the gun and parachute, which was now on the floor near the opening.

Mark began to stir, making his way to his feet. They all saw the parachute lying on the floor waiting to be collected. All three men stare at the parachute, waiting to be taken by the one person who could race toward it the fastest. The three of them stare at it, then look at each other, they were all in a line.

"Forty-five Seconds." This was the call that told all three that they didn't have time to waste, all they had to do was get to the parachute to safety. Instantly they ran toward the goal, Daman just mere centimetres in front of the other two. Mark put out his arm and swung it, knocking Daman into Minin, crashing them both out of the short race.

Mark leaned down with his arm stretched forward to pick up the parachute, hoping to collect it on his way through. Another strong hit of turbulence attacked the dropship, causing him to jump over the prize, the momentum took him to the edge of the opening and out. He fell screaming.

The last two remaining were just standing on top of each other, looking at what had happened. Both were shocked at what they had seen but relieved, knowing they have another chance.

"Thirty seconds," the P. A. once again announced.

Daman lifted himself, forgetting that another person was still inside and walked toward the parachute thinking he was victorious. Minin then lifted himself from the ground, walked after Daman, grabbed him by the back of the shirt and yanked him to the floor. Daman threw his arm out, catching Minin in the face, knocking him to the ground. They began to throw punches, each one connecting. Minin then connected two in a row, the punches taking their toll on Daman. Minin threw one final punch, it connected, knocking Daman out.

"Fifteen seconds," the P.A. screamed out, in what seemed to be louder than any other message that Minin had heard before. Minin lifted himself and walked over to the parachute as quickly as he could, knowing running might result in the same fate as Mark.

"Ten Seconds."

Minin got to the prize and picked it up.

"Nine Seconds."

Connected and made sure it was on the best way he could.

"Eight Seconds."

Walked toward the opening, he turned around taking one last look at Daman, who was still on the ground.

"Seven Seconds."

Daman began to stir, staring back at Minin, he knew he had been defeated and the fate that awaited him.

"Six Seconds."

Minin no longer hesitated, lifted his arm, closed his eyes and fell backward.

"Five Seconds."

Minin began to fall toward the ground, he heard one last faint message from the P.A.

"Four Seconds."

He opened his eyes and looked at the dropship, the last remaining second's pass and it exploded. The explosion was like nothing that Minin had seen before, he expected to see one part explode first then the rest to follow but rather the explosion encased the whole Dropship, showing nothing but a flying fireball. The shockwave hit Minin forcing him to the ground faster.

38

Minin looked at the remains of the Dropship, which now looked like a fireball with wings gliding away from the island. Minin then realised he was still falling and flipped himself around and saw the ground coming closer to him. He pulled the ripcord of the parachute, it opened, slowing his descent greatly. A thought suddenly hit him, *'It's over, being ruled by Daman or even Mark Brockly. It was finally over.'* The plan did not happen as anyone had wanted, they didn't leave the island, but they were free. A part of him was still in shock that it had happened.

The more he thought about it, the more it felt as though the biggest weight was taken from his shoulders. A realisation hit him, he didn't know what to do from now on. One part of him always hoped that one way or another he would be free of Daman's rule but the other part felt as though this was strange and this new beginning shouldn't be. He looked over the Island below him, even though he had seen the Island from this angle before, everything looked different, it felt new, felt free. That feeling of a new beginning now felt right.

Minin made the parachute turn around and head toward the opposite direction, it gave him another view of the burning fireball hurling along the skyline. By this moment, it was no longer over the island but over the ocean, for a brief moment a thought occurred to him, *'could the dropship still have some sort of navigation control and turn back around and recircle to the island like it had done before it exploded?'* But the dropship kept moving further away, eventually dropping out of the sky and landing in the ocean. Steam shooting into the air.

Minin just floated in the sky, he soon realised where the air currents had taken him, he was over his home camp. It looked burnt and blackened but didn't feel as though there was a danger. He was now close enough to the ground that he knew he had no choice but to land here. He kept dropping, till eventually, he was in line with the trees. He kicked his feet, hoping to make some sort of clearing, even though he knew that the burnout trees would make that useless. He made it through the tree line, coming to a sudden jerking halt, the parachute was caught on the trees, Minin just hung there swinging. At first, it felt as though it was a rollercoaster, eventually easing till it came to a stop with Minin hanging in the air.

Minin looked at the ground below him, it looked familiar, he didn't know why. Below him was the charred remains of the outside of his home camp. The only other time he had hung like this was when he had come to the island, then a memory came flashing to him, Hunter, Callum and Hayley were under him at this same location. He had landed in almost the exact same spot as when he had come to the island, he waited, looking at the ground hoping that just like last time, someone would help him. A minute passed, there was not the sound of a person, but a cracking noise, the burnt branch holding him couldn't take the weight this time, it was breaking, without another warning the branch broke, sending him crashing to the ground with a thud on his back.

Minin laid on the ground for a moment, wondering if he had broken a bone, he didn't feel any different than he had before so he lifted himself off the ground. The answer was no, but his back was giving him pain. He freed himself of the parachute, ripping it off his body and slammed it onto the ground.

Minin looked around, it was getting dark and wondered where he should go from here. Then he remembered that everyone else would be in the bunker, even if Hunter and Hayley weren't there, it would be a good place to start. He exited the still chard remains of his home camp and entered into the Freelands.

It felt strange that the Freelands were so quiet and empty of people, even though he had been here plenty of times before with his friends and had not seen anyone else, this time it just didn't seem right, it felt odd and he didn't know why, maybe it was because he was on his own without his friends, he had never been out of home camp without them, or was it that he knew the war or whatever you would call it with Daman was over?

There was scuttling on the ground behind Minin, he turned to see what it was. Three chickens were running behind him. They stopped and began to peck the ground looking for some worms. One quickly lifted a worm from the ground, it was covered in a green and grey coloured dust, the chicken quickly ate the worm and the chickens moved on. Minin realised they were some of the chickens that were in his home camp that must have escaped before it had been burnt down, seeing them made Minin realised once more that this strange feeling he had was simply because of the change that was now occurring.

Minin began to make his way toward the bunker, in the distance was a crater, something that had never been there before and only just been made. Inside was the remains of a body of someone that had just fallen out of the sky. The body was crushed and barely identifiable, there was also no signs of anything that looked like a seat. Minin knew right away it had to be Mark, his body was lifeless, he might have survived falling to another floor inside the Tower but his body couldn't have survived that fall. Minin looked at the body, hoping that there would be no signs of life. A minute had passed, his body was still lifeless. He knew Mark was now dead. Minin moved out of the crater and towards the bunker.

Once Minin had arrived he saw people singing and dancing on the outside, they were celebrating. Once he was close enough, they slowly began to notice him, becoming silent for a moment, then suddenly a cheer erupted as they rushed over, shaking his hand, hugging him in victory. A younger girl, who had pigtails and grey eyes who Minin had not seen before, looked up to him and said, "No-one expected you to live once the Dropship exploded, we didn't see anyone leave the ship before it exploded. We could see everyone else though." Minin knew what she had meant, no one could have survived the explosion and he had just gotten out in time.

Minin just nodded slightly and then entered the bunker and down the entranceway, he would pass people every now and then, all of them stunned at his sight, they then began to cheer, tapping him on the shoulder with smiles as he passed. He arrived in the main living area and once again everyone erupted into cheers, but rather than try to hug or shake his hand they separated to each side, creating a passage leading to the medical centre. They all nodded telling him that was where he needed to go.

Inside the medical centre were Hunter and Hayley, both were clearly upset, hugging each other. They also were under the impression that Minin could not have survived the explosion. They both thought they had lost three friends today as far as their camp was concerned, it was now just back to the two of them.

"None of them died in vain, they helped free us, that's the important thing," Hunter kept saying to Hayley.

"I know," Hayley could only reply through her tears.

Minin closed the door behind him quietly trying to not disturb them. He smiled, hearing what they were saying about him, he knew it wasn't the time to joke but something inside him could not resist. "I didn't think you would miss Daman that much that you would be crying over him," He then began to laugh.

The two of them looked up at him, just like everyone else around the Bunker, they were in shock as though they were seeing a ghost. "How?" Were the only words Hayley could manage to get out of her mouth as she ran toward Minin and hugged him as strongly as she could. The hug lasted over a minute until they broke apart. She then looked him in the eyes pulled him close and began to kiss him, she didn't want it to end. They soon broke apart, Minin had a huge smile on his face. "We can't make excuses for us any longer." She said as they hugged once more. It felt perfect as if it was meant to be.

"Ahhh, should I leave you two alone?" Hunter then asked. They both broke apart forgetting that Hunter was in the room. They looked at him, their smiles were as wide as they could get. Hunter just stood there smiling, knowing that his friend was alive. He walked over and hugged Minin himself. They broke apart then quickly brought Hayley in as well.

"How?" Hayley repeated looking up at Minin. Knowing he had survived made her fears and sadness disappear.

"I jumped from the ship just in time…." Minin then continued to explain what had happened until he got to that point. "… What happened to the two of you?"

Hayley began to tell her story but was so rushed that only parts of it could be understood, "We all got dropped…. everyone landed in different spots…not everyone is here, they've sent out a search party for them…only five of us have made it back so far. When we heard the cheers outside we thought it was someone else."

"Shouldn't they be close to each other?" Minin asked, knowing that everyone was ejected out of the Dropship quickly.

Hunter answered, "once the parachute on the seats opened, Air currents would have taken them all over the place. To be honest, I'm surprised I made it back before some of them myself, but at least they are trying to find them."

"How did you get it to blow up?" Minin asked.

"I wasn't going to let him have the ship. I changed the course to return to the island. I knew the computer still had the failsafe of needing a new place to go, so it destroyed itself rather than return to the Island mid-flight," Hunter explained, happy with what he had done. "I'm just glad that there were spare parachutes."

"What do you mean by that" Minin asked.

"I got the ship to self-destruct without knowing that there were spare parachutes, either way, I wasn't going to let him have the ship. I'm just thankful that there were parachutes for the pilot and co-pilot."

Minin smiled, "Either way he's gone now, I had the last parachute, even if I didn't see him leave the plane before it exploded, the impact would have killed him. Mark is gone too, I saw his body on my way here. We're free of them." They all hugged together once more.

When they broke apart, Hayley began to walk over to the door, she was about to announce the news to everyone. She stopped for a second and looked at Minin, she realised this was his news to tell. "They might be celebrating but they need to know a hundred per cent that he's gone. You do it," She told him.

"No, it's fine. You do it," He replied.

She opened the door and ecstatically shouted out, "He's dead.... Daman is dead and so is Mark Brockly. Tell everyone that we no longer live in fear of them."

Everyone who heard her looked at her in disbelief for a couple of seconds. They then slowly smiled as the news sank in. They then began to cheer, celebrating the news. It spread throughout the bunker like wildfire. She then closed the door relieved, the reality that it had happened was sinking in.

"So, it's over?" Hunter asked one more time in disbelief that it was actually happening.

"Our life on the island?" Minin replied, "No...but free of him...yes."

The three of them hugged each other embracing the happy news. As they began to break free there was a knock on the door. Hayley opened the door, a young boy with a bowl cut, who looked like he must have only just arrived on the island recently was standing there, "You guys have to come out, there are guards at the entrance, lots of them. They don't want to speak to anyone except Minin."

They all looked at each other, they didn't think about the possibility that the guards were regrouping and trying to take control for themselves. The short-lived celebration was over, all three stormed out of the room and headed toward the entrance.

Once outside, a wall of people from inside the Bunker was covering the entrance, they didn't want any of the guards to make their way in. A small gap separated them and the rows of Guards, both sides had every weapon they had, ready to fire at an instant. Minin, Hunter and Hayley made their way through the row of Islanders to the front and stood in front of the wall of guards. Both groups just stared each other down, neither budge, waiting for the other side to make a move.

"I think you wanted to speak to me," Minin said to the group of guards, knowing that if he said the wrong words it could lead to a blood bath from both sides.

A guard close to Minin took a few steps in front of the guards, ending within inches of Minin, close enough to feel his breath. Minin recognised the guard instantly he was the guard with the Goatee. Everyone was still on edge waiting for the other side to make a move. Suddenly those from the Bunker got restless and began to aim at the guards, which in turn made the Guards do the same. The Goatee guard turned to the rest of the guards, "Lower your weapons," He commanded. The guards did as they were told, but only enough so that they were not aiming directly at the islanders, but ready that at any moment they could re-aim.

"My name is Nick Station," The Goatee guard announced. "We're not here to fight. Like the rest of you, we don't want that. As a gesture of good faith, I've told the rest of my men to lower their weapons as you have heard, I'm hoping you will do the same."

None of the Islanders knew if they should trust what Nick had told them. Minin turned around and nodded his head, "Do it," He said. Everyone lowered their weapons to the same degree as the guards.

"Thank you. I appreciate that" Nick continued. "Like yourselves, we are finally free of Daman and just like yourselves, we want peace. Like yourselves, we were only doing what we did from the fear of being punished." Those from the bunker weren't sure what to make of the announcement. Was this a trick and as soon as they began to trust them, they would be attacked, or did they really want peace as he said? Everyone just stayed silent and stared at the Guards. "I know this might seem strange," Nick continued. "If I was in your same position, I wouldn't believe me either. But I have a peace offering that we would like to give to you all." He turned to the back of the group of guards and nodded, two groups of four guards brought two coffins to the front, they place them on the ground and returned to where they were.

"What kind of sick joke is this?" Someone from the Bunker shouted out from the back of the group angrily.

"They're screwing with us," another shouted.

Both comments were enough to force all the Islanders to raise their weapons back at the guards. The guards did the same. Minin knew he had to do something, while he himself didn't like the fact the guards brought two coffins to the bunker, something inside kept telling him that maybe it was a peace offering as Nick had suggested. "Don't shoot," he shouted out to both groups. He walked up to the coffins, opened the left one just enough so that only he could just see inside. It was Tiffany, a tear flowed from his eye. Seeing the guards giving his friend back was enough to convince him that it was a peace offering. He looked up at all the guards and told them, "Thank you." He then turned to the Islanders, "put the weapons down, they're telling the truth."

Nick looked at Minin, "All of us are here because we did something insignificant but the mainland doesn't want to deal with us, we have to make the Island our own. The problem stopping that has been rectified.

Minin thought for a moment, "You want peace from both sides?"

"We don't want sides, we want to live together," Nick replied.

Minin turned around, everyone looked back at him, unsure what to say, their looks told him, *'it's up to you.'* "You know we will fight back if this goes to hell, you know that right?" He said to Nick and put out his hand.

"If anyone falls out of line, if you don't shoot them, then we will," Nick replied and put out his hand and proceeded to shake. "We'll leave you be, we'll let you mourn for your loved ones, but come see us when you are ready," He turned to the guards, "Let's go." The guards all turn around and began to walk away from the bunker.

Hayley grabbed Minin's hand and smiled, "There's peace?" She asked.

Minin turned to everyone and shouted loud enough so they could all hear. "You each had your camps, then there was the Tower but from now on, we are one." Everyone put up a cheer, celebrating the announcement.

39

A few days had passed, until now everyone had celebrated in the sun but now that had changed, rain had come and everyone was now putting their friends that had died to rest. A new graveyard was placed near the bunker. All the fallen would be laid to rest here, no matter where you had come from. Carts with sheets covering the dead were placed next to a grave, this would be their final resting place, except for two.

Minin, Hayley and Hunter walked out of the bunker and proceeded to walk past the waiting graves, their heads down as a mark of respect. They walked away from the graveyard to an open area of the Freelands, the same area where Tiffany had danced when she first came to the island, two more graves were here. They were open, mounds of dirt surround each. On top of the dirt were two shovels, inside the graves were the coffins of both Tiffany and Callum. Standing near those graves looked to be everyone on the Island. Simone, Gin, Michelle, Stephen, Emily, Emmitt, Lukas, Stephanie, Screamer, and Nick. Had all surrounded the graves holding flowers.

Minin, Hayley and Hunter saw everyone standing there, they smiled but were slightly confused as to why. Minin then asked, "Why are you here?" They thought that a couple of people would come but not the crowd that was there.

"Without them, this wouldn't be possible," Simone replied. "We'll pay our respects to your friends first before we say goodbye to the others."

Minin smiled at what she had said, Hayley began to tear up but it was too much for Hunter who began to cry. "We'll get this started quickly then," Minin announced. The three walked to the head of the graves, Hayley in front of Tiffany's, Hunter in front of Callum's, Minin in the middle.

Hayley had wanted to do the eulogy herself but each time she tried to write something she would burst into tears, it was at that moment she and Hunter decided that Minin should do the eulogy. He wasn't sure he would be strong enough but seeing as up until this moment, Hunter had not cried or broken down, he believed Hunter could have taken over if needed but this was not the case. Minin took out a piece of paper from his pocket which contained a few notes that he had written down.

Minin paused, he kept looking at the notes he had written, his hands were shaking, even though he knew that his friends weren't coming back, he didn't want to say goodbye at that moment, he took a deep breath and began to talk. "Today we lay Callum and Tiffany to rest and like everyone, we never want to see this happen. We want another second, another minute, another hour, another week for these people to be in our lives, just that little bit longer….." With each word more tears came, "…..But we don't have that choice, the circumstances of their death were tragic, but the outcome has helped us all." Everyone looked at him and smiled. "I didn't know Tiffany as long as Callum but that didn't matter to me. On this island the people we call family are in short supply but she was family to Haley, Hunter and me. She came to this island scared, not knowing what to do but if given the chance she would have lead us all." Everyone began to chuckle through their tears. "I would have loved to see what she could have become, but it didn't happen and that in itself is a tragedy. As for Callum, he was my brother surrounded in mystery. There's still more I would love to know but will never find out but at least what I do know about him made him one of the best people I will ever know." Minin looked at the piece of paper, he scrunched it up and threw it away, "There's so much I could say about him, he was loyal, helpful, he would help in an instant." Minin's eyes began to swell up with tears, "I want to finish by saying we'll miss them." Minin looked at Callum's grave, "We'll miss my brother," then turned to Tiffany's, "And we'll miss my sister," he then bowed his head, everyone joined him.

After about a minute or so Minin lifted his head, "Thank you," he said with a smile. Everyone began to leave. Those that had flowers began to drop them into the graves and walked off toward the other funerals.

A couple of minutes had passed when Hayley asked, "Do you think we should go to another one and pay our respects?" Trying to hold back her tears. Neither answered the question, they were unsure if they should.

As Gin put his flowers on Callum's grave he spoke up, "No-one expects you to do that. The two that you said goodbye to, they were the two closest people that you had on the Island. If it was me, I'd just stay here, no one will blame you if you don't go."

Minin turned to him, "Thank you," he replied with a smile. Gin then began to walk to the graveyard.

The three of them smiled knowing that their friends helped them turn the island around, helped everyone get their freedom from someone who they were afraid of. The dreams that they talked about that night around the campfire were complete in their own way. Even though Tiffany and Callum had died, their memories would remain and for the rest of their lives that would make Minin, Hayley and Hunter smile.

The End

Dear Reader:

If you have gotten to this point, I can only assume that you have read all the way through the story. Thank you for making it all the way through.

If you have ever read one of these blurbs at the back of a book, you would know that they say the same thing, how hard it is to complete a project like this. And it is true, only having an hour here or there, and the feeling that you are the slowest writer in the world. (If I ever make it big, it will not surprise me to hear that George R.R. Martin say that I need to hurry up and release the next book.) But that's the thing with a story that you truly believe in, you keep at it, no matter how slow you are or what else you have in the world that is more important like your family or the not so important, such as ending up in a Youtube spiral. No matter what happened you'll just keep coming back to it. After all, it was the tortoise that won the race, not the hare.

Even if you read all the way through and thought, *'this was the worst thing I have ever read'*, I still thank you for at least taking the time to make it to the end. If you were on the other end of the scale and enjoyed it, I'm thankful that you enjoyed it.

Thank you and stay safe.

Epilogue

Inside a cave with walls that were damp and dark, the only light was provided by torches with flames. A person wearing a red hood sat on a throne made of mud and rocks. Another who had green face paint was standing next to them. They were looking out into a small crowd, who also had faces covered in green. The person looking over the crowd, who's mouth could only be seen due to the flames. His mouth looked as though he had the same face paint began to speak. Their voice sounding as though it came from a man, "The war with Daman is over, we no longer need to hide."

"The plan with Mark didn't work though," The person standing next to the throne replied.

"Let them have their peace, for now. When they don't suspect it, we will take it back." The hooded man said and began to smile, "We are taking our Island back."

"We're taking it back," The crowd repeated over and over.

The hooded person then said, "They will fear us, this is our Island and we are Tainve."

The small crowd erupted into cheers.

Danny Kylstra was born in 1986 from the Wollongong region of NSW, Australia. He lives with his wife and two daughters. He enjoys reading, spending time with his family and friends and cruiseships.